#3

Dear Grisham
May 6, 2005

RIVER'S EDGE

Books by Terri Blackstock

Emerald Windows

Cape Refuge Series

Cape Refuge
Southern Storm
River's Edge

Newpointe 911

Private Justice
Shadow of Doubt
Word of Honor
Trial by Fire
Line of Duty

Sun Coast Chronicles

Evidence of Mercy
Justifiable Means
Ulterior Motives
Presumption of Guilt

Second Chances

Never Again Good-bye
When Dreams Cross
Blind Trust
Broken Wings

With Beverly LaHaye

Seasons Under Heaven
Showers in Season
Times and Seasons
Season of Blessing

Novellas

Seaside

CAPE REFUGE SERIES

RIVER'S EDGE

BOOK THREE

Terri Blackstock

ZONDERVAN™

GRAND RAPIDS, MICHIGAN 49530 USA

ZONDERVAN™

River's Edge
Copyright © 2004 by Terri Blackstock

Requests for information should be addressed to:
Zondervan, *Grand Rapids, Michigan 49530*

ISBN 0-7394-4525-1

Scripture taken from the New American Standard Bible®, Copyright © 1960, 1962, 1963, 1968, 1971, 1972, 1973, 1975, 1977, 1995 by The Lockman Foundation. Used by permission.

Published in association with the literary agency of Alive Communications, Inc., 7680 Goddard Street, Suite 200, Colorado Springs, CO 80920.

Interior design by Beth Shagene

Printed in the United States of America

*This book is lovingly
dedicated to the Nazarene*

PREFACE

*C*ape Refuge is a fictitious island which I set just east of Savannah, Georgia, on the Atlantic Coast. To research it, I spent time on Tybee Island, a lovely little beachside community outside of Savannah. Many of my ideas for life in Cape Refuge came from there.

There's another island just south of Tybee called Little Tybee Island, an uninhabited marshland and wildlife refuge. For this novel, I turned Little Tybee into Cape Refuge, after a few alterations to the terrain and the coastline. I hope the kind people of Georgia's coast will forgive me.

I owe a big thanks to J. R. Roseberry, editor and publisher of the *Tybee News,* for his help in my research.

ACKNOWLEDGMENTS

*E*ach book I write requires a certain amount of research, and that research often forces me to seek out experts in particular fields. I couldn't write my novels without their help. For this book, I offer thanks to Dr. Steve Bigler and Dr. Tree James, for answering my random questions and brainstorming with me through plot scenarios. I owe a lot to Cissie Posey, who shared her struggles with infertility.

I'd also like to thank two groups of people who have helped my books reach more and more readers—booksellers and librarians. I consider my work a ministry, and I consider you to be my partners in that ministry. Thank you for all you do.

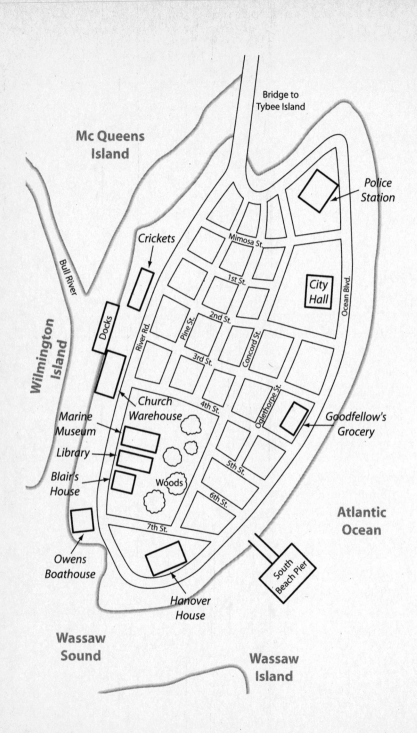

RIVER'S EDGE

CHAPTER

1

*T*he cramps woke Morgan at 3:30 a.m., startling her out of a deep slumber. She'd been immersed in a dream about a little girl on a swing set, her long brown hair flowing on the breeze. She knew without a doubt that the child was the baby she was carrying.

The cramps offered a stark warning, as if her anxiety had shaped into a blunt instrument that bludgeoned her hope.

She sat up, her hand pressed over her flat stomach, and looked at Jonathan, who slept peacefully next to her. Should she wake him to tell him she was cramping, or just be still and wait for it to pass?

She had taken the home pregnancy test yesterday morning, then followed up with a blood test at her doctor's office that afternoon. Jonathan sat in the examining room with her, fidgeting and chattering to pass the time. When the nurse came back with the verdict, he sprang to his feet, muscles all tense, like a tiger tracking a gazelle.

"Before I tell you the results, I need to know if I'm bearing good or bad news."

Jonathan glanced at Morgan, and she knew he was way too close to calling the woman a smart aleck and warning her not to toy with them. "Come on, just tell us."

"But do you want to be pregnant? Is good news a yes or a no?"

Before he could grab the nurse by the shoulders and shake the playfulness out of her, Morgan blurted out, "Yes! More than anything!"

"Are we going to have a baby or not?" Jonathan asked.

"Congratulations!" The word burst out of the nurse's mouth, and Morgan came off the table, flinging herself into his arms, and they yelled like kids as he swung her around.

They agreed not to announce it until today, so they could share that first night of giddy excitement, crushing the secret between them.

They waited until Caleb, their eighteen-month-old foster child, was sound asleep, then went across the street to Hanover House's private stretch of beach. They giggled and danced under the May moonlight, to the music of the waves whooshing and frothing against the shore. When they'd finally gone to bed, they lay awake until close to midnight, wondering if it would be a girl or a boy, and how soon they would be able to see their child on a sonogram. Jonathan held Morgan and whispered about soccer games and ballet, piano lessons and PTA.

Finally, they had both fallen asleep, and now she didn't want to wake him. It was probably nothing. Just something she ate last night. She would have to be more careful now.

But as the moments dragged on the cramping grew worse, and she couldn't ignore it. She folded her arms across her stomach and slid her feet out of bed. She sat up and realized it was worse, even, than she thought. There was blood.

"Oh, no." The words came out loud and unbidden, and Jonathan turned over and looked up at her in the night.

"Baby, what is it?"

She turned on the lamp. "Oh, Jonathan . . ."

He looked at her with an innocent, terrible dread, expecting something, though not clear what. Slowly, he sat up. "What?"

A sob rose in her throat as she pointed to the mattress.

For a moment they both just stared at it, the blood-spot of a dream dying.

Their unformed, barely real, secret baby dying.

Then he jolted out of his stunned stupor and sprang out of bed. "Are you okay?"

"I'm losing it." The words bubbled up in her throat. "Jonathan, I'm losing the baby!"

"We're going to the hospital. Maybe it's not what you think. Maybe they can stop it." He pulled on the jeans hanging over a chair by the bed.

Maybe he was right. Maybe the baby was still there, nestled in its little sac, unscathed by whatever thing had broken loose in her. Or if not, maybe the medical staff could ward off danger, stop the impending doom, give her some magic pill to make it hang on.

She quickly got dressed while Jonathan woke Sadie—their seventeen-year-old foster daughter and Caleb's sister—to tell her of the emergency and ask her to listen for her little brother in case they weren't back when he awoke.

Then Jonathan helped Morgan out to the car as though she were a sick woman who couldn't walk on her own. She tried not to make sudden moves, not to walk too hard, not to cramp so tightly.

But it all seemed out of her control.

"It's okay, baby," Jonathan said as he drove at breakneck speed across the island. "We'll be in Savannah in no time."

Was it already too late? The drive from Cape Refuge to the closest hospital was too far. She cried quietly, staring out the wind-shield, praying that God would intervene.

"God's going to save her," he muttered as he drove. "He has to."

Morgan's face twisted. "Her ... you said *her*." She looked over at him and saw the tears on his face. "You think it's a girl?"

He didn't answer. "God, please ..."

She sobbed as he drove, her hand pressed against her stomach. *What kind of mother am I? I couldn't keep it safe for a day?* Her tears were cold against her face in the breeze of the air-conditioner.

Jonathan's lips moved in some silent monologue—a desperate preacher's prayer of faith and hope—or the angry railing of a seaman who saw terror coming and believed he could head it off with enough threats. His hands clutched the steering wheel, and occasionally he reached over to touch her with fearful reassurance.

Finally, they reached St. Joseph's, and Jonathan pulled up to the emergency room door. He got out and ran to Morgan's side, helped her out. There was blood all over the back of her robe, and some of it had soaked into the seat.

"I need help here!" Jonathan helped her through the sliding glass door. "Please, someone help!"

But Morgan knew there was no help for her baby. It was already too late.

CHAPTER

*T*wo hours later, they rode home in silence, each mired in their own despair. As she'd known he would, the doctor confirmed her fears. She had miscarried her child.

Guilt and anguish ached through her body.

How would Jonathan ever forgive her?

They both wept quietly as the sun rose over the Atlantic, heralding a day that others would find beautiful and welcome. But she would do anything to turn the clock back to this time yesterday.

Jonathan pulled their car into the shade of the red cedars at the end of the gravel driveway. Their house loomed big in the morning light, the yellow paint glowing like the sun, the Victorian trim clean and white. Gus—one of the home's residents—had done some repairs on the house and coated it with fresh paint a couple of weeks ago. The full ferns on the porch overflowed their urns in bright, life-filled green. Impatiens in yellow, red, and purple lined the front of the house, well cared for by the home's other residents. It was one of those chores that helped their charges integrate back into the world after time on the streets or in jail. Cause-and-effect lessons about working hard, taking care, cultivating and nurturing, and reaping good results. The testimony of a job well done.

She spoke that lesson to them so many times, reminding them that obedience to God, self-discipline, and love all added up to blessings too numerous to count.

Yet here she was, a poster child that the opposite was true.

The front door to the big yellow house was still closed. Maybe that meant that no one was up yet. If they were, the door would have been open, letting in light, along with the ocean sounds from just across the street, through the glass storm door.

Morgan hoped no one knew where she'd been. She didn't want to explain this to anyone but Sadie.

Jonathan helped her out of the car and walked her up the porch steps.

Sadie met them at the door, her eyes red-rimmed and worried. "I'm so glad to see you, Morgan!" She threw her arms around her. "I thought you were dying or something."

"I'm sorry we worried you, honey." Morgan held her in a tight, reassuring embrace.

"Jonathan didn't say what was wrong. I saw the blood on your bed . . ."

"I'm fine, really."

"But what's wrong? What happened?"

Her effort not to cry twisted her face. "Honey, I found out yesterday that I was pregnant. And this morning . . . I miscarried."

At seventeen Sadie had seen the dark side of life, and she knew what it meant to grieve. Her expression bore the weight of Morgan's news, and she pulled her back into a hug. "Oh, Morgan. I'm so sorry."

Morgan didn't want the girl to suffer with her, so she tried to hold herself together. "I want you to keep this to yourself. I haven't even told Blair yet. And there's no need for anyone else to know, okay?"

Sadie wiped a tear. "Okay."

Jonathan stroked Morgan's hair. "Why don't you go get changed and lie down? I'll clean up the car."

She nodded and started toward the stairs.

"I changed the sheets," Sadie said. "The bed is clean."

"Thank you, sweetie."

Morgan went in, trudged up the stairs, and took a quick shower to clean up. She got dressed, and with her long, curly dark hair still wet, slipped into Caleb's room. He slept soundly in his crib, his thumb shoved into his mouth. Within the next hour, the eighteen-month-old would wake up and cry out for her. She wished she didn't have to wait.

She wanted to pick him up and hold him, crush him to herself, assuage those maternal hormones that hadn't gotten the news.

She didn't think she could have loved him more if he'd been her own son. But he wasn't.

Caleb Seth Caruso had a mother who was serving time in prison on drug charges. Morgan was merely a temporary caretaker until his mother was set free. She started to weep again, and left the room so she wouldn't wake him. He didn't deserve to see her like this.

She went back into the bedroom. Jonathan was sitting on the bed, his face white, expressionless. "I want you to lie down," he said. "When Caleb wakes up, I'll get him."

"Okay."

"Are you feeling all right? Physically, I mean?"

"Yeah, the cramping is getting better." She hated what that meant.

He sat down and looked at the wall, and she knew that he felt the loss as keenly as she. "We are going to be parents, sweetheart," he said. "I know it doesn't seem like it, but we are."

She nodded. They had been trying for over a year. In the scheme of things, she supposed it wasn't as bad as other couples who'd tried for seven, nine, twelve years. She thought of Ben Jackson—Jonathan's opponent in the mayoral race—and his wife, Lisa. They'd been trying for thirteen.

"Do you want to call Blair?" Jonathan's words cut into her thoughts.

Morgan thought of waking her sister up to tell her this news. It hardly seemed fair. Ever since Blair had bought the newspaper, she hadn't been getting adequate rest. "I'll tell her later."

She got into the bed, and Jonathan pulled the covers up over her and tucked her in. He bent over and kissed her cheek.

When he'd left her alone, she let her control slip away, and wept into her pillow.

Later that morning, the cramping stopped, and Morgan forced herself to get out of bed. She went downstairs, and saw that the kitchen was spotless. Gus and Felicia had gone to work, and Sadie was at school. She saw Karen on the back porch feeding her own baby. There was no sign of Jonathan or Caleb. Maybe Jonathan had taken him with him to do some campaigning today.

His big debate with his two opponents in the mayoral race—Sam Sullivan and Ben Jackson—was tomorrow. Jonathan—who worked as a fishing tour guide, pastor of their small church, and director of Hanover House—had only come into the race a month ago, so he was way behind. The special election was scheduled for three weeks away, and he didn't have a moment to waste. If he won, he'd take office almost immediately, since the town had been without a mayor since the last one had been dethroned by scandal.

She went through the kitchen into the small office where she and Jonathan took care of the business of Hanover House. She sat down at the desk and moved a stack of donations out of her way. The home, a halfway house for people trying to change their lives, was supported by monthly contributions. She had yet to log them all this month, so much had been going on.

She picked up the telephone and dialed her sister's number. When there was no answer, she checked the clock. Ten o'clock. Of course Blair wasn't home. She dialed the newspaper office and got her voicemail. She was probably out tracking down a story, trying to find an interesting angle to the mundane events of the island.

Discouraged, she hung up. She would try Blair again later. But would her sister understand her grief over a baby that she had only known for one day? How could she? No one could understand unless they had been there.

Then she remembered. Someone had.

She thought of the wife of Jonathan's fiercest opponent in the race. Lisa Jackson had been in Morgan's shoes four different times.

One would never have known of her struggle with infertility. It was a secret, closely held. Morgan wouldn't have known it herself, except that she had seen it on Lisa's face when they'd both wound up in the bathroom at a mutual friend's baby shower.

She had recognized those tears, and Lisa had recognized hers. Without saying a word, the two women, whose husbands were political archenemies, had embraced. They'd sneaked out for coffee to comfort each other, and had poured out their hearts about their infertility and their desperate desire for children.

Maybe it would help to talk to her now.

You call me if you need to talk, honey. Day or night, I don't care. And if you don't mind, I'll do the same. These husbands of ours will just have to get used to it.

Morgan knew she'd meant it.

She knew Lisa probably wasn't home, since her real estate business kept her hopping. But she called and left a message on Lisa's voicemail, then tried her at her office. When her taped recording kicked in, Morgan decided to leave a message there too.

"Hey, Lisa," she said in a soft voice, "this is Morgan. Could you give me a call when you have a chance to talk? I really need to share something with you." She paused and tried to control the emotion wavering in her voice. "Something happened this morning. You're the only one I know who'll understand." She hung up and stared down at the phone. She hoped Lisa would return the call soon.

But hours later, Lisa had not called back, and neither had Blair. Jonathan came home with Caleb—he had only taken him for a walk on the beach—and she busied herself with his care and the affairs of the house.

She longed for night and the sleep that would numb her pain, but when it finally came, she lay awake, thinking about the dream she'd had last night about the little girl on the swing.

She prayed that God would let her dream it again.

CHAPTER

*P*olice Chief Matthew Cade—simply Cade to everyone who knew him—came to Hanover House early the next morning. From the look on his face, Morgan knew he hadn't dropped in for breakfast. As Jonathan's closest friend and the love of her sister's life, he dropped in often—but not in full uniform.

He had bad news. She knew that look. It was the same tight expression he'd worn when he interrupted that City Council meeting last summer to tell her that her parents had been murdered.

"I hate to bother you this morning," he said. "I know you're all getting ready for the debate."

She felt like sinking against the wall, raising her arms to deflect the blow. "Something's wrong, Cade. What is it?"

"I'm here on police business. I need to ask you a few questions."

She shivered, and her mind raced with possibilities. She still hadn't been able to get in touch with her sister. Had something happened to her? "Is it about Blair?"

He looked startled at the question. "No, why? What's wrong with Blair?"

"Nothing. I just haven't heard from her. I tried to call her yesterday but never got her."

His face relaxed. "I talked to her last night. She was working late, trying to cover a baseball game and an awards ceremony. She's fine. No, it's about Lisa Jackson."

"Lisa? What about her?"

"Morgan, Ben reported her missing last night."

"Missing? What do you mean, missing?"

"She didn't come home last night, and she missed several appointments yesterday. Important ones, apparently. She seems to have vanished sometime yesterday morning. We're talking to everyone who might have seen her yesterday. She had messages from you on her home and business voicemail. I wondered if you'd heard from her."

Morgan just gaped at him for a moment. "No. She never called me back."

"When's the last time you spoke to her?"

She shoved her long curls back from her face. "Uh . . . a few days ago."

"Did she give you any indication that she was upset about anything? Angry at Ben?"

"No, not at all. Cade, do you think something's happened to her?"

He seemed to consider whether or not to answer that. "Maybe not. I'm hoping she'll turn up today. Maybe she just left town for the night or something."

"But what does Ben think?"

"He seems to think that she's in trouble. He's pretty upset. He claims they hadn't had a fight, but with the stress of the mayoral race and the debate coming up, maybe she'd had enough and he didn't know it."

Morgan knew that was true. But it was more than that. The stress the Jacksons had been under with their fertility treatments was even more significant than the pressure of the race. But she didn't want to bring that up. "I'm sorry I can't help, Cade. All I know is that Lisa isn't the type to take off."

"I didn't think so either."

She walked him back to the door and looked into his eyes. He looked tired, as if he'd been up all night. His black hair looked a little disheveled, and his limp reminded her how recently his own life had been in jeopardy. "Are you okay, Cade? Taking care of yourself?"

"Yeah, I'm fine. Cane helps."

Morgan knew his transition from a crutch to a cane spoke well of his progress. He'd had surgery a month ago for multiple fractures in that leg. It had been set internally with steel rods, but his recovery was not yet behind him. She reached up to hug him. "If you see my sister, tell her to call me."

He smiled down at her. "Will do."

She watched him limp out to his squad car and get in, and she knew Blair would call her soon.

But what would she say when she called? *Hey, Blair. Whatcha been doing? Me? Oh, I found out I was pregnant, then miscarried the next day. Most people get nine months, then a bundle of joy. Not me. Nosirree, not me. My womb is like a tomb, rejecting life and creating death. My womb is a tomb ... my womb is a tomb. I'm a poet and don't know it.*

Tears pushed to her throat again, and she told herself she would have to stop this. She wasn't this way. She didn't think bitter, cynical thoughts. But then, she obviously had a skewed picture of herself. She had pictured herself as a mother, raising a houseful of children—a big family, full of laughter and love ...

But her body had kept secrets about its malfunctions, as if it had other intentions entirely.

Was this anger normal? Had Lisa had these same thoughts of self-hatred, these raging thoughts that she had failed her child?

Morgan hoped Lisa was okay. Maybe she'd been plagued by the same kinds of self-recriminations, the need to escape herself and go somewhere alone to scream out and rail against the world and her body and all those busy, stressed-out moms who could never understand the broken and empty *longing* ...

Maybe Lisa needed her, wherever she was.

Morgan blew her nose and dried her tears, then went to the phone. She dialed the Jackson's house. Ben answered on the first ring. "Hello?"

"Ben, this is Morgan Cleary. I just heard about Lisa."

"Who told you?"

"Cade came by to see if I'd seen or heard from her, since I'd left her some messages yesterday."

"And have you?"

"No. She never called back."

His voice cracked. "I haven't seen her since yesterday morning. She's just vanished. She's not answering her cell phone, but that's nothing new since you can't get a signal on this godforsaken island. She missed several appointments yesterday. She even missed an important ultrasound she had scheduled. She would never do that. *Never.*"

Morgan knew he was right. Lisa would never have missed an ultrasound, now that they'd decided to go through with another attempt at in vitro fertilization. Knowing when to harvest her egg was critical. "Ben, are you okay?"

"No, of course I'm not."

"Look, if you want to call off the debate this morning, I'm sure—"

"I don't care about the blasted debate! Let them declare Jonathan the winner, for all I care. *My wife is missing!*"

He slammed down the phone, and she felt shallow and silly for suggesting such a thing, as if he might have even considered showing up.

"Did I hear Cade?" Jonathan stood in the doorway, holding Caleb on his hip.

"Yes." She hung up the phone. "He said Lisa Jackson is missing. I just talked to Ben, and he's a basket case."

"Missing?"

"The police have been looking for her all night."

Jonathan stared at her for a moment, as if he didn't believe it. "You don't think this is a publicity stunt, do you? To get a few sympathy votes?"

She grunted. "Jonathan, I heard his voice. He's frantic. He doesn't even care about the debate right now. I think we should go over there."

He set Caleb down, and the child toddled over to his toy basket and took out a plastic train. "Morgan, of all people, he doesn't want me over there."

"Then I'll go by myself. He's there all alone, Jonathan. Someone needs to wait with him. And I'm worried about Lisa. She's my friend."

He sighed, as if he couldn't believe she was asking him to do this now. "All right, I guess we can go over for a little while."

She knew he was worried about the debate, which was scheduled for eleven. They still had three hours.

He got that sober, concerned look on his face and touched her chin. "Are you okay? Sure you're up to this?"

"I'm fine," she lied. "Really, I am."

He clearly had no choice but to take her word for it.

CHAPTER

*B*en Jackson's house was one of the more elegant ones on the island, situated near the northeastern point with a backyard view of the Atlantic. Beach property came at a premium on Cape Refuge, but it was well known that the Jacksons had money. That was why he was pulling ahead in the mayoral race.

He'd invested more money than either of the other two candidates. He'd had television commercials running on Savannah stations for the last month, as well as a billboard just off the bridge onto Tybee Island, and another one on the island expressway into Savannah. He had also taken out full-page ads in the *Savannah Morning News* and the *Cape Refuge Journal*. Even Blair had been forced to sell him the ad space that helped create his image as "The Man for the People."

The porch light was on, though the sun shone hot and bright. Ben had probably had it on all night.

She knocked. Jonathan stood behind her, his hands in his pockets. "I can't believe I'm here."

"Jonathan, take off your candidate's hat and put on your pastor's hat. We're here as Christians who care, not competitors."

Jonathan swallowed. "You're right."

Ben opened the door. His face was pale and his eyes were red, with dark circles shadowing them. He hadn't shaved, and his hair was tousled and dirty. "What are you doing here?"

"I wanted to come and sit with you," Morgan said. "You don't need to go through this alone."

He abandoned the door and headed back inside, and Morgan wondered if that was his invitation for them to come on in. She nudged Jonathan and they stepped inside, closing the door behind them.

They followed him into a great room decorated with rich silk draperies and faux-finished walls, with an adjoining kitchen that had a tin ceiling and shiny stainless steel appliances. Ben slumped over the amber granite counter. "What do you want?" He looked up at Jonathan. "Did you want to come over here and gloat that I'm finally getting mine?"

Morgan shot Jonathan a look that pleaded for him to answer gently.

"I would never do that. I came because Morgan said you were upset and you were alone. I thought maybe there was something we could do."

"You could go out and find her!" He ran a shaking hand through his hair. "You could tell me where she is. *That's* what you could do."

"Ben, are you sure she didn't just leave town for the night?" Morgan asked. "Maybe all the stress—"

"Absolutely no way. We were in the process of doing in vitro. It's a huge daily commitment. I have to give her shots the same time every day, pumping her body full of drugs and hormones. She would never go through all that for nothing. Never."

Jonathan sat down and rubbed his hands on his knees. "Those hormones, don't they cause mood swings, maybe even some irrational behavior? Maybe the pressure got to her—"

"She can take the stress," Ben cut in. "She always has. We've tried this three other times, and she was fine. This is a way of life for us. Has been for thirteen years. Yeah, the hormones make her moody. She cries more often than she should. She's irritable and cranky, and sometimes she's angry. Anyone would be when they've had four miscarriages and nothing seems to work. But she's not angry at *me*, and she wouldn't have just taken off when we still had some hope."

He went to the huge window with an ocean view and peered out as if expecting her to swim up with the waves and come dripping across the beach.

"She was in a good mood yesterday morning." His voice lowered. "She made me breakfast, and I took the day off to go fishing. I thought a day of relaxation would help me to get my mind straight before the debate. I got back midafternoon and showered and went to the doctor's office to meet her there for the ultrasound we had scheduled. She was supposed to ovulate yesterday or today. It was critical that we knew when she did. But she didn't show up. And it wasn't until then I started to realize something must have happened to her."

"Doesn't she have a business partner?" Jonathan asked.

"Yeah, Rani Nixon."

Morgan thought of the beautiful African-American woman who had once been a successful New York model. When she'd gotten out of the business, she had moved here to open a real estate office with Lisa, her college roommate.

"I talked to her," he said. "At first she wasn't too concerned. Said that Lisa was probably out showing property, that she'd had several appointments and a couple of closings. But a little while later she called back and said that Lisa hadn't shown up for any of them. She'd heard from several clients who were upset."

"Is that when you called the police?"

"That's right. Chief Cade was here with some of the uniformed cops. Technically, he couldn't file a missing person's report for twenty-four hours, but I filled one out anyway. He probably took it back to the station and sat on it all night."

"No, that's not true," Jonathan said. "He told Morgan he'd been working on it."

Ben rubbed his neck. "He ought to be on leave. He practically just got out of the hospital. He can hardly walk, for Pete's sake, and he's trying to run a police force?"

Morgan saw Jonathan bristle. Revamping the police force had become one of the mayoral race's biggest issues. She hoped they wouldn't start debating now.

"He's as capable of running it now as he ever was," Jonathan said.

Ben went to the window and looked out again. "That's exactly what I'm saying. He never was capable. Our illustrious former mayor was his uncle. Nepotism, pure and simple. The whole family is corrupt. He's not qualified to do that job, and it's time somebody else was appointed."

"When he finds Lisa, you'll change your opinion," Jonathan said. "Meanwhile, I'm calling off the debate."

Ben threw up his hands. "I don't care."

Jonathan looked at Morgan, and she knew he realized the urgency of the situation. This was no publicity hoax.

Ben Jackson was scared to death.

CHAPTER

*B*lair Owens's morning walk always provided the last bits of peace in her day, before she started chasing down stories for the newspaper that came out three times a week. The newspaper business was new to her. For the past several years she had worked as a librarian, and only bought the paper a month ago. While she was widely known as a research whiz who could chase down facts like a greyhound after a rabbit, being a librarian had suited her specific paranoias. The burn scars that covered the right side of her face made her uncomfortable in public, but when she'd bought the paper, she'd been forced outside her walls. It took some getting used to, but she was finding that her new duties suited her personality even better.

She trudged through the sand and grass on the river side of the island to Cricket's, the little hole-in-the-wall diner on the dock where she had breakfast each morning. Often her walk had a payoff at the end, when she found Cade sitting at the counter, sipping his coffee as if waiting for her to come in.

She hoped he would be there today. It had been a month since that first kiss between them, and ever since she'd walked around with butterflies in her stomach, wondering if it had meant as much to him as it had to her. Though he'd been spending a lot more time with her since then, she didn't want to assume anything. Word had gotten around that she and Cade were a couple, and people on the island were beginning to treat them as one. But in truth, she wasn't sure *what* they were. They had never expressed their feelings in words, but Cade's treatment of her had changed from intense friendship to flirtation. Not having that much experience with that type of relationship, she found herself feeling like a bumbling kid who had a crush on someone out of her league.

She got to the screen door of the small diner and pushed inside. Cade sat at the counter, wearing his khaki uniform. He swiveled on his stool at the sound of the door and smiled at her. She couldn't explain the thrill that went through her.

"Hey there," she said in a voice that she hoped sounded friendly and cool. She fought the urge to lean over and kiss him, to touch his freshly shaven jaw or run her finger over his ear.

"I was hoping you'd come in before I had to leave."

"Where you going?"

"Work." He turned back to the counter as she sat down. "Colonel, get Blair a cup of coffee, will you?"

She studied Cade as the Colonel got her a cup. He looked as if he hadn't gotten much sleep last night. Had the pain kept him awake? She'd seen the struggle he encountered going from crutches to that cane, forcing himself to walk on the surgically repaired fractures, his bones held together only by the steel rods the surgeons had inserted. "You look tired."

"Yeah, I didn't get much sleep last night." He sipped his coffee. "Been working on a missing person case."

"Who's missing?"

"Lisa Jackson," the colonel said over the bar.

Blair looked up and caught her breath. "Ben Jackson's wife? She's *missing*?"

Cade sipped his coffee and nodded. "Yeah. It's pretty much common knowledge now, since we've been questioning people all over the island."

"Ben too," the proprietor said. "He was in here drilling everybody who came in last night. I'm thinking they probably had a fight and she ran off for the night. She'll turn up this morning, and they'll get it all worked out, I reckon. They have to. Neither one of them would want to jeopardize the mayoral debate."

Blair took her coffee and turned back to Cade. "How long's she been missing?"

"Not quite twenty-four hours, best we can tell. But I didn't see any point in waiting after Ben reported it. If she shows up today, so much the better."

She thought that over as she took a sip. "The stress of this debate probably got their tempers flaring. Ben can't be easy to live with right now."

"He's convinced something happened to her."

"Well, we both know that Ben's usually wrong. Does make for a more interesting story about the debate, though. I was picturing a big front-page article with a bunch of sound bites from their dogfight this morning, but now I can talk about missing wives and the stress this has put on the families. Heaven knows, it's been stressful for mine. Morgan has been so tense you can hardly talk to her. You'd think Jonathan's been in politics for years."

"Don't exploit it, Blair. There's not a story there yet."

Blair tried not to look insulted. "Me? Hey, I just report the truth. You know I don't embellish."

"Every journalist embellishes, and your imagination is right up there with the best of them."

"You know I'm fair." At least, she hoped he knew. Before, when she had lived by her own set of rules, she might have exaggerated for the sake of subscriptions. But her life had changed. Just weeks ago, she had given her life to Christ, and everything had changed. Now, even in her work, she tried to live by the biblical principles of honesty and love. It wasn't always easy—sometimes she just didn't get it—but God was teaching her.

Cade slipped off the stool and got his cane. "I've got to go."

She tried to hide her disappointment. "You don't have time to eat?"

"I had a bowl of cereal at home." His voice dropped to a deep bass as he leaned in close to her ear. "I just came to see you."

She smiled up at him, knowing that her feelings flashed like neon through the transparency of her eyes. He grinned as he limped out the door, letting the screen door bounce behind him.

When she turned back, she saw the Colonel grinning at her. "What?"

He started to chuckle. "You've got it as bad as he does."

Laughing softly, she brought the cup to her lips and hid behind it, hoping the Colonel hadn't read Cade wrong.

CHAPTER

6

There was bad blood between Cade and
Ben Jackson, but Cade knew he had to put it out of his mind
during the course of this case. He couldn't dwell on rumors
and stretched truths, on Ben's unfounded criticism of his
department and Ben's promises to fire Cade if he was
elected. If anything, Cade had overcompensated on Lisa's
case to prove he wasn't holding anything against him. Most
departments wouldn't even start a search until she'd been
missing twenty-four hours, but Cade had a special interest
in missing persons since he had so recently been one himself.
It didn't matter that Lisa's husband was out to destroy him.

Cade knew Ben would have called him if he'd heard
from Lisa, but he decided to go by his house after leaving
Cricket's, just to update him on the search. He found Morgan and Jonathan there, and while it surprised him that
Ben would have let Jonathan into his house, he was glad
the man wasn't alone. Morgan was known as one of the
chief comforters on the island—one of the first to show
up after any tragedy with a casserole and a hug.

Jonathan, who had grown more compassionate since becoming a pastor, would have a harder time comforting his political rival. But Cade knew his buddy was up to the task.

Ben looked even worse than he had last night. His eyes had a wild fear about them and his hands trembled, but he seemed grateful when he learned just how much the police department had already done to find Lisa.

He rubbed his stubbled jaw and looked up at Cade with misty eyes. "Listen, about all the stuff I've said about you during this campaign—"

"Don't worry about it, Ben. None of that matters. I'm just here to do my job."

Ben looked more humble than Cade had ever seen him. "I'm just saying that if I'd known I was going to need you like this, I sure would have been a little more careful what I said."

Morgan patted his shoulder. "Cade's not the type to hold grudges. You'll find her, won't you, Cade?"

"We're giving it everything we've got. But I need to go over some more things with you, Ben."

Ben nodded, as if anxious to cooperate. "Of course. Anything."

Jonathan got up. "Look, we'll be leaving now so you guys can talk." He reached out to shake Ben's hand. "Let us know if you need anything, okay?"

Morgan gave Ben a hug. "Please, if she turns up, would you call us? We're going to get everybody to pray."

Ben rubbed his face. "I appreciate that."

"And we're not going to be debating without you," Jonathan said. "I'm calling it off."

"You don't have to do that. Sam will revolt."

"Of course I'm gonna do it. This is serious. He'll get over it."

Ben couldn't have looked less interested. He just fixed his eyes on Cade, clearly ready to begin. Cade got the feeling that the mayoral race was the farthest thing from Ben's mind.

CHAPTER

7

*M*organ was quiet as they drove home.

"You okay, babe?" Jonathan asked.

She leaned her head back on the headrest. "Yeah."

"You were thinking about the baby, weren't you?"

She closed her eyes, hoping they'd look less haunted. "I was actually wondering if God still answers my prayers. Will he hear my prayers for Lisa, when he didn't hear my prayers for the baby?"

Silence fell between them. She was glad he didn't spout out some pat answer about how God heard but had a different plan. Even if it was true, she didn't want to hear it right now.

"Is it ever going to happen, Jonathan?"

"Of course it is." His voice sounded as weak and uncertain as hers.

She leaned her head against the window. "I'm not so sure. It took so long to get pregnant, and now this. There's got to be something wrong." She looked back at him.

"Jonathan, I think it's time for us to make an appointment at the fertility clinic."

He pulled into the driveway and cut off the engine but made no effort to get out of the car. "Don't you think it's too soon? It's only been a little over a year."

"If it's too soon, they'll tell us. Meanwhile, I just want some tests. I want to know if there's something wrong that can be fixed before much more time passes."

"You've got plenty of time left on your biological clock, Morgan. You're only twenty-nine."

"But I want a big family, and I don't understand why I can't get pregnant when teenagers do after one indiscretion. I need to know what's wrong with me."

He looked out the window for a long moment, staring at the wax myrtles along the driveway, their branches reaching up to the sky. Blair's car sat in the driveway. Was Sadie filling her in on the miscarriage? She hoped not.

"It could be me, honey." His words came out raspy, uncertain.

She shook her head. "You know that's not true. I was pregnant. I'm the one who lost the baby."

"But the bottom line is, something's going wrong with *us*. And if you feel like you need to go to the fertility clinic, I'm with you."

She had expected a fight. "Are you sure, Jonathan?"

"Of course I'm sure. Why wouldn't I be?"

"All the reasons you've said before. It seems like once we start on this cycle, it's hard to stop."

"It's worth a try, baby. Just one appointment. We can find out what our options are. Then we can decide if we want to go on." He squeezed her hand. "That okay?"

She wished the decision had made her feel better. It was simply a step, not the cure. "Yeah." She looked up at the porch. Her big ferns spilled over their hanging pots, cascading almost to the floor, in need of water. She suddenly felt too tired to tend to them. "Guess it's time to tell my sister what happened yesterday."

Jonathan looked as though he dreaded that as much as she did.

They went in and found Blair in the kitchen with Sadie and Caleb. The baby was in his high chair, shoving dry Cheerios into his mouth as he banged his spoon on the tray.

Blair was munching on a carrot and glanced at the Braves T-shirt Jonathan wore. "You're not wearing that to the debate, are you? Don't you realize this is the most important day of your political life, Jonathan?"

He headed for the phone. "There's not going to be a debate today, Blair."

She caught her breath and looked at her sister. "Because of Lisa Jackson?"

Morgan nodded. "How did you know?"

"I heard about it at Cricket's. Sadie said you'd gone over there. Is this for real?"

Morgan went to the coffee pot. It was still warm, so she poured a cup. "She's still missing. Ben's crazy with worry."

"You're sure it's not just some trumped up attempt to get attention?"

"Yes," Morgan said. "If you'd seen him, you wouldn't even ask. Besides, Lisa's not a publicity hound. She wouldn't have gone along with a scheme like that."

"She would if he tied her up and locked her in a room."

Morgan turned back to her sister and shot her a withering look. "That's not funny, Blair."

Blair looked as if she'd been unfairly judged. "Hey, I'm just saying people will do strange things for politics."

"This is not political," Morgan said.

Jonathan got off the phone and came out of the office. "Well, there's no way to completely call this off without going to the rally and making an announcement there. We're going to delay it a week, possibly two, depending on the availability of the Pier."

"Darn." Blair threw down her carrot. "I really hate that. I was all set for you to pull ahead in the race today." She looked at Sadie, who sat next to Caleb and was staring at Morgan as if she expected her to burst into tears. "Sadie, I guess you and I can chase down the Lisa story today. See if we can find out anything."

Sadie had worked briefly for the previous owner of the paper, so Blair had hired her to help out after school and on weekends. She had proved to be a valuable employee. But Sadie looked as if something was troubling her.

"I was thinking . . . since the rally's off, do you think I could go to Atlanta and see my mom? I haven't seen her in about a month. We've been so busy, and she doesn't get that many visitors. It always cheers her up when I come."

Blair shrugged. "I can do without you. The paper doesn't even come out until Tuesday. I'm sure I can cover everything by myself today."

Morgan smiled at the girl. "You can take my car, honey. Give her a kiss from Caleb."

A grin broke out on Sadie's face, and Morgan realized how much the teen still missed her mother. Saturdays were the only days that Sadie could go visit. The fact that it was a six-hour round-trip made it prohibitive on any other day.

"Before you leave, Sadie, I need to talk to Blair upstairs. Can you watch Caleb for a few minutes?"

Sadie gave her a knowing look. "Sure. Come on, Caleb. Come with me while I get ready to go see Mommy." Caleb toddled off, holding Sadie's hand.

Blair got up and studied Morgan's face. "Everything okay?"

"Let's go talk." Morgan was quiet as she led her sister up the stairs. She could hear Karen—one of the home's residents—changing her baby's diaper in her room, talking to the seven-week-old infant in a soft, sweet voice. She had turned out to be a devoted mother to Emory—not something Morgan would have expected from a former crack addict.

Morgan led Blair into their parents' old room. Though they had died months ago, Morgan had left their room just as it was. The scents in the pillows and the curtains had long ago faded, but the room still filled them both with comfort when the grief got a foothold.

Morgan sank onto the bed.

"Sis, are you all right?" Blair whispered.

Morgan pressed the corners of her eyes, trying hard not to cry. "I had a miscarriage yesterday."

It took a moment for the words to hit full force. "A miscarriage? You were pregnant?"

"I'd only found out the day before. We were going to announce it yesterday."

"Oh, honey." Blair sat down on the bed next to her and pulled her into her arms. "I am so sorry."

Morgan laid her head on Blair's shoulder. "I tried to call you several times yesterday, but I never got you."

"Why didn't you leave a message? I would have called back."

"I don't know. I guess I couldn't decide whether I really wanted to talk or not. Oh, Blair, I really wanted to be pregnant."

"I know you did." Blair grabbed a Kleenex box from the nightstand and handed one to Morgan, then wadded one up for herself. "I don't even know what to say."

"There's nothing to say. It just is."

"At least you know you can get pregnant now."

Morgan wished Blair hadn't said that. "What good is it to be able to fertilize an egg and have it implant into your uterus if you can't make it hold on? Lisa's had four miscarriages. She's been trying for thirteen years. What if I'm going to be like that?"

"You're not, okay? It's nothing like that."

Morgan blew her nose. "I don't know, Blair. I have a bad feeling."

"Well, don't." Her voice held a determined certainty. "You're perfectly fine."

"I miss Mama." Morgan's voice broke off, and Blair pulled her back into her arms and let go of her own emotions. "I miss her so much."

"Me too," Blair whispered. "She would know what to say. She wouldn't spout off like I do, without a thought."

"Words aren't the answer," Morgan told her. "But she would pray. Mama was the world's best prayer warrior."

"Now, that I can do," Blair whispered.

*M*organ recognized the angry voice at the front door as she and Blair came downstairs.

"I heard you're planning to call off the debate. Who do you think you are, making that decision without even asking me?"

Morgan looked at Blair.

"Sam Sullivan," they said at the same time.

Sam was the third candidate in the mayoral race—the one who wrote the book on cut-throat campaigning. Morgan might have known he wouldn't take the cancellation well.

She reached the bottom of the stairs and joined Jonathan at the door.

"Lisa Jackson is missing," he was saying. "Under the circumstances, we could hardly have gone on with it."

"You and me could have done it." The tips of Sam's ears turned pink. "If somebody can't show up, that's his tough luck. But this was supposed to go off. We have advertisements up all over town—*paid* advertisements, I might add. It ain't right to call it off without consulting everybody involved."

Jonathan shook his head. "We can put it off, Sam. It won't hurt a thing."

Sam looked like a good-ole-boy version of Rodney Dangerfield, with his flattop and his don't-get-no-respect attitude. "You think you're pretty smart, don't you, Jonathan? Throwing us off guard like this when we were all prepared. You know darn well that Ben Jackson'll do anything for publicity, and this is the biggest stunt he's pulled yet."

"I thought of that," Jonathan said, "but I really don't believe that's what's happening here. I was with him this morning."

"I knew it!" Sam threw his hands up. "So you two are in cahoots then. I might have known. And if you don't think I'm gonna let this be known to every reporter in the area—"

"Milk it for all it's worth," Jonathan said. "Knock yourself out. If you want to look like a man who doesn't have an ounce of compassion, go for it."

"I have a good mind to hold that rally anyway. To stand up there by myself and take advantage of the opportunity."

"Like I said, knock yourself out." Jonathan swung the storm door open to let Sam out. "Nice of you to drop by, Sam. Sorry you have to leave so soon."

Sam spotted Morgan and Blair standing in the doorway. "Blair Owens, you better write about this in that paper of yours! Tell 'em how he talked to me. You can't play favorites."

Blair crossed her arms. "I'm on it, Sam."

He marched out the door, grumbling something about derailing this election and suing for the advertisement money. Jonathan let the door bounce shut behind him.

Blair chuckled. "That man is like a caricature of himself. Every reporter's dream."

Jonathan ground his teeth together. "Coming into my house and chewing *me* out. He can have at it. I hope he does prance down to the Pier and show his true colors."

"Are you going to show up and make the announcement?"

"You bet I am," Jonathan said. "And if Sam tries to stand in my way, the crowd will see what he's made of."

CHAPTER

9

*T*he drive to the prison, which was located one hour east of Atlanta, seemed farther every time Sadie made the trip. She passed the time listening to music, but by the time she got there she dreaded having to drive home again.

She went through the degrading hoops necessary for security—emptying her pockets, removing her shoes, enduring a search that left her feeling humiliated—then took her place at one of the visiting booths as she waited for them to get her mother. She hadn't been able to hug her mother in a year, since her arrest and felony conviction on drug charges. A panel of smudged glass separated them, and they had to talk via the telephones that hung on either side of the glass.

The atmosphere was not conducive to a relaxing visit. Every conversation in the room could be overheard. The glass partition didn't go to the ceiling, only high enough to prevent contact. Angry voices and expletives flew around her. She sat with rigid muscles, as if ready to defend herself from sudden assault.

In the booth next to her, a man cursed into the phone, and she could hear the inmate's angry reaction as she hit the glass with her fists, causing Sadie's own booth to jerk. The woman shrieked at her visitor, and for a moment Sadie thought the inmate might come over the partition and latch onto his neck.

Sadie fought the urge to run out. If she did, her mother would be crushed.

She watched through the glass as two guards came to quiet the inmate. The woman swung at one of them, and in an instant, they had wrestled her to the door, no doubt escorting her to lock-down where she would feed her rage.

"Leave her alone!" Her visitor was on his feet, shouting. "She didn't do nothin'. I got the right to visit my wife!" He kicked his chair, and it fell against Sadie. She sprang up and tried to move away.

Another guard pushed her aside and escorted the rabid husband out. Sadie watched until he was gone, afraid he would run back in and wreak more havoc. She felt small and fragile—and close to tears—as she sat back down to wait for her mother.

Other conversations around her were thankfully less heated. A baby cried at one of the booths, and a two-year-old had been set free to run around barefoot on the dirty floor.

There was no air-conditioning, and the room was approaching eighty degrees. The heat did nothing to help the smell of backed-up sewage in the bathroom or the heavy scent of body odor on the stagnant air.

The door opened, and Sadie saw Sheila step in and look from window to window. When she saw Sadie, her face lit up. That look made all of this worth it.

Sheila grabbed the phone and sat down. "Hey, baby—" she touched the glass—"I thought you couldn't come today."

Sadie put her hand against the glass. Her side was sticky. "My plans changed at the last minute. How are you?"

Her mother looked good, in spite of the brown jumpsuit she'd worn every day of her incarceration. Her hair was pulled up in a pony tail, making her look younger than thirty-two. Sadie knew most people thought they were sisters, rather than mother and daughter. Sadie was the result of a teen pregnancy, and her upbringing bore that out.

"How's Caleb?" her mother asked.

Sadie pulled the current pictures out of her pocket and pressed them against the glass. "I took this one earlier this week. Look how curly his hair's gotten. He's always real busy and talks a lot. You should hear him. He's a real scream."

Her mother's head tilted at the sight of the pictures, and she got tears in her eyes. "I wish you could bring him to see me."

"It would be too hard, Mom. The ride is too long. He'd never be able to stay in his car seat that long. And when we got here, you wouldn't even be able to hold him."

Sheila wiped a tear. "Maybe we could get special permission. Some of the girls here have been able to do that. One of my cell mates had a baby right here in jail two months ago. They took it from her the next day, but they let her hold her baby sometimes when her mother brings her. I could get the chaplain to work it out for me. They listen to him."

Sadie sighed. She couldn't imagine subjecting her little brother to this place. "We'll see, Mom. Maybe we can work it out sometime. But I'll leave you these pictures."

"Did you get my letter yet? About my lawyer?"

Sadie shook her head. "When did you send it?"

"Two days ago. You probably would have gotten it today." That smile came back to Sheila's face. "Baby, I'm not getting my hopes up or anything, and I don't want you to either, but I found out that the legislature just passed a law to help overcrowding in the prisons. For nonviolent crimes, they're letting people out after serving only twenty percent of their sentence. I'm not sure whether my conviction falls within the right timeline. I may qualify and I may not. My public defender is looking into it."

Sadie almost jumped out of her seat. "You mean you could get out?"

"It's possible. I have four more years. If I fall under the twenty percent rule, I could get out now. But don't get your hopes up, baby. It may not work out. Hardly anything ever does."

Sadie's heart was pounding. "Mom, that's great! What if it *does* work out? You could be free."

Sheila leaned in to the window and giggled. "Wouldn't that be a miracle?"

"God's given us miracles before, Mom."

Sheila's eyes grew misty again. "Yeah, he has."

"Oh, Mom, you would love Cape Refuge. It's so beautiful. Probably the most beautiful place on earth. At least, it's the most beautiful place I've ever seen."

Sheila paused for a moment. "Baby, I don't know if I want to come to Cape Refuge."

Sadie's heart deflated. "Why not? You don't want to go back to where we were before."

"Tell you what. We'll just cross that bridge when we come to it."

Sadie thought about that statement as she drove back to Cape Refuge. She couldn't consider the thought that her mother might choose to go back to Atlanta if she was released early. Somehow, she had to talk her into coming to Cape Refuge and starting a new life.

There simply was no other option.

She prayed that God would have mercy on her mother and give her this second chance that no one had expected. Then she imagined Sheila walking along the beach with her, barefoot in the sand, swinging little Caleb between them, and splashing his feet in the water. She pictured her being serene and happy, like Morgan, taking care of her family and watching over them.

It was a picture far removed from the reality she had known before her mother went to jail, but she hadn't given up on the hope that she could change.

"Please let it happen, Lord," she prayed as she drove. "Change Mom's heart, and give her a new start."

10

*D*etective Joe McCormick, the only detective on Cade's force, had not been with Cade last night when Ben reported Lisa missing. Since she still hadn't been found, and the possibility that she'd met with foul play increased with each passing hour, Cade decided to bring McCormick in. Maybe something in Ben's story would send up a red flag in the detective's mind.

McCormick took notes as Ben went over his story again. When Ben finished, McCormick studied his notes. "Where were you fishing yesterday, Ben?"

"I took my boat and went out to the reefs."

"Catch anything?"

"Yeah. Six black sea bass. They're in the freezer."

"Then you took the time to clean them before you went to meet Lisa?"

"Yeah. It didn't take that long. Then I showered and headed to the doctor's office."

"How long were you out there?"

"Until about two. Appointment was three-thirty."

"Did you communicate with her at all from the time you left Cape Refuge until you came back?" McCormick asked.

Ben shook his head. "Not at all. She had all these appointments scheduled. It was a big day for her. She was closing on some houses and looking forward to that appointment. And I don't have to tell you that our cell phones don't work on the island. When she's in Savannah I can usually get her, but not here."

"Was she worried about anything—upset at all?"

He shrugged. "Just the usual."

"What usual?" McCormick asked.

"Well, you know, we were both stressed about the debate, and she was worried about whether this in vitro would work. She had this big-deal Hollywood producer coming, and she was supposed to help him scout locations for his newest movie."

"I've got his name," Cade said. "We're questioning him today."

"She never made it to that appointment. Rani said she had to fill in for Lisa."

McCormick rubbed his chin as he studied Ben's face. Cade knew what he was looking for. The husband always had to be considered a suspect when a wife met with foul play, but so far, Cade hadn't found any guile in Ben's body language or glitches in his story. They still weren't sure there had been any foul play.

"Had a lot on her plate, huh?" McCormick asked.

"Yeah, but she always does."

Does. Present tense was a good sign.

"I expected her at home when I got here because we were going to ride to the fertility clinic together, only she didn't show up. So I called her at the office. Rani hadn't seen her. Nobody'd seen her, but I didn't worry. I figured she'd meet me at the doctor's office. There was no way she was going to miss it." He stopped talking and rubbed his mouth hard. "It wasn't until I got there that I realized something must have happened to her. That's when I started getting worried."

Cade heard a car door slamming outside, and Ben sprang up and lunged for the window, as if expecting to see Lisa getting out of her car. But it wasn't Lisa. A television van from Savannah had parked in front of the house, and a camera crew was setting up. Cade saw the coiffed correspondent trudging across the lawn to the door.

"It's the press," Ben said. The disappointment hung over him like a lead cloak. He dropped back into the chair. "I thought it was her."

Cade watched him cover his face and fight tears. He didn't know how to comfort the man, but he felt sure this wasn't an act. The worry and dread seemed genuine.

The bell rang. "Do you want to talk to them?" Cade asked softly.

Ben slid his hands down his face and looked toward the front door. "I guess it might help. Get the word out."

It wasn't the answer Cade expected, but he saw the wisdom behind it. Maybe it was a good idea.

Ben went to the door and told the reporter that he'd be out in a minute to give a statement, then he turned back to Cade and McCormick. "I need to figure out what I'm going to say."

"Find a picture of her to give them," Cade said. "Describe her car and when she was last seen. That kind of thing."

Ben grabbed a framed picture off of an end table. "This one should do." His hands trembled as he took it out of the gilded frame. He looked scattered, as if his mind raced with pleas for his wife. "Are we finished here?"

Cade looked at McCormick. He nodded. "Ben, last night we checked all the hotels on the island, to see if she might have checked in. She didn't. Today we're checking the hotels in nearby towns. Are there any other towns we should check? Any family members she might have gone to stay with?"

"No. I talked to her parents in Cordele last night, and they haven't heard from her. She's an only child. There's no place I can think of where she would have gone."

"We're putting a statewide APB out on her car, and I'm going to ask South Carolina and Florida to do the same. Maybe someone will spot it." Cade got up and reached for his cane. McCormick followed him to the door.

Ben stopped them at the door and grabbed Cade's arm, his desperate gaze locking into Cade's. "Find her, Cade. She has to be all right."

Cade knew better than to give him meaningless assurances. "We'll do everything we can, Ben."

Ben's face sagged with the heaviness of his fear. "Look, would you two mind going out and standing with me while I make my statement? They might want to ask you a few questions."

"I'm not going to give a statement," Cade said, "but our presence will let them know that we're looking."

The three of them stepped out into the front yard, and the television camera started rolling. Cade saw Blair's car pulling up, and she hurried up the yard, as if she didn't want to miss a thing.

He hoped the publicity would bring Lisa home and that later they would all feel like idiots for making so much out of nothing. Yet he had no intention of resting on that assumption. If he had anything to say about it, Lisa would be found today.

CHAPTER

11

*H*er friend's disappearance haunted Morgan all morning, and she finally decided to drive to Lisa's real estate office to talk to her partner. Rani Nixon's Mercedes Roadster was the only car in the parking lot, and Morgan supposed that the staff must be off on Saturday.

The sun blazed on the black asphalt, its heat radiating upward. She was glad the debate wasn't going to be today. She still felt weak from the miscarriage and had dreaded standing out at the South Beach Pier, trying to look perky in ninety-five-degree heat.

The cool air from the air-conditioner blasted her as she went into the building. She stepped into the quiet waiting area and looked around. Morgan had never been in here before, so she wasn't sure where Rani's office was, but she could hear the woman's low voice from one of the offices at the back. She went to the doorway and saw the woman talking on the phone. Rani saw her and lifted a hand in a wave, then held it there as if telling her she'd be right with her.

"Yeah, look, if she does come by, would you please have her call? We're all very worried about her." Rani sniffed and wiped her nose with a wadded ball of tissue.

Morgan looked away, feeling as if she'd stepped in on an intimate moment.

"We hope not too. Yeah, I know."

Morgan looked up at her again, a sense of awe falling over her at the strikingly attractive woman. Rani Nixon still looked like a cover model. With her Halle Berry features and short-cropped black hair, she looked as if she should have a mob of paparazzi following her around. When she'd given up her career five years ago and moved to Cape Refuge to work with Lisa, she had been an instant success. Everyone wanted to do business with the celebrity. Her reputation, her money, and her aggressive nature had all added up to skyrocketing success for their real estate business.

Rani got off the phone. "Morgan, isn't it?" She stood up, her five-feet-ten-inches making Morgan feel dwarfed.

"Yes." The woman had a Wall Street handshake, and Morgan was intimidated. "It's good to see you. I just wanted to come by and talk to you about Lisa. I'm really worried about her."

"You and the rest of us. I haven't slept all night. I've been worried sick." She motioned for Morgan to sit down, and Rani took her chair again. "So how did you come to hear about it?"

"I left some messages for Lisa yesterday, so Cade came to question me this morning about whether I'd talked with her. I hadn't. She never called back."

Rani shook her head and leaned forward. "I have a bad feeling, Morgan. A real bad feeling."

That wasn't what Morgan wanted to hear. "Why?"

"Because she had a million things going on yesterday. Trust me, she wouldn't have just bagged them. I spent the whole day trying to do spin control and cover for her, and that never happens. And the kicker is she missed her doctor's appointment."

"At the fertility clinic." Morgan wanted Rani to know that Lisa hadn't kept that secret from her.

"Yeah, she's practically psycho about those things. Her body's pumped so full of hormones that if Ben's one minute late for one of those appointments, she just about goes ballistic. No way did she just decide to skip town and not go."

"Well, that's the thing. Don't you think those hormones just may have pushed her over the edge?"

"Hey, she's moody, but she's not crazy. I meant she was psycho about the appointments, the fertility, the whole baby thing. It's an obsession with her, you know? I didn't mean that her hormones were really making her crazy. A little irritable maybe. A little moody. And come on, she missed half a million worth of commissions yesterday. No way that would happen."

"Was there any place she went where her car might have broken down or something?"

"There's no telling. Her car hasn't turned up, so we don't know." She dug into her drawer and came up with a cigarette and lighter. "You don't mind, do you?" she asked as she lit it. She took a drag and blew the smoke out in a stream, then tossed the lighter back into the drawer. "Lisa hates when I smoke in the office. I've been trying to quit, but it's impossible with this stuff going on."

Morgan tried not to cough.

"Anyway, if the cops know what they're doing—and frankly, I'm not so sure—they're interviewing everyone she was supposed to meet with yesterday."

Morgan ignored the comment about Cade's police force. "They'll find her. I know Cade real well. He's very good at what he does."

"Let's hope you're right. But with one detective and a half-crippled chief, I'm skeptical. If Lisa's all right, she would have called by now. If she could get to a phone, that is. If this blasted place could just get a cell phone signal—I've never heard of anything so primitive. It almost kept me from moving here. And it hurts with selling real estate, I can tell you. People prefer to go somewhere else if they can't even make a call."

Morgan didn't bother to mention that they always had Ma Bell. "Did she have a cell phone with her?"

"Yes, and I've tried to call it a million times. She's not answering. If she were off the island somewhere, she'd at least check her voicemail." She brought the cigarette to her lips again. "I swear, I think he had something to do with it."

"What? Who?"

"That Ben." She blew the smoke toward the ceiling. "I wouldn't put it past him."

Morgan just gaped at her. "Are you suggesting he would hurt Lisa?"

Rani gave Morgan a conspiratorial look. "I'm not accusing him of anything, okay? I'm just saying, there's been trouble in paradise for a long time."

Morgan didn't know whether to be relieved or concerned. If it really had been a fight, then maybe Lisa was off nursing her anger. Maybe she'd be back.

Rani tapped her cigarette on an ashtray shaped like a manicured hand. "Lisa comes in here a few weeks ago with tears in her eyes. She'd just collected the mail in her office, and you'll never guess what she found."

Morgan couldn't imagine. "What?"

"A letter from a woman who claimed to be Ben's lover."

Morgan's mouth fell open. "You're kidding."

"The woman told her that she'd been having an affair with Ben for months and that he'd been promising that he was going to leave Lisa."

"Who was it from?"

"That's just it." Rani leaned on her desk, her gaze locking into Morgan's. "There was no signature and no return address. The letter was postmarked Cape Refuge. No clue who sent it."

"Did Lisa confront Ben?"

"Of course she did." Rani stubbed out her cigarette. "That jerk just told her he had no idea where the letter had come from, that it was a bunch of lies. He told her that if she didn't believe him, she could hire a detective to follow him around. She bought it."

"Did she hire the detective?"

"No. She convinced herself he was telling the truth. She figured he wouldn't be working so hard at trying to have a baby with her if he planned to leave her. And besides that, he seemed to be available at a moment's notice. Not like he was hiding anything." She waved her hand in the air. "They were doing this temperature thing, checking her body for ovulation, all this stuff, and whenever she'd call him, he'd drop whatever he was doing and meet her—at home, at the doctor's office, wherever she needed him. He also convinced her he'd never do such a stupid thing when he was trying to run for mayor. It would ruin his chances in a town like this."

"Well, that does sound reasonable," Morgan said. "Ben is always worried about image. You'd think he wouldn't be so stupid as to have an affair when so much was at stake."

"You would think." She set her chin on her hand and let out a long sigh. "But I wasn't believing it. I've seen this kind of thing before. People *are* stupid when they're cheating. And then she got more letters."

Morgan frowned. "How many?"

"Three or four more. And every time, he denied it, but I think Lisa was starting to get wise. The last one really concerned her, though, and I could see on her face that her faith in him was starting to falter. I tried to convince her to call his bluff and hire a detective just like he'd suggested, but I don't think she ever did."

Morgan felt sick. Maybe the pain she'd seen on Lisa's face so many times hadn't just been mourning over her infertility. Maybe there was something much deeper.

"Rani, have you told the police about this?"

Rani lit another cigarette. "I've been going around and around about it. I didn't know if I should, because it opens a whole new can of worms. And if Lisa hasn't just run off, they might assume she has and stop looking."

"Cade wouldn't do that. You have to tell them. This is relevant information."

"If Ben has any decency, he'll tell them himself."

"Not if he's hiding something." Morgan thought back over Ben's countenance this morning. Did he look like a guilty man, someone who'd been having an affair, cheating on his wife, lying to her all along? No. The truth was, he had been beside himself, panicked over the disappearance of his wife. It couldn't have been an act.

Or could it?

"The thing is, even if he was having an affair," Rani said, "I don't think he would have killed her."

Morgan shivered. "*Killed* her?"

"Well, yeah. I mean, to get her out of the way so he could be with his lover or whatever."

Morgan had considered that Lisa could be dead, but only as a fleeting thought. Now, the idea that Ben might have done it disturbed her more than she could explain. "Rani, you have to tell the police."

Rani stared at her for a long moment, turning the idea over in her mind. "I guess you're right. I wonder if she kept those letters in her desk. They came here, after all. Maybe I can find them." She slid her chair back and walked out, her perfume trailing in the air behind her, mingling with the smoke.

Morgan followed her into Lisa's office. The walls looked like polished marble, and the carpet was a deep wine color. Tiffany lamps accented the antique desk and the sitting area. Morgan could just imagine Lisa making deals in an office like this.

Rani pulled out the drawers and searched through them until she came to the bottom drawer and found a box of letters.

"Bingo. Pay dirt." She pulled the letters out, then tossed them onto the desk. "Take a look if you don't believe me."

"Uh . . . no. I don't feel comfortable doing that. Let's just take them to Cade. Let him read them."

Rani shrugged. "Okay, maybe they do have some relevance. Let me get my purse."

When Rani had locked the office, Morgan looked at her. "Do you want me to follow you there and talk to Cade with you?" She felt foolish for asking. Rani was tough, assertive. She didn't need anyone to hold her hand.

But the woman surprised her. "Yeah, it might not hurt to have a little moral support, if you don't mind."

Morgan followed the Roadster to the police station, thinking about those letters and praying that they didn't mean something terrible had really happened to Lisa. Was Ben Jackson grieving over his wife's disappearance—or his own guilt? Was he covering for a lover who might have taken matters into her own hands?

The questions filled her with nauseating urgency. She only hoped Cade could answer them.

CHAPTER

*T*he stage on the beach next to the South Beach Pier had been built for the rally, decorated with the American and Georgia state flags. It was wired to blast the debate for hundreds of yards. The crowd had already assembled when Jonathan pulled up in his car and found a parking place in the spot reserved for the candidates. Sam Sullivan was already there, working the crowd, wearing a light blue seersucker suit and a Panama hat that made him look like Rodney Dangerfield impersonating Harry Truman.

Art Russell—one of the City Council members—met Jonathan in the sand before he reached the crowd.

"Jonathan, are you really calling this off? We have vendors here selling food and drinks. A lot of people went to a lot of trouble. The square dancers are all here in full costume, ready to perform."

"We have to call it off, Art. It's not right to hold a political rally without all the candidates."

"But Ben had the choice to show up."

Jonathan kept walking. "No, he didn't. His wife is missing. I'm not going to take advantage of it, and neither is Sam."

Art looked back at the crowd. "You know he's planning to take the stage himself."

"Not if I can stop him."

Jonathan didn't bother to shake any hands as he walked through the crowd and right up onto the platform. Sarah Williford, the council member who was going to introduce them, was already sitting in her spot as if afraid that someone else might get it. The woman, looking as though she'd stepped out of a sixties commune, had dressed for the occasion in a flowing dress, which looked like it was made of cheesecloth, and a pair of flat sandals.

Jonathan didn't bother to speak to her. He went straight to the microphone and tapped it. "Excuse me, could I have your attention, please? Everybody, could I have your attention?"

Sam Sullivan cried out, then made a beeline through the crowd. In his hurry, he almost stumbled up the stairs.

Jonathan ignored him and kept talking. "Ladies and gentlemen, I'm afraid we're going to have to call off the debate. Ben Jackson won't be able to make it. It seems that his wife, Lisa, has been missing since yesterday." A wave of surprise whispered over the crowd. "We'll reschedule the debate for two weeks from today, since it wouldn't be right to do it without him at a time like this."

By now, Sam was on the stage. He glared at Jonathan like he had hijacked the spotlight and grabbed the microphone out of his hand.

"We need your help and the help of anybody else on this island who's so inclined," Sam said. "Lisa—bless her heart—was last seen yesterday morning. If any of you have any information about any sightings of her yesterday at any time of the day, we would ask you to call the Cape Refuge police and report it. It's not a time for politics. It's a time for working together, to help a brother in need."

Cade stood back gaping at the man. Did anyone really buy this sudden concern? He hoped the people saw through Sam's self-sacrificing act.

Jonathan took the mike back. "I spoke to Cade before coming here, and he said we're going to need a lot of volunteers to search the island. Since all of you are already assembled here, I'm going to open up a table over to the side here where people can sign up to help."

"When did she go missing?" Ronald Myers shouted from the crowd.

"Sometime yesterday," Jonathan said. "No one's sure yet."

"I saw her Wednesday," Fran Lincoln said. "She was in line at the bank, and we struck up a conversation. She was in a real big hurry to get away."

"Everybody's in a hurry when they talk to you," someone returned. Jonathan saw her ex-husband snickering at the back of the crowd.

"I'll bet Ben campaigned her right outta her mind," Bo Patterson suggested. "She's prob'ly curled up in fetal position on some shrink's couch."

Half the crowd laughed, and the rest expressed indignation.

"I hope it's something simple like that," Jonathan said. "But she needs earnest prayer right now. In fact, I'd like to lead us in that."

Most of the people bowed their heads, and a hush fell over the group. Jonathan made a petition for Lisa's safety and Ben's comfort. When he'd said *amen*, he looked over at Sam. His opponent—an avowed atheist—looked as if he might grab Jonathan by the throat and wrestle him to the ground.

"So, Sam, do you have something you'd like to add?"

Jonathan could have sworn smoke was coming out of the man's ears. He wondered if he'd invoke the "separation of church and state," but Sam was too shrewd for that. Too many of his constituents believed in God.

"Just that I'll be helping at that table too. Maybe we can divide up and take groups out to search various areas."

Jonathan smiled and looked down at his feet. Sam wasn't going to give him the opportunity to show his leadership skills all alone. He figured it could only help.

He stepped off the stage and went to the table that had been set up to give out campaign flyers. He wasn't sure where Cade would want them to start looking, but from the number of people assembling to get in line at the table, he knew that they would have a good start on searching for Lisa today.

"Jonathan, a word with you, please."

Jonathan looked at the man who had stepped to the front of the line. He looked familiar, but Jonathan wasn't sure where he'd seen him before.

"Vince Barr, of the *Observer*." The man reached across the table to shake his hand.

"Of course." Jonathan remembered the sleazy reporter for the tabloid based in Savannah. He'd been amused at some of his recent headlines. One claimed that George Bush had been kidnapped and replaced by an alien—complete with pictures of the offending space ship in the sky. Usually mayoral debates in small towns weren't up his alley.

"It's about Lisa Jackson's disappearance. I heard about it on the police scanner, and I've been trying to get information for our Tuesday issue. Have you spoken to Mr. Jackson?"

Jonathan wasn't about to tell this man a thing. "I thought you guys just made stuff up. You don't really do interviews, do you?"

He grinned. "Of course we do interviews. This is serious news."

"Yeah, but it's not national."

"They didn't think Laci Peterson's disappearance was national either, but you never know. It's always good to have a leg up on things just in case something comes of it. So did you talk to him?"

"Yes, I talked to him. He's very upset."

"Do you think he'd grant an interview?"

"I really couldn't say." Jonathan turned to the line of volunteers forming and passed a legal pad across the table. "If you'd all just sign in, I'll try to get word to Cade that we're ready to start looking where he tells us."

"How well do you know Lisa and Ben Jackson?" the reporter cut in.

Jonathan shot him another look. "Well enough."

"Were they happy? Had there been any trouble in their marriage?"

"I don't know any of that. They seemed happy."

"What kind of man is Ben Jackson?"

Jonathan didn't like where Vince was going with this. "If you don't mind, I'm busy. But you can sign up as a volunteer, if you want. The search itself will be a story. Maybe there's even an alien or two involved."

Vince chuckled again and started to back away. "Thanks anyway. I'm sure I'll find someone who'll give me information."

CHAPTER

*B*en Jackson owned a fleet of shrimp trawlers and a shrimping warehouse on the Savannah dock, one of many operations in the industrialized area that serviced the marine commerce. Since adult white shrimp spawned near the shores in May, it was a busy time for his captains and crews.

Cade knew Ben oversaw the warehouse operations and the shipping of the shrimp to other states, but he wasn't here today. Cade had driven here in hopes of talking to his employees, to feel them out about the possibility that Ben had a mistress.

Rani's revelation about the letters had changed his thinking about the case. Sympathy for Ben had kept him from exploring the man's possible guilt in his wife's disappearance, but the letters forced his hand. If they had, indeed, been written by his mistress, then Ben could be hiding much more than infidelity. The letters provided motive for two different people to want Lisa out of the way. If there truly was another woman, Cade was determined to find out who. The more he knew, the better equipped he'd be when he confronted Ben about the letters.

One of the rigs had just returned with its catch from a run up the South Carolina coast, so no one noticed right away when Cade came into the warehouse. The crews busied themselves with deheading, sorting, and packing the catch in ice. Though the place was clean and cool, the smell of shrimp filled his nostrils and attached itself to his hair and clothes. He looked around at the dockworkers on Ben's payroll. They were mostly tough, rugged men with foul mouths—which pretty much ruled out the possibility that Ben had a mistress here.

Cade identified the supervisor in charge of the shift and headed toward him. The man looked as if he hadn't showered in days. He wore an old charcoal gray T-shirt with big sweat rings under the armpits. Someone nudged him as Cade approached, and he met Cade halfway across the floor.

"Thought I might see the po-lice here today. I'm J. B. Hutchins, Ben's operations manager."

Cade introduced himself. "Why did you expect the police?"

"What with Lisa missin' and all. TV stations were here, snoopin' around about Ben. Only fittin' that the po-lice would show up, askin' questions." He could see that the man was excited by the day's events.

"What kind of questions did the press ask you today?"

"You know, stuff about their marriage and whatnot. Whether Lisa was depressed."

"And what did you tell them?"

"I told them they were a solid couple. Happily married, far as I could see. I didn't see Lisa all that much."

"J.B., was there anybody else in their lives, somebody who might have threatened Lisa or . . . might have come between them at any point?"

"Come between them?" J.B.'s voice echoed over the warehouse. "You mean like an affair or somethin'? Heck, no. Lisa would never do that."

His immediate assumption that Cade was talking about Lisa surprised him. "What about Ben?"

J.B. let a laugh echo over the room. "No way. Ben ain't the type to do that. He has a one-track mind. Like with this mayor's race, it's all he thinks about. He's like that with his marriage. He'd never go with no other woman."

"Was there anybody who might have been angry at Ben or Lisa? Angry customers? Disgruntled crewmen?"

"Not that I know of."

"No threats? Nothing out of the ordinary?"

"Naw, none." He stuck his hands into his back pockets. "What do you think? She got kidnapped or somethin'?"

Cade evaded. "We're still investigating. Looking at every possibility." He saw J.B. look toward the door, and Cade glanced behind him.

Blair stood at the doorway. He wondered how much she'd heard.

"Grand Central Station," J.B. muttered. "People comin' and goin' all day today, askin' all sorts of questions. I'll be glad when she gets found."

"Listen, if you think of anything, give me a call at the station, will you?"

"Sure, I will." J.B. reached out to shake his hand and then headed back to the crew.

Cade limped over to Blair and grinned down at her. "What are you doing here?"

She grinned back. "Same thing you are. Snooping around. Digging up dirt."

Cade grunted. "That's what you think I'm doing?"

She didn't answer that. "So what's this about Ben having an affair?"

Cade's grin crashed. "Where did you hear that?" He had explicitly instructed Morgan and Rani to keep that to themselves.

"You were asking like you thought maybe it was a possibility. You must know something."

He wasn't sure he believed that was how she knew, but he tried to rally. "You misunderstood, Blair. I only came here to see if anyone knew anything about Lisa."

She turned her face up to him, that maddening determination sparkling in her eyes. "Come on, Cade. Ben's your first suspect. That's a no-brainer."

"We don't have any suspects yet, Blair. We don't know that a crime has been committed."

"Yeah, and that's what they said when *you* were missing."

She had a point. He dropped his voice to a near whisper. "That's precisely why I'm not taking this lightly."

Her eyes squinted, and he felt she could see right into him and read his every thought. "So who is she?"

"Who is who?"

"The other woman. You obviously think Ben was having an affair."

He sighed. "Blair, your creative auditory skills amaze me. And that intuition of yours is sometimes wrong."

"Sometimes. But not often."

It was true. He knew it, but he wasn't about to encourage her. "I've got work to do." He started limping toward the crew.

"Have you found Lisa's car yet?"

"No, it hasn't turned up. Hopefully that's because she's driving it." Sighing, he turned back around.

"Are people out looking for it?"

"Of course they are. In fact, Jonathan's organizing a search party. We're going to comb the island this afternoon. I have men from the Sheriff's Department, the Highway Department, the State Police, and the Savannah and Tybee police departments on their way to help out."

She pulled out her notebook. "One more question."

He turned around and she stepped closer. She was a whole head shorter than he. He happened to know that her shoulder fit right under his. If he pulled her against him, she would hear his heart beating.

But her personality seemed to put her at eye level. "What question, Blair?"

Her eyes lost that eye-of-the-tiger glint, and her face softened. "You're not overdoing it, are you? With the leg, I mean."

He was glad she *couldn't* hear his heart. "I'm chief of police. I'm doing what I have to do, injury notwithstanding."

"You didn't answer my question."

He looked toward the activity of Ben's workers. A gentle smile pulled at his lips. "I'm fine, Blair. Thanks. How about your skedaddling on out of here so I can interview some people? A woman's life could be at stake, and every delay could cost her."

"Are you running me off?"

"Yes, I am."

"All right, but I'm coming back when you leave. By the way, thanks for the lead."

He might have known. "I didn't give you a lead, Blair."

"If I find out her name, do you want me to tell you?"

He groaned. "What if she's just a figment of your imagination?"

"I'll find that out too."

He tried to get serious. "Blair, a man's reputation is at stake, and he has enough problems right now."

"Not to worry. I'm not out to ruin anybody. But I'm still going to dig. I think I'll go talk to some of Lisa's friends, see what they know."

He knew Rani would be among them. Blair would know about the letters within the hour. "Guess I can't stop you."

"Got that right."

Sighing, he started back toward the crew.

"Take care of your leg, okay? Don't go tromping through the woods looking for her. There are plenty others who can do that."

"I'll call you later." He wouldn't let himself look back at her as he walked away. She clearly enjoyed driving him crazy.

And as aggravated as he was at her, he had to admit he enjoyed it a little, too.

CHAPTER

14

*R*ani Nixon let the top down on her Roadster as she flew through town. Her bones felt weary from not having slept the night before. She'd spent too much time dialing and redialing Lisa's cell phone, yelling messages for her to call and put them all out of their misery. She'd gone to every property that Lisa might have shown the day she disappeared, searching every room and praying that she wouldn't come upon Lisa's body. But so far she had no clues as to where her best friend was. So this morning, when the telephone call came from the psychic, she agreed to meet him without hesitation.

His name was Carson Graham, and though she didn't know him, she had done a quick search on her computer and found a webpage that described the services he performed. He did palm readings, astrological charts, and tarot cards, and his bio claimed he had helped the police solve several cases through doing psychic readings on victims.

"I just wanted to offer my services," he'd told her. "Perhaps you could bring me something of Mrs. Jackson's—something she wore that I could use to do a reading."

Rani had frowned and clutched the phone. "Why did you call me and not the police or her husband?"

"I tried calling her husband," he said. "I kept getting his voicemail, and I don't know how to get in touch with him. As for the police, I used to help the department all the time until Chief Cade was hired. Let's just say he hasn't needed my services, and I didn't think he would be open to my helping with the case, but I know I can at least generate some clues."

Rani liked the sound of that. One good clue and they could find Lisa. She was sure of it. "What do you need? I'll bring it to you."

"Just something of hers, something personal. Something she wore or used a lot. Whatever you have in your possession."

"I have a sweater," she said. "She left it in my car the day before when we were previewing properties."

"That would be perfect."

"Where can I meet you?"

"How about if you meet me at Winston's Restaurant? You can buy me lunch, and I won't charge you for my services."

She hadn't thought about a charge, but she figured it was worth it. She'd pay anything to know where Lisa was. "All right. I'll be there in twenty minutes."

"Just ask the hostess for me," he said. "She'll lead you to the table."

Rani got to the restaurant a little while later, holding Lisa's sweater folded over her arm.

The hostess led her to Carson Graham. He looked like he belonged on an infomercial for Ronco products. His goatee needed trimming and his hair needed to grow. She suspected he shaved his head as an offensive against his baldness.

She greeted him and handed him the sweater.

"I took the liberty of ordering you coffee," he said. "I didn't know how you take it."

"Black's good."

"What about lunch? Would you like to order before we get started?"

She really didn't want to be bothered with food right now. "You go ahead. I'm not hungry."

"From the looks of you, you could stand a good meal." His laughter was inappropriate and a bit too loud.

At five ten, Rani had always been bone thin. When she'd worked in New York, she had learned to eat high-protein and low-carb to stay lean. She'd kept the diet ever since. She preferred lean meats and salads over the breads and pastas that everyone else considered staples. "I'll pass, thanks."

"Gonna make me eat alone?"

She saw that her lack of appetite was distracting him. She was going to have to order. "Okay, I'll eat something."

He called the waitress over and placed an order big enough to feed a baseball team. When it was her turn, she ordered a salad.

The waitress hurried off, and Rani turned back to the man. "Tell me, can you see anything yet just from holding the sweater?"

He smiled and brought it to his face, taking in a deep breath. "Actually, I think I need to be alone so I can concentrate."

She wished he'd take a to-go box so he could get on with it. "When will you know something?"

"I think later today. I realize that time is of the essence."

"You don't have any impressions yet? Nothing?"

"I told you, I have to be alone."

She sank back into her chair. What if she was barking up the wrong tree? But what could it hurt, giving a psychic a chance to find Lisa? It was as good as any other leads they had.

"Tell me about your friend." He took a long sloppy drink, dribbling some on his chin. "Any information you give me might help me to get a better handle on her."

She dug into her purse. "I brought a picture of her. You've probably already seen it on the news."

"Yes. She's very pretty."

"You got that right." Rani handed him the photo. "She's my best friend. I've known her since college. We were roommates the whole four years. Then we each kind of went our separate ways, had our own careers for a while. She got into real estate, and I was in modeling. When I decided to leave New York, she asked me if I'd like to come here and go into business with her. I did, and we've been together ever since."

"Tell me, what kind of person was Lisa?"

Rani didn't appreciate the use of the past tense. She hoped he hadn't come up with that from some kind of psychic vibration. "Lisa *is* a wonderful person. She's devoted to her husband. She's ambitious, efficient, diligent, vibrant, effusive . . . all the things that spell success. That's what Lisa *is*."

He leaned in, his eyes squinting. "Did she have any dark secrets she was hiding?"

That aggravated her. "Look, I don't have to tell you this stuff. Either you know it or you don't. You said you could find her based on something she owned. I'm hoping you can do that. If you can't, I want that sweater back."

"Of course. I didn't mean to step on any toes. I was just trying to get a feel for her."

"Yeah, well, it's not my job to fill in the blanks for you. Either you're for real or you're not."

"I assure you, I'm for real. You'll see."

The waitress delivered their food, and Rani watched him dive in. He wasn't even insulted by her doubt in him. Maybe that was a good sign.

With a mouthful of baked potato, he said, "Perhaps I should tell you a little bit about my background."

"Yes, that would be helpful."

He swallowed and took a long swig of iced tea. "I've known since I was a boy that I had some powers. ESP, some people call it. I seemed to always be able to find lost things, and I knew things about people that no one had told me. When I got into college, I joined a parapsychology club and started to meet other people like myself. We sort of encouraged each other and helped each other develop our gifts."

Rani's anger started to fade. This was the kind of thing she wanted to hear. It sounded authentic.

"You claimed that you had helped the police solve crimes before. Which crimes?"

"Oh, there've been quite a few." He buttered his roll. "I gave the Atlanta police clues one time that helped them find a sniper who was terrorizing the citizens, and two or three times I've given Savannah police information that has led to convictions of bank robbers, kidnappers, drug dealers. Before Chief Cade was here, I used to help Chief Baxter from time to time. He wasn't one to give me a lot of credit, but I think I was helpful in a number of cases."

Rani smiled. *Perfect.*

"When Elizabeth Smart was missing, I had a vision that she was with a man and a woman. Saw her wearing a burka-type thing on her head, and I knew she was alive."

"Did you tell the police?"

"Yes, I called them, but that wasn't much to go on. Turns out I was right, though."

Rani was impressed. "Is that documented?"

"What? Who Elizabeth Smart was with? Of course it is."

"No, I mean your phone call to the police."

He breathed a laugh. "I doubt it. Like I said, it wasn't a lot to go on. I didn't have a location or a name. Since it wasn't a real physical siting, they didn't put much stock in it."

He went on about other cases he'd solved, and by the time he'd finished eating, she was a believer. She was glad she'd come.

As he took Lisa's sweater and went toward his van, which had "Palm Readings" in big letters on the side, Rani shook his hand. "You'll call me the moment you have something?"

"Of course I will."

"And don't worry about the police. If you have a lead, I'll make sure they follow it."

"Good deal."

She hurried back home to wait for his call.

15

*T*he phone call Rani had been waiting for came an hour later. She saw Carson's name on her caller ID, and she snatched up the receiver. "Hello?"

"It's Carson," he said.

She'd gone back home and paced her living room a thousand times since lunch. "Have you got anything?"

"Yes, I'm afraid I do. But I'd rather not discuss it over the phone. Do you think we could talk in person?"

Rani hesitated. What could be so bad? She cleared her throat and swallowed hard. "Okay. Do you want me to come to your place?"

"Yes. Do you know where it is?"

"The palm reader's shop on Ocean Boulevard?"

"That's right."

"I'll be right over."

She drove too fast, her heart pounding. If the news was good, wouldn't he have told her over the phone? Did guys like Carson ever deliver good news? Then she thought of Elizabeth Smart. He'd had good news then, if anyone had listened.

She pulled into the parking lot in front of his small eggplant-colored house. There was a painted sign out front that had been faded by the sun. It read, "Palm Reading and Tarot Cards—$20." She went up the steps and knocked on the door. He answered quickly.

His face was sober as he invited her in.

The front room looked as if it had been decorated by an elderly spinster. The walls were paneled in dark laminate, and the furnishings were old enough to need replacing, but not old enough to qualify as antiques.

She stepped into the front room. It smelled of strawberry candles and incense, and the lights were too dim. She turned to face him. "Tell me."

"Sit down." He pointed her to a plush easy chair. Her heart raced as she sat down, terror taking her breath away. He took the seat across from her. They were almost knee to knee.

She couldn't wait any longer. "So what did you find out?"

He picked up the sweater he had lying on an end table and moved it around in his hands. "Rani, I'm really sorry. I hate to be the bearer of bad news."

Rani wilted back. She knew it. "Just spit it out. Come on."

"I'm afraid your friend is dead."

Rani had expected it—had even rehearsed it—but now she found that it hit her in the gut.

"That's what you saw? That she's dead?"

"I saw more than that. I'm sensing that there was foul play of some kind, though I can't say exactly what the nature of it was. When I hold the sweater, I just feel a lot of tension and fear."

Rani sat up straighter, blinking back the tears in her eyes. He could be wrong . . . He could be blowing smoke, conning her. He probably didn't know what he was talking about.

"I believe I know where she is. In a vision, I saw her car going into the water about half a mile east of Bull Bridge."

Fear rammed its fist into her chest again. This was more specific than she'd expected.

"I believe if you find that car, you're going to find her. Tell the police to search there first."

She got up, trying to think. Lisa wasn't dead. The man was a fraud. Just an evil, conniving, con artist trying to get his name in the paper. She tried to believe it was a hoax, but her heart wasn't buying. She looked down at a statue of a Buddha on a table, trying to think.

"I tried to get more," he said. "But it just didn't come to me. It's hard to know how these visions work. Sometimes I get parts of things, sometimes wholes. I guess the important thing, though, is that we notify the police."

Rani nodded and started digging through her purse for her keys. Then she realized she already had them in her hand. "I'll go straight there from here."

"If you need me to talk to them, I will, but as I've told you before, Chief Cade doesn't like me very much."

Rani wanted out of there. She started for the door. "I'll handle it."

"And would you do me a favor? Let me know if and when you find her?"

Nodding absently, Rani headed back out to her car and closed herself in. She sat there for a moment, staring at the steering wheel.

Lisa wasn't dead. He was flat wrong.

She pulled out into traffic, wishing for numbness. It couldn't be true, yet what if it was? What if her friend was dead at the bottom of the river?

She couldn't make herself go to that place for fear she would find her. Instead, she drove to the police station as fast as she could.

CHAPTER

16

*C*ade had gone to the site where Lisa was supposed to have shown property yesterday—a plot of land on the edge of some forest land, on the eastern side of the island. Rani got the location and decided to go there and tell Cade herself what Carson Graham had said. If she gave the information to someone else, it might be ignored.

She found the site easily. Cars lined the street out in front of the land, and a table was set up near the road, where police officers were registering volunteers and giving them instructions. She tromped in her high heels through the grass, right up to the table.

"You'll need to change your shoes, ma'am," a young cop said. "It's rough treading in those woods."

"I'm not here to search. I need to speak to Chief Cade."

"He's busy right now."

She leaned on the table and glared into his face. "Go find him and tell him it's Rani Nixon, and that I have information about where Lisa is!"

The cop sprang up. "Okay, just stay here for a minute."

She paced back and forth in front of the table, waiting for Cade to come out of the house. In a moment, he emerged, looking fatigued and distracted. His limp was more pronounced than it had been earlier.

"What is it, Rani?" he asked. "Have you heard from her?"

"No. Cade, I need to talk to you privately."

He looked concerned and motioned for her to walk with him. Taking her away from the crowd, he said, "Okay, Rani. What is it?"

Rani shoved her fingers through her cropped hair. "Cade, I know this is going to sound crazy, but this man named Carson Graham contacted me. He's a psychic and he told me—"

"Hold it." Cade raised a hand to stop her story. "I'm not buying anything Carson Graham told you. That guy is a complete fraud."

She hesitated, gaping at him. "He *told* me you didn't like him, but that doesn't matter. I just need you to listen to what he said."

"Rani, that guy tries to get in on every investigation. Trust me, he just gets in the way. Every now and then he hits on something that's vaguely close to the truth, and then he takes full credit for it when the crime is solved. You can't believe a thing he says."

"Okay, maybe he's just a lying jerk. But what if he's right?"

Cade looked down at his cane. "Okay, Rani, what did he tell you?"

"He told me she's dead." She burst into tears. "That she's in her car at the bottom of the Bull River, half a mile east of the Bull Bridge."

Cade sighed. "Rani, I can't send divers to a place based on some psychic's vision."

"Just go over there. Wouldn't you see something if a car had gone into the water? I mean, wouldn't there be tire tracks or something?"

He seemed to consider that. "All right, Rani. I'll go over there myself and have a look. That's all I can promise you. I'm not wasting a lot of my department's resources on one of Carson Graham's wild-goose chases."

"Good enough. I just want you to see. I don't want it to be true."

CHAPTER

17

$\mathcal{C}$ade drove to the Bull Bridge, clocked out a half mile to the east. The land along the river was largely protected by the state's Department of Resources, which had laid down strict rules about the homes built along the river. They hadn't approved many of them before the DOR decided no more could be built—much to the delight of the few property owners, who knew their property values would shoot higher because of the rarity of riverfront homes.

The homes were widely spaced, with hundreds of yards between them. They were secluded and built among the trees, maintaining the integrity of the land along Bull River.

He left his car and walked through the trees until he reached a place where he used to come fishing as a boy. It reminded him of the place where Andy and Opie fished during the whistling theme song of *Andy Griffith*. He walked along the dirt patches and grass, looking down toward the meandering river and scanning the ground for any signs of Lisa.

He didn't even know why he was wasting his time. Some people on the island bought Carson Graham's lies hook, line, and sinker. He had a nightclub psychic act that wasn't doing so well. When tourist season was hopping, business picked up, but rumor had it that the proprietor was thinking about bringing in a magician to replace Graham.

As long as his lies were just part of a nightclub act or a palm reading business, Cade had decided the man wasn't all that harmful, but this took the cake. Exploiting a woman's disappearance by preying on the people who loved her beat everything.

He kept walking, leaning on his cane, wishing he could go home and put ice on his leg. Each step made it ache more, and he felt it swelling against his pant leg. He had a two-bit psychic to blame for this. A psychic who had sent him on a wild-goose chase. He was probably hiding and watching, laughing it up that Cade had followed up on his tip.

He started to turn back, then stopped as something caught his eye. Tire tracks dug into the bank, going right into the river.

He stood there a moment, staring. Was it possible Carson Graham had gotten it right this time? Was it just a coincidence? Was there really a car at the bottom of that river?

He studied the tracks and saw footprints mashed in next to them. This wasn't a place to put a boat in—the launch ramp was only a mile down. The half shoe prints looked as if someone had pushed hard against a heavy weight.

He had no choice now. He was going to have to find out.

He went back to his car and radioed the Department of Resources to ask if they could send divers over with sonar equipment. They would be at Cape Refuge within the hour.

He then set about to cordon off the tire tracks and footprints until they could study them for evidence, in the event that a car . . . and Lisa . . . were found on the bottom of that river.

Blair knew they must have found something when she heard Cade's voice on the police radio, ordering all units to a place a half mile east of the Bull Bridge. She'd been on her way to photograph the search on the eastern side of the island, but now she turned her car around and headed to Bull River.

Squad cars from Cade's department and the Chatham County Sheriff's Department blocked off the road in front of a cluster of trees. She couldn't see what was going on behind them, but there was clearly a lot of activity. She saw Rani arguing with an officer at the edge of the crime scene tape, so she got out and crossed the grass.

"Rani, has there been news on Lisa?"

Rani turned around. She was frantic, almost hysterical. "You bet there has! But they won't let me in. I can't see anything."

"What happened?"

"I got a tip that Lisa's Lexus had gone into the river right here. I gave the tip to Cade, but he didn't believe me until he came over here to check out the place. He must have found something!"

Blair scanned the landscape. Maybe she could find a place with a view of the water ... It was forest land for as far as she could see right now, with no houses in sight. But Blair knew there was a house a couple hundred feet away on the other side of the trees. The house had a view of a portion of the river directly behind it. She knew it had a pier, and it might give her a view of what was going on upriver.

"Who gave you the tip, Rani?"

"Carson Graham, that's who."

Blair turned back to her. "The palm reader?"

"He's a *psychic*, Blair, and he did a reading on Lisa today."

"Come on. You're kidding me."

"Hey, I was a skeptic at first too. And I'm praying he's wrong. But look at all this!"

Blair dropped her notepad. This was going to be a wash. She didn't even know why Cade would entertain anything that guy said. She heard a helicopter overhead. Shading her eyes, she looked up and saw the chopper with the word *Observer* on the side. The tabloid hadn't missed a beat to get the best seat in the house.

"I heard someone say they're using sonar equipment to look for the car," Rani said.

Blair couldn't believe they would go to all this trouble for a hoax. "Wow, they must really think she's there."

"She is! I just know it!"

Blair looked around. "I've got to get a vantage point, even if I have to go across the river."

"I'm coming with you," Rani said.

"There's a house down the way," Blair said. "Do you happen to know who owns it?"

"Oh, yeah. It belongs to Melanie and Andy Adams. I sold it to them."

Blair knew the couple. "Great. Let's go ask them if we can use their pier."

They went back out to the street, where a crowd of other reporters and onlookers had formed. No one was getting past the police line.

Blair led Rani toward the house, hoping no one else had already thought of this. She went to the door and knocked. Melanie, a nervous-looking blonde, answered quickly. "Hi."

"Melanie, I don't know if you remember me . . ."

"Of course I do. Nobody ever forgets you, Blair."

Blair thought that was a reference to her scars, but she tried not to dwell on it. "Melanie, would you mind if we go out on your pier to see if we can tell what the police are doing?"

"The police?" Melanie's face changed, and she looked out past them.

"Yes. They're looking for Lisa Jackson, and apparently they think she's in the water. We don't know for sure what they've found, if anything."

"Lisa Jackson? Here?" Her face drained of its color as she peered at the police. "Well . . . sure. Yes, you can use it. I'll come too." She came out with Blair and followed her and Rani around the house to the pier.

As they walked around Melanie's yard, Blair bit her lip. Maybe this wasn't going to help after all. Privacy hedges lined the sides of the property, and forest separated Melanie's yard from where the police worked. Their part of the river was on a narrow bend that restricted their view to the right or the left.

Blair saw a few people with television cameras across the river, trying to get pictures of the search. She hurried out onto the pier, looked to the left, and saw one of the search boats on the water. "Yes! We'll see some of it, anyway."

Rani came and stood beside Blair. "They haven't found her. They wouldn't still be looking if they'd found her."

Melanie stood behind Blair, gazing off toward the activity. "I hate this. It's freaky. My husband is going to die when he hears about this."

The heat was intense, steaming off of the water. Blair slowly sat down on the boards. "This could take a while. We might as well get comfortable."

"I don't want to be comfortable," Rani said. "My best friend might be in that water."

CHAPTER

*W*e got something!"

The yell came out over the water, and Cade went as close to the bank as he could without getting wet. The call came from one of the boats in the middle of the river, a little to his right.

"What is it?" he asked into his radio.

The response crackled. "Sonar's showing a big object, straight down. We're getting the divers down there. Might be a car."

He prayed that it wouldn't be. From here, he could see Blair sitting on the Adamses' pier, her hand shading her eyes as she watched the activity. Rani towered behind her, standing next to Melanie.

Then the call came. "It's a car, Chief. A Lexus XL330, and there's a woman's body in it."

Lisa. His heart slammed against his ribcage, and he stood there a moment, trying to process the reality.

Ben . . . how was he going to tell him? Should he get him over here or tell him later? Would someone else get to him first?

He went to Alex Johnson, who was holding back the crowd. "Alex, do me a favor and go get Ben. Pick him up and bring him here."

The young cop looked as if he'd rather be beaten. "Really, Chief? You want him to see this? What do I tell him?"

"Just tell him we may have found her car. Nothing else."

Alex rushed away, and Cade called the medical examiner's office and told him to hurry.

He went back to the bank and waited.

The radio crackled. "Chief, what do you want the divers to do?"

"Just hold tight. We need to leave the body in the car so we won't disturb the evidence. The ME is on his way, and the Georgia DOR will have to pull it out."

It looked as if the search for Lisa was over.

But this wasn't the way he'd expected it to end.

CHAPTER

By the time the DOR tugboat was in position to pull the car up, a huge crowd had gathered. The media, trying to get a better shot, had collected on the opposite side of the river with cameras, and a news helicopter circled overhead. Cade saw Jonathan and Morgan with baby Caleb, tearfully arriving on the scene. Alex brought Ben back with him, and he stood, pale, face full of dread, as he watched the DOR working to pull the car up.

Cade had roped off the area around the crime scene to keep the evidence from being disturbed. Finally, the cable began to creak and squeal as the tail of the vehicle came up out of the water. It was Lisa's burgundy Lexus.

And then he saw her as the front end was lifted out—Lisa Jackson, still strapped in by her seatbelt, her hair floating in the murky water-filled car . . . exactly where Carson Graham had said she would be.

The boat moved the car to the bank, then lowered it hard onto the grassy area a hundred feet from where it went in, so as not to disturb the tracks and footprints. They opened the door, and the water gushed out.

The sight of Lisa in that car hit Cade in the gut. For a moment he stood there, staring at her through the wet windshield as if there were some possibility she would begin to cough. He told himself to move, to look for blood or a gunshot wound or evidence of suicide or foul play—to do *something* befitting of a police chief who'd just discovered a body—but he couldn't catch his breath.

The medical examiner moved into action, checking for any sign of life. "No pulse," he said.

"She's not dead!" Ben's words cracked out over the area. "Help her, you idiots!" Ben broke through the barricade of officers keeping him back and wrestled his way to the car. Cade tried to hold him back, but he fought to get to her door.

"She's not dead! *Do* something!"

"Ben, you can't touch anything! You'll compromise the evidence."

"*Lisa!*" He began to shake, and the anguish on his face cut through to Cade's soul. "Dear God, who did this to her?" Ben started to sob, and Cade felt torn between offering comfort to the man and dragging him away. "Please . . . maybe there's a pulse."

Cade pulled him away. "Ben, she's dead."

The words seemed to drag the strength right out of the grieving husband, and Ben covered his face and wailed out his pain.

Cade turned away. He had work to do; he didn't have time to fall apart.

"You can't just leave her like that," Ben cried. "Get her out of there!"

"We will as soon as we can, Ben. Just stay back, okay?"

There was too much that had to be done before they could move her. The detectives had to take pictures of the car from every angle, with her exactly as she'd been found. Everything was critical, from the fact that she wore her seat belt, which didn't sound like something a suicidal person would do, to the angle of any gunshot wound or injury that might explain how she died. If she was killed and then pushed into the river, the killer might have left some clue behind. They couldn't risk losing that by moving her.

Ben was led back to the shade, where Cade could hear the anguished sounds of his grief.

McCormick came to stand beside him. "You think his grief is for real, Cade?"

"Looks real to me. My gut tells me he's not responsible."

But his gut couldn't dictate his conclusions. The evidence would have to do that. He looked at the body, still in the car. There would be many questions answered there, and many new questions raised.

He hated investigating homicides, but someone was going to have to do it. There was a killer out there somewhere, and Cade wouldn't rest until he found him.

Blair couldn't see what was happening, but she heard yelling, and the one boat she could see drifted out of sight around the bend. She decided to try to get a little closer.

The three of them followed the river line at the back of Melanie's property. There was a small path between the trees and the river bank, cutting right to the place where the police worked.

They got around the bend, and finally had a clear view of them pulling the Lexus out.

Rani cried out. "Lisa's car!"

Then Blair heard Ben's wailing and watched as he tried to get to the car.

She knew Lisa was there.

Rani screamed out her despair and denial, then bolted out of the trees toward the car too, but she was wrestled back.

Ben was weeping in a crowd of police, standing back from the scene.

Blair didn't know what to do. They needed pictures for the paper, but somehow, it seemed cruel and opportunistic to snap them now.

She saw that Morgan and Jonathan had been allowed past the crime scene tape and were trying to comfort Ben. He staggered toward them and fell into Morgan's arms, and she held him for a long time.

Blair blinked back her tears. No ... she wouldn't take pictures now.

Others found no problem with photographing the scene. Vince Barr of the *Observer* had gotten through the barricade somehow and was using his telescopic lens to get pictures of Lisa inside the car. Where was his helicopter? Had he parachuted out or just taken a leap into the water? She wouldn't put either past him.

She sidled up beside him. "Don't you think you've gotten enough, Vince? You're not really going to publish pictures of her dead body, are you?"

"What do you think?" he asked with a smirk.

She thought of the JonBenet Ramsey case and the pictures his rag had published of the murdered child. Yes, he would indeed publish them. "Don't you have the slightest bit of integrity, Vince?"

He lowered the camera long enough to shoot her a smarmy grin. "Don't be such an amateur, Blair. Integrity doesn't pay the bills. Graphic pictures do."

I didn't think she was dead. She was somewhere in trouble, but not dead. Not Lisa." Ben's words
seemed to echo in the large great room of his home.
Jonathan and Morgan had managed to convince him to
let them bring him home, and now they wondered what
comfort they could give the man in his shock.

"She would never have killed herself. *Never*. She had
no reason . . ."

Morgan wondered if he was right. Could her despair
over her marriage have driven her to suicide? Had the hormones and the stress over the IVF procedure and the mayoral race pushed her over the edge?

"I can prove it!" he said suddenly. "Have you seen
the nursery?"

She wiped her face. "No."

"Let me show you." He started through the house,
his gait angry and determined, his breathing hard. She and
Jonathan followed.

Ben led them into a sage-colored room, with a junglelike mural painted on the wall and characters from Disney's *Jungle Book* hidden among the trees. A custom crib with legs that looked like little tree trunks sat in the center of the room, and a green rocker and chaise lounge sat at angles across from it.

"Lisa did all this herself." His voice was raspy and trembling. "She wouldn't take her life when we were right on the verge . . ." He sat down in the rocker. "Having a baby was what she lived for. It was her goal . . . and we were close to reaching it. If I'd known that she wouldn't live to see it, I wouldn't have let her waste all those years."

"But you didn't know," Morgan whispered. "How could you know?"

He reached out for the bed, touched the sheets, then crumbled again. "Who did that to her? I can't even imagine."

The assault of those words surprised Morgan, reviving her own helpless, rabid, broken questions in the aftermath of her parents' murders. Jonathan seemed to sense her memory and set a gentle hand on her shoulder.

Morgan shook herself out of her own stroll down murder lane, and drew on her store of tried and true helps in tragedy. "Ben, is there anyone you want me to call?"

Ben looked up, his face stricken. "Oh, God help me, I have to call our families."

"I could do it, Ben."

He shook his head. "No, I have to. They have to hear it from me."

As he picked up the phone, Morgan went back into the kitchen, and she and Jonathan prayed quietly for those poor family members he called.

CHAPTER

Lisa Jackson hadn't killed herself. Cade was certain of that. The medical examiner had ruled out suicide almost immediately. The marks on her neck indicated that she'd died of strangulation with a telephone cord they'd found on the floor of the car. Because there was no water in her lungs, it was clear she died before entering the water. The lividity on her skin—the purplish pooling of blood at the lowest points of a corpse—indicated that she was killed before being placed in the car.

Cade tried to puzzle the pieces together. Had someone come into her home after Ben left, murdered her, loaded her body into her own car, and driven her into a river in broad daylight? Granted, it had gone in at a secluded part of the river, in a place where no one was likely to see. Still, it seemed like a tremendous risk ...

Unless the driver of the car had been its other owner. If Ben killed her and drove her across town, no one would have noticed anything out of the ordinary. He would simply have driven through the trees to the quiet fishing hole, strapped her into the driver's seat, put the car in neutral, and given it a shove into the water.

But why would he kill her? Could it have anything to do with those letters?

And what about Carson Graham? How had he known where Lisa could be found?

Could *he* have committed the murder?

The shoe prints were a clue, but they hadn't gotten a match just yet. They'd determined the prints came from a size eleven men's shoe—the same size Ben wore.

Cade put Ben's house under surveillance until he could get over there to question him further. If Ben was guilty, he didn't want him making a run for it.

While the forensics team from the State Police worked the crime scene, Cade went to pay Carson Graham a visit. He pulled up on the dirt parking lot in front of the peeling blue house, and before he could knock, Graham opened the door. He grinned as if he'd been expecting him. "You found her body, didn't you?"

Cade hadn't expected him to be quite so delighted with the find. "I want to talk to you, Graham."

"Certainly. I'm always eager to help. You know that."

Cade walked into the dark house, which smelled of incense, and looked at the lit candles clustered around the room. A few fake Tiffany lamps provided a little more lighting, but the place had a carefully created air of dusty mystery.

The man lowered himself into a Chippendale chair and gestured for Cade to take the one facing him across a small round table. "Want me to do a reading for you, Cade? Perhaps I could aid in finding the killer."

"No, thanks." Cade took the seat, studying the man's face. "How did you know, Graham? The truth."

"I saw it in a vision. That's a fact. I wish I'd seen the identity of the killer, but I'm afraid I didn't."

Cade cleared his throat and leaned forward. "Where were you yesterday morning, Carson?"

"I was right here, sleeping late. I didn't have any appointments, and I'd had a late show over at the Frankfurt Inn the night before."

"Do you have any witnesses who could vouch for that?"

"Well, I didn't have anyone in bed with me, if that's what you mean. My wife worked a double shift at the hospital that night and didn't get in until almost noon yesterday. But I can guarantee that you won't find anyone who saw me anywhere else. Ask the neighbors. My van was here all day." The arrogance on his face faded somewhat. "I know it's hard for you to believe, Cade, but psychic phenomena are real. I've never met Lisa Jackson in my life. All I know of her is what I've seen on the news—and the vision I got when I held her sweater."

Cade stared at the man for a moment, knowing in his gut that Carson was somehow involved in Lisa's death. He might not have killed her, but he felt certain he knew who had. How else would he have directed them to her body? "Graham, what size shoe do you wear?"

The man looked surprised at the question. "Size nine. Why?"

Cade studied his feet. He wore a size ten himself, and Graham's feet did look smaller. He figured he was telling the truth.

Graham seemed to sense Cade's thoughts and he almost looked amused. "You're not going to pin this on me, Chief. I'm a bona fide psychic, whether you can deal with that or not. My advice to you is to embrace that knowledge and use it to your advantage. I'm more than happy to work with you on future cases. Of course, we both know that after the election, you may not even have a job."

He had guts. Cade would give him that much—though he didn't think much of his intellect. Provoking the police chief wasn't wise when one was tied up with a murder case and had no alibi. Cade got up. "Don't leave town, Graham. We might want to question you again."

"I have no place to go. Don't worry about it."

Cade couldn't help worrying as he limped through the door.

"You take care of that leg now," Carson called out behind him.

Cade got into his car and glanced back up as he drove away. Carson Graham stood outside his front door, arms crossed, chuckling like a man who'd just won the lottery.

*D*espite his suspicions about Graham, Cade had no choice but to center his investigation on the other main suspect—Ben Jackson. The grieving husband was inconsolable when Cade and McCormick showed up at his house with the news that strangulation had been Lisa's cause of death.

Morgan and Jonathan tried to comfort Ben, but anger, rage, and grief all booked time on his face, glazing his eyes with tortured visions. "My Lisa, she didn't have any enemies. Everyone who knew her loved her. Who could do this? *Why?*"

Cade didn't even try to answer those questions. "Ben, Lisa was killed before she was put into her car. It may have happened here."

Ben's face changed, and he looked around him, his eyes rapidly darting around the room, as if looking for some sign that a killer had been here. "In my house? You think he came in here and murdered my wife?"

"We can't say for sure. But we'll need to search your house."

"Of course, yes. That's fine. If the killer was here, maybe some evidence was left." He walked to the back door and looked down at the lock. "Nothing was stolen. I would have noticed. And there wasn't any sign of a break-in." He swung around and settled his wild eyes on Cade. "Do you think it was someone she knew? Someone she let in willingly?"

"Those are questions we're asking, too. We'll know more after we've had time to go through the house."

"Go ahead. The sooner the better. I want you to find him, Cade. I want to know what happened . . ." His face twisted in his anguish.

Cade looked at the floor. McCormick gave him a quiet moment, then said, "Ben, we need to sit down with you and go over a few things."

"Anything," Ben said. "Anything you want to know."

Jonathan got up. "We'll go, Ben, so you can talk to them."

Morgan's face mirrored Ben's pain as she gave him another hug. "Ben, call us when they're finished. We don't want you to be alone."

Ben was unresponsive as Morgan and Jonathan whispered goodbyes and left. Instead, Ben kept his eyes on McCormick, seemingly anxious to talk. "Okay, go ahead. What do you want to ask me?"

McCormick pulled out a stool at the counter, but Ben kept standing. In a quiet voice, McCormick asked him the question that had plagued Cade all day. "Ben, is there something you failed to tell us about your marriage?"

Ben clearly looked perplexed. "Like what?"

"Like the letters Lisa got from someone claiming to be your mistress?"

Ben groaned and pulled out a stool. Dropping into it, he rubbed his face. "I might have known. Who told you that? Rani? Had to be Rani."

McCormick didn't answer.

"Ben, who is she?" Cade asked.

"Nobody! I'm telling you, I was not having an affair. There *is* no other woman."

"Then how do you explain the letters?"

"Exactly the way I explained them to Lisa. Some crackpot was trying to cause problems for me before the election."

"You realize that if you were seeing someone, we'll find out." McCormick's tone was still soft, steady. "It wouldn't be wise to withhold that kind of information, Ben."

Ben leaned forward and locked his eyes into McCormick's. "I told you, I'm not lying. There is no woman! Trace those letters. I'd *love* to see where they're from. Maybe it was a way of luring Lisa somewhere. Maybe the killer sent them."

Cade just stared at him for a long moment, studying his face and his body language for some sign of guile, but he saw none. "Ben, was there anyone who might have had designs on you? Anyone who may have harbored some secret fantasy? Anyone you'd gotten to be close friends with, even if it was platonic?"

"No. I'm a busy man. I don't have time for stuff like that."

"Did Lisa believe that?"

"Of course she did. She knows how I am. She had no reason to suspect that I was having an affair until those letters started coming."

"And then she did suspect it?" McCormick asked.

"Well, yeah, she suspected it when she first got them. She came home all upset, crying her eyes out, accusing me of all sorts of things. It took some doing to convince her that they weren't true. And then they kept coming. Every week I had to mount a new defense, but ultimately I always convinced her."

Ben leaned back in his chair. "The last letter came a few days ago. I think by the time that one came Lisa resolved herself to the fact that it was a pack of lies. It wasn't an issue. We had other things to think about."

Cade could see that Ben wasn't going to change his story. They'd know more when they sent the letters out for a handwriting analysis and tested them for fibers and prints.

"You know, you should search her office, too," Ben said. "If he didn't do it here, maybe it was there. Or some other clue . . . Last night I went there and checked her desk for a note or anything, or a notation on her calendar. I didn't find anything, but maybe I missed something. I don't even know what to look for."

"We plan to do that," Cade said. "But for now, we'll need you to leave the house. Where will you be in case we need to contact you?"

Ben breathed in a ragged breath. "At the office, I guess. Do I need to stay overnight?"

"Probably," Cade said. "We're going to be a while."

"All right. I'll pack a bag."

Cade felt a surge of pity for the man. If he was innocent, he was being run from his home even as he struggled to absorb his shock. On a night when he would need to curl up with Lisa's things, he was exiled to a cold warehouse that smelled of shrimp. "You could probably stay at Hanover House if you wanted. Morgan and Jonathan wouldn't want you sleeping on a cot somewhere."

"I'll be fine. I have a lot of phone calls to make. I have to make arrangements . . ." He looked around as he spoke, as if trying to decide what to take with him. "I think I need to be alone. I need to think . . ."

Thinking was just what Ben didn't need to be doing. Cade walked with Ben to his bedroom and watched as he packed a few things into a small suitcase.

As he watched Ben pull away in his car, Cade turned all of the man's reactions and behaviors over in his mind. There was nothing there to indicate that he was lying. At least, nothing apparent.

"What do you think?" McCormick asked him.

Cade looked back at his detective. "I don't know. He's acting like a man who's just lost his wife."

"Yeah, seems genuine to me, too. But you know things aren't always the way they seem."

Cade knew that better than anyone, so he pressed past his own gut feelings and called for the detectives the State Police had loaned him to help with the search of the house.

CHAPTER

I know the timing is bad, mon, but you'll be seein' why I don't want to wait to say what I got to say."

Gus and Karen had been waiting on the porch for Morgan and Jonathan when they'd gotten home, and had followed them into the kitchen with solemn looks on their faces.

Jonathan shot Morgan a look, and she wondered what to brace herself for now.

"Sure, Gus. Is something wrong?"

The Jamaican fidgeted with a button on his shirt as he sat down at the table. Karen took the seat next to him. He cleared his throat, as if preparing to make a speech.

Gus had lived there for over a year since getting out of prison, and in that time he'd grown into a man of integrity and character with a good job and a future, ready to stand on his own. He planned to move into his own apartment within the next couple of weeks, and Morgan knew she was going to miss him terribly. But it was time. It was clear that something romantic was developing between him and Karen, and dating among the residents was forbidden.

"Nothing wrong." He grinned at Karen, and she grinned back, and suddenly Morgan knew.

"Don't tell me—" Jonathan smiled—"let me guess. When you move out, you want permission to date Karen."

Gus took Karen's hand in his. "Not exactly, mon. I don't want your permission to date her. I want your permission to *marry* her."

Morgan caught her breath so hard that she almost choked. Jonathan touched her back as she coughed her way through the shock. She got up and grabbed a glass from the cabinet, filled it with water, and threw it back. Able to breathe again, she turned back to them.

"You all right, babe?" Jonathan asked.

"Yes. I'm sorry, I just . . . Wow. I didn't expect that." Gus and Karen were beaming. She forced herself to smile.

Now it was Jonathan's turn to clear his throat. "Well, I have to say . . . This is uncharted territory for Hanover House."

"I know it is, mon. It's uncharted for us, too."

Morgan searched her mind for the right response. Just a few weeks ago, Karen had come to them nine months pregnant, fearful that her baby's abusive father would endanger her child. She had a history of drug addiction and had served time in prison. Though she had done well in their program so far, it was no guarantee that she was strong enough for marriage.

"Gus, we appreciate you coming to us," Jonathan said, "and we're happy that the two of you want to commit to each other. But Karen, you've only been here a few weeks. I'm not sure you're ready for this kind of thing. You thought you were ready to stand on your own when you got out of prison, but you've said yourself that you backslid and went back to your old ways."

"Not the drugs," Karen said. "I didn't go back to the crack. I been clean of drugs for three years now, so it's not like I have that calling to me. I did get weak and wound up pregnant with Emory. I know all that, Jonathan, but this is different. Gus is the kind of man I been dreaming of. He's a good man, who can take care of us. And he loves Emory."

"Emory needs a daddy, mon," Gus told Jonathan. "You know he does."

Jonathan couldn't argue with that. "The thing is, I don't want Karen to always turn to a man for her security. I want her to learn to lean on Christ."

Karen took Jonathan's hand and made him look at her. "I am leaning on Christ. I really am, Jonathan. And Gus will help me. You told me a husband is s'pose to be a spiritual leader. Gus is a strong man who loves the Lord. He'll help me grow, like you help Morgan."

"But you haven't known each other but a few weeks," Morgan said. "Wouldn't it be better to take some time to date and get to know each other better?"

Karen let Jonathan's hand go and put her hands over her face.

But Gus wouldn't give up. He put his arm around her shoulders. "We do know each other, Morgan. We been spendin' lots of time getting to know each other. Nothin's happened, so you don't have to worry, but we been around each other a lot. I seen what kind of mama she is to Emory. She's a good woman. I know all I need to know."

Karen slid her fingers down her face and met Morgan's eyes.

Silence passed between them, and Morgan just stared at both of them. "We need to pray about this."

"We been praying already, Morgan, ever since we knew we were in love." Gus took Karen's hand in both of his. "And what we came to is that we need your blessing. If we don't get it, we'll wait until we can."

That surprised Morgan even more. She looked at Jonathan and saw that he was equally moved. "You would do that? Wait, just because we wanted you to?"

Karen nodded. "If we knew you'd been praying about it and still felt we should wait, then we would. If we're s'pose to do this now, like we think God is telling us, then he'll tell you, too. I know

I still need what I can get at Hanover House. I need the Bible study and the structure. It makes me strong. I like being part of your family."

"We thought of two ways to go about this," Gus said. "We could get married and I could stay at Hanover House. I could just give up my room and move in with Karen, so's she could stay in the program. Or she could move in with me in my new apartment and come back here for the Bible studies every day."

They heard the front door open, and Morgan knew that Sadie was home. "Let us pray about it, okay? We want what's best for you. We really do."

"We know you do, Morgan," Gus said. "And I want what's best for Karen and Emory, whatever that is, but I want to start thinking of her as my wife, and him as my son. The apostle Paul said it's better to marry than to burn with lust."

Morgan thought she might choke again, so she grabbed her glass and went for more water.

"But lust is not a good reason for marriage," Jonathan said. "That's not what Paul meant."

"That ain't all, mon," Gus said. "I love this woman. I want to spend my life with her."

Morgan gulped the water down and turned back to them. When Jonathan met her eyes again, he was grinning. She couldn't help answering that smile.

"Well, I have to say that it's good to have some happy news," she said, "after all that's happened today."

Sadie stepped into the kitchen, looking haggard from her long drive. Morgan went to kiss her on the cheek. "Hey, sweetie. Come in and I'll fix you something to eat."

"No, I got something on the way." Sadie looked around. "Am I interrupting something?"

"No," Gus said. "We just be talking, Sadie. We're done. How was your trip?"

"Long." Sadie went to the refrigerator and got out a drink. "How was your day? Did anything happen with Lisa?"

Morgan's fragile joy for Gus and Karen faded. "They found her body at the bottom of the river."

Sadie spun around. "Oh, Morgan. I'm so sorry . . . Are you okay?"

"Yeah, I'm fine."

"Her poor husband. How is he?"

"Not well. He's taking it hard." She didn't want to talk about it now, so she changed the subject. "Sit down and tell us about your visit. Was your mom okay?"

"She was great, and she had some good news. Well, *maybe* some good news. She may be getting out early."

Morgan wasn't sure she'd heard her right. ".What? How?"

"Some new law that says nonviolent offenders only have to serve twenty percent of their sentence because of overcrowding in the prison. She's not sure if she qualifies, but her lawyer is looking into it."

A fifth of her sentence? Morgan looked at Jonathan, quietly passing her concern to him. If that was the case, her time served would be all that was required of her.

Jonathan leaned on the table. "Sadie, I don't want you to get your hopes up about this. Morgan and I have been working in prison ministry for a while. It happens all the time—the inmates hear rumors about new laws and think they're getting out early. Mostly, they're disappointed. They want to be released so bad that they cling to every remote hope that comes along."

Karen agreed. "It's true. Whole time I was in jail, I just knew that I was gon' get out the very next week. First I thought somebody would post my bond. Then when they didn't, I thought I could get my public defender to file for a motion to reconsider. Then I tried to figure out ways to work off my sentence, get house arrest, whatever. Never did happen. Half the time I couldn't even get the lawyer to come see me."

"Me too," Gus added. "You turn into a mathematician when you're in the can. You get your time, minus time served, and then you get a day's credit for every day you work, time off for good behavior, and then the sixty percent law or the forty percent law, or the possibility of parole, or a mistake in the DOC office . . ."

"And it never added up the way we thought."

Morgan thought Sadie might cry. "Honey, it's something to pray about."

"But it could work out." Sadie's pleading expression broke Morgan's heart. "Maybe it will. Maybe God's just giving her a second chance. He does that. I know he does."

Morgan took her hand. "Of course he does. He's the author of second chances."

Morgan could see from the girl's face that they had ruined her hopes. She wished she had just kept her reservations to herself.

"I'm tired," Sadie said. "I think I'll go on up to bed and read for a while."

Morgan hoped she wasn't going upstairs to cry. "Honey, I'm sorry we brought you down."

"Yeah, Sadie, we didn't mean to do that," Karen said.

Gus's face softened. "We hope your mama does get out. It happened to my cell mates sometimes, just never to me."

"It's okay." Sadie looked back at Morgan. "I'm sorry about Lisa. I know she was your friend."

"Thank you, sweetie."

"Good night, everybody." Sadie left the room, and silence fell over them all.

"She's right," Karen said quietly. "God does give lots of second chances." She reached for Gus's hand again.

Morgan knew they had an awful lot to pray about that night.

CHAPTER

25

*W*ell, there's no blood," McCormick said after five hours of searching the house, "but that's no surprise since there weren't any open wounds. But the telephone doesn't bode well."

Cade had to agree. They had found a phone without a cord in the living room, suggesting that the murder weapon had come from the house. If Ben had removed the cord to kill her, wouldn't he have thought to replace it? Even if he'd forgotten, he would have been reminded each time the other phones in the house rang.

As they'd searched the premises, they'd found a good deal of evidence suggesting that these two people had a future together. They hadn't found a thing suggesting marital discord or even a struggle of any kind.

They bagged a truckload of things that might later prove to be evidence, vacuumed the floor for fibers, and dusted for fingerprints. They confiscated her computer and canvassed the neighborhood for anyone who might have information.

And then they found the shoes.

They were the same size as the shoes that made the prints at the crime scene, with the same Nike design on the bottom. But it was a common running shoe, so the find didn't mean that Ben had been the one to push his wife into the river.

Unless the lab could prove that the dirt on the bottom was the same dirt that had been on the riverbank.

The officers also sealed off Lisa's office and confiscated Ben's boat and car. He handed everything over freely and got a rental car to drive.

By ten-thirty, Cade put night-shift officers outside the real estate office and the Jackson home to stand guard so he and McCormick could call it a night. They would all need some sleep if they were to make any sense of the evidence they'd gathered.

It was after eleven when he got into his truck, wincing as he pulled his swollen leg in. He sat behind the wheel for a moment and stared out the window into the night.

He was bone-tired and drained, yet he didn't want to go home. His day felt unfinished. He needed to see Blair.

She was probably in bed already, sleeping soundly, but it wouldn't hurt to drive by and see if the lights were on.

He drove down Ocean Boulevard, his eyes scanning the moonlit beach and the businesses along the road. Did a killer lurk there somewhere? Was he laid up in one of the condos along the beach, or watching the local coverage of his murder on a hotel room TV?

Anger surged through Cade. He loved this town and the people who lived here and he wanted to protect them from evil, but sometimes evil slipped through anyway.

He rounded the island, where the road was darker along Wassaw Sound. Some of the houses were dark for the night, with lone porchlights the only security other than a locked door.

But Blair's house was still lit up, and relief flooded through him as he pulled onto the gravel parking lot she shared with the library. Maybe she'd waited up, hoping he'd come by. Warmth flooded through him at the thought.

He went to the door and tapped lightly on it. He saw her pull the curtains up from the window. She opened the door and smiled out at him.

"Hey." The word was soft, drawn out, packing more punch than a simple greeting. It said she was glad to see him, that she'd been hoping he would come.

"Sorry it's so late." He leaned against the casing.

She looked sleepy and disheveled in a pair of sweat pants and a wrinkled T-shirt. "It's not too late. It's exactly the right time." She took his hand and pulled him in, and he felt the stress of the day melting away as he entered the warm glow of her living room.

"Sit down," she said. "Your leg is killing you."

He hadn't realized how badly he was limping, but he didn't argue. He sat down, and she got a cushion to put his leg on. "Here, prop it up. You want some aspirin?"

"No, I'll live." He slid down, resting his head on the back of the couch. It was the most comfortable he'd been all day.

She sat down next to him, pulling her feet beneath her. "Rough day, huh? Did you find anything in the house?"

"Blair, you know I can't talk about it."

"I know. But I've been doing a little searching on my own. You might be interested in a few things I came up with. But if you don't want to talk about it ..."

He grinned. This was her way. She played that game of *you-scratch-my-back-and-I'll-scratch-yours* whenever there was an important investigation going on. The truth was, she usually had better information than he did. She had a gift, one that law enforcement officers would kill to have, and he didn't discount it.

"Okay, Blair. Tell me."

Clearly delighted that he'd taken the bait, she shifted to face him fully. "Okay, so I'm looking around town and interviewing people to find out who might have seen Lisa Jackson last. Lo and behold, Alan Freeman told me that maybe Lisa went looking for Ben's girlfriend."

"That guy? Alan Freeman is a well of misinformation," Cade said. "You know that. He thinks he's an expert on everything."

"I realize that, but I wanted to know where he heard it, so I drilled him as hard as I could, and I found out that he heard it from some of the women in the ladies' book club. Well, I don't have to tell you, I know every one of them, so I got on the phone and started calling around. Every single one of them had heard rumors of Ben Jackson's affair. No one had a name. No one knew anything except that there was some mystery mistress."

Cade sat up straighter. "Yeah?"

"Finally, I traced the rumor back to Sarah Grady, and she refused to tell me who told her."

Cade's hopes crashed. "Blair, you're starting to sound like one of those high school girls on the telephone."

"I know, but don't you see, Cade? It's not just the rumor that's important." Her eyes widened. "It's where the rumor *started*. Tracing this rumor back to its roots is going to take us either to the mistress or to the person who started the rumor, who ultimately may have written the letters."

Cade closed his eyes and sighed. "I didn't tell you about any letters."

She waved the comment off. "My sister let it slip out when I called her this afternoon."

Cade might have known. "Morgan knew better than that."

"Don't worry. She was horrified after she did it, but I'm pretty good at prying information out of people. She hardly had a chance."

"She still shouldn't have given you that kind of information. You're the media, for heaven's sake."

"Well, don't blame her. Her defenses were low. She's really depressed today and she was hoping I'd find the killer."

"You? I'm the one leading this investigation!"

"Yeah, but she knows I'm just like you. I don't give up until I have answers that make sense."

He rubbed his eyes, realizing he was more tired than he thought. "So did you follow the rumor mill any further?"

"Not quite, but tomorrow I'm going to get to the end of it, I can promise you that. Either there's a mistress or there's a liar trying to stir up trouble. Either one could be our killer."

Cade chuckled softly and stroked her hair. "I'm glad you're on my side."

"I'll keep you updated, even if you don't return the favor. And Cade, go easy on Morgan. She's not herself today."

Cade relaxed his head back again. "I guess the murder rocked us all."

"It's not just that. It's something else. Just between you and me, Morgan had a miscarriage yesterday."

"What?" He dropped his leg and sat up straight. "Jonathan didn't tell me she was pregnant!"

"They had just found out. Hadn't even told *me* yet."

"Oh, no." He thought of the blow that must have been to his best friend and his wife. "That's awful. I need to call him."

"Not tonight. They're exhausted. But see, that's why she called Lisa, because Lisa's been infertile all these years, and they'd gotten to be friends through that common bond. Morgan wants a baby so bad."

Cade knew Jonathan yearned for a child too. His poor friends. They must be heartbroken. "I wonder what went wrong."

"They don't know. They're making an appointment with the fertility doctor Monday. The same one Lisa was seeing."

"Sims?" Cade had heard plenty about the doctor from Ben today. He got comfortable again and propped his leg back up. "I've heard he's pretty good." He reached up and pushed Blair's hair back from her face. He knew she didn't like it when he did that. Her self-consciousness about her scars made her hide behind that hair, but he liked having a clear view of her eyes. "Do you ever think about having children?"

Those scars turned pink, and she looked away. "Sometimes. It's hard to picture—me, as a mom. I'm probably better aunt material."

"I can picture it," he whispered. "You'd be a terrific mom."

She studied his face—a million thoughts and twice as many emotions flashing across her features, but for once, she didn't voice them. Instead, she got up. "You want something to drink?"

She was changing the subject, so he let her off the hook. "Yeah, I'll take some water."

He watched her retreat into the kitchen, wondering why the thought of motherhood would seem so foreign to her. She'd had a wonderful mother of her own, and while she didn't have the "earth mother" traits Morgan had, she was devoted and nurturing to those she cared about.

After a moment, he got up and followed her into the kitchen. Leaning against the counter, he watched her fuss over putting ice in the glass. He met her eyes and saw her swallow. Then she looked away and let her hair fall back along her face.

If only she understood how beautiful she was.

"Come here." He took her hand and pulled her toward him. She came, looking up at him with those wide eyes that seemed so uncertain—even a little afraid—as if she might be misreading his interest and making a fool of herself.

Slowly, he bent down and slid his fingers through her hair, against her soft neck. Her pulse raced against his fingertips as she melted in the kiss. She caused a longing deep inside him, a sweet homesick pull for some home he'd never had. It made him ache.

When the kiss broke, he kept his forehead against hers and let that ache linger.

It wasn't safe, the two of them here . . . alone like this, with these feelings that seemed bigger than the strength he had.

"I'd better go."

"Why?" Her question was a breath against his lips.

"Because I really want to stay." He kissed her forehead. "You know?"

She breathed a soft laugh. "Yeah, I know."

He pulled himself away, got his cane, and went to the front door. Blair followed him, her hands in the pockets of her sweat pants, as if she couldn't trust them at her sides. He opened the door, looked down at her, but couldn't think of a thing to say. Finally, he drew in a deep breath, then let it out in a rough sigh. Then with a soft grin, he said, "Good night, Blair."

"Good night," she whispered.

He didn't kiss her again—didn't dare—for fear he'd never get out that door. But his heart hammered as if he had.

He hoped he would be able to sleep tonight.

Blair lay in bed, staring up at the ceiling, a soft smile on her lips. She'd had sleepless nights thinking about Cade before, but usually her thoughts were dismal and hopeless. This time they held a giddiness that she'd rarely experienced in her life.

Cade made her feel so pretty. She would never have believed that anyone would think such a thing, yet every time he looked at her with that soft grin in his eyes, she saw herself as a beautiful woman. Was it possible that someday her scars wouldn't even be an issue, that she would go through an entire day without thinking about them?

Or was she just setting herself up for a humiliating heartbreak?

Almost frantic at the thought, she slid out of bed to her knees and sent a plea up to heaven that the Lord wouldn't let her overestimate Cade's feelings for her. She didn't think she could stand his rejection.

She had loved Cade far longer than she'd been willing to admit to herself, and while he'd shown signs that he'd been interested as well, he'd never made a single gesture toward her until after she'd embraced Christ. He had cried at her baptism four weeks ago when Jonathan immersed her at the beach across the street from Hanover House, with the congregation of their church gathered around for the occasion. She came up out of the water feeling clean and triumphant, and the crowd burst into cheers. Cade was the first to hug her as she came dripping onto the shore.

She sensed he'd been praying for her for a very long time.

Her salvation was like the dawning of day to her, moving from a life of dull gray to one of bursting yellows. She understood the term *born again*. As a babe in Christ, she felt the new life God had spoken of in his Word.

Cade was an extra blessing, one that she would have to take as God decided to give. She couldn't rush this, anymore than others could have rushed her salvation.

Yet waiting was hard, and it made for lots of restless nights, especially when possibilities loomed like dormant dreams stirring themselves awake.

Could Cade really feel the same about her?

She decided to hope just this once, and that hope turned into another prayer. Maybe God would smile on her and give her this desire of her heart.

CHAPTER

26

*B*lair got to Cricket's an hour before church the next morning and took a booth in case Cade joined her. After breakfast, she would walk across to the Church on the Dock that met in the old warehouse. Her parents had planted the church years ago, and after they died, Jonathan stepped into the role of pastor. Blair had only returned to its pews last month after staying away for years. Now the act of worship was something she looked forward to.

She wondered if Cade would even have time to come by this morning, much less worship, with the investigation still in its infant stages. She hoped he'd rested his leg and gotten some sleep last night.

She was on her second cup of coffee when he came in. He looked exhausted, but his eyes lit up with that contagious light that made her see herself in a new way.

"I can't stay," he told her as he slipped in across from her.

"I know. You look tired. Did your leg keep you up?"

"Among other things." His grin brought the heat rushing to her face. "Listen, I wanted to talk to you about what you're writing."

"Okay."

"Paper comes out Tuesday, right? I want you to mention that the police department has a tip line and that we're waiting to hear from anyone who may have seen Lisa's car Friday. We especially want to know if someone else was driving it."

"You got it. I'll put it on the front page."

He pulled an index card out of his pocket. It had the number on it.

She took her notepad out of her bag. "So, where's the car?"

"We moved it to the crime lab in Savannah. Forensics is going through it."

"And the autopsy?"

"They'll be doing it tomorrow. I plan to be there when they do."

"You'll update me, won't you? I don't want to put the paper to bed tomorrow night until I've got the latest info."

"You know I'll tell you what I can."

"Coffee, Cade?" the Colonel called from the bar.

"Yeah, a tall one to go, Colonel."

Blair leaned on the table, fixing her eyes on Cade. "So, tell me about Carson Graham."

Cade laced his fingers in front of his face. "That's the other thing I wanted to talk to you about. I meant to bring it up last night, but . . . I got sidetracked."

She looked down at her coffee and moved her stirring stick around. Should she joke about last night or pretend it hadn't happened? Feeling awkward, she chose the latter. "Weird, huh? How do you think he knew?"

"Good question."

"He told Rani he'd helped the police before. Is that true?"

"The guy's a pest," Cade said. "Apparently he gave Chief Baxter some no-brainer tips before I was here and claimed credit for solving those crimes. We're talking vague stuff, nothing specific.

Anybody could have come up with the same tips if you just gave it a little thought."

The Colonel brought Cade's coffee, and Cade busied himself adding sugar and cream. "He tries to get involved on every major crime. Even when your parents were killed, he had some cockamamy story about who he thought did it based on some vision he'd had. None of it panned out."

"But he was right on the money this time. I mean, don't you find that bizarre? You can't seriously attribute that to luck."

Cade sipped his coffee. "What *can* you attribute it to, Blair?"

Blair thought it over for a moment. "Maybe God? Maybe God's speaking to him. Or even through him."

"God doesn't use psychics."

"But what about the spiritual gift of prophesy? Isn't that the same thing?"

"Not at all." He sipped through the plastic top. "The Bible forbids us to go to psychics. Psychics and sorcerers and those who do what the Bible calls *divination* are an abomination to God."

Blair didn't remember seeing that in the Bible. "Are you sure?"

"Of course I'm sure. Pull up that Bible program of yours and do a search. You'll see."

"So you're saying that if a psychic can't be of God, then he must be of Satan?"

Cade shook his head. "I'm not even sure it's that spiritual. I mean, think about it. Half of what they predict is based on common sense and probable outcome. When a woman says that her husband all of a sudden wants a divorce, that he's been staying out all night, it's kind of a no-brainer to suggest that he might be having an affair. Based on that probable outcome, the so-called psychic makes a prediction. And *voilà*, it turns out to be true. That doesn't mean he has any special powers."

Blair leaned back, processing that. "But what about the cases where they are specific and turn out to be right?"

"Well, even if they did have *some* power, if the Bible forbids it, then it can't be of God."

Blair wasn't sure she could attribute it to Satan, either. Carson Graham didn't seem evil. She would have to look that up on her own and see what the Bible really said.

"Just do me a favor, Blair. When you write about him, please don't make it sound like he cracked the case. Every desperate person in town will be lining up for a reading from him. We both know that's not where they're going to find answers."

"I'll only report what happened, Cade. Just the facts."

CHAPTER

*B*lair didn't hear from Cade again that day, and by Monday, she knew he was probably working on the investigation around the clock. She spent the day interviewing people about the murder, trying to find out if Ben indeed had a mistress. She continued to trace the rumor back to its origin, but hadn't reached it yet.

Sadie came after school to help her lay out the paper. When she had to go home to study for exams, Blair stayed at the office, proofing every article one more time.

Finally satisfied that it was ready, she kicked her shoes off and padded in her sock feet back to the printing room to start the presses. The person who had owned the newspaper before her only had a weekly edition. Ever since Blair took over, there was too much news to settle on once a week, so she'd put out an edition each Tuesday and Friday. That meant that Monday and Thursday nights she got little sleep. In the past few weeks, as more subscriptions had sold, she'd been able to draw more from the wire services and news syndicates. She'd also occasionally paid a few stringers, who brought in stories that interested them, and Sadie, who was gifted in both journalism and photography.

The mayoral race kept things going strong. Blair even got a lot of comments from islanders that they'd canceled their sub-scriptions to the *Savannah Morning News* since her paper seemed to have everything they needed to keep them up-to-date.

She got the printer started. Maybe she should sell the equip-ment and start hiring an outside printing company to do this part of her job. But then she couldn't make changes at the last moment, and she needed that flexibility.

It would be several hours before the newspaper would be printed, and then she'd have to bundle the stacks and have them ready for the paperboys who would report at 5:00 a.m.

She pulled one of the front pages off the printer. She hoped Cade wasn't upset by the headline: "Psychic Leads Police to Body." There were two pictures on the front, one of Lisa Jackson and the other a photo of Carson Graham that Blair had pulled from his website. She had tried rewording the headline, but she couldn't tell the story of police finding the body until she told how they knew it was there. It was headline material, and all the other papers were reporting it as such.

She had to keep the integrity of her paper by giving the read-ers all of the facts. They expected it of her, after all. Surely Cade wouldn't find fault with that.

CHAPTER

*"*L*isa Jackson Found Dead—Husband's Footprint Found at Crime Scene.*"

Cade stared at the headline of the *Observer*, the national tabloid whose weekly issue had come out that morning. How had Vince Barr known about the shoe print?

He grabbed his cane, got up, and, waving the paper, went into the squad room. "I want to know who leaked this, and I want to know *now*!"

Billy Caldwell rose from his desk. "What, Chief?"

"*'Husband's Footprint Found at Crime Scene'*! Who told this reporter that?"

Alex Johnson and McCormick emerged from the interview room, and Sarah, the dispatcher, looked up at him with wide eyes. "I didn't even know about it, Chief."

Cade swung around to Johnson and McCormick. "I want to know who did it so I can personally end his career in law enforcement and arrest him for interfering with an investigation."

"Whoa, Chief." McCormick held out his hands, as if calming a bucking horse. "You don't know it was one of us. It could have been one of the borrowed investigators. There were enough people working the scene."

Cade flung the paper across the room. "We don't even know for sure that it was Ben's shoes that made those prints! And here they are publishing it in a national tabloid!" He grabbed the paper back up and saw the articles further down the front page. *"Local Psychic Helps Police Find Body."* Carson Graham's picture had a place almost as prominent as Ben's or Lisa's.

When he turned to page two, his heart felt as if it would slam right through his chest, alien-style. Pictures of Lisa's dead, wet body, slumped in that car dripping with seaweed, filled half the page. He ripped the page in two and flung both halves down. "This is all we need. A media circus making Lisa Jackson into a freak show and Ben into a homicidal maniac." He pointed to the cops in front of him. "No one talks to the media about this case, do you hear me?" His staff nodded, and he turned to Sarah. "Get on the radio and tell every one of my men that. No one talks to the media—or they lose their job. No second chances. Tell them I'm not playing."

He went back into his office and sank back into his chair. The phone was ringing, and no one out there was answering it. It was probably a reporter. He felt like ripping the cord out of the wall and throwing it across the room.

He leaned his elbows up on the desk and looked down at today's copy of the *Cape Refuge Journal*, which had also come out this morning. Its headline was almost as bad as the *Observer*'s.

"Psychic Leads Police to Body."

As if on cue, Alex stuck his head around the door. "Uh, Chief, Blair's here to see you."

Great. He'd been wanting to talk to her, too. "Send her in."

Blair bolted in, looking like she hadn't yet been to bed. "Cade, I just saw Vince Barr's article. Why didn't you tell me about the footprint?"

"Because it's not public information, Blair! I don't know who told him, but when I find out, somebody's gonna lose their job! Barr's reporting of it was irresponsible."

Blair sank into a chair. "And that surprises you? That a tabloid would be irresponsible?"

"Speaking of irresponsible ..." Cade got up, came around his desk, and closed his door. He picked up the *Cape Refuge Journal*. "What do you call this?"

She grunted. "The edition I stayed up all night to get out. What's wrong?"

"It's the headline that's wrong!" He flung the paper back down. "You gave this psychic undue credence, Blair. I asked you not to!"

"Cade, you asked me not to make him a hero, and I didn't. Did you even read the article?"

"I didn't have to. The headline says it all."

"No, it doesn't. The article explains what happened. Cade, if I didn't report it, I'd be the only one. The *Savannah Morning News* reported it Sunday."

"But our residents expect more from you. They expect accuracy. For you to back up what they said just makes it look true. You could have found another angle. '*Police Find Body in River*' would have been fine, but that's not sensational enough."

Blair got up and faced him squarely. "Okay, is that it? That you didn't get credit?"

That did it. He felt as if his body was going to implode right there. "It's not about credit, Blair," he said through his teeth. "It's about the fact that my job is already pretty much on the line. If anybody but Jonathan makes mayor, I'm out of here. How do you think it makes me look to be taking advice from some two-bit con artist?"

"You didn't take his advice. You followed up on a lead. You were doing your job, and that's what I wrote!" She picked up the paper and shook it out. "Here—" she poked her finger at a paragraph—"right here, I said that you were skeptical about the lead, but when you followed up you saw evidence that a car may have gone in the river. The fact is that you would not have seen the tire tracks if it hadn't been for Carson Graham. That's all I said. I have to do my job, Cade, just like you have to do yours. You can't expect me to hedge on the facts. I put your tip line on the front page. I quoted you and told how you'd gotten others in from different departments to help with the search. You're the real hero here."

"I'm not trying to be the hero!" He grabbed the paper out of her hands and stuffed it into the trash can. "I'm trying to solve a murder! It's not about me. It's about an innocent woman who was strangled to death in our town. But you and Vince Barr and all those other reporters have made it a freak show, with Carson Graham as the star. Giving away key bits of evidence that no one but the police were supposed to know—"

"Then it's true about the footprints?"

"I don't believe this." She was still playing reporter, using their argument as another chance to get a scoop. Chewing his lip, he went back to his desk, trying to calm his anger. Slowly, he lowered back into his chair. "This interview is over, Blair. I have nothing more to say."

The anger on her face matched his as she bent over his desk. "It's not an interview, Cade, and you know it. I just asked you a question. I'm not Vince Barr. I'm not the one who printed pictures of her corpse, so you can stop taking it out on me."

"I'm not taking it out on you."

"I bought that paper so that I could report the news in this community with integrity and intelligence. I use my Christian principles in deciding what goes into that paper, and you know it. I don't appreciate your implications that I'm irresponsible or opportunistic."

He wondered if his own face was as red as her scars. "Christian principles, huh? Then tell me why you would help that fly-by-night fortune-teller elevate his name. I'm absolutely amazed that you spent so many years dissecting Christianity because it didn't make sense to you, but you're accepting that guy's claims without a second thought. Did you read what the Bible says about guys like him, Blair, or did you just blow that off?"

She straightened. "I've been busy, just like you have. Are you questioning my Christianity?"

"I'm questioning your knowledge of the Bible. If you knew what it said about psychics, you wouldn't be giving this guy a standing ovation."

The words hit dead-on. "You act like I've joined a cult or something. I just wrote an article. And it's not a big surprise that I'm not as well versed in the Bible as you are when I've only been a Christian for a month! But none of that has anything to do with my reporting the facts. He told you where she was. That's all there is."

"How did he *know*?" Cade wanted to hit something, but he knew the raised voices were already giving his men enough to talk about. Blasted paper-thin walls. They'd probably heard every single word. Whose idea was it to turn a laundromat into a police station, anyway? "Did you ever question that, Blair? How did this so-called psychic know where she was?"

Her face changed. "So you think he was involved in her death?"

He couldn't believe that had come out of his mouth. He needed some sleep, some Advil for his aching leg . . . and while he was at it, a resolution to this murder case. He took in a long, deep breath and lowered his voice. "I don't know, Blair. All I know is that God didn't give him a vision. But when his show packs in more people this week than the churches packed in Sunday, you can pat yourself on the back for advancing the cause of the crackpots."

He got up, came around the desk, and opened the door. "Now I've got work to do."

He stormed past the officers at their desks, pretending to be busy as if they hadn't heard the exchange. Pushing out the front door, he went to his truck and got in.

Blair was coming out as he backed up and pulled out of the parking lot. He was more determined than ever to find the killer and solve the puzzle of Carson Graham's involvement before this whole thing got out of hand.

CHAPTER

29

As tired as Blair was from her all-nighter, she found herself unable to sleep when she went home. Anger seethed through her at the things Cade had said, but more than that, she felt stark disappointment that he'd walked out on her.

They'd argued before, but not in the last month, since the two of them had gotten closer. She'd wondered if they still had that kind of fight in them. His accusations made her livid. Did he doubt her faith because of a headline? Did he consider her a superficial Christian because she hadn't had time to study what the Bible said about psychics?

She tried to swallow back her anger and, taking his challenge, went to get her father's Bible. She took it to her laptop, sat at the kitchen table, and pulled up her Bible program. She keyed in a few words and began flipping through the Scriptures that spoke on the subject of psychics.

Deuteronomy 18 had much to say on the subject. She turned to that place in her father's Bible, and read aloud.

"There shall not be found among you anyone who makes his son or his daughter pass through the fire, one who uses divination, one who practices witchcraft, or one who interprets omens, or a sorcerer, or one who casts a spell, or a medium, or a spiritist, or one who calls up the dead. For whoever does these things is detestable to the LORD; and because of these detestable things the LORD your God will drive them out before you. You shall be blameless before the LORD your God. For those nations, which you shall dispossess, listen to those who practice witchcraft and to diviners, but as for you, the LORD your God has not allowed you to do so."

She sat back and stared down at the page. It was clear what God thought about the practices of people like Carson Graham.

But did that mean that he was a fake? If he didn't get his vision from God, where *had* he gotten it? What had given him the power to see where Lisa's body lay?

She closed her Bible and stared at a spot on the table. Maybe Cade's suspicions were right. Maybe Carson had inside knowledge that had nothing to do with psychic powers. Maybe he *had* been involved.

She checked more of the passages that came up on her computer screen. In 1 Samuel 28 Saul had consulted a medium, and the woman brought up the dead Samuel, who prophesied Saul's death. If that woman had the power to bring someone back from the dead, was it just a one-time fluke for God's purposes? Had she been a fraud up until that point, then been stunned when Samuel appeared? God had used a donkey before to speak his truth. Was it so far-fetched that he might use a woman he considered wicked to speak Samuel's prophecy?

Or did she really have special powers apart from God, who would never have gifted her with something he considered detestable?

She read about the spiritists and magicians who couldn't recite Nebuchadnezzer's dreams, and how Daniel did so through the spirit of prophecy. Had those spiritists been able to do so before?

Finally, she found the passage in Acts 16 in which a fortune-teller followed Paul around for days, yelling out that he was a "bond servant of the Most High God." She had spoken the truth, yet Paul had turned around and cast a demon out of her. Immediately, she'd lost her power to tell fortunes.

So what did that tell her? She got up and walked around the kitchen, trying to think it through. Apparently some psychics really did have demonic power to do the things they did, though it sounded like they could not see the future. Deuteronomy 18: 21–22 said, "You may say in your heart, 'How will we know the word which the LORD has not spoken?' When a prophet speaks in the name of the LORD, if the thing does not come about or come true, that is the thing which the LORD has not spoken."

If they really had power to see the future, then they wouldn't ever get it wrong.

But did they have the power to see visions of things that had already happened? Did demons, who knew the evil that had already happened to Lisa, put that vision into Carson's head?

She went back to the Bible, determined to mold her anger at Cade into something productive. She would study until she got to the bottom of this, and then she would show Cade that his implications about her faith were unjust and untrue.

Knowledge could only help.

CHAPTER

30

Lisa's fertility doctor, Alan Sims, the one who had worked with her and Ben through their long, arduous struggle to have a child, wasn't at his clinic. His receptionist told Cade that Sims had taken the day off to attend Lisa's funeral that afternoon.

Cade found the man's home on Cape Refuge—a three-story Tudor-style house situated on an acre in one of the more upscale neighborhoods in town. Since he'd been personally interviewing everyone who'd been scheduled to see Lisa on the day of her murder, he needed to talk to the doctor to see if he had any insights to give him about her death. It was the kind of thing McCormick might have done better, but he was tied up reviewing the evidence that had been taken from Lisa's car and body, so Cade had come himself. It was welcome work since he couldn't stand the thought of sitting in his office, stewing about Blair's article and dealing with phone calls from the press.

He rang the front bell and waited. After a moment, the doctor himself answered. "Chief Cade?"

"Dr. Sims, I'm sorry to bother you at home, but your office told me you'd taken the day off. Do you mind if I come in and talk to you for a minute?"

"Sure, come on in." Sims was unshaven and smelled of whiskey. Barefoot and wearing a wrinkled T-shirt and a pair of jeans, he led Cade into his living room. A shirt lay wadded on the couch, and several pairs of shoes and socks lay on the floor. A plate, several glasses, and some wadded napkins cluttered the coffee table.

"Excuse the mess." He grabbed some newspapers off of a chair so Cade could sit down. "My maid is AWOL, and my wife has been in Europe for the past week. It doesn't usually look like this. This thing with Lisa really shook me up. I haven't even been able to think clearly." He sat down on the couch, and Cade took the chair. "You build a relationship, you know? She wasn't just a patient. She was a friend."

"I can imagine," Cade said. "I'm afraid I didn't know her very well myself. Dr. Sims, could you tell me about the last time you saw her?"

He set his elbows on his knees and raked his hands through his hair. "That was the day before she disappeared. I saw her every day last week. We were doing daily sonograms so we'd know exactly when she ovulated. We had to know when we could harvest her egg. Timing is critical."

"Did she ever mention any problems or turmoil in her life? Or anyone she might be afraid of?"

"Not really. Fighting infertility is a very long road and it's not always pleasant. The Jacksons had a lot of disappointments and were under quite a bit of stress, not to mention all the drugs that she was on and the pressure that Ben was under with the election."

Cade thought of those letters again. "Did Lisa ever express concerns about her marriage?"

"Not really. I know he had asked her to wait until after the election to do the last IVF. But she felt panicked, like her time was running out. Every month counted. I had noticed a little more tension between them lately." He stopped, ran his hands down his face, and looked at Cade over his fingertips. "Chief, do you think he killed her?"

Cade wasn't going to answer that. "Was there anything in Ben's character that would make you think he was capable of that?"

His hands went back through his hair. Cade noticed they were shaking. "You never know what anyone's really capable of, do you?"

CHAPTER

31

And now to comment on this bizarre murder case in Cape Refuge, Georgia, Vince Barr of the *Observer* joins us via satellite. Welcome, Vince."

Blair caught her breath and turned up the television. Had FOX News really asked the sleazy tabloid reporter to talk about Lisa's case?

"This morning your paper called this case to the attention of the national media," Shepherd Smith said. "It seems that this woman named Lisa Jackson turned up missing just days ago, and then her car was found in the river."

"That's right, Shep," Vince said, as if he was a regular on their show instead of some two-bit paparazzi looking for an alien behind every bush. "And the interesting thing about this case is that a psychic is the one who led the police to her body. He apparently was given a sweater that belonged to Lisa, and from that he got a vision. He told her closest friend where her body could be found."

As he spoke, FOX flashed pictures of Lisa Jackson on the screen.

"And the sheriff listened to him, and indeed, her body was found there, in her car."

"He's not a sheriff!" Blair bit out to the television.

"Tell us about Lisa Jackson," Smith said. "I understand she was a real estate maven in the area."

"She was, and a very popular one, at that. Her business partner is former model Rani Nixon—"

"Rani Nixon? One of the highest paid models in Manhattan just a few years ago. So that's where she wound up."

"That's right. She went into business with Lisa when she retired from modeling."

Blair couldn't imagine what he thought Rani had to do with anything, but she supposed that had probably been a part of his pitch to FOX when he'd tried to sell them the story.

The photos of Lisa stopped flashing, and the camera went back to Vince. He looked like he'd dyed his hair overnight. He'd been decidedly grayer yesterday.

"Lisa and her husband had been married for twenty years," he went on, "and by all accounts, seemed happy. They had gone through years of infertility treatments and were, in fact, about to do their third in vitro procedure when Lisa disappeared."

"Vince, in your article this morning, you said that the husband's footprints were found at the scene where her car went into the river."

The helicopter footage of the search for Lisa's body came on, then the tape from across the river, and then closer up of when he'd taken pictures of the body. Blair thought of grabbing a vase and slamming it into the screen, but she decided to wait until she saw him face-to-face.

"Yes. They found shoes in his house that matched the prints."

"Is this confirmed?"

"Anonymously. I got this tip from a very reliable source."

"And they're putting her time of death at midmorning, isn't that right? So do they think he just drove her car there with her dead body in it and pushed it into the river in broad daylight?"

"The site where she went in is a pretty isolated area on the river. He could have easily done it without anyone seeing him. And apparently did."

"Have any arrests been made yet?"

"Not yet, Shep. Understand, this is a very small sheriff's department, used to dealing with car thefts and parking violations. If it weren't for Carson Graham's psychic reading, they'd probably still be searching for her."

"Thefts and parking violations!" Blair threw the remote across the room, then went to the set and punched the power button to turn it off. Hadn't Cade solved four murders in the past few months? She couldn't watch another moment. She hoped Cade hadn't seen that. He would be more enraged than he already was, and she didn't blame him.

Suddenly she realized that she wasn't angry at him anymore. Her feelings of defensiveness over him spoke volumes.

How dare that man minimize Cade's competence?

She thought of what Cade had said about her making Carson Graham out to be a hero. He was even more of a hero now, and he would probably be invited onto every news show in the country after this.

Could Cade be right about his involvement being more than just a psychic vision? Could the psychic have had something to do with Lisa's death?

She decided her first interview of the day would be with Graham himself. She called him, and he answered on the first ring.

"Carson Graham. How can I help you today?"

She swallowed. "Carson, this is Blair Owens. I was wondering if I could come by and talk to you this morning."

"Would you like a personal reading or is this newspaper business?"

She rolled her eyes. "Newspaper. I'd like an interview."

"Well, certainly." His syrupy, soft voice was reminiscent of a funeral director. "I have some time right now if you could come on over, but I can only spare a few minutes. I'm getting quite a large number of media requests today."

She hurried over and pulled up into the gravel parking lot of the old house, situated on Ocean Boulevard just off of the Tybee Bridge, one of the busiest roads on Cape Refuge, where every gullible soul who came in or out of town would see his sign. She shivered as she looked up at the place, wondering if she should be afraid. She could be walking into danger on several levels. If Carson was a fraud, and really was involved in Lisa's death, he could be dangerous. And if he wasn't a fraud but a real psychic, were there demons hovering around him? She wished she knew more about the spiritual aspects of his "gift."

Carson Graham met her at the door. "Blair, so good to see you." He took her hand in both of his. "Come in, dear. Would you like coffee? Coke?"

"No, thanks. I'm good."

Withdrawing her hand, she looked around at the candles clustered around the room, their light flickering eerily against the wall. The smell of incense almost made her sneeze.

"You sure keep it dark in here."

"That's for privacy and concentration. I'll open the drapes if you'd like."

She shrugged, as if she didn't care one way or another, but she was glad when he did. As light filled the room, she realized it didn't look nearly as elegant as she'd thought. Dust particles danced on the sun rays, revealing the scratches and age in most of the cheap furniture. Shabby without the chic.

He sat down across from her. "Thank you for the headline today, Blair. It was such a pleasant surprise. My work is usually done behind the scenes. I don't expect that kind of credit."

She cleared her throat. So Cade was right. "I just reported the facts. But today I was thinking about doing a piece on the process behind being a psychic. Where you got your gift, how you've developed it, what exactly you see . . . that kind of thing."

"Of course. And I'm glad you used the word *gift*. It really is that, you know. A gift from God."

Blair hadn't expected that. Her eyebrows came up. "God, huh? So you believe God is the one who gave you this power?"

"Of course he did. He's the one who opens my eyes to see, if you will."

Blair jotted that down. *Eyes to see.* Bible lingo. "So tell me about your average vision. How does it work?"

He shifted in his seat. "Well, to tell you the truth, it comes in different ways. Usually, I'll take my subject's hand, and impressions just begin flooding my brain." He reached out for her hand. "May I?"

"Maybe some other time."

He laughed softly. "Oh, a skeptic, huh? Well, you know, I don't always *have* to touch that person to get those impressions. Sometimes they come without it. Like now, for instance. I'm sensing that you're in love."

She tapped her pencil on her pad and hoped her scars weren't flaming. "Is that right?"

"Yes. I sense that it's a strange feeling to you, because in the past you haven't let yourself be that vulnerable. And you never thought romance was in your cards. But let me tell you, Blair. It is."

Part of her wanted to follow this lure—see if he could tell her where her relationship with Cade would lead. But wasn't it becoming common knowledge? After their first kiss, which happened in front of dozens of police officers, hadn't word spread all over the island?

"You've been hurt in the past. You've suffered intense grief."

She sighed and propped her chin on her hand. "Come on, Carson. Everybody in town knows I lost my parents."

"But your scars have caused you no end of grief, haven't they? You put on the air of a tough broad, but the truth is that all you've ever really wanted was someone of your own to love you."

Now she knew her scars were flaming. She felt her chest tightening, her heart ramming against it. "Could we get back to the interview?"

"This *is* part of the interview, Blair. I'm showing you how this works."

"I didn't come here for a reading. I'm here as a reporter."

"Don't worry, I won't charge you. He is going to marry you, you know."

Her heart jolted. "Who is?"

"This person you're in love with."

She stared down at her notepad as an unexpected wave of anger surged up inside her. Why Graham's words angered her so, she wasn't sure. Tapping her pencil on her paper, she gritted her teeth. "On the day after Lisa's disappearance, Rani Nixon came to see you. Is that right?"

"Yes," he said with a condescending smile. "She gave me Lisa's sweater. I took it home and sat alone, right here in this room, holding that sweater. And that's when I saw where she was."

"So, did you go into a trance or something? An out-of-body experience?"

"No trance. I just saw impressions of her in her Lexus, going into the water. Very similar to the one I see of you in a wedding dress."

She stared down at her notes and forced herself to go on. "How did you know exactly where on the river she was?"

"I just knew. It's very hard to explain, Blair. I saw her dead in the water, and I just knew exactly where it was. Half a mile east of the Bull River Bridge. I know it sounds crazy. But that's the way it is."

She thought back over those Scripture passages she'd read this morning. "Carson, you mentioned that your power came from God. What religion are you?"

He seemed to stiffen. "I'm not really into religion, Blair. Not organized religion, anyway. I worship God in my mind. My body is his temple. And I like to think that the people who come to me for readings, whether it's here or at my show, feel that their experiences are very close to religious experiences."

That was telling. So his belief in God was ethereal. "Do you believe in heaven?"

"Yes, of course."

"What about hell?"

"I believe in a hell on earth. How else can you describe poverty, death, depression?"

"No hell," she jotted down. "Okay, so how about Satan?"

He chuckled as if he knew exactly what she was getting at. "Are you trying to figure out if I'm demon possessed?" He seemed genuinely delighted. "Look at me, Blair. Do I look evil?"

She had to admit he didn't. A little silly, maybe, but not evil.

"My power does not come from the Devil or demons, Blair. I'm gifted by God. It's as simple as that. God wanted Lisa to be found, and so he used me to do that."

Blair jotted that down verbatim, but didn't know if she would use it in her article. Cade was right. There would be readers who would conclude that Carson was a prophet from God.

"Blair, I think that God wants you to be happy, and he's going to use me to help you with that, too."

Again, anger pulsed through her. How dare he try to hit her vulnerability—and in the name of God!

"He's already thinking about marriage, Blair. This man you love can't imagine a life without you. I see a proposal in your very near future."

Her heart began to swell with hope, but then she remembered the Scripture. She wasn't supposed to listen to a psychic or believe in his prophecies. Besides, if he could really read Cade's feelings right now, he would see only anger . . . not romance.

"I have to go." She got up and shoved her pad back into her bag. "I think I have all I need."

"You work too hard, Blair. Yet you have the potential to turn the *Journal* into a daily paper of great import. I advise you to hire a staff to help you and shoot high. I can already see the *Cape Refuge Journal* in a four-story building with dozens of employees. You're familiar with the old South Farm Insurance Building, aren't you? I see the *Journal* occupying that building, Blair."

She paused for a moment and looked up at him. She had never thought of using that building. It was too big. It seemed too soon to think that big.

"You must not be hindered by your logic."

It was as if he could read her thoughts.

"I see your circulation being far greater than the population of this island. You must be bold, fearless in your expansion. You must make daring decisions without looking back."

She felt the pull of his vision, the hope of his promise . . .

. . . and suddenly realized how seductive his words could be. No wonder millions of dollars a year were spent on psychic hotlines.

She started to the door, and he followed her. "You should come to my show one night. Then you could really see me in action. You could be my guest."

"Maybe sometime I will. Thanks for the interview, Carson."

"So will this be in Friday's issue?"

"Maybe. I don't know for sure."

She got to her car and pulled out of the parking lot as fast as she could. As she drove away, she understood how easily people could be taken in by him.

He told them exactly what they wanted to hear.

CHAPTER

*T*he funeral was held in Savannah at an
old, opulent church that Ben and Lisa had rarely attended.
Seated in the pews was a Who's Who of the wealthiest
people in the area. Morgan almost felt out of place.

The priest clearly didn't know Lisa. He talked about
her in generic terms, read Scripture that had little to do
with her, and gave a sermon on the battle between good
and evil. She supposed that was his vague reference to
Lisa's killer, and that the good was a veiled reference to
God. How sad that at a time like this, the man of the
cloth could give them nothing more than that.

Rani Nixon had been asked to give Lisa's eulogy,
since she was her oldest friend. Rani had on a sleek black
dress like something she would have worn on the cover of
Vogue, with a sheer black sari thrown around her shoulders. Despite her sophistication and prideful carriage, she
looked as fragile as blown glass.

Morgan prayed that the woman could get through it
without tears.

Rani strode to the pulpit and stood there looking out at them, as if waiting for the camera to snap. Finally, she spoke. "Lisa Jackson was my best friend." Her mouth quivered at the corners. "I met her in college, when we were assigned together as roommates. I was this tall, lanky, skinny black kid who expected someone of my race as a roommate. Lisa came in, and the first thing she said was, 'You're black.'" Rani smiled weakly. "She always did have remarkable insight."

The crowd laughed softly, and Morgan's tension melted away. Rani could do this.

"I told her that if she had a problem sharing a dorm room with someone of a different race, I would be glad to go to the housing director and ask him to move me. She looked at me for a minute and said, 'It's not your race that worries me. It's your size. I was really hoping we could share our wardrobes.'"

Morgan smiled. That sounded like Lisa.

"She hugged me then, and we began to unpack, and before the day was over, she'd found four or five of my blouses that she could wear." She paused. "I don't think I ever saw those again."

More laughter. This was perfect. Since the murder, she'd only been able to dwell on the negatives in Lisa's life. It was good to remember the things that brought smiles.

Rani's smile faded, and her mouth trembled as she tried to hold back her tears. "We continued to live together for the next four years. We told each other every secret, concocted schemes together, and suffered through the ups and downs of romance. I remember the night she met Ben."

She stopped then, staring down at her notes, her nostrils flaring because of the struggle going on within her. "She said it was love at first sight. That he was her knight in shining armor. That she knew . . . nothing bad could ever happen to her if he was in her life."

She lost the battle with her tears then, and her face twisted with pain. Wetting her lips, she looked out at Ben, sitting in the front row. "Did you know that, Ben? Did you know she trusted you that much?"

Morgan touched Jonathan's hand, and he squeezed. She glanced at Ben in the front row and saw that his shoulders were shaking as he wept into his hands.

Blair, who sat on the other side of Jonathan, leaned up to meet Morgan's eyes. *What is she doing?* her eyes asked.

"Lisa will be deeply missed." Rani went back to her notes. "My life will never be the same without her. No one's will, not if they knew her well."

She went back to her seat, wiping the tears off her face.

Morgan breathed a sigh of relief. For a moment there, she had expected something more. A confrontation, perhaps, given Rani's feelings about Ben and the letters.

Unfortunately, the danger was not over. As they all got into their cars for the funeral procession to the grave site, Morgan stopped Rani. "Do you want to ride with us, Rani?"

Rani's eyes followed Ben into the limo at the front of the line. He was weeping again and hugging a mourner. Rani's face tightened at the sight. Morgan wondered if she'd heard her.

"Rani?"

"What? Oh, no, I think I need to ride alone."

"Are you sure?"

"Yeah." She clipped off to her Roadster and slipped behind the wheel.

"She's right on the edge of losing it," Jonathan said.

"And she's sure he did it." Morgan realized she could hardly blame her. The letters didn't make Ben look good.

Yet Ben's grief seemed authentic. He was clearly broken, just as he'd been the day Lisa had been found.

They drove in the silent procession to a new memorial garden that wasn't yet sprinkled with graves.

Ben had chosen a lovely spot for Lisa's burial—on a hill beneath the shade of a sprawling oak tree and near a summer garden of marigolds, periwinkles, and brightly colored pansies. It was a soft reminder that life flourished, even where death was planted.

The graveside service was brief and somber, and after the priest had given his final words, Ben got up and hugged Lisa's weeping parents. They clung to each other before the casket, sobbing openly.

Morgan looked at Rani, saw that her eyes were dry. She sat with her hard eyes fixed on Ben, her lips tight across her teeth. She was a powder keg about to explode . . .

"Stop it!"

Everyone turned to look at Rani, as she came out of her chair. Tears stained her dark face. "You're not fooling anyone!"

Ben let go of his in-laws and turned his wet face to Rani. "What?"

"Everyone here knows you're the one who put her in that car and shoved her into the river!"

Morgan gasped and reached for Rani. "Honey, don't—"

Rani jerked out of her grasp and strode toward Lisa's parents, who looked at her as if they'd just plunged into a new dimension of their grief. "He killed your daughter, Mr. and Mrs. Hinton. I know he did!"

Ben stepped toward her. "Rani, I know you're upset. We all are. But you can't go accusing me like that. I loved her."

Rani slapped him.

Morgan gasped as he stumbled back, almost falling.

"Are you crazy?" he shouted.

"You were having an affair!" She grabbed his shirt and shook him. "Who was she, Ben? Is she here? Did *she* make you do it?"

"Rani!" Lisa's mother said.

"That's a lie!" Ben cried. "It's not true!"

"Did Lisa finally get wise and threaten to leave you before the election?" Rani railed. "Did you kill her for the votes, Ben? Is that why Lisa's dead?"

Someone tried to restrain her, but she jerked away. Throwing her hands over her mouth, she ran back to her car.

Everyone stood frozen as Rani screeched away.

Morgan turned back to Ben. He stood there alone, sobbing as he looked around. "I didn't do it," he said softly. "I would never kill her. She was my bride. The letters were a lie." He broke down, and several friends came to hold him up.

Morgan couldn't escape that image of Rani's active rage, and she couldn't help wondering if she was right.

CHAPTER

33

*B*lair rode back to Cape Refuge with Morgan and Jonathan. "That was unbelievable. Dramatic, but unbelievable. And I saw Vince Barr there. I'm sure he was taking notes."

Morgan looked back at her. "Don't be flip, Blair. It was very sad."

It was a day for reprimands, Blair thought. She was getting tired of it. She decided to switch gears. "Someone needs to tell Cade what happened. Jonathan, I nominate you."

Jonathan looked at her in the rearview mirror. "Me? Why not you?"

She sighed. "Because I don't think we're speaking."

Morgan twisted in her seat and looked back at her. "What happened?"

She sighed. "Today's paper happened. He went ballistic over the headline."

Morgan sent Jonathan a knowing look.

"Oh, don't tell me. You two are hot about it, too?"

"Not hot," Jonathan said. "But we wondered what you were thinking."

Blair leaned up on the seat. "Okay, so the headline rubbed you all the wrong way. It's no reason to question my Christianity."

"He did that?" Morgan asked. "Oh, Blair."

Blair leaned back and looked out the window. "He was furious at the *Observer* for telling about the shoes and printing those pictures, so he took it all out on me."

"He was probably just frustrated," Jonathan said. "His job's in jeopardy, you know. He doesn't need more fodder for his critics. But that's no reason for him to question your faith."

She thought of the things Cade had said that morning, and the pain came back again. "He did," she said softly. "Made me wonder if he's doubted it all along. I guess all this time he's been thinking that I faked a religious experience just to get his attention."

"Honey, he knows better than that."

"No, he doesn't, Morgan. I mean, if I was gonna do that, I'd have done it long before now. And can't he see that I've changed?"

Jonathan considered her words. "Of course he does. He just got his feathers ruffled. He's probably just tired and cranky."

"I'm the one who hasn't slept." Blair was quiet for the rest of the ride home. She wondered if Cade had nursed his anger for her all day.

When they reached Hanover House, a Mercedes Roadster sat in the driveway.

"Uh-oh," Morgan said. "Rani's here."

Blair perked up and got her notepad out of her bag. This could be interesting.

As they pulled up next to her, Rani got out of her car. Her eyes were red and puffy, but she had managed to pull herself together. "I need to talk to Blair," she announced as they opened the car doors.

Blair got out of the car, bracing herself. "What is it, Rani?"

Rani faced off with her, towering above her. "Don't write about what I did at the funeral, Blair. Please. It wouldn't serve any purpose."

"Rani, you did it in public, right out in front of everybody."

"But I just lost it! I don't want that in the papers. The gossip will be bad enough without you confirming it."

"I wasn't even the only media there, Rani. This is a case of national interest now. Vince Barr from the *Observer* was there."

"I'll deal with him. But right now I'm asking you. Blair, please. If you have any decorum at all . . ."

Morgan and Jonathan turned to her, their eyes echoing Rani's pleading. So many critics, she thought. So many self-proclaimed editors.

"Okay, I won't write it. But this is the last time you or anyone else is going to tell me what to print."

Rani let out a breath.

"Are you okay?" Morgan asked her.

Rani shook her head. "No, I'm not. He killed her, Morgan. I know he did." She glanced back at Blair. "Off the record."

"Off the record, off the record," Blair mocked under her breath as Morgan led Rani to the porch. Why did people think *off the record* absolved them of any responsibility for the things they blurted? Didn't she have to agree that it was off the record? Weren't they supposed to say it *before* they spouted out revelations? Maybe she hadn't been in journalism long enough, but she knew manipulation when she saw it.

Rani sat down on the swing, and Morgan took the seat beside her, patting her hand like the proverbial earth mother.

"They should have arrested him by now," Rani said. "Or at the very least, identified the other woman. They have the shoes. The letters. They should test them for fibers, fingerprints, handwriting. I watch *CSI*. I know what they can do. What are they waiting for?"

"They're going through all the evidence," Blair said. "They're not equipped to do this without outside help. The force is too small and their budget isn't adequate, which is why we need a new mayor. One who'll give enough money to the police force so they can do their jobs better."

"So what have you found out, Blair? Sometimes reporters can get to the heart of things faster than the police can."

Blair shook her head. "I haven't gotten any closer than the police have. And if I did, I wouldn't tell you two, because you'd try to talk me out of reporting it."

"Rani, I know how things look. But I really don't think it's Ben," Morgan said weakly. "I'm a good judge of those things, and I've been around him a lot in the last few days."

Blair almost laughed as she came up the porch. "No, you're not! You're a terrible judge. You think with your heart. You let people convince you that they're good when they're really not. And do I need to remind you that just a week ago you thought Ben Jackson was the scum of the earth? You remember, Morgan. When he was putting up all those signs and running those ads, throwing hundred dollar bills around like they were M&Ms, while you and Jonathan could barely get fliers into the hands of the voters?"

"So we were competitive with him. It wasn't like we thought he was a killer!"

"And speaking of the election," Blair said, "I don't think Jonathan should stop campaigning just because of this. It's too important. He's got to win this race. He should get back to work this very afternoon. Door-to-door, shaking hands, person-to-person."

Morgan bristled. "It doesn't hurt to take a few days off of campaigning to honor someone who's just lost his wife."

"You don't see Sam Sullivan taking time off."

Morgan threw up her hands. "Fine. Let him move ahead. I'm tired of this whole mess."

"Me, too." Rani sat there a moment as if trying to hold herself together. "I really miss her. I keep wanting to pick up the phone and tell her stuff. Who am I gonna talk to now?"

Blair looked down at her feet. She knew that feeling. There were still times when she picked up the phone to dial her mother. She wondered how long that would last.

She looked back at Rani. Was she just seeking friendship and someone to talk to, or had she really come by to shut Blair up?

Maybe Blair would get to know Rani better, when all of this died down. They had a few things in common now, after all. By the time it was all behind them, they each might need a friend.

CHAPTER

Cade found that the lab report on Ben's shoes answered the questions the media had already answered. The dirt on the shoes *was* the same dirt found at the scene where Lisa's car had been pushed in. That, added to the phone cord that had come from Ben's home—the same cord that had been used to strangle Lisa—as well as the alibi that couldn't be confirmed, gave Cade probable cause for an arrest, and the DA had insisted that he go ahead and bring Ben in.

He'd hoped to make the arrest quietly, but there were already dozens of media standing outside Ben's place, taking pictures of every person who came or went. They shouted questions at Cade and his officers as they went to the door.

Ben opened it before they could ring the bell. He took one look at Cade, then threw up his hands. "What do you want?"

Cade stepped inside, out of the sight of the reporters. Johnson and Caldwell came in behind him. "Ben, we have a warrant to arrest you for Lisa's murder—"

"Cade, I can explain the shoes. They were in her car. I left them in there the day before when we went for our appointment. She picked me up at work, and I changed my shoes because I didn't want to wear dirty tennis shoes to the doctor. The killer must have gotten them out and used them to set me up."

"Ben, we found them in your bedroom, under your bed."

"I didn't put them there! Don't you understand?"

Cade nodded for Johnson to cuff him. "I'm sorry, Ben."

"Cade, don't do this! You know I didn't kill my wife!"

Cade didn't like doing it, especially when he still had such deep reservations about Ben being the killer, but he couldn't go by his gut. He had to go by the evidence, and the DA had given him orders.

He hated parading Ben through the reporters, allowing them to get pictures of the grieving husband whose life had been twisted into pieces. If Ben turned out to be innocent, Cade wasn't sure he would ever forgive himself.

"Is this about the shoes, Sheriff?" Vince Barr called out through the cameras.

Cade turned back to him. "I'm not the sheriff. I'm the police chief. At least get your facts straight before you go on national television with your wild tabloid stories, Barr."

As he got Ben into the squad car and drove him away from the circus, Cade vowed he wouldn't rest on this arrest.

Until he was absolutely convinced that Ben was guilty, he would keep looking for Lisa's killer.

CHAPTER

*T*he fertility clinic had a cancellation for Wednesday afternoon. Morgan had been thrilled to get in so soon, but then it hit her that the cancellation might well have been Lisa's daily appointment.

Jonathan seemed as nervous as she as they stepped into the clinic that they hoped would change their lives. Women and men of various ages sat around the room, paging through magazines or talking softly. One woman with a baby sat in the corner, a testimony to the success of the clinic.

Morgan felt a surge of hope. Maybe one day she would come in here with her own baby in her arms. She checked in and filled out the paperwork, and then they waited.

She grew more tense as the moments ticked by, and when her name was finally called, she almost jumped out of her seat.

The nurse led them to the doctor's office. He wasn't there yet, so she looked around at all his medical degrees.

A bulletin board with baby pictures hung on the wall behind their chairs. "Look, Jonathan."

He turned and looked up at the pictures, some of them of multiple births. "I think we're in the right place," he said.

Dr. Sims came in after a few minutes. He bore a strong resemblance to Mark Harmon, the actor, and he had kind eyes. He greeted them both warmly, then took his seat behind the desk. "I saw you at Lisa's funeral yesterday," he said in a quiet voice. "Were you good friends?"

"Yes, we'd gotten to be over the last few weeks. She's the one who wanted me to come see you."

He adjusted himself in his seat, then looked down at Morgan's file. After a moment, she realized he was struggling with his emotion.

"It's terrible what happened to her." He rubbed his eyes and cleared his throat. "It's such a tragedy. And what happened at the funeral yesterday . . ." He brought his troubled eyes to Morgan's. "You don't think he actually killed her, do you?"

The question surprised Morgan. "We've been with him since before she was found. He's a wreck. I can't imagine that he did."

He stared at the file again, unseeing. "I considered them both friends. When you see somebody as often as I see some of my patients, for years at a time, and you know their deepest longings and you're trying to help them fulfill them . . . you get close to them." His voice broke, and he clasped his hands in front of his mouth. "It's very hard."

"We feel the same way, Doctor," Jonathan said.

He sat up straighter, took a deep breath, then scanned her records. "Well, you certainly have reason to come here. Anytime you've been trying over a year to get pregnant and it hasn't happened, one has to wonder why."

"We're not sure that we're ready to go the whole infertility route, Doc," Jonathan said. "We just want to know what's wrong. Then we'll decide if we want to pursue it."

"Of course. That's what I recommend to all my patients. You have to know what your options are. The first thing I'd like to do is to test Jonathan to see if his readings are normal."

"Me?" Jonathan asked. "But Morgan's already been pregnant. Wouldn't that mean that things are all right with me?"

"It's routine, Jonathan. It's an easy test, just to make sure you don't have a problem that, combined with Morgan's, is making it harder for her to get pregnant. If nothing's wrong with you, then we'll do what's called a hysterosalpingogram for you, Morgan."

Morgan had never heard of that. "A what?"

He smiled. "We call it a hysterogram for short. It's when we shoot dye into your uterus and fallopian tubes to check for blockages. That'll tell us if the problem is with you. Then we'll know how to proceed."

"So when can we get started?" Jonathan asked.

"Well, we can test you today, Jonathan, if that's all right."

"Of course." Morgan laughed. "I didn't expect to jump in so soon."

"Why wait?" Sims' voice softened. "I'm very hopeful that you're going to have a baby soon, and this time, you'll carry it to term. In fact, I feel this is a personal goal. Lisa died before she could ever hold a baby in her arms. Let's make sure that we get it right with you."

CHAPTER

*S*o you think this is going to work, huh?"

Blair had come over to Hanover House to hear about the doctor visit, but her question was heavy with skepticism.

Morgan sat at the table, Caleb in her lap. The child was finger painting with chocolate pudding and working on a picture that Morgan held still. It looked like mocha chaos, but Caleb was thrilled with the effort.

"I don't know. We'll see what the test results show."

"Is he going to put you through the hormonal wringer, like he does all those other women?"

"I hope not."

"See?" Caleb cried out, indicating that he was finished.

She kissed Caleb's chubby cheek and picked up his picture. "Look how beautiful this is. Caleb, this is the best picture you've done! Blair, isn't this wonderful?"

Blair grinned and ruffled the child's hair. "Caleb, that's beautiful," she said in a delighted voice. "It looks like the inner workings of a headache."

"Blair!" Morgan grinned. Caleb thought it was high praise. "We have to let it dry now."

"More," he said.

"All right. I think you've got enough pudding for five more on your hands." She got another piece of manila paper and set it in front of them. As Caleb began slapping it with his chocolate-blobbed hands, Blair set her chin on her palm.

"So is this doctor going to make you jump through hoops?"

"I hope it won't come to that. We won't know anything until he sees the test results, and maybe they'll tell us everything. Maybe it's just a mild case of something that they can fix. A blocked tube or something. He'll find it. I know he will."

"Morgan, maybe you just haven't given it enough time. Maybe you're jumping ahead of God."

"I don't think so. I think he's given me this doctor to help me with the process. He does work through doctors, sometimes."

"Of course he does, but I don't want to see you get as caught up in this as Ben and Lisa were."

Caleb finished his picture again and began licking his hands. His face looked as if he'd been bobbing for apples in a bucketful of cocoa.

"I'm serious, Morgan. You're not going to make this an obsession, are you?"

Morgan took the baby to the sink. "Lisa and Ben were desperate to have a baby. They were doing whatever it took. What's wrong with that?"

"I'm not sure, but there needs to be balance."

"Well, let's see if you feel the same way if you ever have trouble getting pregnant."

Blair almost laughed. "Me? I can't even keep a relationship, much less do the family thing."

"What do you mean, you can't keep a relationship? Hasn't he called?"

"Nope. I haven't talked to him since he chewed me out yesterday."

Morgan cleaned Caleb up, then set him down. He toddled to his toy basket. She regarded her sister. "Are you okay?" But she could see that Blair wasn't.

"I could have sworn we were getting closer. He was over Monday night, and we had a real tender moment there . . . But now I think he's lost interest. I can't believe he questioned my faith."

Morgan wiped the pudding off the table, then rinsed her rag out over the sink. "He didn't mean it."

"Yes, he did. All these years he's known me as a proud unbeliever, and I guess that's a tough image to shake, but I would never fake my conversion. I don't do that kind of thing, and he knows it."

"Maybe you've blown his silence way out of proportion. Maybe he's just busy. He knows what you're like, and he knows you've changed." She dried her hands. "Besides, I think he's secretly been in love with you since before you believed."

"In love?" Blair uttered the words with astonishment. "He's never told me he loved me, and there's not one thing to indicate that he had feelings for me then."

"No, not one thing. More like a dozen things. I could see it in his eyes. It was pretty clear, even though he never would have made a move. He takes the Bible very seriously when it says not to yoke yourself with unbelievers."

"Well, I'm not an unbeliever now. It's maddening, this feeling of being at his mercy. All these years I was content knowing that I was going to be alone, that no man would have me because of these hideous scars."

"They're not hideous."

"And finally, now I've had a taste of what it's like to be in love. I don't much like being that vulnerable."

Morgan just smiled. "He'll call you, Blair. You know he will."

"When?"

"I don't know when, but he will. Just give him a little credit, okay? He's not the type to just dump somebody without telling them."

"But we never had an understanding or anything. Can you dump someone that you've never had any kind of commitment to?"

"Cade would never lead you on if he didn't intend to follow through."

"Well, he's not leading me on now. I'm just sitting here like an idiot, waiting for a phone call. I hate that."

"I know you do, but you do it very well." She laughed. "He's going to call eventually, but right now he's just stressed out. You'll hear from him soon enough."

The telephone rang, and Morgan laughed. "Maybe that's him now."

Blair grunted. "Fat chance. Maybe the results of your tests?"

"Too soon." Morgan picked up the phone. "Hello?"

"May I speak to Morgan or Jonathan Cleary?" It was a man's voice, crisp and rapid.

"This is Morgan."

"Morgan, this is Anthony Hammond. I'm the attorney for Sheila Caruso."

Morgan caught her breath. "Yes, what can I do for you, Mr. Hammond?"

Caleb started pounding a wooden spoon on his toy piano. Morgan motioned for Blair to distract him.

"I wanted to let you know that Sheila's going to be released in a little over a week."

Morgan froze. "*What?*"

Blair picked Caleb up and looked at her. "What is it?"

Morgan held her hand up to quiet her. "How can she be released in a week? She was supposed to be in for four more years."

"The legislature issued a new law a couple of weeks ago that nonviolent offenders only have to serve twenty percent of their sentence. She's already served that."

"Yes, I heard that might be a possibility, but I didn't think—" His words ricocheted through her head, making her dizzy. She groped for a chair. "What are her plans, Mr. Hammond? Regarding her children, I mean."

"I'm not sure yet, but she plans to contact her daughter soon. I just felt you should be notified, as the foster parent of her children."

When he hung up, Morgan set the phone back in its cradle. Her mind raced with images of her foster children being dragged away. She took Caleb from Blair and held him tight.

"Sheila's getting out?" Blair asked in a whisper.

"That's right." Her voice sounded as if it came from someone else. "Next week."

"No way! Morgan, what are her plans?"

"I don't know." She choked the words out. "But she's going to want her kids."

Caleb touched her face. She took his hand and kissed it. "She can't take him back, Blair. She's not ready to be a mother."

"Oh, Sis." She reached out to Morgan, pulling her into a hug. "What are you gonna do?"

Morgan tried to think. She couldn't let it happen. Sheila was not equipped to care for Caleb. Her irresponsibility had almost gotten both of her children killed.

"There's only one answer. She'll have to come here. We'll just have to convince her to do that, and then she can mother Caleb as much as she wants to, right here in our home. And so can I."

"Do you think she will?"

"We'll just have to convince her." Fear took hold of Morgan's heart, for she knew Sheila might have other plans.

CHAPTER

*T*he test was the hardest and most important one Sadie had taken all year. She had studied her brains out, and she had a headache and a cramp in her hand from writing the essay questions.

Already half the class had turned their exam papers in. All she had to do was take the test up to her teacher and tenth grade would finally be behind her. Then she could work full-time for Blair for the summer and stop worrying about the stress and dread of being a seventeen-year-old sophomore.

She finally realized she had done her absolute best and couldn't improve on any of her answers, so she got her books and turned the test in.

"Thank you, Sadie." Mrs. Whitlow smiled at her. "Have a good summer."

She walked out into the hall. Lockers were slamming in celebration as students came out of their exams, exhilarated that school was over.

But no one was happier than she. She walked up the corridor, wishing she'd never have to see this place again. She had begged Morgan to let her homeschool next year so she could work more hours for Blair. Neither Morgan nor Jonathan liked the idea.

But she hadn't given up. If being a seventeen-year-old sophomore was bad, being an eighteen-year-old junior was sure to be worse. She had come to Cape Refuge a sixteen-year-old ninth-grade dropout, running for her life from her mother's drug-addicted, violent boyfriend. Everyone in the school knew of her checkered past, and her few attempts at fitting in had been disastrous. Her hours at school were among the loneliest of her life.

When she got home, she heard the sounds of Caleb laughing in the kitchen and baby Emory crying upstairs. She loved those sounds. It sounded like a family, a warm contrast to the social chills she got at school.

"I'm home!" she cried out.

"Hey, sweetie." Morgan came out of the kitchen. She still didn't look good since her miscarriage—her face was pale, and she'd lost a few pounds. Sadie knew she wasn't eating or sleeping much. She hoped Morgan was really all right. "How was your exam?"

"Not bad. Now I'm free." Sadie set her backpack near the bottom of the stairs so she could take it up when she went.

"I have some good news for you."

Sadie examined her face. Morgan didn't look like she had good news. She seemed to be balancing on the edge of tears. "What?"

"It's about your mother." She planted a smile on her face. It was a valiant effort, but it didn't reach to her eyes. "You were right. God is giving her a second chance."

"She's getting out?" The words burst out of her.

"Next week," Morgan said.

Sadie let out a scream and began jumping up and down. She hugged Morgan. "Did you talk to her?"

"No, her lawyer called."

Sadie squealed. "Oh, my gosh! I bet she's just freaking out." She ran into the kitchen and found Caleb sitting among several pots and pans that he banged on with his favorite wooden spoon. She grabbed him up and kissed him. "Caleb, Mom's coming home!"

He giggled, though he didn't have a clue what she was talking about.

"Mom's coming home!" She swung around to Morgan. "She's coming here, right?"

Morgan's smile faltered. "I don't know, honey."

"But she has to. We can't leave." Only then did Sadie understand the reason for the tension on Morgan's face.

"She's welcome here," Morgan said.

"Oh, Morgan, do you think she'll come?"

Tears came to Morgan's eyes, and she took Caleb out of Sadie's arms. "I hope so."

Any other possibility seemed too far-fetched to consider. Sadie thought of her mother coming here, seeing the beautiful house, and soaking up the love and warmth of the family. She had never really had that before. "She will. I'll convince her. Don't worry, Morgan. It's going to be all right. I'll go visit her Saturday and talk her into it. Where else would she go?"

With that, she ran up the stairs and began to clean up her room, to prepare for her mother.

CHAPTER

*H*ow do you people work in this place? Can you at least turn up the air-conditioner?"

Cade looked at the cocky detective at the back of the group. He'd had to cram all of the crime scene investigators—three from the State Police, plus McCormick and himself—into the small interview room at the police department. It wasn't big enough for this many people.

"Yeah," someone else complained. "Place feels like a boiler room."

"Or maybe a laundromat." The three guest detectives laughed.

Cade didn't find it amusing. "We're trying to cool it down. I'll make this fast." He stood in front of the dry-erase boards he had temporarily hung on the wall and pointed to the column with "BODY" at the top. "Strangle marks on her neck. No other bruises or cuts, no signs of a struggle. The medical examiner put her death at ten-thirty Friday morning. She was dead before she went into the water."

"So the husband is in custody?" one of the detectives asked.

"That's right. The DA wanted me to bring him in, but the truth is, he doesn't have enough of a case to convict. And I'm not entirely convinced the husband's the killer. The letters, shoes, and telephone cord do seem to implicate him, but he claims that the shoes were in her car at the time of the murder and that the killer must have brought them back to his house and put them under the bed where we'd find them."

"That's a stretch."

"Yeah, it is," Cade admitted. "And then there's the phone cord that came from their house. And we have the letters. Don't yet know where they came from, but we have handwriting analysts working on that. Either there was another woman, which certainly could be the motive, or someone was trying to sabotage Ben Jackson's marriage . . ."

"Or his campaign," McCormick added.

"Have you considered one of his opponents?" someone asked.

"Could be," Cade said. "Alibi's iffy. And he's been pretty cut-throat during this campaign."

"What about the other one?"

"Jonathan Cleary?" Cade knew Jonathan hadn't done it, but he didn't want to appear biased. "Has a strong alibi. His wife had a miscarriage that morning. They were at the hospital, then he didn't leave her until later in the day. The residents of their house are witnesses."

A knock sounded on the door, and he opened it. Alex Johnson stood there with an uncomfortable look on his face. "Uh . . . Chief. You may want to take a look at this. That *Observer* guy is on FOX News again."

Cade groaned and stepped into the squad room. The television was on in the corner, with the volume turned down low. Video was playing of Ben's arrest, of Cade walking him through the crowd to the squad car, and of Cade's comments about not being the sheriff.

Vince had made him look like a jerk. Cade turned it up and heard Vince talking over the video. "... rumors that Ben Jackson was having an affair. It seems that the other woman had been writing letters to Lisa, telling her about the affair. According to her friend Rani Nixon, Lisa had confronted her husband about the affair, but he convinced her it was a hoax."

Cade just stood there, frozen, trying to stay calm. In the reflection of the television screen, he saw that all of the detectives in the meeting had come out and were watching it, too.

He brought his hand up and raked his fingers through his hair. He was glad Vince Barr wasn't within his reach. He might have actually given the national media a new story to cover.

Cade turned back to the men. "I guess the meeting's over. McCormick, tell them what we need from them."

His jaw flexed as he went into his office and put his foot up on the desk. If he could keep the media out of his way long enough to conduct this investigation, they might actually figure out who the killer was.

The media would try Ben in the court of public opinion, before they even had a case that could convict him. Meanwhile, if Ben wasn't their guy, the real killer was getting a good laugh out of the whole blasted thing.

CHAPTER

39

*T*he test results cleared Jonathan of blame
for their fertility problems, which laid it squarely at Morgan's feet. Dr. Sims scheduled a hysterogram for the next
day and assured her they would know more after that.

Morgan knew she should be grateful that the first test
had shown no problems, but a heaviness lay over her heart
at the thought of the road they were headed down.

When she saw Sam Sullivan's car pulling into the
driveway, she thought of meeting him at the door and
warning him that Jonathan was on his boat, trying to earn
a living, and that she wasn't in the mood for his harassment today.

Instead, she met him out on the porch and forced
herself to greet him like she would any other visitor.

He looked as if he'd just won the lottery. "Did you
hear that Ben has been taken off the ballot?"

Morgan crossed her arms. "Where did you hear
that?"

"Down at City Hall. There was a question on whether he qualified to run, given his arrest, but apparently he told them to pull him out of the race. Looks like it's just Jonathan and me now. We've officially rescheduled the debate for a week from Saturday."

"That's fine, Sam. That'll be three days before the election."

He chuckled and rubbed his hands together as if he couldn't wait to take Jonathan on. "Sure he's up to a one-on-one?"

Morgan tried to smile. "I'm sure he's ready, Sam."

He started back to his car, but stopped before getting in. "Oh, by the way, did you hear about the deal I just made for a cell phone tower on the island?"

Her smile faltered. "No, I didn't."

"I sold them some of my land. Prime real estate. We'll have cell service out here before we know it."

He winked like a car salesman and got into his Mercedes.

Morgan watched him drive away. So that was his ace in the hole. He would become the island hero by giving the people something they wanted.

It would be hard to compete with that. She only hoped the people had sense enough to see past it.

CHAPTER

40

$\mathcal{C}$ade hadn't planned to come to the City Council meeting tonight. He had enough to do and didn't relish wasting time with this group of gabbing, self-important council members, but they had demanded his presence and an update on the investigation.

He asked them to put him first on the agenda so he could get in and out quickly, but as was always the case, they ignored his wishes, bickering about when the next meeting was going to be and who would be introducing the candidates at the upcoming debate.

He looked at his watch and wished they would hurry.

Finally, they came to an agreement, and Art Russell banged his gavel.

"Next on the agenda tonight we'd like to address some questions to Chief Cade. Cade, would you mind stepping up to the microphone, please?"

Cade looked around. Other than council members, there were only six people in attendance tonight. "What do I need a microphone for, Art? There's nobody here."

"Very well. Stay where you are. We wanted to talk to you about this investigation and how much it's costing Cape Refuge."

Sarah Williford had a Tootsie Pop in her mouth. She took it out to address him. "Cade, you're way over your department's budget on this."

"That's right," Cade said. "I never budgeted in a murder. Since I only have one detective in the department, I had to go to outside departments to do the crime scene investigations. And yes, they do have to be paid for the overtime hours. Some of that money will come from the state, and some of it will come from their own departments, but we are going to have to come up with some of it."

"How long are you going to need those folks?" George O'Neal asked from the end of the table. He must have been out fishing today, for his skin was ridiculously red. "You've made an arrest. Looks like you could send them on their way."

"Come on, George. We're going to use the help as long as we need it. There's more to an investigation than making an arrest. I can't short-circuit this investigation just to save the city a few bucks."

Sarah piped in. "I'm just saying that you don't have to drag it out if you already know who did it."

Cade cleared his throat and tried to stay calm. "Sarah, I'm not going to try and explain to you the finer points of investigating a homicide. You're just going to have to trust me to do my job."

"We're just saying you don't need an outside group to help you solve a murder that's already been solved."

"This is why your days as chief are numbered," Art Russell muttered.

Cade ground his teeth, the muscles in his jaw popping, and considered handing them his resignation right then and there, but he couldn't let pride and emotion guide him. "I have no intention of discussing the details of this case in front of this body. And I will not close an investigation just for your convenience or your budget. Now, if you'll excuse me, I have work to do."

Cade turned and limped back to the door he'd come in and prayed again that Jonathan would be elected mayor, before the business of this town got further out of hand.

CHAPTER

Cade sat at his desk, staring down at the paperwork he had to deal with before he could get back to the investigation. Anger still beat through him at the City Council's audacity.

What did they expect him to do? With a force of fourteen people, including himself, it was impossible to evaluate the evidence from the car, the body, the bank of the river, the Jackson house, Lisa's business, Ben's boat, and all the other possible crime scenes, without outside help.

"Hey, Chief. Somebody here to see you."

Cade looked up at Alex. "I'm kind of busy."

"It's Lisa Jackson's parents."

Cade sat back hard and rubbed his eyes. He couldn't send them away. They were probably crazy with grief over their daughter. He looked around. He had reports stacked up on the chair in front of his desk and three feet of files on his desk. If he moved anything, he'd lose his whole train of thought.

He could meet them in the interview room, but first he'd have to remove the dry erase boards he'd been charting the investigation on. He couldn't let them see them.

"Alex, do me a favor. Go in the interview room and turn those boards to face the wall. I'll take them in there."

"Will do, Chief."

Cade got his cane and limped out of the office. The couple stood at the door, looking awkwardly around. The woman, who appeared to be just over sixty, had a vacant expression in her eyes as she stared at the air. Her fingers rubbed her white collar nervously. Lisa's father wore an expression that hovered between despair and indignation.

"Mr. and Mrs. Hinton, I'm Chief Matthew Cade," he said in a soft voice. "Sorry to keep you waiting."

Lisa's father shook his hand. "Al Hinton. My wife, Marge."

Cade led them into the interview room and gestured for them to sit down. He closed the door and took his seat at the table. "Mr. and Mrs. Hinton, first let me say how sorry I am about your loss."

Mr. Hinton cleared his throat. "We need to know if . . . we need to understand . . ."

"Why would Ben kill our daughter?" Marge blurted.

Cade knew that Ben's arrest had to make their tragedy double-edged. "Mrs. Hinton, your son-in-law is innocent until proven guilty. I can't really discuss the details of the investigation."

"Just tell us, is it true about the shoes and the letters?" Al asked in a raspy voice. "That's all they're talking about on the news."

Cade thought of Vince Barr and all the damage he was doing to this case. "There were some shoes found in Ben and Lisa's house, and they matched the footprints at the scene of the crime."

"And there were letters from some girlfriend?"

"We don't yet know who those letters were from or even that they were true."

Mrs. Hinton got up and stared down at him through raw, swollen eyes. "Chief Cade, we've loved Ben all these years. He's like a son to us. We can't imagine he would do such a thing, that he would hurt our daughter when he seemed to love her so much."

"Has he said why?" Al asked. "Has he given any indication of what might have caused this?"

Cade wanted very much to tell them that he wasn't convinced that Ben was the killer, that he may indeed be the devoted husband they believed, but doing so would undermine the district attorney and make things even worse than they were already.

"Would you like to see him and ask him yourself?"

Al looked like he might seize the opportunity, but Marge began to cry harder. "I can't look him in the eye, knowing he might have hurt Lisa. I can't sit there and listen to him lie."

Cade got up and went around the table to Mrs. Hinton. He bent down to her and touched her shoulder. "Ma'am, I can tell you that the investigation is not over. We're still gathering evidence, still getting tips. All the pieces of this puzzle aren't in place yet. It could be that things will change. When's the last time you spoke to your daughter?"

"The night before she disappeared." She dug into her purse for a tissue and dabbed at her nose. "She called and was anxious over the IVF. She felt it had to work, that it was her last chance to get pregnant."

"Did she mention anything else she was upset or worried about?"

"No, not at all. We talked about my arthritis. I dominated the conversation." She stopped and tried to rein her emotions in. "I wouldn't have, if I'd known it was the last time I'd ever talk to her. I would have told her I loved her. I would have listened more."

Cade wished he could take off his chief-of-police hat, and just hold her hand to comfort her. "Don't you think she knew you loved her?"

Al put his arm around her, and she laid her head on his shoulder and wept. "She knows, Mother. Lisa knows."

Marge looked up at Cade, her eyes pleading. "Do you think she suffered, Chief Cade? Do you think it was a horrible death?"

"No ma'am," he whispered. "It looks like her death was quick." He didn't know that for sure, but it was the only thing kind enough to say. "Mr. and Mrs. Hinton, whoever did this to your daughter will be brought to justice. I'll see to it here, and God is going to see to it in the next life."

But it didn't satisfy the mourning couple. He supposed nothing ever would.

CHAPTER

*H*e met her on the Internet, and next thing we knew he had run off to South America to marry the girl. Brought her back with her four kids, both parents, and a bedridden grandmother who we've been supporting ever since. If that ain't bad enough, her ex-husband comes high-tailin' it after 'em, threatenin' to kill my boy."

Morgan lay on the hospital bed, watching the IV drip into her arm, grateful for the conversation going on just beyond the curtain. The unsuspecting nurse had gone to prep the woman for surgery and been treated to the saga of her family. Morgan had to admit it was fascinating and got her mind off of the hysterogram. She hadn't slept last night, fearing the procedure and what it might reveal.

When it was time, they wheeled her into a sterile room and sedated her with an amnesiac drug. The next thing she knew, the procedure was over, and she had no memory of it. Jonathan was with her. He helped her get dressed, then they waited for the results.

When Dr. Sims came in, he looked cheerful. Hope fluttered to life in her heart.

"How are you feeling?"

"Okay," she said. "Do you have my results?"

"I sure do." He took the rolling chair and sat down in it, crossing his legs. "I think it's good news again. There were no blockages, no endometriosis, nothing evident to keep you from getting pregnant."

"Yes!" Jonathan punched the air.

Morgan knew she should be happy, but she couldn't muster any joy. "Nothing? Nothing at all?" She tried to swallow the constriction in her throat and turned her troubled eyes to Jonathan. His excitement deflated visibly. "I was hoping you'd find something you could fix. But if you didn't, do we just go on like this? Unable to get pregnant, then when I do, losing the baby?"

"I understand your feelings, Morgan." The doctor smiled and patted her knee. "We're not finished yet. We're going to take some blood from you before you go home. We'll do an FSH test and see what your follicle-stimulating hormone level is. We'll see if that could be the problem."

Jonathan squeezed her hand. "And what if it is that?"

"Well, that would mean that you're having trouble producing enough eggs. We can put you on a hormone called Pergonal, which may help you with that, and there are a number of options." He looked into her face. "Morgan, I'm not going to give up until we see a baby in your arms. You got that?"

Morgan tried to smile. "Thank you, Doctor." She glanced at Jonathan. "But I'm also worried about the cost of all this. Being self-employed, we don't have very good health insurance. We're not even sure it'll pay for the hysterogram. If we don't find something soon, I'm not sure we can afford to go further."

"We'll go further," Jonathan said. "We'll go as far as we need to. We may just have to take time between tests to save up."

"I'm sure we can work something out," Sims said. "Just get with my bookkeeper, and she'll give you some options." He grinned and winked at Jonathan. "Of course, if you're elected mayor, you'll be on the city's health insurance. Some policies even provide for one or two IVF procedures."

Morgan hadn't thought of that. She looked hopefully at Jonathan.

"Guess it would be one of the perks of the job."

"Now all you have to do is get elected." Sims started from the room. "You've got my vote." He looked back at them before closing the door. "I'll send someone in to take your blood, Morgan. We'll call you with the results sometime Monday. Chin up, okay? You're going to be a mommy before you know it."

CHAPTER

43

I'm comin' home, baby!" Sheila Caruso
stood on the other side of the prison's visitation glass the
next day, her arms raised in a victory celebration.

Laughing, Sadie slapped her hands against the glass.

Morgan smiled at the exchange. Though Sheila was
being released in just a few days, Morgan had decided to
come with Sadie to visit her today, hoping she could help
her talk her mother into coming to Hanover House.

Sheila was still a pretty woman, even with the lines
of years of drug abuse etched onto her face. Her hair was
a golden blonde and shone as if she'd used some fifty-
bucks-a-bottle conditioner on it. Her eyes were as blue and
round as Sadie's. When Sheila grabbed up the phone, Sadie
put her receiver between her ear and Morgan's, so they
could both hear her.

"I'm getting out!" Sheila yelled. "Can you believe it?"

"Mom, I'm so excited!"

"I was sitting in my cell feeling sorry for myself, and
my lawyer comes to visit me. So I come down here and he

tells me and I just went, like, nuts, jumping up and down and hollering. They threatened me with lockdown if I didn't shut up."

Morgan tried to jump in. "We're really excited for you, Sheila."

"Mom, you remember Morgan."

"Of course I do. Hey, Morgan."

Morgan took the phone. "Sheila, I wanted to come with Sadie today because I wanted to let you know that we would love for you to come and stay with us when you get out. Sadie and Caleb are doing very well at Hanover House, and we were really hoping you would join them there. That would give you time to get on your feet, get a job, and save some money."

"Yeah, Mom. It's a beautiful place. You'd really like it."

The zeal in Sheila's eyes seemed to go dull as she clutched the phone. "Are you sure you want me to?"

"Yes," Morgan said. "We have a vacant room. And it's a great answer because you could be with Caleb and Sadie without uprooting them."

Sheila began to jitter. "I've thought about it some. But I don't know if it's the right thing." She looked at Morgan through the glass. "Don't get me wrong, now. I'm so grateful to you and your husband for all you've done for my kids. I really am. I'm just not sure what I want to do."

Morgan's heart sank. *Please God ...*

"Caleb's really happy there, Mom." Sadie's voice was tight and louder than normal. "It would really hurt him if you moved him now."

Sheila shook her head. "But he's my son. He needs to get to know me again."

"He will!" Morgan's words burst out on a rush of fear. She swallowed and tried to steady her voice. "He is your son, Sheila. I just thought we could make it a little easier for him—"

Sheila sighed. "I didn't even think you would take somebody like me without making me fill out an application, get a bunch of references ... or something like that. Hanover House doesn't take just anybody."

Morgan's chest had locked tight and her breathing was shallow. She tried to stay calm. "It's true, we do have an application process, but since we already have your children, we're going to make it easy for you. You'll still have to abide by our rules and follow our structured program. We are a Christian home, Sheila, and we try very hard to give the people who come to live with us a new way of life. We give them a foundation in the Bible so that when they're on their own, they can live by those principles. And best of all, it's free. You can stay there without charge until you start working, and then we have a sliding fee for room and board until you're able to live on your own."

"Abiding by the rules," Sheila repeated. "See, that's the thing. I've been abiding by rules for the last year now. I don't think I'd like it too much to have somebody telling me what I can and can't do."

Morgan kicked herself for choosing the wrong words. If she hadn't mentioned rules, maybe it would have gone down easier. "So often people who get out of jail wind up in desperate situations, unable to pay their rent or buy food, and the stress of life outside causes them to go back to drugs. We've had a really high success rate with people standing on their own and never going back to jail after they get out of our program."

"It's a really good program, Mom," Sadie said. "The house is beautiful, and it's in the greatest town in the world, and the people in the house are like a real family."

"But I *have* a family."

Panic hit Morgan like a tidal wave. Sheila was going to take Caleb and Sadie away. That little boy would be ripped out of his home, away from the people he loved.

For the second time, she would lose a child.

"Mom, what's wrong?" Sadie asked. "Don't you understand how great this is? Where else do you have to go?"

"I have friends who can help me get started. Until I get on my feet."

Sadie's look broke Morgan's heart. "But you know what those friends do to you! Mom, I don't want you to go back down to that again. Being dependent on those people who call themselves your friends. Getting involved with some guy who treats you awful and ruins your life. And ours, too."

Morgan put her arm around Sadie to calm her, but then she saw the possessive, bitter look on Sheila's face. She let her go.

"I won't do that again, baby. I've learned my lesson."

Morgan thought of telling her that she wouldn't have to follow the rules if that was what was dissuading her. She could come and go as she pleased, do anything she wanted, if she would just let her keep Caleb.

But she knew better.

Her mouth trembled, and she knew she couldn't hold back the tears any longer. She didn't want Sheila to know how desperately she wanted this. She sensed that would play against her.

"Tell you what," she said. "I'll leave you and Sadie to talk about this alone. If you have any questions, I'll come back and talk to you before we leave."

Sheila put her face in her palm, and Morgan knew Sadie's expression had hurt her, too. "I'll just be out in the front room if you need me, Sadie."

She hurried out of the room before the tears assaulted her. By the time she reached the waiting room, she was sobbing. She found a chair at the back of the room and sat down facing the wall. Covering her face, she wept quietly. No one around her seemed to notice or care.

In the visitation room, Sadie tried not to cry. "It would be cruel to take Caleb away from Hanover House." Her voice was soft, careful. "He's really bonded with Morgan and Jonathan."

Sheila's face hardened. "He's mine, not theirs."

"I know, but it's going to take time for him to warm up to you again. You said yourself that he doesn't know you."

Sheila looked wounded. "And how will he *get* to know me if they're around all the time?"

"He will, Mom. He takes to people. He loves everybody in the home. He'll warm right up to you."

"I want him to know that I'm his mother, and she's not."

"Mom, he will know that eventually. But he's been with them longer than he's been with you."

"That's not my fault!"

Isn't it? Sadie wanted to say. Wasn't it all her fault for putting her drugs and her men above her children?

Sheila leaned forward, clutching the phone to her ear. "Baby, listen to me. Just think about if we went back to Atlanta. We could be a family again, just the three of us. If you came with him, Sadie, he'd be fine."

"Me? To Atlanta?" She finally lost her battle with her emotions. Tears came to her eyes. "Mom, I have a life in Cape Refuge. I love my job, and I don't want to leave Hanover House. It's the only safe place I've ever lived."

Sadie's tears seemed to push Sheila over the edge. "If they're around, he's *never* going to turn to me. I'll never really have him back!"

Sadie saw the desperation in her mother's eyes, and suddenly her anger melted away. "Mom, we didn't expect you to be out for four more years. It's a God thing that you're getting out early. Morgan and Jonathan taught me that the Lord restores the years that the locusts ate."

"Locusts? What do *locusts* have to do with anything?"

"It means that all the years that were lost to prison or abuse or addiction can be given back. He can help you start over. But you need to do it his way."

Sheila wiped the tears from her face. She was still so pretty, Sadie thought, even in prison browns.

"Baby, I know you don't have a lot of faith in me, but I'm different now. I've been clean from drugs for almost a year."

"You couldn't help being clean, Mom. You've been locked up. You don't know what it's going to be like when you're back in Atlanta and all your old friends start coming out of the woodwork, and you have the stress of trying to hold down a job and raise a baby."

"But I'll have you to help me, Sadie."

Sadie sat back in her chair and stared at her mother. She wanted to be with her more than anything, but setting up house-keeping with her in their old neighborhood was like moving back into the garbage dump after sitting at the king's table. Going back would be suicide.

"Mom, if it weren't for Morgan and Jonathan, we both might be dead right now. Please, just say you'll try it. What could it hurt?"

Sheila crumpled then and began to cry, and Sadie wished she could go through the glass and hold her. She had always been her mother's caretaker, the one who comforted, the one who let her off the hook.

She prayed she wouldn't do it this time. "Caleb will love you, just like he did before. But make yourself a *part* of his life. Don't just snatch him out of it."

Sheila sat there crying like a teenager with a broken heart. "I love you, Sadie," she said finally. "But you're putting me between a rock and a hard place."

Good, Sadie thought. "Maybe that's the only place where we'll all be safe, Mom. Between that rock and that hard place."

CHAPTER

*C*ade was still angry at Blair, but the truth was, he missed her.

He had run into Jonathan campaigning in town, and he'd mentioned that Blair was babysitting at Hanover House. "Why don't you go by and give her a hand?"

Did his best friend know about their fight? "I'm kind of busy, buddy."

"Come on, man. You can take five minutes."

Now he found himself driving by Hanover House, looking to see if Blair's car was still there. She'd been as busy as he had for the last few days. Several times he'd driven by her house, but she never seemed to be home. Did she miss him? Was she nursing her anger at his reaction to her article . . . ?

Or did she even notice he hadn't been by?

He started to pass the house, like some teenage kid on a drive-by. Then he kicked himself and pulled into the driveway.

He went up the porch and heard chaos through the storm door. Caleb was crying at the top of his lungs, the telephone was ringing, and the buzzer on the oven was shrieking out. Worried, he didn't bother to knock. As he stepped inside, something shattered on the kitchen floor.

He bolted into the kitchen.

Blair stood there with her back to him, dancing screaming Caleb on her hip and staring down at the shattered glass. The phone kept ringing. "It's okay, kiddo," she was saying. "Come on, calm down. You're dealing with an amateur here."

"Is everything all right?" he yelled over the noise.

She swung around at Cade's voice. The glass crunched under her shoes. "Oh, thank goodness you're here!" The phone kept ringing and the buzzer shrilled out over Caleb's screams. "Here. Please, can you hold him for a second? Watch the chocolate on his face."

Cade leaned his cane against the wall and started to take the child.

"Watch out, there's glass on the floor." She thrust the filthy baby into Cade's arms and ran to the buzzer. The phone kept shrilling as she took a pan of smoking brownies out of the oven and dropped the pan into the sink with a clank. Smoke filled the kitchen.

She crunched to the phone. "Hello?"

The baby kicked and screamed in Cade's arms, crying to be put down, but there was no way he could set him down with the glass on the floor. He slid toward the back door and opened it to air the room out, then slid through the glass to the sink. He turned on the water and grabbed a paper towel. With his arm around Caleb's waist, he turned the child face out and swiped the wet paper towel over his face. His cries rose an octave.

"No, I need to get someone over there right away," Blair said into the phone. "It's the first cell phone service on the island. I can't. I've got to babysit. Please, can you cover it for me? No, Sadie can't go. She's out of town today. You've been wanting me to hire you, Jeff. Just do this story and we'll talk."

Caleb kept crying, so Cade lifted him over his head and wiggled him, trying to make him laugh. The baby looked tortured.

Blair propped the phone between her ear and shoulder, and crunched to the refrigerator. She grabbed out his little cup and handed it to him. Caleb knocked it out of her hand.

"Oh, brother," she whispered. "No, I wasn't talking to you, Jeff. Would you? Oh, thank you! You're a lifesaver." She grabbed the broom and started sweeping the glass.

Cade lifted the baby again, trying to make him catch his breath. The smell that wafted past his face made Cade catch his, instead. "So *that's* it, huh?"

Blair put her hand over the phone. "What's it?"

He held the baby out in front of him. "Dirty diaper."

"Great. Morgan keeps them upstairs."

Cade glared at her. "Surely you don't expect me to—"

She held out a hand to stop him. "Yes, Jeff. Drop the film by here when you're done, all right? And make sure you get statements from the cell phone company. I suppose you'll have to get one from Sam Sullivan, too, and also some of the citizens who are there."

He'd have to go for it. Holding the baby out in front of him, he left the kitchen and carefully started up the stairs. Without his cane, it was slow going. The child kicked and screamed, his face as red as the chocolate-covered shirt he wore.

He found Caleb's room and laid the baby on the changing table. His crying covered the scales as Cade took his dirty diaper off. He found the covered garbage pail and dropped it in.

The smell was lethal. How did people do this? He looked around, and saw nothing with which to clean the baby up.

Caleb kicked and cried, and Cade tried to keep him on the table while he looked on the shelves beneath him, searching for toilet paper. There was none.

What was he going to do now?

He was the chief of police, for Pete's sake. He had averted disasters, chased criminals, solved murders. Changing a diaper couldn't be that hard.

But why didn't Morgan have toilet paper nearby?

He would have to go get it from the bathroom, he decided. Instead of taking Caleb with him, he picked him back up and put him in the crib, hoping he wouldn't sit his dirty bottom down. "Just stand there, bud. Don't touch anything. I'll be right back."

Caleb began rattling the side of the crib like a psychotic prisoner.

"Come on, Caleb," he called from the hallway. "Can't you just cooperate a little? I don't know what to do here."

He limped to the bathroom and grabbed the roll of toilet paper off its holder, then hurried back into the nursery, trailing tissue behind him. He grabbed the baby back up and took him back to the table. He tried to wipe his bottom, but it wasn't easy.

"Give a guy a break," he said in a soft voice. "Come on, bud, I just want to clean you up."

"I'm so sorry, Cade!"

He turned to see Blair at the doorway, looking as frantic as he felt. She'd brought his cane.

"He needs a bath," he said. "I can't get him clean."

"Did you try the baby wipes?"

Baby wipes. Of course. He'd seen the commercials. She grabbed out the box that was conveniently placed on the shelf below the changing table, and took over.

"I'm so sorry I left you with him! He's really been pretty good most of the morning, then the universe kind of exploded. About the same time as his bowels, apparently." She got him clean, then grabbed a fresh diaper. Caleb finally stopped crying.

"Why isn't he potty trained?"

Blair grinned. "Because he's only eighteen months old. They don't potty train them until at least four or five."

"You're insane. They start school at four or five, and I don't know any teachers who have to change diapers."

"*I'm* insane? You're the one who tried to clean him up with toilet paper!"

Cade started to laugh, softly at first, but then the laughter bent him over. It was contagious, and Blair caught it. She set Caleb down before she dropped him.

The two screamed out their laughter, and Caleb stood there smiling up at them. Cade tried to stop laughing, but it had wound itself within him, sapping his strength. He saw that Blair had the same problem. Tears rolled down her face as she fell against him.

It was the most beautiful sight he'd seen in days.

Blair wiped her face. "You didn't say why you came by," she said as her laughter played down. "Did someone call 911? Report us for disturbing the peace?"

He drew in a deep breath. "Jonathan told me you were here."

Her laughter settled, and her eyes grew wide. "And you came anyway?"

"Yeah—" he grinned—"I came anyway."

He wanted to kiss her, squeeze the breath out of her, and beg her to update him on every minute of her days since he'd seen her last.

But Caleb made a run for it.

"Oh, no, you don't, kiddo!" Blair started after him and grabbed him up.

Caleb screamed with glee as she hoisted him on her hip again. She started down the stairs. "Come on, let's go outside where we can't destroy anything."

Cade followed her down and out to the backyard. She set the boy down, and he ran to his big plastic gym. Sighing, she dropped into one of the lawn chairs. Cade dropped into one next to her.

"So, how are you?"

"Okay," she said. "You?"

"Better now."

She smiled at him, and he realized how much he'd missed those bright eyes. "Jonathan told me Caleb's mother's getting out of jail."

"Yeah," Blair said. "Morgan's really depressed. If she doesn't talk Sheila into coming here, I don't know what she'll do."

Cade looked at the boy, who chattered to himself as he climbed the three-step slide. "I'm praying for her."

"Me too," she said. "I do that now, you know. Pray, I mean. Now that I'm a Christian and all. A real one."

Cade hated himself for ever suggesting she wasn't. "I know you are, Blair. I didn't mean what I said. I was just mad."

"No kidding."

He smirked. "I'm still ticked that you gave credence to Carson Graham, but I'm man enough to forgive you."

"And I'm woman enough to accept your apology."

"Apology?" he said. "I'm not apologizing."

"And I'm not admitting wrong."

He couldn't help smiling. "You make me crazy, you know that?"

"You've mentioned it before."

He watched Caleb try to go up the slide the wrong way. "So, what're you doing tonight?"

"What have you got in mind?"

"I wanted to drop by Carson Graham's show, just to see how he operates. Want to come?"

"I don't know. The Bible calls that stuff detestable. You should look it up."

Touché. "I'm not going for entertainment, but I want it to look like I am."

"So is he a suspect?"

"Let's just say he's a person of interest. I'm not entirely sure Ben's the right man. And that's off the record."

Blair locked her eyes on him as she considered his offer. "What time will you pick me up?"

CHAPTER

45

*C*aleb was sleeping when Morgan and Sadie got back. Morgan went upstairs to check on him. The child lay face down, his cheek mashed against the mattress, his thumb in his mouth. Did his mother know he was a thumb sucker? Would she let him do it or slap his hand away?

She leaned over the crib rail and picked the boy up. He stirred awake, his face warm against her neck. She carried him into her room and laid him gently down on the bed. He put his thumb back in his mouth and began sucking again as she curled up next to him.

Stroking his little head, she began to cry. *Please, Lord. Don't take this baby away from me.*

Even if Sheila did come to live with them, Morgan's days of mothering the baby would end.

Did she even have a choice?

What if he's the only baby I ever have?

She touched her stomach and wondered how it would be to feel the swell of a baby, the flutter of his movement, the kick from a little foot. Even the morning sickness would be welcome.

She cried into the pillow and prayed that the results of her hormone test would be good news, and not further deplete her hope.

Monday morning, when Morgan and Jonathan went to learn the results of her FSH test, she knew the news was not good. Dr. Sims met them in his office, a grim expression on his usually pleasant face.

"As I told you before I did the test, the follicle-stimulating hormone enables your ovaries to produce eggs. Whenever the FSH level is over twenty, it tells us that your ovaries may not be working like they should."

"What was my level, Doctor?"

"Forty-two."

She felt as if he'd thrust a fist into the middle of her stomach, knocking the breath out of her.

Jonathan took her hand. "So, what does that mean? Will we be able to have children?"

The doctor sighed. "I never say never."

Morgan's heart plunged.

"At this point, I usually put a patient on Pergonal, which helps stimulate follicle growth. In your case, with such high numbers, I think a more aggressive approach might be in order."

"Aggressive?" Jonathan asked.

Morgan tried not to cry. "But I don't understand. My miscarriage didn't have anything to do with my eggs, did it?"

Dr. Sims got up and came around the desk, and sat on the edge of it, facing them like a friend instead of a doctor. "Morgan, we don't know for sure what caused your miscarriage, but it may have had to do with the maturity of the egg. My goal in treating you would be to stimulate the follicle production with Pergonal, harvest the egg at the right time, and then fertilize it in our lab."

Morgan couldn't believe she was hearing him right. "Are you suggesting in vitro fertilization?"

"That's exactly what I'm suggesting. We've had a tremendous success rate with this procedure."

"Wait a minute." Jonathan looked as if he'd been threatened. "I thought IVF was a last resort, for people who had no other hope. I thought you were supposed to try everything else first."

The doctor shrugged. "Some do, but I realize how much the two of you want a family. While you're trying other things, Morgan's biological clock is ticking."

"Dr. Sims, she's only twenty-nine. It's not like her time is running out."

"Can I be honest with you?" Sims asked in a soft voice.

"That's what we want, Doc."

"Lisa tried everything else first. By the time she and Ben decided to try IVF the first time, she was pushing forty."

It made sense. Morgan looked up at Jonathan, wishing he wouldn't reject the idea outright. They needed to listen, at least.

"How much money are we talking about for a procedure like that, Doctor?"

He went back around the desk and sat down. "It varies. Insurance usually doesn't cover the retrieval of the egg, the embryology lab, or the transfer of the embryo. The cost in my office usually averages ten thousand dollars, depending on several factors."

Jonathan looked sick.

"What if it's not successful?" Morgan asked. "Would other attempts be included in that price?"

"No, that cost is per treatment. It's a very high-tech procedure, and it's expensive. Most people think it's worth it when they're holding that baby in their arms."

Morgan couldn't imagine coming up with ten thousand dollars for something that might not even work. She met Jonathan's eyes and saw the helplessness there.

"We could never afford that," he said. "No way."

"Some of my patients take out loans. Mortgage their houses, that kind of thing. There are ways to make it work. I haven't known a single couple to regret the sacrifice."

Tears were coming, and Morgan couldn't stop them. "I never thought it would be this way. I thought I'd get married and have a baby, then another baby, and another . . . Infertility never crossed my mind."

Dr. Sims looked as if he hurt with her. "Morgan, I know this is difficult. I can tell from the short times I've spent with you that you would be a wonderful mother. We're going to make it happen, okay?"

Later, as they drove home, Morgan wept quietly.

Jonathan took her hand. "Honey, it's going to be all right. If God wants us to have a baby, we will."

That was just it. What if he *didn't* want them to? "I feel kind of like Sarah," she said, "working it all out in my own way. Is Pergonal my Hagar? Is IVF my Ishmael?"

"What if it's God's provision?"

"Why would he need to provide that way, when he could just touch me and make me conceive? He's the one who creates life. Why can't he create it in me?" She looked over at Jonathan and saw the tears brimming in his eyes.

"Are you saying we just need to trust?" Jonathan asked. "To wait for God's timing?"

"I don't know! What if we do that and never have a baby and realize that we missed the opportunities he gave us?"

"We could adopt, if it came to that."

"That takes years, too. I want to be pregnant, Jonathan. I want to have a baby that looks like us. I want to be able to say, 'You're just like your father.' And I don't want any biological mother coming to take him back."

"It wouldn't be the same as having a foster child. An adopted child would really be ours."

Silence fell over them as Morgan thought of little Caleb. She knew she had it in her to love a baby that wasn't biologically hers, but she wasn't ready to give up the idea of having her own child. "Caleb's not ours, and we're going to lose him."

"No, we're not," Jonathan insisted. "Sheila will come. You'll see."

"But I wanted to be his mother."

He reached over and pulled her into his arms, and he held her for a long time.

"I have to surrender," she said finally. "I have to just surrender to whatever God is doing. I have to believe it's the best thing."

"Honey, if God wants us to do the whole infertility thing, he'll show us. We'll have peace about it. We have to be open to seeing the signs when he gives them. But in my heart, I see you as a mother, Morgan, and I see myself as a father. It's going to happen, honey, one way or another. If we have to do these treatments, we will. If we have to go to some foreign country to adopt, we'll do it. We'll do whatever is necessary to have the family that I know God has planned for us. We're going to go through this together, whatever we decide."

Morgan looked out the window, her heart sending up pleading prayers for help.

Even with all the best science had to offer, Morgan knew God was their only real hope.

CHAPTER

46

*B*lair had trouble deciding what to wear on her pseudo-date to Carson Graham's show. She hated herself for being so self-conscious and vain, when she'd once had such contempt for women who spent too much time in front of the mirror.

She settled on a pair of white slacks and a pink blouse, one she'd bought on a whim when she'd been starry-eyed about Cade. Sitting in front of the mirror, she put on her makeup, paying careful attention to her eyes. She wanted to knock his socks off tonight, even if they were going for business.

But it was almost hopeless.

She put her hand over the right side of her face, imagining what she'd look like without the scars. She might have been print-ad pretty, like her sister. Pageant material. Drop-dead gorgeous.

She moved her hand and saw the whole picture, the same face Cade saw each time he looked at her.

She parted her hair on the side and brushed it to fall in front of her scars. If it hung just right and shone just enough, maybe he would be distracted from her scars.

The doorbell rang and Blair turned away from the mirror. She wouldn't look at her reflection again for the rest of the night. There was no use ruining a perfectly promising date.

The sight of Cade made her heart jolt. He wasn't in uniform tonight. He wore a pair of jeans and a pullover shirt—and a gentle smile on his face. "Hey there. You look nice."

She fought the urge to turn her face away. "Thanks. So do you."

He stepped inside and bent down to kiss her. Then slowly, he swept her hair back from her face, exposing it fully. His gaze swept over her face—all of it—and if she hadn't known better, she would have believed there was pure pleasure in his eyes.

Her heart beat like a jackhammer as he took her hand and escorted her to his truck.

He is going to marry you, you know. Carson Graham's prediction came back to her, fluttering like a hummingbird through her heart.

She tried to put it out of her mind, but it was there, a hope spoken aloud, stamped on her subconscious, always lingering in her mind.

No matter how often she told herself the man was a fake, she still hoped the psychic knew what he was talking about.

CHAPTER

47

*T*he club at the Frankfurt Inn was filling up fast, and Blair wished they had come earlier to get a decent table. She followed Cade through the crowd to a small table in the back corner of the room.

"Can you believe this crowd?" he muttered as they sat down.

"Yeah. Looks like Lisa's murder was a real boon to Carson."

"It's the big break he's been waiting for." Cade's eyes scanned the crowd at the many familiar faces. He saw George O'Neill and Harold Delaney, two of the town's city councilmen, sitting near the front with frosty mugs of beer.

"Is that Bruce over there?" Blair pointed through the people.

Cade looked and saw the newest member of his police force sitting at a table full of friends. He sighed. "Great. Even my own men are buying into this stuff."

Blair's eyes swept over the crowd. A couple of church members sat at another table, watching them as if wondering what would bring them here. She supposed she couldn't blame them for their curiosity. "If this guy's a fake, he sure has a lot of people fooled."

"*If* he's a fake?" Cade breathed a laugh. "He is one, Blair. He's a con artist and a liar."

The lights flickered, indicating that the show would begin soon. Blair looked toward the stage as people hurried to find seats. Was Cade right, and so many others wrong? *He is going to marry you, you know.* Graham had been right before. The pianist sat down at the piano at the side of the stage and began a Broadway-type intro that quieted everyone.

Blair spotted Rani coming in, and when she saw them, Rani made a beeline toward them. She smelled of cigarette smoke and Obsession perfume. "Hey, guys. Mind if I share your table?"

"Sure," Cade said. "Pull up a chair."

She sat down and grinned at them both. "I'm so glad to see you two here. Finally, you'll see what Carson is all about. I've been to his show every night since I met him. It's fascinating. Tell the truth, Cade. You're starting to believe, aren't you?"

Cade bristled. "No, actually, I'm not. I'm just here to watch."

A spotlight came on as the music crescendoed. The manager of the Frankfurt Inn walked onto the stage and introduced Carson Graham as if he were a rock star.

The crowd applauded enthusiastically and the curtains parted. Carson stepped out, arrayed in a purple sequined coat with a red satin shirt. His head, freshly shaved, shone in the lights.

He clutched the mike like a nightclub singer. "Thank you, thank you everybody. Thank you for coming."

Rani clapped so hard she almost came out of her seat. Blair just looked at Cade, noting the tension on his face.

"Ladies and gentlemen, my beautiful assistant, Amber—who also happens to be my bride—is coming around the audience with a velvet bag right now. She'd like for you to throw in personal objects. If you have a cigarette lighter or a pen, a pair of glasses—anything—just throw it in. But beware! When I pull your object out of the bag, I might be inclined to tell some of your deepest, darkest secrets."

A nervous chuckle went across the room, and then Graham's wife—who Blair knew held a job as a nurse at a Savannah hospital—came into the audience with a velvet bag. A spotlight followed her around the room as people dropped in their objects.

"Wanna put anything in to test him?" Blair asked Cade on a whisper.

"No, I don't."

"I have something." Rani dug through her purse as the wife headed in her direction. She pulled out a big tortoise-shell barrette. "It's Lisa's."

Cade stiffened even more. "Do me a favor, and don't let them know it's hers."

"Okay, but he'll know. You'll see."

Amber came to their table, and Rani dropped the barrette in. After accepting a few more items, she pranced back up to the stage and handed the bag to Carson.

Carson sat on a stool, which had been spray-painted gold, and reached in for the first object. He pulled out a handkerchief and held it by one corner with two fingers.

"I hope this isn't used." Laughter rippled over the crowd. He shook the cloth out, revealing a flower embroidered at the center of it. "I'm sensing that this handkerchief belongs to a woman." Again, laughter.

He laid it across his knee and stroked his hand across it. "A very pretty woman. I'm seeing bright sunshine associated with this handkerchief. This could be a woman who works outside, maybe spends a lot of time at the beach."

A woman at one of the tables began to laugh, and the group around her began to whisper.

"Rocket science," Cade muttered. "We live on the ocean."

"Is this yours?" Carson asked the woman.

"Yes," she said as the spotlight sought her out.

His face sobered. "You've recently been to a wedding or a funeral. Am I right about that?"

She caught her breath. "Oh, my gosh. Yes, I've been to a wedding."

"How hard is that?" Cade muttered to Blair. "Everybody's been to a funeral or a wedding."

"You met a man there," Carson went on. "He might have been in the wedding party ... or maybe just a guest. Is that right?"

"That would cover just about every man there," Blair whispered.

Rani shushed her.

"Yes. He was an usher."

"And some romance may have developed."

The woman hesitated, but he kept going. "Not really a romance, but just some interest ... maybe a little chemistry?"

She smiled as if she'd been caught. "Maybe."

"I think that man that you met may actually be someone you need to get to know a little better."

Her eyebrows came up. "Really?"

"I see another wedding in your future. Only this time you're the one wearing white."

The group at her table began to laugh raucously. The crowd applauded.

Cade leaned over to Blair's ear. "And how can you refute anything he just said? All you can do is wait to see if it happens. Smoke and mirrors. And if she gets married, she'll think he got it right. He predicted her walking down the aisle in white."

Blair thought about his prediction about her own marriage. It had been specific, that Cade would propose. But was it such a stretch? Wasn't it what she'd hoped for? If it happened, did it mean that Carson Graham was gifted or that he was just a good guesser?

Or was he off-base altogether since there had been no mention of any kind of commitment between them, much less marriage?

Blair watched as Carson pulled out an unsmoked cigarette with lipstick stains on the filter. He held it up, took a sniff of it, and turned it around in his fingers. "This belongs to someone who is trying to quit smoking."

The crowd chuckled.

"But this person is also grieving over the death of someone she loved."

"Oh, he's right!" a woman said, and the spotlight quickly found her. "Yes, that's true."

"It was someone very close to you."

Blair thought that could apply to her. In fact, it could apply to almost everyone.

The woman paused, as if not sure whether to help him or not. "My mother," she blurted out.

"You've got to stop blaming yourself," he said suddenly.

The woman just stared at him, stricken.

Blair's mind raced critically ahead. Wasn't guilt a natural aspect of grief? Didn't everyone who'd lost a parent blame themselves for something they hadn't done?

"You have regrets over the way you treated her," Carson said. "You want to know if she's forgiven you. But she wants you to know that there's nothing to forgive."

Whether he'd hit the nail on the head or not, the audience sat spellbound, hanging on every word.

"What, is he a medium now too?" Cade whispered.

Carson came out into the audience and made his way to the woman. He handed the cigarette back to her. "You've also been sad that your mother won't be at your wedding."

The woman gasped. Blair looked at Cade.

"Engagement ring," Cade whispered. "Either that, or she's a plant."

Maybe . . . but maybe not.

"She wants you to know that she will be there. She's not going to miss it for anything."

The woman began to cry, and the man next to her pulled her against him.

Rani turned back to them with tears in her eyes. "Isn't he wonderful? He's given her so much comfort."

Blair didn't say anything.

Carson dug into Amber's bag again. This time he came up with the barrette Rani had dropped in.

Cade shot Rani a look, reminding her not to react.

"How can you think he's not for real?" she whispered. "He told us where she was!"

"Please, Rani," Cade whispered. "Just sit tight. See what he says."

"All right, but only to prove it to you."

Carson stood among the tables, holding the barrette to his head. "This barrette belongs to a blonde woman. I'm picturing a pretty woman with blondish hair."

Blair looked at Cade. Lisa was a brunette.

Rani looked distressed.

"Kind of a sandy blonde, with a little brown. Highlights of auburn."

"He didn't mention gray," Cade muttered under his breath.

Carson looked around the room, as if reading the faces to see whom this might belong to. "I get the impression this barrette belongs to a very troubled person."

Cade glanced at Rani, saw that it was taking all her effort not to respond.

"Who put this in here?" he asked finally. "I need to see you. I'm getting some very vivid impressions . . ."

Rani looked back at Cade, but he slowly shook his head.

"Don't want to tell me?" Carson shrugged then and dropped the barrette back into the bag. "Let's move on to something else."

Rani shot Cade a condemning look. "I should have stood up."

"Why?" Cade whispered back. "If you had stood up, he would have known right away that it was something to do with Lisa. That's all that's been on your mind lately."

Blair leaned toward Rani. "If he was for real, Rani, wouldn't the object have told him something?"

"He said he got some vivid impressions! Maybe they were too vivid. Maybe he just had more scruples than to blurt them out."

"Or maybe he was drawing a blank," Blair said.

Rani sat there for a few moments longer, as Carson made more educated guesses about the people whose objects had been in that bag. Finally, she got up and strode out.

"Guess she's mad," Cade said, "but maybe she learned something."

They watched as Carson demonstrated his performance skills and his keen ability to read body language. But it clearly wasn't magic.

When they were finally driving home, Blair looked over at Cade. "If the guy's a fraud, how did he know where Lisa's body was?"

"That is exactly what I intend to find out."

CHAPTER

*S*he's coming!" Sadie's cry shook the walls of Hanover House the next day. "Mama's getting out tomorrow, and she's agreed to come here!" She bounced down the stairs and into the kitchen, and she grabbed Caleb off the floor. "Caleb Seth Caruso, your mommy's coming home!"

Morgan felt the staggering relief taking hold of her, but even as it did, a profound sadness followed. "Are you sure she's coming here?"

"Yes. She called collect and said that they're releasing her tomorrow! I can't believe it," she squealed. "I'll have my whole family back together. This is the new beginning that Mom needs."

It was the new beginning Sadie needed, too. Maybe there would be healing for her in Sheila's release, but Morgan couldn't imagine it being best for Caleb.

Or for her.

As soon as she was able to get away without Sadie wondering why, she slipped out and drove to Blair's house. She needed for her sister to pray with her.

Blair saw the pain on her sister's face the moment she let her in. "Oh, no. Sheila refused to come?"

"No, she's coming tomorrow." Tears hung in Morgan's eyes, ready to shatter. "I know I should be happy, but I'm scared, Blair."

Blair was struck by the frantic expression on Morgan's face, the smear of mascara under her eyes as if she'd cried on the way over, the nervous way she kept wiping her hands on her jeans and sliding them into her pockets.

"Sit down," Blair said.

Morgan pulled out a chair at Blair's kitchen table and dropped into it. Blair wished she had some cookies to offer her, like their mother would have done. If not cookies, then wisdom. But she didn't have much of that, either.

Morgan was the wise one, the more mature Christian, the one who cast her cares before the Lord and left them there. Morgan had prayed so often for Blair, but it was only recently that she had been able to ask for prayer in return. Blair was glad that pattern had been broken.

"What specifically do you want me to pray, Morgan?"

"That I'll love her." Morgan wiped the smear of mascara under her eyes. "That I'll be a bigger person. I'm so disappointed in myself, Blair. I should want what's best for Caleb, not myself. If I can give Caleb back his mother and teach her how to parent him, then I'd be glorifying God. But I have these selfish thoughts."

"How does Jonathan feel?"

Morgan shook her head. "He's worried, too. But I'm Caleb's primary caretaker. I do everything for him. How can I turn it all over to her?"

"Morgan, that's a natural response. You need to stop beating yourself up."

"Do I? Or am I just an ungrateful wimp?"

"No, Sis. You have a tender mother's heart that's just about broken in two. One side for your miscarried baby, and the other side for Caleb.

Morgan lost it then, and Blair pulled her into her arms and held her for a long time. She needed to pray. A fierce sense of responsibility gripped her, and she started to pray aloud. She felt the Holy Spirit directing her thoughts and words, administering a healing balm over her sister's heart.

When they'd finished praying, Blair let her sister go. "Sis, you rescued Caleb and Sadie from pure evil. You've loved them and given them things that they've never had before. Even if the day comes when Sheila takes them away, I know you would do it all over again."

"Of course I would."

"It's going to be all right. You're just like Mama. You give and give, and every time it glorifies God. Sometimes it's going to hurt. Break your heart, even. But you'll keep doing it, because that's the way you are."

Morgan reached for her again, and they wept together until there were no more tears.

Later that day, Morgan lay on the bed, curled up next to Jonathan.

"It's gonna be okay, baby," he said. "I know it is. We'll make it work. God is looking out for Caleb. He's going to take care of him."

"But I want to take care of him."

"You will. Sheila will need your help. She'll be grateful for it."

Morgan wondered if that was true. The woman she'd seen in jail a few days ago didn't seem grateful or even willing to let Morgan help.

"You know, we need to talk about where we're going to put her."

"I was thinking Mrs. Hern's room, since she's gone to the nursing home."

"Or Gus's room."

They hadn't had the chance to really consider Gus's request. "I guess we need to talk about that, don't we?"

"Yeah," Jonathan said. "I've been praying about him and Karen a lot."

"So have I. What do you think?"

Jonathan sat up and leaned back against the post at the foot of the bed. "Ordinarily, I would say that it's way too soon for Karen, that she needs to finish our program, that she doesn't need to take on the responsibility of being a wife."

"But this isn't an ordinary situation."

"No, it isn't. Karen has the baby, and Emory needs a father."

"Gus would love to be his daddy," Morgan said. "He's been around since he was born. I have no doubt in my mind that Gus is ready to handle the responsibility of a family. If they stay here, then Karen can finish the program, and we can help her with her parenting skills and give her a solid foundation to overcome her addictions once and for all."

"Besides," Jonathan said, "I hated to see Gus leave. He's like family."

Morgan smiled. "Then we're going to give them our blessing?"

Jonathan sighed. "Are we crazy?"

"I don't think so. I mean, I've been thinking that maybe this was all part of God's provision for Karen and Emory. Maybe he brought her here so that she'd meet Gus. Emory's father is a violent, abusive drug dealer who had no intention of marrying her, and even if he did, he'd put Emory in danger. Maybe God was taking care of her by making Gus fall in love with her."

Jonathan reached across the bed and kissed her. "As if we didn't have enough to do, now we've got a wedding to plan."

"Let's go tell them!"

They hurried downstairs and found Gus and Karen sitting on the sun porch with Emory.

"You guys don't have time for lounging around when you have so much to do," Jonathan said.

Gus got up. "You need help with something, mon?"

"You bet I do," Jonathan said. "I need help figuring out where we're going to have your wedding."

Karen screamed and shot out of her seat, and they all threw themselves into joyful hugs.

CHAPTER

49

*T*he Tuesday issue of the *Observer* was even more sensational than the one the week before. McCormick had brought it to Cade in his office, and Cade had lost his appetite for breakfast. He scanned it now as his coffee slowly got cold. It was packed full of articles about Ben and Lisa's life together, about the journey their infertility had taken them on, about the rumored affair ...

Vince Barr had more pictures of Lisa's wet, dead body in her car, pictures of her parents at the funeral, an article about Rani's outburst last week, and a lengthy interview with Lisa's best friend, in which she accused Ben of the murder again.

He chronicled the searches of Ben's home, car, boat, and business, complete with interviews with each of his employees, defending his character and denying that he'd ever had another woman.

He even profiled Ben's opponents in the election, with questions about whether Jonathan or Sam might have had anything to do with the murder.

He was thorough, imaginative, and left no stone unturned.

Too bad one of those big networks who kept interviewing him about the case didn't just hire him so he could turn to the scandals of politicians and athletic stars—and get off Cade's back. Cade knew Barr wasn't about to let the case go until he'd milked it for everything it was worth.

When Cade finished scouring the tabloid, he turned to Blair's new issue, which had also come out today. She'd handled things tastefully and accurately, in contrast to Vince's fiction, though she hadn't sold nearly as many copies.

It wasn't fair, but it would be all right. Blair would build her circulation, and eventually she would give even the Tampa paper a run for its money. He knew her potential. She could do anything she set her mind to.

Blair perused the *Observer*, gritting her teeth at the things Vince Barr had reported. The man had gall.

She set the paper down and looked around at her cluttered office. She'd been up most of the night trying to get the paper out. She was exhausted. She didn't know how much longer she could keep up this pace, and for all the work, she still put out a less-than-stellar little paper that few took seriously.

She'd been thinking about hiring a night staff—maybe two or three people to handle the printing—since she'd bought the paper. But ever since Carson Graham had made the prediction about her buying the South Farm Insurance Building, her imagination had been running wild. What if she really could expand that much, start putting the paper out every day, and grow her circulation to all of Georgia rather than just the island? She was good enough. Her investigative skills, coupled with her research and writing skills, could catapult her to the top echelon of the media in no time . . .

Not that she was listening to Carson. She knew better than that. The idea had already been in her mind somewhere, dormant. A dream planted by God. Carson simply awakened it.

Inspired by the vision, she decided to drive over to that vacant building, just to see. She crossed the island and found the building, which had been vacated when the insurance company had moved to bigger facilities in Savannah. A "For Sale" sign sat on the front lawn. Rani and Lisa's real estate company had listed the property.

There was no way she could afford it, but it had been on the market for a long time. Maybe they would consider some sort of lease.

But even that would be out of her budget, wouldn't it?

Her heart began to pound, and her mind began to calculate. She had spent every penny she had in savings to buy the paper. It had been a good investment, but she had nothing left. Still . . . there might be a way if God was in this . . .

But that was the question, wasn't it? Was this a seed planted by God, or was it something else entirely?

She drove back home, muscles drawn tight by the anxiety of dreaming too big, the stress of wanting more than was in reach. It wasn't like her to be greedy, to take shortcuts to success. If she had to go into deep debt to expand, if she had to scheme against her own accounting, if she had to take such tremendous risks when she'd barely gotten the paper off the ground—then she was pretty sure this wasn't of God.

Until she was sure it was, she would put the plans on the back burner. But keeping herself from thinking about them might not be all that easy. Her Pandora's box of dreams was open now. She didn't know if it was possible to close it again.

CHAPTER

50

*M*organ rose Saturday morning while it was still dark and went downstairs to gather herself before Caleb got up. Karen was already up, sitting out on the sun porch nursing Emory.

Morgan put a pot of coffee on, then stepped out to join her. "Good morning. You're up early."

Karen smiled up at her. "Emory woke me up. If I can get him to sleep till five I'm happy. Besides, I'm so excited about the wedding, and there's so much to do. I couldn't hardly sleep anyway."

Morgan hugged her. "You sure you can get it all together that quick? A week from Saturday is awfully soon."

"I'd do it today if I could. I can't believe how the good Lord has blessed me."

When the couple had chosen to have it so soon and asked to have it at Hanover House, Morgan and Jonathan pointed out that it was impossible to do much in preparation. The debate was this Saturday; the election Tuesday.

But Gus and Karen didn't want any flowers other than the ones already planted in the front garden. Melba Jefferson, a dear friend of the family, got the news and immediately volunteered to make Karen's wedding dress. They wanted it simple and sweet.

Church members offered to help with the food, the music, and the chairs on the front lawn, and Jonathan would conduct the ceremony. Morgan just hoped it wouldn't rain.

"So are you getting ready to go get Sadie's mama?"

"I am." Morgan sat down next to her. "It's a three-hour drive, so I hope to get off early. Jonathan's staying behind to do some campaigning."

"You want me to keep Caleb for you?"

Morgan thought about that for a moment. "I'm trying to decide whether to take him with us or not."

"It's a long trip. Three hours, one way."

"I know, but when I put myself in Sheila's place, I think how anxious she must be to spend time with him. She'll want to hold him the minute she's free. She could sit by him in the backseat and bond with him. I think he'll be okay if we make frequent stops."

"That's sweet of you to think of her, Morgan. I know this is hard for you."

Morgan hated being so transparent. "I want her to be happy here. I want to give her every opportunity to be what her children need her to be."

"That's what you gave me," Karen said. "A chance to start over, get my life right. And watching you mother Caleb has taught me how to be a mama to Emory."

Ironic, Morgan thought. Here she was, not even a mother herself, modeling motherhood to the mothers who would live in the house. That heaviness fell over her heart again. "Well, I guess I'd better get Sadie up, and I need to go through the clothes we've had donated. Sheila may not have anything to wear."

"Guaranteed she's not the same size she was when she went in. I was two sizes bigger when I got out."

That had been the problem with virtually all of the women who came here from jail. They'd spent whatever money they'd earned working in jail on candy bars and junk food at the commissary. It helped anesthetize the grief, boredom, and loneliness. She went to the closet where they kept the donated clothing and picked out a couple of outfits in different sizes close to what Sheila probably wore. She was still slim, but she'd been nothing but skin and bones when she'd been arrested.

Help me to think of her today, Lord. Not me.

If she could focus on her, maybe she would get through the day without falling apart.

Sheila was waiting in the holding room in the prison when Morgan, Sadie, and Caleb went in. She still wore her brown prison jumpsuit, dingy white socks, and the fluorescent orange flip-flops that were issued to all the inmates.

Sadie carried Caleb in, and the moment she saw her mother she let out a joyful yell. Sheila bolted out of her chair and threw her arms around them.

Morgan stood back, holding the clothes over her arm. Sheila took Caleb and covered his face with kisses.

It was as it should be.

"He's so big. Look at him. He's grown up. He's not a baby anymore."

The child stared up at his mother, as if he didn't quite know how to react. Morgan prayed he wouldn't cry.

"His hair has a curl. I didn't know he had curly hair."

"I sent you pictures, Mom," Sadie said. "Don't you remember seeing the curl?"

"It's not the same." She ruffled his hair and kissed him again. He smiled—miraculously . . . beautifully. "Look at you, smiling at your mama. Oh, you're so different in person, Caleb! Do you even remember me?"

Of course he didn't, Morgan thought. He'd only been a few months old when she'd been arrested.

She stepped up then. "Sheila, we're so glad you're coming home with us."

Sheila looked as if she could have floated out the door. "Well, I'm ready to get out of this place, only they won't let me go in the state-issued jumpsuit."

"I brought you some clothes. I wasn't sure of the size, but one of these should work."

Sheila took one of the pairs of jeans with her free hand and held it up to her. "You people are unbelievable, you know that? I'm just blown away."

"Go change, Mom," Sadie said. "I can't wait to get you out of here."

Reluctantly Sheila handed Caleb back to Sadie and, giddy with excitement, disappeared into a bathroom.

When she'd finished dressing and signed all of her paperwork, they left the depressing building. Morgan unlocked the car and opened the door to the backseat. "I thought you'd want to sit next to his car seat. Here, I'll put him in."

"I can do it. I remember how to put a kid into a car seat."

Morgan didn't like hearing Caleb referred to as a kid, but she knew loving parents did it all the time. She got into the driver's seat as all three Carusos lined up in the back.

They had scarcely gotten to the highway back to Savannah, when Caleb started to cry. Morgan listened helplessly as both Sadie and Sheila tried to calm him.

She glanced into the rearview mirror. "Maybe we should pull over. He might need to be changed. We need lunch, anyway."

"I can change him," Sheila said quickly, and before Morgan could stop her, she had unclipped his car seat and pulled him out. "He just wants his mama, don't you, Caleb?"

Alarms went off in Morgan's head. "He really needs to be in the car seat, Sheila. It's dangerous to have him out of it. It's also against the law."

"Well, what are they gonna do, put me back in jail for holding my own baby?"

Morgan swallowed and decided to pull over at the next exit.

Caleb didn't like the new arrangement, so he cried louder, kicking and bucking to get out of her lap. He was just about to break free when Morgan pulled into a McDonald's. "We can eat and let him play for a little while. He'll probably be ready for a nap by the time we get back into the car."

She could see the frustration on Sheila's face, and she told herself to have compassion. Sheila was trying, after all, even if her methods were a little wrong.

Caleb got sleepy after lunch and fussed until Morgan finally took him. He laid his head down on Morgan's shoulder and began to suck his thumb. She saw the disappointment on Sheila's face, so she tried to distract her. "I'll go change him. If you guys need anything, there's a big convenience store next door." She pulled out a twenty dollar bill and handed it to Sheila. "I'm going to pull the car over there and get some gas."

Sheila's face changed, and mother and daughter hurried across to the store, like best girlfriends on a shopping spree. It had been over a year since Sheila had been in a store. She would probably head straight for the Cokes, as the residents often did. Then she'd get some mascara, if they sold it, maybe some lip gloss. Things that made her feel human again.

Morgan tried to get her bearings. She changed Caleb and hooked him back into his car seat. "Go to sleep, sweetie," she said, kissing his forehead. "You're being such a good boy."

His eyelids began to close even as she got into the driver's seat and pulled over to the gas pumps. She looked toward the door and saw Sadie coming out. Her face was pale, and she looked as if she might burst into tears.

"What is it, honey? Is everything okay?"

Sheila came out then. A lit cigarette hung from her mouth. She held a brand new pack in her hand.

Morgan glanced back at Sadie.

"I told her, but she wouldn't listen. Morgan, please don't get mad."

Sadie got into the car. Morgan waited for Sheila to reach her. "Sheila, if you read the rules of the program at Hanover House, you know that smoking is forbidden."

"Well, we're not at the house yet. Don't worry. I won't smoke in the car."

"I'd rather you didn't smoke at all."

Sheila huffed and took the cigarette out, exhaled a long stream of smoke. She looked poised to argue, but then seemed to think better of it. Dropping the cigarette, she stomped it out.

"I don't want you bringing the pack home, Sheila."

Sheila sighed. "Well, you paid for it. You want me to just toss it?"

"I'd appreciate that."

Her face was tight as she dropped it ceremoniously into the trash can, then got back into the car.

"Thank you, Sheila." Morgan took the nozzle out and put the gas cap back on.

Sheila didn't answer. She just closed the door hard.

Morgan didn't know why she felt like crying as she got back into the car. This happened almost every time they got a new resident. They were always happy and grateful to be accepted, but as soon as the rules and the reality sank in, they began to resent Morgan and Jonathan. Usually, if they could just stick it out for the first month or so, the resentment would eventually fade, and the real work could begin.

But she wanted it to be different with Sheila. Her children were watching.

Sheila seemed to be sulking as she sat next to her sleeping child. Her arms were crossed, and she stared out the window as Morgan pulled back onto the interstate. Sadie was just as quiet.

As she drove, Morgan realized they were walking a tightrope between strict adherence to the rules and the knowledge that Sheila could leave, taking Caleb if Sheila felt provoked. Morgan couldn't let her love for the child temper her expectations. It wouldn't help Sheila change her life. It wouldn't do her any good at all. Since the other tenants had to follow the rules, it wouldn't be fair to bend them for Sheila.

If Morgan were still pregnant, everything would be different. Maybe it would be easier for her to let go. Or maybe not.

After a while, Sadie tried to get her mother's mind off of her anger. "Mom, there was a murder a couple of weeks ago in Cape Refuge. I've been helping Blair cover it for the paper. This woman, Lisa, was found in her car at the bottom of the river . . ."

This woman, Lisa, Morgan thought. Her friend, who had been barren. She wondered if this third treatment would have helped Lisa conceive, if she had been close to seeing her dreams come true.

Maybe they could still come true for her. In vitro was a drastic approach so soon in her infertility struggle. But maybe the doctor was right. Maybe they needed the big guns first. She didn't want to wind up like Lisa, with an empty womb and an empty crib where Caleb used to be.

When she got home, she would tell Jonathan she wanted to try. Somehow, she would come up with the money. But Dr. Sims was right. She couldn't put a price on having a family.

Whatever it cost, she would figure out how to get the money. Even if it meant mortgaging Hanover House.

CHAPTER

51

*H*ave you seen this autopsy report?"

McCormick's question cut into Cade's thoughts as he studied Carson Graham's phone records. "No. Anything we didn't know?"

McCormick came in and dropped the report on his desk. "You might want to take a look at it."

Cade glanced down at the long report. It would take him a while to read it.

"Look under General Health History. The part about her uterus."

Cade scanned the pages until he found that section. "What's a bicornuate uterus?"

McCormick sat down. "I looked it up. It's when the uterus is split in two parts, and there's a wall between them. It causes a woman to miscarry early in her pregnancies, which is obviously why Lisa was never able to have a baby. Read on."

Cade looked back down at the report. Keith Parker, the medical examiner, had made a notation. "Subject's IVF procedures were misinformed and suggest malpractice."

Cade froze. "Malpractice? Why?"

"I don't know, but I thought it was worth following up on."

"I'll call Keith." He dialed the number and waited as the call was routed to the medical examiner. "Yeah, Keith, this is Cade from Cape Refuge."

The ME sounded rushed, busy. "Yeah, Cade. What can I do for you?"

"Listen, I was just looking over your report on Lisa Jackson, and I wanted to ask you about something. You mentioned that Lisa had a bicornuate uterus."

He was quiet for a moment, and Cade pictured him fumbling through her file. Finally, he spoke. "Yeah, that's right."

"Are you sure about that?"

"Absolutely. I saw it myself."

"You mentioned that her IVF procedures suggested malpractice. What did you mean by that?"

"I mean that any doctor who performed an in vitro procedure on a woman with a bicornuate uterus was either stupid or a fraud. Her problem was not in conceiving. She simply couldn't carry a baby for very long."

Cade tried to follow what this meant. "So is it possible her fertility doctor didn't know this?"

"Hardly. It's a birth defect. He would have seen it in a hysterogram, which is one of the earliest tests he would have done on her. He also would have seen it in any laparoscopy. And he would have done those in the first two IVF procedures when he harvested the eggs. No way he didn't see it."

Cade locked eyes with McCormick across his desk and changed the phone to his other ear. This couldn't be right. Had Sims lied to her?

"Keith, can this be corrected?"

"Sometimes it can."

"Then why wouldn't the doctor have done that?"

The ME hesitated. "The only reason I can think of is that there's more money in stringing her along. Three procedures would cost over thirty thousand dollars, and that doesn't even add in all the other treatments he'd tried on her over the years. He had a long-term money bag there, and much of it didn't have to go through insurance companies. It was cash out of pocket."

Cade felt sick. Could someone really be that manipulative? That evil? To drag someone's hopes and dreams through such trials just for a buck?

When Cade hung up, he told McCormick what Keith had said. "I think it's time to interview Sims again."

McCormick agreed. "You think he had anything to do with her death?"

Cade drew in a long breath. "I wouldn't rule anything out. But even if he didn't, he could be lying to all his patients. He has no business practicing medicine. And because of Lisa's murder, he's going to be exposed."

"Looks like we have *two* major crimes to investigate," McCormick said.

Cade nodded. "I think I need to call the DA."

CHAPTER

*S*adie didn't like the distant, restless look she saw in her mother's eyes as night began to fall. So many times she had anticipated Sheila seeing Hanover House for the first time, with its garden of color lining the front of the house and the big, luscious ferns spilling onto the porch. It looked like something from one of those foggy dreams of heaven, a picture of hope. The reality of a home.

But Sheila didn't catch that vision. Even when they showed her the room Sadie had worked so hard to fix up for her, Sheila's gaze strayed to the window, as if she scoped out her escape.

"I know it's all really stressful to you, Mom. Being in a strange place and having so much expected of you. But it's going to be all right. You'll get comfortable in a few days. Caleb will get to know you."

"I don't see why he has to go to bed so early. He was down before dark."

"It gets dark pretty late this time of year. He's little. He needs his sleep."

"You used to stay up till after midnight," Sheila said. "It never hurt you any."

Sadie didn't want to tell her that many of the choices Sheila had made about her childhood had hurt her. "He's got a routine. It's good for him."

Sheila turned to look at her. "What does he call her?"

"Who?"

"Morgan. Does he call her *Mama*?"

"Usually he calls her *Mo*. I guess it's his shortened version of Morgan. Sometimes *Mo-mo*."

"It sounds awfully close to Mama." Sheila's voice sounded hollow, and in it Sadie heard the waver of fear.

"It doesn't matter what he calls her. It matters that he's happy. It's good that there are people like Morgan and Jonathan, Mom. They can love without expecting anything in return."

Sheila gave her a faint smile. "It's just that it makes the rest of us look bad. I don't need any help with that." She turned from the mirror and sat down on the bed. "I'm easily replaced, you know."

Sadie's heart broke at the words. "How can you say that? You haven't been replaced."

Sheila's eyes rimmed with tears. "I've always been a problem to the people around me. Even when I was a little kid, and my mama was going through her string of men, I was always in the way. They farmed me out to everybody they knew. Aunts and uncles and neighbors and foster homes. Nothing—nobody—was ever really mine."

Sadie sat down next to her. "I'm yours, Mom. I always will be. And so will Caleb."

"But can you see why I don't want to be here? I'm in the way again, in a place that's not mine, trying to fit back into my own family. The people here only know me as an ex-con, a drug addict, a terrible mother. How can they see me as anything else, when that's what I am?"

"Mom, Morgan and Jonathan think everyone is worthwhile. Take Gus Hampton, for instance. He's been in prison most of his adult life for everything from armed robbery to drug trafficking. They took him in here and helped him change his life. Now he has a good job, and next Saturday he's marrying Karen. You met her downstairs. The one with the baby. Karen has been in and out of prison, too. She came here pregnant, fearing for her baby's life if she stayed with her violent boyfriend. But Morgan and Jonathan gave them both that new start, showed them what a real home and family are supposed to look like. They've loved them like family. And Felitia, she was in prison too, before she came here. Same story. Drug addictions. She's clean now and doing really well. If you let them, Morgan and Jonathan will help you start a new life. Think of it, Mom. They helped me start over when things were really bad."

Sheila brought her tear-filled eyes to Sadie's face. "You're different, baby. More confident. More mature. You sure didn't get that from me." She pulled Sadie into a hug.

Finally, she let her go, and her gaze strayed back to the window. "Go for a walk with me, Sadie. Show me this island paradise you've been writing me about."

Sadie couldn't think of anything she wanted to do more.

CHAPTER

53

*B*en Jackson's mistress is a business owner somewhere on this island." Clara Montgomery wiped her oiled cloth over the antique dresser she had gotten at the Methodist church bazaar, and looked up at Blair. "You mark my word, she's someone we all know."

Blair had come by to pick Clara's brain about the mystery woman, since Clara was the biggest gossip in town. It seemed that everyone in town had heard the rumors, but no one had a name. "Come on, Clara. You know everything that goes on in this town. Don't you even have some idea?"

"It's a well-kept secret, that's all I know. I gleaned as much as I could from the hints I've gotten from people all over the island." She got finished wiping the wood and turned to an iron headboard propped against the wall. "Did you see this, Blair? It's lovely, isn't it? It would look so pretty in your bedroom. Especially if you were to get married. That brass one you have right now is a little too feminine for a macho man like Cade, don't you think?"

Blair gasped. She didn't know whether to deny the rumor about a wedding with Cade or ask how the woman knew about her bedroom furnishings. "Clara, Cade and I are not engaged!"

"Just a matter of time, dear. Just a matter of time."

Blair decided to get out of there before Clara "gleaned" anything more. She said a hurried goodbye and rushed out to her car.

For a moment, she sat behind the wheel, letting Clara's words sink in. Was this confirmation that Carson's prediction was real? Could Blair really count on a wedding?

If so, why weren't things moving faster? Why wasn't there a commitment? Why hadn't Cade ever uttered a word about love or marriage?

Was she simply being an idiot to put any stock at all in Carson's or Clara's assumptions?

As she pulled out of the parking lot of the Trash to Treasures Antique Shop, she glanced across the street to Carson Graham's house, with its huge, faded Palm Reading sign. The dirt parking lot seemed full of cars. She wondered if his visitors were media or people lined up waiting for readings.

Then she saw the front door open, and Carson stepped out with Vince Barr. What was he doing there? Digging up more dirt for his new television career? Manufacturing more lies?

She decided to ask him herself, so she pulled across the street. Carson went back in, and Vince crossed the parking lot to his car. Blair pulled in front of him and rolled her window down.

"Anything going on I should know about, Vince?"

He grinned. "Don't you wish?"

"Hey, I'm just trying to learn from the professionals. Don't tell me you were just getting your palm read."

He leaned into her window. "Carson's the man of the day. Everybody wants a piece of him. You'll have to stand in line."

"Oh, I'm not that interested in Carson. I'm more interested in Ben Jackson's alleged mistress."

"Have you got a name?" His question suggested he didn't.

She decided to play that game. "Maybe."

He grinned. "Did Sam Sullivan finally spill it?"

Blair shifted her car into park. Sam Sullivan? How did he figure into this? "I don't reveal my sources. You know that."

Vince straightened up and peered down at her. "I should
have listened to him when he came to me three weeks ago, wanting me to do a story on the affair to blow Ben out of the campaign."

Blair almost caught her breath. So Sam Sullivan was behind
the rumors. No wonder no one knew the woman's name. There
probably *wasn't* a woman. He'd probably made the whole thing
up just to ruin Ben's chances in the campaign.

"I told him I wasn't interested in local politics," Vince went
on. "The *Observer* is a national publication. It didn't pique my
interest until Lisa turned up missing. Come on, Blair. You got a
name, tell me who it is."

"I don't have a name, Vince. I don't even know if I believe
there was an affair. Her name would have come out by now if
there really was someone."

"Then why are you wasting my time?"

She had expected as much. She watched him get into his car,
and she turned hers around before he could pull out.

Cade needed to hear about this. If Sam Sullivan had anything
to do with these rumors, then maybe he wrote the letters—and if
Sam wrote the letters, maybe he'd been involved in the murder.

She found Cade in a briefing session with McCormick and
some of his men. He looked happy to see her when she came in,
and he took her into his office.

"I found out some things that might be of interest to you,"
she said, taking the chair across from his desk. "It's about the
alleged mistress. I've been digging around town, trying to find out
who she is. No one knows, Cade. No one. Wouldn't you think
someone would know something if Ben were having an affair?"

"What are you getting at?"

"I'm thinking that maybe it really is all a hoax. But who's
behind it? Cade, do you know whose name kept coming up as I
was questioning people about this rumor?"

"Who?"

"Sam Sullivan. He told Vince Barr about the affair even before Lisa went missing, hoping to derail Ben's chances in the campaign. Maybe he also sent the letters."

Cade sat back hard and stared at her for a moment. "So what I need to do is get a sample of Sam's handwriting and compare it to the letters."

"Just what I was thinking. Do you think he just did this to make Ben look bad during the election? Or could he have had something to do with the murder?"

Cade leaned his head back on his chair and stared up at the ceiling.

"Just what you need, huh? Another suspect."

He ran his hands through his hair. "You don't know the half of it."

"Anything I can do?"

He leaned on his desk, rubbing his face until it was red. Looking at her over his fingertips, he said, "There might be."

"What?"

"Tell me about Jonathan and Morgan. Have they been seeing Dr. Sims?"

The shift in subject surprised her. "Yes, as a matter of fact."

"And what has he told them?"

Disappointed that he wasn't going to enlist more of her help in the investigation of Sam and the letters, she sighed. "Well, he's told Morgan that she has a problem producing eggs. They're considering their options."

"Has he suggested any big procedures?"

Blair didn't really know if she should be sharing this. "He suggested in vitro. I think Morgan's considering it."

"I thought so." Cade got up, went around his desk, and closed the door. He bent over her chair, inches from her face. "Blair, I think Sims is a fraud. I need Morgan and Jonathan to help me prove it."

"A fraud? What do you mean?"

"I mean that I want her to get a second opinion. Have those tests done again."

"Why?"

He sat on the edge of his desk. "Blair, this is off the record. You can't repeat it to anyone, and you sure can't write about it."

Off the record. Again. She considered objecting, but figured silence was a small price to pay if this involved Morgan. "Okay, I won't. Cade, what is it?"

"Lisa's autopsy showed that she had what's called a bicornuate uterus. It's a condition she had since birth, and it kept her from being able to carry a child. Yet Sims never told her what her real problem was, and the IVF procedures wouldn't have helped. He lied to her for years, when surgery might have helped her, and he milked a lot of money out of them in the process."

Blair caught her breath and slowly got to her feet. "Do you think he's been lying to Morgan?"

"The procedures are expensive, Blair. He deals with desperate people who are willing to do whatever it takes to have a baby."

She felt her scars burning, tears stinging her eyes. Had he given Morgan false hope? Had he preyed on her greatest fears?

"So . . . what? Do you think he's the killer?"

Cade drew in a deep breath. "I've got a medical fraud milking desperate people out of their money; I've got a mayoral candidate who may be stirring up scandals behind the scenes; and I've got a supposed psychic with inside information. Three con artists, and a husband with a weak alibi and a pair of dirty shoes. One of them could be the killer. But I don't know which one."

CHAPTER

54

As Cade waited to hear back from the DA's office, he studied the phone records for the Jacksons' telephone number for the days prior to and since Lisa's disappearance. He'd hoped to see a pattern of calls to Ben's mystery mistress, but there didn't seem to be any. But there was one call the morning of her disappearance that caught his attention.

She'd gotten a call from a Dr. Ralph Anderson.

He looked up the practice on his database and saw that it was from another fertility clinic in Savannah. Had Lisa sought another opinion? If so, did Ben know about it? And if she had gone to another doctor, why was she keeping her appointments with Sims each day?

Cade went into the jail at the back of the small building and found Ben lying on his cot. He had been subdued ever since he'd locked him up, with no outbursts of rage and no desperate pleas for freedom. Now and then Cade had come back here to check on him and had heard his deep, wet weeping. He told himself that the man's grief didn't necessarily proclaim his innocence. Guilty people could grieve, too.

But Ben wasn't crying now. He lay perfectly still, as if he slept with open eyes. He made no move at Cade's approach.

"How ya doing, Ben?" Cade asked him.

"How do you think?"

"Ben, I need to ask you something about Lisa."

That got his attention. Ben sat up and looked at him. "What?"

"It's about her infertility treatments. I need to know if Lisa ever sought a second opinion from another doctor."

Ben slumped over, set his elbows on his knees, and rubbed his stubbled jaw. "As it happens, she *had* decided to get a second opinion. She went the week before her disappearance to a doctor named Anderson in Savannah. He just gave her the runaround."

Dr. Anderson. The one the phone call had come from that morning. Cade pulled a chair close to the cell bars and sat down. "Could you tell me what prompted that?"

"Yeah," he said. "We were going to the Resolve support group—a support group for infertile couples—and there was a woman in the group who convinced her to do it. She claimed she'd gotten a second opinion and that doctor had found what was wrong with her husband, something that Dr. Sims hadn't found. It was something minor that could be fixed in surgery, and now the woman was pregnant. Lisa thought it was worth a try, though she wasn't entirely sure she needed to give up on Dr. Sims. That's why we didn't cancel any of our appointments, and we were going ahead with the protocol."

"And how did he give her the runaround?"

"Well, he gave her a hysterogram and some other tests, but then she couldn't seem to get the results. Sims always gave them to her on the spot. But it was like an act of congress with Anderson. She'd just about given up on him."

"Are you aware that Dr. Anderson called your house the morning of Lisa's death?"

"No." Ben got up and came to the bars. "How do you know?"

"Phone records."

Ben stared at him for a moment as he processed the information. "He must have called after I left. Maybe he gave her the results of her tests."

Cade wondered if he had finally told her about the problem with her uterus. Had his phone call prompted Lisa to confront Dr. Sims?

"Can you go see him, Cade? Find out what he told her? Maybe it had something to do with what happened to her."

Again, Cade's gut told him he had locked up the wrong man. He got up, put the chair back. "I will, Ben. That's first on my agenda today."

CHAPTER

*C*ade found Dr. Anderson's office on the fourth floor of a building that housed dozens of medical practices. From the looks of the decor, every practice there was established and lucrative. He found the sign that said "Women's Diagnostic Health Clinic" and saw Anderson's name listed as one of three doctors in the practice.

He pushed open the heavy mahogany door and stepped into the big waiting room. It was full of couples of various ages—from their mid-twenties to mid-forties— talking quietly and flipping through magazines that probably didn't interest them.

Some of them looked up at him, and he wondered if he should have worn his uniform. He went to the reception desk and waited for the receptionist to slide open the glass panel. "I'm Chief Cade with the Cape Refuge Police Department—" he showed her his badge—"I need to see Dr. Anderson as soon as possible."

The receptionist looked fascinated at his credentials, and a little frightened—the way one might look if Mike

Wallace came into the office with the 60 *Minutes* crew. "Of course. Come this way."

He followed her back into Dr. Anderson's office.

"Have a seat, Chief Cade. He's with a patient, but I'll tell him you're here. Unless it can't wait. I could go get him right now . . ."

"No, that's all right. He can finish with the patient."

She looked relieved, as if that meant that he wasn't in any kind of trouble. She closed the door, but Cade didn't sit down. Instead, he perused the framed degrees on the wall behind the doctor's desk, the pictures of his family. His wife looked about forty-five. They had two boys that looked college age. From the other framed snapshots around the room, he gleaned that they played baseball.

The door opened, and a small man with a bald head and a lab coat that looked too big for him came scurrying in. "Sorry to keep you waiting, Chief Cade." He closed the door behind him, then reached out to shake Cade's hand. "I've seen you on television."

Cade didn't know what to say to that. He'd never wanted to be a celebrity. He sat down, and Anderson took the seat behind his desk. It looked a little too high for him. "Then you know that I'm investigating the murder of Lisa Jackson. I understand she was a patient of yours."

"As a matter of fact, yes. She just came to see me the week before her death. I was shocked when I saw that she'd been murdered."

"I was wondering if you could tell me why she got a call from your office the morning of her disappearance."

"Oh, yes." Anderson reached into a stack on his desk and pulled out Lisa's file. "I had called her that morning with the results of her tests. Spoke to her myself."

Cade sat up straighter. "Is that right?"

"Yes. You see, she'd been through all these fertility treatments, very painful and difficult procedures, literally for years. But when I did her hysterogram I saw immediately why she'd never had a child."

"A bicornuate uterus," Cade said. "It showed up in the autopsy."

"That's right. I should have told her the day I did the test, but I decided to wait until I had all of her results. I was reluctant to accuse Alan Sims of lying to her. I tried to fathom how he could have made a mistake like that. But it was impossible. He had done the same tests on her, so he knew what I knew."

"And you told her that morning?"

"Yes. It was a difficult thing to tell her. She could have had surgery years ago. The surgery has a high rate of success. But now, at her age, she had other factors against her. I told her we could still try, that there was much more hope with the surgery than there was with IVF."

"Doctor, if there was fraud involved, is it possible that he could have pulled it off without help from his nurses and technicians?"

"I suppose it's possible. I understand Sims does all his own lab work, instead of using outside labs like I do. If he falsified her results, it may be that no one knew."

Cade studied the man's face. "Dr. Anderson, why didn't you come forward with this before?"

The man leaned back in his chair, crossing his hands in front of him. "I decided to take a different approach."

"And what would that be?"

"I launched an inquiry with the American Medical Association. That's how we physicians normally do things, Chief Cade. They have means for investigating these things, and if Sims is judged to be guilty of fraud, the appropriate authorities will be notified."

"I understand that, Doctor, but I would think that Lisa's murder might have made you rethink that approach."

He sighed. "Perhaps it should have. But I have a very busy practice, and I admit I didn't give it that much more thought. Once Lisa died, I figured her reproductive system wasn't an issue anymore. Surely you don't think that this had something to do with her murder."

"I don't know that, but right now everything is relevant."

Cade got a copy of her records and left the office, deep in thought as he drove back to Cape Refuge. On his way back he radioed McCormick at the station.

"Yeah, Chief, what you got?"

"I want you to go to get a list of every person scheduled to see our man on May 16." He hoped McCormick understood. The police scanner wasn't all that private, so he didn't want to spell it out.

There was a moment of silence, then McCormick came back. "Good idea, Cade. I'll get right on it."

*B*lair heard Cade's call on her police scanner. She recognized his attempt to keep his orders private from those like her who listened in. Dozens of private citizens had police scanners and kept up with the calls—retired or off-duty cops who still wanted to be a part of things, reporters like her looking for stories, and stringers hoping they could rush to crime scenes and get pictures to sell to her paper or others.

Who was *our man*? Was Cade telling McCormick to get the patient list from Dr. Sims' office for the day of May 16 or the list of clients Carson Graham had seen? Or did this have something to do with Ben or Sam Sullivan's business appointments?

It was unlikely he was talking about Ben or Sam, since they weren't in businesses that relied on frequent appointments. No, it had to be Graham or Sims, and since he'd just told her about suspecting Sims of fraud, she decided it was probably him.

Did he think that one of the patients had killed Lisa, or was he simply looking for a witness? Had he come to the conclusion that Sims was the culprit?

She went by the newspaper office to check her messages before deciding which story to cover next. There was one from the postmaster about the post office closing on Wednesday afternoons. "Would you put a notice in the paper that they'll have to do their mailing on Wednesday mornings instead, Blair? I don't want any angry residents banging on our doors."

Amy Matheson had left her weekly update about her daughter's latest accomplishments. "Blair, I'm sending you a picture and a paragraph about Courtney's soccer team's win last week. Also, I thought I'd stick in the list of the straight-A honor students from the high school. Courtney was among them, of course. Next week she's in the Chatham County Junior Miss Pageant. I know you'll want to cover that."

Blair sighed. Amy would love it if Blair devoted every page to her daughter. She needed an entire staff to keep up with these mundane stories. If she ever did expand into a daily, statewide paper, maybe she wouldn't need this kind of drivel to fill up the pages.

She waited for the next message. "Blair, it's me." It was Morgan's voice, flat and listless. "I wondered if you could come by and house-sit while I go to Dr. Sims this afternoon. I'm not comfortable leaving Sheila here alone with Caleb, and Jonathan's going with me. Sadie's here too, but I would feel a lot better if you were here. I have to be there at three."

Blair wondered why she was going to Dr. Sims. She hadn't had an appointment scheduled. Unless . . .

Blair's heart jolted. Had her sister decided to do something drastic? Was she going to tell him that she wanted in vitro?

She didn't bother to call her back. Instead, she called Cade's cell phone, hoping he was still in Savannah and could get the signal. When he picked up, she burst out of her chair.

"Cade, this is Blair. I hope I'm not interrupting anything."

"No, I'm just driving back. What's up?"

"It's Morgan. She's made an appointment to see Dr. Sims this afternoon. I'm afraid she's decided to go through with the in vitro. She needs to know what you told me."

He hesitated for a moment. "What time's her appointment?"

"Three o'clock."

"It's one now. Tell you what, I'll go straight to the house, and we'll tell her together. Maybe she can keep that appointment and help us out a little."

Blair grunted. "No, Cade. She's too fragile right now. She might not be able to handle it."

"Don't underestimate your sister, Blair. She's almost as tough as you are."

CHAPTER

57

*M*organ stared out through the glass window in the kitchen, across the sun porch to the backyard. She could see Caleb chattering while he played on his plastic playground. Sheila stood back, as if she didn't know how to involve herself in his play. Morgan hoped she wouldn't let him fall.

She started to turn away, but just as she did, she saw Sheila bring something to her mouth. Was that another cigarette?

Morgan opened the screen door and stepped out, letting it bounce shut behind her. Sheila jumped and dropped what she'd been holding, but a thin cloud of smoke lingered around her.

Morgan almost didn't say anything, but then she realized that Gus and Karen and Felitia had all been smokers too, when they'd come. They all quit as a requirement of living in the home. If she let Sheila get away with it, how would she face them?

She stepped down the steps into the yard. "Sheila, you were smoking."

Sheila stepped on the butt, hiding the evidence. "No, I wasn't."

Morgan picked Caleb up. "He's never been around cigarette smoke, not since he's been with me. He doesn't need to be inhaling that stuff."

"Hey, I didn't do it, okay? I'm being falsely accused."

Morgan touched her arm and moved her aside. The butt lay on the ground like an indictment. "Then what is that?"

Sheila shoved her hair back from her face. "Look, there's no sin against smoking. I haven't done anything wrong."

Morgan tried not to react in her anger. She swallowed back her ire and took a deep breath. "Sheila, I really want this to work. Not just for Caleb and Sadie, but for you, too. We're not asking that much of you. We'll give you a nice place to live, food and clothing, and all the time in the world to be with your children. You don't even have to work until you get your bearings."

The screen door opened and Blair called out, "Hey, Sis."

Thank goodness Blair had come. Now she could leave without worrying. "I'll be in in a second," she called. Blair went back in, and Morgan turned back to Sheila.

Caleb was fighting to get down. Morgan set him on his feet, and he bolted back to the playground.

Sheila sighed. "Look, I'm sorry. I won't smoke anymore. It's just stressful, this whole thing. I know I've been clean for a year, but I still have those cravings for . . . the drugs. And the cigarettes. I figure there's no harm in the cigarettes." She shoved her hair back from her face. "Oh, man. I can't believe I just told you that. You can't understand those cravings."

"No one's judging you, Sheila. Almost everybody who comes here has them, but I really believe the cigarettes make the cravings worse instead of better. Just the smell of matches starts the cravings in some people. In order to change your life, things have to be different. It's my job to help you with that. Don't you want to do better by your children? Don't you want to stop letting yourself down?"

Sheila's face softened, and she looked helpless as she stared back at her son. "Of course I do. I'll do better. I promise."

Morgan sighed as she went back into the house. She didn't want to talk to Blair or anyone else about all the negative feelings pulsing through her. She had only been at this for a few months, since her mother had died. Before, she had just helped her parents deal with the problems the residents presented. She had watched and learned, but when they died, she had felt called to take over. But she wasn't a seasoned veteran, and she wasn't as wise as they were. She could only draw on the wisdom of the policies they'd set in place, and the strength she drew from her Bible study and prayer early each morning. Without that, she knew she would have closed the home months ago.

She stepped back into the kitchen and saw Blair waiting for her. She heard men's voices in the front room. "Is Jonathan home?"

"Yeah, he drove up when we did. He's talking to Cade. Morgan, we need to talk to you in private."

"What about?"

"It's about Lisa. Let's go into the parlor."

What now? Morgan followed Blair into the parlor and listened, horrified, as Cade told them about Lisa's uterus and the second opinion she'd gotten.

"Whoa, wait a minute," Jonathan said. "You're telling us that Sims is a liar? A fraud?"

"It looks that way," Cade said.

Morgan felt as if an eighteen-wheeler going ninety miles an hour had just broadsided her. She stared in front of her, searching her memory of every encounter with the doctor for some sign of guile. He'd seemed so sincere, so down-to-earth, so compassionate. He'd acted as if he really wanted them to have a child. For Lisa . . .

"He manipulated Lisa, lied to her, kept her from getting the help she needed that would have helped her get pregnant? How could anyone be that cruel?"

Blair spoke quietly, as if she feared setting Morgan off. "I told Cade that you had an appointment this afternoon. I wanted him to share this with you before you invested any more into this."

Tears came to Morgan's eyes. "We were going to have IVF. He convinced us that was the best thing."

"Can we trust him with the results of the tests?" Jonathan asked. "Any of them?"

"I wouldn't," Cade said.

New hope blossomed inside Morgan. Maybe he was wrong about her hormones. Maybe it wasn't as bad as he'd made it sound. Maybe she *could* have a family.

Jonathan got up and went across the room. He turned back, rubbing his tanned neck. "Wow. This is unbelievable. What do you want us to do, Cade?"

"I want you to keep that appointment today. Tell him you've decided to do the in vitro. I'll put a wire on you, Jonathan, so we can record whatever he says. I want you to ask specific questions. Get him to tell you Morgan's condition again. Ask who does the ultrasounds, who fertilizes the egg after its harvested, which labs they work with, and how long before you get the results."

"I'll go along with this," Jonathan said, "as long as he doesn't touch my wife again. I don't want him doing anymore tests or injecting anything into her or drawing blood—"

"That's fine. I just want him to indict himself with his words."

"I can't promise I won't reach across that desk and throttle him."

Morgan knew her husband wasn't exaggerating. "Jonathan, we can't do this if you act angry."

"She's right, man," Cade said. "I need you to stay calm. Act like you would have before. He thinks he's getting away with it."

Jonathan's jaw popped. "Do you think he killed Lisa?"

Cade rubbed his face. "I don't know. We may be talking about two different cases that have nothing to do with each other.

But it's real coincidental that Lisa found out on the same day she disappeared."

Morgan sat down. "I'm going to be sick."

Jonathan looked down at her. "Honey, are you sure you're up to this?"

"You *bet* I am—" She bit the words out. "If he killed my friend, or even just lied to her—or to us—he needs to be stopped."

Cade got up. "I'm going to get you an appointment with Dr. Anderson, Lisa's other doctor. He's going to do some preliminary testing of you and Jonathan and see if he can confirm what Sims has already told you. Will you do that, Morgan?"

"Of course. Just tell me when to show up."

CHAPTER

58

*M*organ's heart hammered out a triple-time cadence as she followed Jonathan into Dr. Sims' waiting room. As always, the room was full. How many people in here were clinging to false hope, and how many had been lied to about their conditions? She fought the urge to scream out that they needed to flee from this office and get second opinions immediately. She hoped they would know to do so when Cade got through with Sims.

Jonathan guided her to two of the last available seats. Morgan's palms were wet. She hoped the doctor didn't try to shake her hand. She glanced at Jonathan. He wore a dress shirt and jacket, not his usual attire, but it helped hide the wire that Cade had put on him. It wasn't visible at all. There would be no reason for the doctor to suspect anything.

She glanced around for something to read—anything to keep her hands and eyes busy while they waited—and found a copy of the latest *Cape Refuge Journal*. She picked it up and saw the picture of Lisa Jackson on the front page.

"That's so sad about Lisa Jackson." The woman next to her pointed to the picture. "She was a friend of mine."

"Really? How did you know her?"

"From here. I used to see her here from time to time. We had a lot in common."

Morgan didn't want to get into her own relationship with Lisa. Her throat was too tight, and her heart still sprinted. She hoped her nerves didn't show on her face.

"Life is so short," the woman said. "You just never know what's going to happen. Here she was, struggling so hard to have a baby, and if she had gotten pregnant, she wouldn't have even lived to see it be born."

The irony had not escaped Morgan, either. "Maybe all those babies she miscarried were waiting for her in heaven."

The woman got tears in her eyes. "That's a nice thought."

"Yes, it is." Morgan smiled and patted her hand.

"I saw her the morning she disappeared."

Jonathan put his hand over Morgan's and leaned forward to see the woman. "You saw her that day? Are you sure?"

"Oh, yes. I'll never forget that."

"Where did you see her?" Morgan asked.

"Right here. In this very office."

Morgan couldn't speak, so Jonathan did. "But I read that the appointment she missed was for that afternoon."

"Oh, she wasn't here for an appointment. In fact, the doctor wasn't in until after noon. I just came in to get some blood work done. Lisa came storming in. She looked like she was fuming."

Morgan turned and looked at Jonathan. This was new information. Even Cade didn't know about this.

The woman lowered her voice. "She didn't even speak to me. She walked right past me to the receptionist's desk and told them that she needed to see the doctor immediately. They told her he wasn't in, that he was off that morning, so she hurried back out.

That was the last time I ever saw her. The next day, when I heard she was missing, I was stunned."

"Did you hear her say where she was going?"

"No, nothing."

"Was she alone?" Morgan asked.

"Yes, as far as I could tell. I didn't see her drive away, though." She sighed. "I've thought about it a million times. Maybe if I'd stopped her, asked her what was wrong, invited her for a cup of coffee ... maybe she wouldn't have gotten murdered."

The nurse came to the door and called out, "Laura Gulley."

The woman next to Morgan sprang up, whispered goodbye, and headed back to see the doctor.

Morgan stared at Jonathan. Whispering, she said, "The question is, did she find the doctor after she left here?"

"I hope Cade is getting this," Jonathan said in a low voice.

CHAPTER

59

"So you've decided to try IVF!" Dr. Sims looked almost jubilant at the decision. He sat down at his desk and folded his hands in front of him. "Tell me what prompted this decision."

Morgan swallowed and looked at Jonathan. He took her hand. She was trembling. "Well, it was a very hard decision, but you convinced us it was the right thing. I'll be thirty soon, and I want so much to have children. Not just one, but three or four. Maybe even more. I'm ready to get started."

"And how do you feel about that, Jonathan?"

Jonathan was calmer than she was. She could feel the heat of his anger in his hand. "I wasn't so sure. For one thing, we'll have to mortgage our house to do this. We just barely make ends meet as it is. I'm not sure it's the right thing to do. Are you sure it's not too soon to try this?"

Sims took off his reading glasses and leaned forward on his desk. He looked like a pastor, counseling them on their covenant. His eyes held no guile. He seemed compassionate, caring. Could he really be a liar? A killer?

"It has to be your call," he said. "I can't really say what's right for you. All I know is that Morgan's FSH is too high. Her ovaries are not producing mature eggs on their own. They need help. Even if you did manage to conceive, more miscarriages could happen. If we harvest mature eggs and fertilize them outside her body, there's a greater chance that she could carry the baby to term." He turned his hands palms up. "But you do have the option to wait. We can do it a year from now. Two years."

"But even if it works," Jonathan said, "won't we have to do it with every child we have?"

"Maybe she would have multiple births," he said with a grin. "One of my patients had triplets just last night. She sold her car and cashed in her 401(k) to pay for it, but she has no regrets. None at all. She was almost forty, though. If it had happened ten years ago, it would have been much better for her. She waited until it was the absolute last resort. I'm glad she finally went through with it."

"And then there's Lisa." Morgan hadn't expected the words to come out of her mouth. "She'd had two procedures and none of them worked."

"I had every hope that the third one would. We were so close. We had gotten her FSH levels low enough and were ready to harvest the egg. And then this."

Morgan fought the urge to ask him if Lisa had found him that morning, if she'd confronted him about her misshapen uterus and the false hope he'd given her, and all the money he had taken from her. She bit her lip until it almost drew blood.

He went on about what she could expect from the drugs he would give her and when he estimated the procedure could actually take place. Morgan sat like a statue, her hands folded in her lap. As he went on, she prayed that Cade would get enough from this conversation to lock the man up for life.

Jonathan interrogated him like a pro, probing him with pointed questions, making the man talk long enough to hang himself. "Do you use a lab, Doctor, or do you do everything yourself?"

"We do it here, in the office. Most doctors do have outside labs, but I've hired some of the best technicians in the area, and we do all our own work. I'm very hands-on. I see the results immediately, and I oversee all of it. I do a lot of the actual lab work myself. Morgan, you've come to the best possible place to make your dreams come true. Do you believe that?"

She hesitated for a moment. "I want to," she whispered.

"Good. You're going to have to trust me. But I won't let you down."

60

*R*iley Holmes, Chatham County's DA, was new to his office, and while he was tough in the courtroom, he was more cautious than most of the cops in his jurisdiction would have liked.

"I do think you're onto something here, Cade," he said, looking down at the report Cade and McCormick had brought him. "But I don't think we'll have probable cause to arrest Sims for medical fraud until we get confirmation that he lied to not one, but many patients. Any lawyer could make a case for a doctor making a mistake. Interview some of his patients, get them to go for second opinions, subpoena his records, his lab reports—"

"We'll do that," Cade said. "But before we give him a heads-up on the fraud thing, I want to question him about whether Lisa found him that morning or not, and I want to get his alibi."

Holmes nodded. "Yes. We don't have enough on the fraud case, and we have even less on the murder. I need something concrete, guys. I can't even get a grand jury indictment with any of what you've brought me. You're close, and I know you're headed in the right direction—but you still have a lot of work to do."

Cade had known that would be the answer. He looked at McCormick, whose expression was irritated but not surprised.

"Meanwhile," McCormick said, "he's going to keep seeing patients."

"All the more incentive for you to get your work done quickly."

Cade almost laughed as they left the office—as if they hadn't been working night and day with every resource they had already.

"The man's got a point," Cade said as they strode back to their car. "We don't want to make an arrest only to have some slick lawyer get it thrown out of court."

McCormick only grunted as they got into the car.

CHAPTER

61

*T*he Saturday debate for the mayoral race brought out hundreds of Cape Refuge citizens. Morgan supposed that was a good thing for Jonathan since he hadn't had the advertising budget that Sam Sullivan had. Hopefully, some minds would be swayed today.

It was a nice day. The temperature was low, hovering around seventy-five to eighty degrees, rather than the usual ninety-five. Even though the weather forecast had predicted rain, there wasn't a cloud in sight.

Annabelle Cotton's Dance Club was on the stage, the ladies decked out in their frilly square-dancing skirts and their Mary Jane shoes, and their partners wearing short-sleeved white shirts with sweat rings under the arms. They danced with gusto to Otis Peabody's calls. Some of the audience danced along, missing the calls and laughing with glee.

Jonathan was too busy mingling to dance, so Morgan just stood near their campaign tent and clapped to the music, trying to keep her mind off the events of the last few days and on the task at hand. As she did, she kept her eyes on Sheila and Caleb. Sheila had taken the toddler down to the water and held his hand as he romped in the waves licking at his feet. They were, indeed, bonding. Morgan had to give Sheila credit for being attentive to the baby. She hoped Sheila didn't take her eyes off him today. So much could go wrong in a crowd at the beach.

She looked for Sadie through the crowd and saw her with her camera hanging from her neck. Blair was paying her to photograph the event for the paper. She seemed deep in conversation with Matt, the guy who helped out at the florist shop while he attended college in Savannah. He was a nice kid, a Christian, and Morgan hoped that something might come of it. Sadie needed a young man to find her attractive, one who wasn't controlled by his hormones, but she hoped the girl wouldn't get too busy with him or her pictures to forget about Caleb and her mother. Morgan wanted her to jump in if Sheila turned away for a second.

Ben Jackson's absence was conspicuous. The stage looked different than it had two weeks ago for the original debate. Instead of three microphones and three chairs, there were only two. Instead of an organized debate moderated by an objective party, it looked as if Sarah Williford was going to moderate, which meant it would probably turn into more of a back-and-forth between the two candidates themselves. Morgan hoped Jonathan was prepared, but with all the other distractions, she feared he wasn't.

"It's all set up, Morgan."

She turned and saw that Gus had set up the table under Jonathan's tent and was unpacking stacks of campaign flyers and cards. Karen sat in one of the folding chairs behind the table, holding Emory.

"Thank you, Gus."

"I'm going to get my bride-to-be something to drink. You want something, too?"

Morgan smiled and winked at Karen. "No, thanks. I'm fine."

She turned back to the square dancing, wishing she felt more festive. She needed to be mingling, talking up Jonathan's ideas, and sticking close to his side. But she couldn't seem to drag herself out of her depression.

Blair stepped into the shade of the tent. "So where's Cade?"

Morgan looked around at the people. "I haven't seen him."

"Guess he decided not to come since he's one of the issues they'll be debating." Blair's disappointment was clear. "He should have shown up to defend himself, though."

"Don't worry, Jonathan will defend him. He probably did the right thing, staying away. Besides, he's really busy, isn't he?"

"Yeah. The DA's got him jumping through hoops." Blair paused and gave Morgan a long look. "Are you okay, Sis?"

"Yeah. Just a lot on my mind." Her eyes strayed back to the water. Caleb had plopped down in the wet, packed sand, and Sheila was helping him make a little mountain. Morgan hoped he didn't try to eat any of it.

"Stop watching them. He'll be all right."

Morgan forced her eyes away. "I know he will."

Blair stroked her back as if wishing she could offer something to lift Morgan's spirits. She needed to look happier, Morgan thought. The candidate's wife shouldn't look so melancholy.

The music ended and the square dancers curtsied and bowed. The crowd whistled and applauded.

Then Councilwoman Sarah Williford—decked out in a hot-pink sundress and a big straw hat—took the stage, clapping as the dancers exited. "Thank you, dancers. Annabelle, you work wonders with this group. I went to the high school prom with ol' Jake Pryne, and doggone if my toes weren't black and blue. You've turned him into a Fred Astaire."

The man laughed and gave another mock bow.

"Welcome to the Cape Refuge mayoral debate," she said over the PA system. "Will the candidates please come to the stage?"

She saw Jonathan shaking hands with the people he'd been talking to, and quickly he ran up to the stage. Sam Sullivan took his place as well. Sam had worn a big Hawaiian shirt and a gold chain around his neck. He had an even tan and little round white circles over his eyelids. It was a tanning bed tan, Morgan thought, carefully planned for the purpose of looking like one of the islanders. But Morgan knew he rarely spent time outdoors. He was a white-collar, at-his-desk kind of businessman.

Jonathan's tan was real, from all the hours he spent out at sea on his fishing tours. He wore a white short-sleeved dress shirt, which probably had been a mistake since sweat rings were already visible under his arms. She hoped he looked more like a citizen who wanted to serve than a politician who wanted to take over.

"In case you guys are hungry," Sarah said into the microphone, "we have hot dogs over here to the right, only a dollar apiece, courtesy of Mac's Hot Dog Stand, and the Colonel from Cricket's has graciously offered to sell us drinks over here to the left. And Nemo from the concession stand down the beach has offered us cotton candy and popcorn."

"Give me a break," Blair said under her breath. "This is a forty-five-minute debate, for heaven's sake. What, are we gonna starve to death?"

"It's a town event, Blair," Morgan said. "Food makes it more festive."

Morgan glanced over at Sheila again. Caleb was on his feet, sand sticking to the back of his diaper. He walked toward the water, and Sheila did nothing to stop him.

Morgan caught her breath and started toward them, but suddenly Sheila got up and grabbed him before he could get slapped by a wave. His mother was doing fine—so why didn't that make her happier than it did?

"All right, ladies and gentlemen," Sarah Williford said. "I hope you all realize the importance of this debate. Since we're without a mayor right now—due to his run-ins with the law—the newly elected mayor will be sworn in just a few days after the election and will begin serving immediately. The direction of our town hangs on your decision."

"Would you get on with it, Sarah?" somebody yelled from the audience. "It's getting hot out here."

Sarah lifted her chin and kept talking. "As moderator of this debate, I'm going to start off by asking the candidates to comment on several issues. The first issue concerns the police department. We've heard Sam Sullivan saying that he would like to revamp it, that he's not satisfied with how it's running. Jonathan Cleary seems to be happy with the status quo. Sam, would you go first and please comment on your stand on this issue?"

Sam moved his heavy frame up to the microphone. "As most of you know, I'm for getting Chief Matthew Cade out of our police force and bringing in some new blood with more experience. Cade was fine when all he had to take care of was an occasional car theft and disturbing the peace violations, but in the last year we've had five murders here, including Lisa's—God rest her soul—and as far as I can see, they're not letting up."

"Oh, brother," Blair bit out. "Somebody needs to throw a tomato at that guy."

Morgan touched her arm to calm her. "Don't say anything, Blair. Let Jonathan refute that."

The scars on Blair's face burned crimson.

Sam raised his hand dramatically. "And to make matters worse, he's running this city into some serious debt by hiring outside people to help with this investigation, even though he's already arrested the killer, my former opponent. Every day that goes by is costing this city thousands and thousands of dollars. I say it's time we got somebody who knows what they're doing in here and get the police department back on track, where it can protect our citizens and our money."

Sullivan stepped back from the microphone. Jonathan came forward, and slid his hands into his pockets. Morgan knew that he was nervous.

"As most of you know, I have great faith in our police department. Three of those murders that Sam just referred to were very personal to me. As most of you know, my mother- and father-in-law were the first two victims, and one of our residents at Hanover House was the third. Chief Cade and his police force worked as professionally and as quickly as any police force I've ever seen to bring those cases to a resolution, just as he's done on the other two cases."

"Way to go, Jonathan," Blair muttered.

"As for the money he's spending, if I'm elected mayor, this town will get behind our police force and stop balking about giving them the resources they need to fight crime. The department is still housed in a laundromat, for Pete's sake, and their cars are all over ten years old. There is all sorts of technology available to them, but their computers are outdated. We need to hire more officers and send them to schools where they can get more training and certifications. I say we need to keep Cade in office and support him wholeheartedly."

"How you gonna pay for all that, Jonathan?" Sam mopped his forehead with a handkerchief and stuffed it back into his pocket. "You plan to raise property taxes?"

The crowd muttered disapproval, and Morgan saw the tension on Jonathan's face. "No, I'm not. The town can mark my word. We get enough taxes from our citizens, but under my leadership, the City Council will stop wasting it."

Applause and whistles and yells roared up from the crowd, and Morgan found her spirits lifting. Jonathan could hold his own with Sam. The voters were seeing what he was made of.

Sam Sullivan's smug smile seemed to say he would shoot down Jonathan's little victory as soon as he got the microphone back.

Sarah Williford went on to ask them about parking on the island, about tourism and their approach to it, about real-estate development, and the kinds of businesses they should attract to the island. Sullivan got his licks in regarding the cell phone company he had already wooed to the island, taking absolute credit for the fact that the tower would be completed and Cape Refuge would have cellular service within a matter of days.

Morgan glanced around to see where Caleb was. She saw that Sadie had him now. She was standing back from the crowd with a concerned look on her face. As Morgan watched Sadie's eyes scan the crowd, she realized the girl was looking for her mother.

Morgan looked around, searching the crowd for Sheila's face. "Blair, do you see Sheila?"

"No, and frankly, I need Sadie to be taking pictures, not watching her brother."

"I'll get him." Morgan cut through the people and got to Sadie. "Honey, where's your mother?"

Sadie looked close to tears. "I'm not sure. She gave Caleb to me and said she'd be right back. Maybe she went to the bathroom or something."

Morgan took Caleb from her arms and kissed him on the cheek. He was getting hot. He needed to be in the shade before he got sunburned. Had Sheila done as she'd reminded her and put sunscreen on the boy?

"Morgan, I know she didn't run off. I'm not sure where she went, but she'll be right back. I know she will."

"Why don't I take Caleb and go stand under our tent? He needs something to drink."

"Okay, and I'll go look for Mom. I'm sure she's around here somewhere." Sadie took off her camera and handed it to Morgan. "Will you give this to Blair, in case she needs to get something? Tell her I'll be back in a minute."

CHAPTER

*T*he moment the debate was over, Blair saw
Vince Barr, complete with a cameraman, conducting interviews among the people. Since he was a print journalist—
and she used that term loosely—he'd have no reason to film
unless he planned to sell the video footage to the news chan-
nels. He was probably drilling townspeople on their opinions about the murder and why Ben may have done it,
whether there were others involved, or whether the police
even had the right person. Anything he could find to keep
the story going.

She hoped no one said anything stupid. Heading to
her car to change the film in Sadie's camera, she cut
through the line of cars in the parking lot and heard gig-
gling from Carson Graham's Palm Reading van parked
under a tree. As she hurried by, she glanced over.

Sheila sat in the doorway with a bottle of beer and a
cigarette in one hand. Carson held her other one and
seemed to be studying her palm.

"So there you are, Sheila!" she called as if she'd been look-ing for her.

The woman dropped her cigarette as if it had stung her. She pulled her hand from Carson's and set the bottle down behind her in the van.

Blair stepped between the two. "My sister's been looking all over for you."

Sheila didn't get up. "I told Sadie I'd be right back."

Blair reached into the van and pulled out the beer. She held it up to Carson. "So, what are you doing, Carson? Contributing to the delinquency of one of the Hanover House residents?"

"Hey, I didn't know she lived at Hanover House."

Blair gave a sarcastic grunt. "You didn't see it in her palm?"

He smiled. "Let's just say hers wasn't as clear as yours was."

Sudden shame swept through her.

"So you had a reading too, huh?" Sheila seemed amused.

"No, I did not. I went there to interview him."

Graham's smug grin told her he enjoyed her discomfort. "I gave her one on the house."

"You did not read my palm," Blair bit out. "And any pre-diction you made about my life was unsolicited."

Sheila was laughing now. "Don't be so defensive, Blair. I believe in it, too."

Blair felt the fight deflating out of her. "I *don't* believe in it! And you're changing the subject."

Sheila got up. "Okay, so I saw his 'Palm Reading' sign on his van, and I asked him to give me a reading. He had an ice chest with beer, so I took one. It's not the end of the world. You don't have to tell Morgan."

Blair couldn't believe the gall of the woman. Sheila turned back to Carson. "Look, I'll see you later, okay? Feel free to call anytime. I could use the diversion."

Carson chuckled. "Maybe I will. We can finish your reading."

Blair's chin shot up at the man. "Where's your *wife*, Carson?"

He stiffened slightly. "She's here, over with the crowd. I haven't done anything wrong, Blair. By the way, I saw you and Cade at my show the other night. Hope you enjoyed it."

Sheila breathed a laugh then, as if he'd just knocked Blair down, and started to walk away. Blair launched out after her and stopped her before she reached the sand. "What is wrong with you?"

Sheila swung around. "What do you mean?"

"I mean you have a lot of nerve doing this after Morgan has been taking care of your children for the last year. You're throwing her kindness back in her face. You had no place else to go and you know it. If you had gone back to Atlanta, you would have gone right into the arms of some other man who would get you back hooked on drugs and abuse you in every possible way. And if history repeats itself, he might also abuse your children. But instead, you get to come here to a place that's practically paradise on earth and live in a house that you would never have even *dreamed* of living in before, where your child is getting an education and your baby has been cared for and loved. All you have to do is abide by certain rules of their program, which are designed for *your* good. But you can't even do that!"

"I have a life, okay? I'm not some Hanover House robot. I get to think of myself sometimes."

"Isn't that what got you put in jail? Isn't that what almost got your daughter killed? Maybe it's time you started thinking of your children for a change and doing what's right for them."

"How is my drinking an occasional beer and smoking a cigarette wrong for my children? It has nothing to do with them."

"It has *everything* to do with them," Blair said, "because if Morgan and Jonathan throw you out of the home, it's not just you who's going to lose out. It's your children."

Sheila grit her teeth. "If I leave Hanover House, my children are going with me."

Blair threw up her hands. "*That's* what I'm talking about. There's no way on earth you could think that was best for them, not by any stretch of the imagination. They're going to lose, and you're going to lose, too. Why can't you be grateful for all Morgan and Jonathan have done for you and just abide by a few little easy rules?"

Sheila took a step closer, her face inches from Blair's. "I don't have to take this stuff from you. I'm not your inferior. You're not better than me just because you came from that family."

"I know I'm not better than you. Just a couple of months ago I was a lot like you—a sham who considered myself wise. I was stupid enough to believe the world's lies. I didn't want to be accountable to God, but you know what? I was anyway. And so are you. If you could stop being stupid, you might actually make something of your life!"

Sheila just stared at her as if Blair had struck her in the face. Blair tried to take a deep breath. It wasn't exactly the way Morgan would have shared her faith, but it was the best Blair could do.

"You know—" she tried to calm her voice—"by all rights, you should have been in jail for four more years. The fact that you got out early was a gift from God. Look at your life, Sheila!"

"Mom!"

Blair turned and saw Sadie coming toward them. Sheila's expression changed and she started toward her daughter. "Hey, I was just on my way back."

Sadie was clearly upset. "Where were you?"

"I was looking for a bathroom."

"There's one on the Pier. All you had to do was ask me."

"Next time I'll know."

Sheila shot Blair a look that told her to keep her mouth shut, and started walking back to the crowd. Sadie exchanged looks with Blair. She clearly knew something unpleasant had occurred, but she just followed her mother back to the group.

Blair stood there a moment, wondering why she felt like a faithless hypocrite. Here she was, holding up Sheila's shortcomings like a mirror, forcing her to look into it. But she didn't want to look at her own.

The shame that someone like Carson Graham had seduced her with his uninvited reading and caused her to dwell on it, hope for it, even plan for it, sickened her. Wasn't she stronger in her faith than Sheila? Didn't she, indeed, know better?

She saw Jonathan greeting people at his table. Blair swallowed and followed Sadie and Sheila to his tent. When Sheila marched in and took Caleb out of Morgan's arms, Jonathan excused himself. She started away, but he grabbed her arm. "Sheila, have you been drinking?" he asked quietly.

"Of course not. Where would I get alcohol?"

"I don't know, but you smell like beer and cigarettes."

"What is wrong with you people?" Sheila said. "Even if I did, I'm not going to hell just because I smoke a cigarette and drink a beer!"

"Of course not," Jonathan said. "Beer and cigarettes are not what keep you out of heaven, but they are things that will keep you out of Hanover House."

"Fine," Sheila spouted back. "Just let me know when you want me to leave, and I'll pack my bags."

She stormed off, Caleb on her hip.

Morgan looked helplessly at Jonathan.

"Is she a piece of work or what?" Blair muttered.

"Did you see where she was?" Morgan asked.

"Oh, yeah. She was in Carson Graham's van, sipping on one of his beers."

"That's it." Jonathan's voice brooked no debate. "She's out."

A look of stark-raving fear came over Morgan's face. "No, Jonathan! We *can't* throw her out."

"Either she abides by the rules or she doesn't. Look at Karen and Felitia and Gus. They're following the rules. What if they see Sheila breaking them and getting away with it?"

She had told herself the same thing, but when it came right down to it, she couldn't risk losing Caleb. "Sheila's different," she whispered harshly. "She's Caleb and Sadie's mother."

Jonathan just stared down at her. "Morgan, you can't possibly think that we should back down."

"We didn't throw Sadie out when she broke the rules."

"That was different. Sadie was our foster daughter. She was just a kid trying to grow up. Sheila is *not* a kid. She supposedly wants to change her life, but if I don't see any commitment from her, I am not willing to give her a free ride."

He went back to his constituents, forcing himself to look cordial.

Morgan turned away and looked at Blair. "What am I going to do?"

"I don't know, but I had a little talk with her. Maybe some of what I said will penetrate."

"What did you say to her?"

Blair looked back at Sheila and saw that she was whispering through her teeth to Sadie. There was anger on her face, and she knew that her words hadn't made a difference. Why should they, when she was no better than Sheila?

"Well, I sort of witnessed to her. In my own way."

"You did?" Morgan asked hopefully. "Good, Blair. Maybe coming from you, she'll listen."

"Yeah, well, my methods leave a little to be desired, I think, and I haven't exactly painted myself as the shining role model."

"What do you mean?"

"Nothing. Never mind." Blair hoped it hadn't done further damage.

Karen approached Morgan from the crowd. "Morgan, Gus is gonna take me and Emory home. It's getting too hot out here, and it's time for Emory to go down for his nap."

Morgan nodded. "Would you see if Sheila wants to go with you and take Caleb? He's looking a little peaked himself. You can take our car and we'll get a ride."

"Sure."

They watched Karen approach Sheila. Sheila looked their way, squinting in the sun. She nodded as if she was anxious to get away from this place.

"Are you okay, Morgan?" Blair asked.

Morgan sighed. "I've got to be. Jonathan needs me."

CHAPTER

*B*lair found Sadie sitting at the end of the Pier, staring down into the water. She sat down next to her. "Want to talk about it?"

Sadie had been crying, but she tried to hide it. "I don't know why she's being like this. I'm afraid she's going to leave—or get thrown out."

Blair thought about Jonathan's decision to throw Sheila out but decided not to mention it. Maybe Morgan would talk him out of it. "She's just adjusting."

"She needs Jesus," Sadie whispered. "He's all that's really going to change her life."

Blair looked out across the ocean. Three sailboats drifted on the horizon, and toward the west she saw a schooner and a speedboat crossing paths. "It can happen," Blair said. "I'm a living example. I found myself at my lowest point of desperation, panic-stricken, with nowhere to turn, feeling like my life was totally out of my control. That was when I looked to Christ. That was when he saved me."

Sadie nodded. "Me too. My mother's been like that for a long time. Her life has been out of her control and she's been at her lowest point. She says she's a Christian, but I don't really think she gets it. I saw her at that psychic's van. She'd rather get her palm read than pray."

Blair's throat was dry. She swallowed hard. There it was again—that shame. She didn't know why. Sadie knew she'd gone to interview Carson Graham—but she didn't know that she'd paid him any heed. She would be so disappointed if she knew.

Blair was disappointed with herself.

The warm wind blew through Sadie's hair as she studied Blair for a moment. "What was it that worked for you, Blair?"

"People were praying for me," Blair said. "Lots of people who loved me were praying hard. Those prayers were heard, Sadie. If you pray for your mom, God's going to hear."

"But will he answer?" Sadie asked.

Blair picked up a piece of hot dog bun someone had dropped next to her on the Pier and tossed it into the ocean. "I don't know the Bible as well as my sister and my parents did, but I was raised on it just like Morgan was. I didn't always heed it, but I did hear it. I always heard that the Lord answers prayers that glorify him and are according to his will. If you pray for your mother to know Christ, God's going to answer that prayer. It's not his will for any to perish. So why wouldn't he answer that?"

"I hope that's true," Sadie said. "What a family we could have if Mom believed and lived for Jesus. I wouldn't have to worry about her so much, and I wouldn't have to worry about Caleb. She would always want to do the right thing for him, even if it meant staying at Hanover House with Morgan and Jonathan."

A strong gust of wind blew the hair back from their faces. Blair saw a dark cloud moving in from the horizon.

"Looks like it's going to storm, after all," Sadie whispered.

Blair gave the girl a hug. "We've survived storms before, haven't we?"

Sadie got up and looked back toward the crowd. Tears still ran down her face. "Can you do without me, Blair? I really need to get back home to keep an eye on Caleb and my mom."

"Sure, go ahead. I can take it from here."

She watched Sadie head back up the Pier. The girl was clueless about who she had asked for spiritual advice.

Blair turned back to the water and thought of the way Carson's predictions had gripped and manipulated her mind, the greed and ambition and discontent they had fostered in her. Suddenly it was clear to her—none of that had been from God. They were sinful pipe dreams that, if pursued, might destroy all the blessings she had.

Her flesh was still so weak. She loved Jesus and had given her life to him, but avoiding sin was still harder than she thought.

She started to cry as the sky grew grayer and the wind whipped harder against her face.

"You okay, Sis?"

Blair hadn't heard her sister coming. Quickly, she wiped her face and looked back. "Yeah. You?"

"Not really." Morgan had been crying too, and her nose was red. She set one foot on the bottom rail and leaned on the top one.

Blair sighed, put her arms around Morgan's neck, and laid her head on her shoulder.

"We're some pair," Morgan whispered. "You're not crying over the Sheila thing too, are you?"

Blair let her go. "No, that's not it. But it's going to be all right. You'll talk Jonathan out of throwing her out."

"How, when I know perfectly well that she *should* be thrown out?"

"Maybe this was a wake-up call for her. Maybe it's just what she needed to straighten up."

Morgan didn't answer. The wind kicked up her long brown curls, and she pushed them back from her face. "So if you weren't crying about Sheila, then what's wrong?"

Blair pulled herself up and sat on the rail, her back to the ocean. "I'm crying because I don't understand why I'm such a weak Christian."

"What? You're not weak."

"Oh, yes, I am. I'm horribly weak." She looked toward the crowd still milling around on the beach. Anabelle's clogging class had taken the stage in their red and white checkered dresses. "Morgan, the other day when I went to interview Carson Graham, he made some predictions."

"What kind of predictions?"

"About my business and my relationship with Cade. He told me that I was going to expand my business to a statewide paper, and that Cade and I would get married soon. Ever since, I've been thinking of increasing my staff—not just by two or three people— but by dozens. Buying property, new equipment, going from twice a week to every day . . ."

Morgan looked at her like she was crazy. "Blair, you know you're not ready for that. Buying the paper in the first place was a huge step, and it's only been a few weeks."

"I know, you're absolutely right. But I've been thinking about it anyway . . . wanting it. Trying to figure a way to make it work. My ambitions have become greedy and unrealistic, just because of him. When I was a librarian, I never had these kinds of ambitions. I just loved my work. If they hadn't practically fired me, I'd still be perfectly content stacking books and doing research."

"They didn't fire you. You quit."

"Only because they were unhappy with my work." She slid down from the rail and turned around, looking out at the water. "But that's beside the point. What is wrong with me, listening to that guy? He also told me that Cade and I would get married, and now I've been picturing myself walking down the aisle, impatient about our relationship . . . I keep thinking about when he's going to propose, like it's some kind of destiny and he's just not getting with the program. For all I know, he may not feel that way about me. We haven't made any commitments or even talked about our feelings."

"Blair, you've only been dating for a little over a month. It's not time. There are steps you have to go through. You can't just jump straight to the wedding. This kind of thing can't be short-circuited—not unless you're both ready."

"Exactly," Blair said. "And rushing things is not Cade's style, and it's not mine, either. Instead of shopping for wedding gowns I need to just enjoy the way things are developing now. But these ambitions—these crazy hopes and dreams—are making me crazy. If it weren't for Carson, I never would have been thinking this way—and that's why I'm so upset. How is it that he affected me that way?"

"Well, it probably has something to do with your listening to him in the first place. The Bible says somewhere that the pagans listen to those who practice witchcraft and to diviners, but you—meaning believers—are not allowed to."

"It's Deuteronomy 18," Blair said. "I read it. Didn't sink in, though, apparently. And the really sick thing is that I caught Sheila getting a reading, and I acted all shocked and judgmental, and then Carson made it sound like he had read my palm too. Boy, did that make her smug."

"Oh, no."

"Yeah. Only, for the record, he did not read my palm. I didn't ask for his predictions and didn't want them. But she thinks I went to him for that. And as much as he affected me, I might as well have." Tears sprang to her eyes again. "I'm no better than her, and she knows it. Morgan, I'm so sorry."

Morgan shook her head and pushed Blair's hair out of her eyes. "Sheila has a lot of problems. You're not the cause of them, Blair."

"It's just that I hate myself for falling for it." She swallowed back the tears in her throat, and looked at her sister. "Morgan, do you remember when we were little, and Mama would wake us up and walk us through 'putting on' our helmet of salvation, our belt of truth . . ."

Morgan nodded. "Our breastplate of righteousness, and our shoes of peace."

Blair smiled. "When we headed out the door to school, she would hand us our shields of faith and our swords of the spirit, like she expected us to run into some angry fallen angels on the way to the bus."

Morgan laughed. "And you would use that imaginary sword to stab me and throw your invisible shield like a Frisbee."

"I'd forgotten that." She laughed softly, but then her amusement faded. "Guess I never took it all that seriously, but it never made sense to me. I might as well have been putting on an imaginary crown and fairy wings. But now I see that I need that armor. Our struggle is not against flesh and blood. It's against the rulers and principalities. Apparently even against the psychics."

"That's right," Morgan said. "Mama knew what she was talking about."

"But I still don't understand how you get it. The only armor I have lying around is the imaginary kind. No pretend armor is going to stop the enemy's arrows. It certainly didn't help me against Carson."

Morgan looked surprised that she would ask such a thing. "Sis, you do have the armor. But maybe it's just weak. Look at it piece by piece. The helmet of salvation—you got that the minute you gave your life to Christ. You don't have to pretend to put some imaginary steel cap on your head in the mornings. It's already there."

Blair thought about that for a moment. "Okay, I'll buy that, but what about the rest? The belt of truth, for instance. I sure didn't know truth when Carson was telling me what I wanted to hear."

"The truth is in God's Word. You get it from studying it, learning it, knowing what it says. Not whipping it out of some pretend closet."

"I guess that's the problem. I don't know the Bible that well, and even since I became a Christian, I haven't spent that much time reading it."

"That's easy to change. As for your breastplate, you do have that protection, because you exchanged your sin for Christ's righteousness . . . and your shoes of the gospel of peace—"

"They don't fit very well," Blair cut in. "Because my peace quotient is low. All I've had lately is anxiety and discontent. How can I take peace to anyone else when I'm in such a mess?"

"Again, you study God's Word, make it a part of you. But the shoes are about spreading the Word, telling others about the peace you've found. You have something they need."

"So what about the shield of faith? How do I strengthen mine?"

"You have to feed it the things that make it grow stronger. Again, you have to study God's Word as if it were your very lifeline. Because it is."

Blair looked out across the water and saw that the clouds were starting to break up, revealing a fissure of bright blue sky. Morgan was so wise. Blair knew she was right, that the armor was there for her taking, if only she spent time learning God's Word and getting to know him better.

"Okay, so I'm protected if I do that. But what about the sword? It's the only offensive weapon, but I don't feel like I'm any threat at all to the enemy."

"As you get to know the Word of God, front to back, layer upon layer—hunger for it, breathe it—that sword will get sharper and more effective. If you don't arm yourself with God's Word, it's about as effective as that imaginary one you used to poke me with."

Blair felt hope seeping back into her heart. Maybe all wasn't lost. "But then why did Mama wake us with that every morning? Like it was something we could do that day?"

"She wanted to remind us what we had, and maybe she assumed that we were more spiritually mature than we were, that our weapons and armor were ready. But the truth is, you have to build up those weapons before you need them, so you'll be ready when you're face-to-face with someone like Carson Graham."

"You're right. I was unarmed with him. Completely unequipped." She looked down at the waves crashing past the posts. "I guess occasional curiosity about something in the Bible doesn't cut it, huh? And neither does regurgitating what someone else told me. Not even if I hear it from you or Jonathan, or even Cade."

"You're getting it, Sis. It's a hands-on project, and you're responsible to keep your armor in good condition. You're a member of God's army, and that's what a good soldier does."

She deserved a court-martial, a dishonorable discharge, or maybe even a firing squad. "That does it. I'm not going to be found unarmed again. The next time the Devil tries to attack me, he's gonna have a real fight on his hands." She considered her sister for a long moment. "Maybe I need to be in the Hanover House program. Your graduates come out more grounded in their faith than I am."

"God's growing you, Blair, and you're letting him. You're not kicking against the goads, like Sheila."

Blair realized she'd been mouthing off about her own problems when her sister was hurting. She settled her eyes on Morgan. "What are you going to do?"

Morgan's tears filled her eyes again. "I don't know. I honestly don't. But please pray for me—and for Caleb and Sadie. God's worked miracles in our lives before. We could use another one, right about now."

CHAPTER
64

*A*lan Sims was in much better shape than he'd been in the last time Cade had interviewed him. Cade and McCormick found him at home. Though it still looked cluttered, it was cleaner than it had been just after Lisa's death.

"No, I didn't see Lisa the day she disappeared. I told you she canceled that appointment."

"One of your patients told us that she saw Lisa come into your office that morning."

Sims looked startled. "That morning? No, it couldn't be. I wasn't working that morning."

"That's what she said," Cade went on. "They told her you were off, and she left. She said Lisa looked angry and upset and that she was intent on speaking to you. You sure she didn't come to find you?"

Sims huffed and poked his chin in the air. "*Quite* sure. As I said, I would have told you something like that."

"Dr. Sims, what were you doing the morning Lisa Jackson disappeared?"

"I was here, puttering around in my yard. My wife went to Europe for a month, and I've been building her a fountain in the backyard to surprise her. Would you like to see it?"

Cade looked at McCormick, and the detective got up. "I would. I've thought of building one of those myself."

Cade knew his detective wanted a look at more of the house, the back door, the yard, anything that might offer him a clue.

Sims led them out and showed them the finished fountain. There was no way to tell when it was built, though it did appear new.

"Was anyone with you that morning?"

"No. My maid, Kylie, had already taken the day off. Up and quit after that. I was here alone and kind of enjoying it."

"Did anyone see you at any time that morning? Did you talk to anyone on the phone?"

"Yes, my office called a couple of times, but I didn't leave the house until about noon."

"When your office called, did they tell you that Lisa had come in looking for you?"

"Of course not." He led them back in. "I get angry patients in all the time. They go ballistic when they start their menstrual cycles after they hoped they were pregnant. Talk about PMS. You haven't seen the half of it until you've worked with angry, hormonal, infertile women."

Cade knew the doctor expected him to laugh, but he couldn't bring himself to do it. He wished he could nail him with questions about Lisa's second opinion, about the results that suggested he was a fraud. But he couldn't. Not yet. He couldn't risk having him go back to the office and start destroying evidence.

"They certainly don't notify me of every one of them. Besides, they knew I was seeing her that afternoon. Whatever she came to see me about could have waited."

"Don't you find it odd that she would have come in that morning when she could have waited until her appointment?" McCormick asked. "Sort of sounds urgent, doesn't it?"

He rubbed his jaw and nodded his head. "Yes, it does. I wish I'd had the chance to find out what it was about. But I didn't, officers. I didn't."

Later, Cade and McCormick sat at their desks and conducted phone interviews with patients who'd been to Sims' office the day of Lisa's death. So far, only the woman Morgan met in the office claimed to have seen her that morning. The receptionist and all of the nurses had denied seeing her. Either Sims had warned them to lie, or it hadn't really happened.

After he'd talked to a dozen or so women, he hung up and studied his notes. McCormick stuck his head in Cade's office. "Have you gotten anything yet, Chief?"

"Nothing to work with. You?"

McCormick looked down at his own list. "Afraid not, and everybody I'm talking to thinks this doctor hung the moon. You wouldn't believe the loyalty."

"Well, who can blame them? A lot of these women have invested a number of their biological years in this man. To admit that he may have cheated them would be admitting they had wasted a lot of time and money."

"You don't think this guy's *responsible* for their infertility, do you?"

Cade shook his head. "Who knows? Maybe he's just in the business of giving false hope. Or maybe he doesn't lie to all of them. Maybe it's just a select few."

"What a sleazeball."

Cade picked up his phone again. "The DA is considering subpoenaing his office for his patient files. He's reluctant to do it until we can come up with a little more evidence. Before he shuts the guy down, he wants a smoking gun."

"Let's hope we can find one before he uses it again."

CHAPTER

65

Sheila took advantage of Caleb's nap time to make some phone calls. Since Jonathan and Morgan were still at the Pier, and Karen was lying down while Emory napped, she knew she wouldn't get caught if she slipped into that master bedroom that no one used and called her friends in Atlanta.

She closed the door quietly behind her. Sadie had told her this was the bedroom of Morgan's parents who had been murdered less than a year ago. The family had left it like a shrine, with all their belongings still in place. It was downright creepy, but it had a telephone.

Sheila sat down on the bed and dialed her best friend in Atlanta.

"Hello?"

"Marlene!" She kept her voice low. "You'll never guess who this is."

Marlene paused for a moment. "Sheila, is that you?"

"Yes, it's me. I'm out of jail. Can you believe it? They let me out early. Some law by the legislature. Whoever thought those people were good for anything?"

Marlene gave a hoarse victory yell. "Well, when are you coming home, kid?"

"That's just it. I'm not. I had to come to Cape Refuge to be with Sadie and Caleb. I'm staying in a home that's almost like a prison itself. I really miss you guys. What's going on there?"

"I've got a new guy," Marlene said. "His name's Harley, and he moved in with me last week. I'm glad you're not here. You'd probably steal him from me."

"Well, why don't you bring him east and let me check him out? I could use some company, and you could probably use a little beach time."

"We might do that," Marlene said, "only I'm working weekends now and most nights. Harley had a good job, but he got laid off a couple of weeks ago. I'm trying to keep us both above water."

It sounded like a typical scenario. The men in Marlene's life—Sheila's too, for that matter—had always had trouble holding jobs. "Man, I'd give anything to come home."

"Hey, if you do, you can stay with me. I can clean out the back room. It'll be just like old times."

"What about Sadie and Caleb? I can't leave without them."

"Hey, we can work it out. I love babies." She'd had three of her own, but two had been removed from her home and the other one lived with his no-account father.

The door opened, and Sheila jumped. Morgan stepped into the room, staring at her as if she'd caught her stealing from her purse.

"What are you doing in here?"

Sheila dropped the phone. "I just wanted to see what was in here." She fumbled for the phone, then quickly hung it up. "It's a nice room. Why doesn't anybody ever use it?"

Pain flashed across Morgan's eyes. "It's off limits, that's why. I don't want anybody in here."

"Okay, okay." Sheila got up and started to the door.

"You were on the telephone."

Here it came. Sheila stopped in the doorway. "Yeah? So?"

"Sheila, you're allowed to make local calls, and we have phones all over the house. Why did you come in here to make a call?"

"Because I wanted my privacy."

Morgan picked up the phone, pressed redial, and read the readout. "Privacy to make a long distance call to Atlanta?" She hung the phone back in its cradle.

"I just wanted to talk to my friend."

Morgan struggled with tears in her eyes. Sheila couldn't imagine why. Was this just a battle of wills? Morgan hated losing that much?

"This was my parents' room." Her voice rasped as she got the words out. "I don't like for anybody to come in here except family."

Sheila didn't know why that stung her. Sadie had talked so much about Hanover House being a family, but she had known it couldn't be true. People didn't treat strangers like family. Especially not people like her.

"I've had a hard time with their deaths," Morgan whispered. "I want . . . I need . . . to leave things in here exactly as they left them. It gives me comfort."

Sheila didn't want to see Morgan's grief. It was better if she kept her distance. She started toward the door.

"Sheila, the home is supported by donations and the money that Jonathan makes on his fishing tours. We barely make ends meet as it is. We can't afford long distance bills for the residents."

"Then add it to my list of broken rules and throw me out. My friend says I can come and live with her. She has a room for me, and Sadie and Caleb will be happy there. The more I think about it, the more I think it's a really good idea."

Morgan just stared at her. "Sheila, why are you so hostile?"

"Hostile? *Me?* You're the one riding me about everything."

Morgan sat down on the bed and started to cry. "I'm begging you, please don't do this to Caleb and Sadie."

"I'm not doing anything to them except clearing their heads! You've brainwashed them both. If I get them out of here, it might be the best thing that ever happened to them."

"What are you doing, Mom?"

Sheila swung around and saw Sadie standing in the doorway. How much had she heard?

"I was just having a few words with Morgan." She left the room and headed for her bedroom. Grabbing the bag she'd brought from jail, she pulled open her dresser drawers and started packing. There wasn't much, since even the clothes on her back were borrowed. Sadie came in behind her. "I've decided I'm leaving here. I've had enough. Marlene says we can move in with her. All I have to do is call her and tell her to clean out the back room. Pack your stuff."

She looked over her shoulder at Sadie, and saw that she was crying now too. She softened. "Honey, it'll be fun. You remember Marlene, all the times we used to have."

"I won't go with you, Mom. I'm staying here."

Sheila stopped packing and turned back to her. "How can you say that? After all this time that I've been in jail, not able to see you . . . ? Are you trying to break my heart?"

"No. I'm trying to change it."

"Well, you can't change me! There's nothing wrong with me. I know what you're afraid of. You think I'm going to go back to drugs, but I'm not, Sadie. I'm stronger now. I've been sober all this time, and I know I can do it."

"You knew you could do it last time too, Mom, only you didn't. Jack came along and he ruined you, and you wound up in jail." She smeared the tears across her face. "You can go, if you have to, Mom, but you'll go alone. I won't let you take Caleb."

Sheila stood stiffer now, facing off with her. "You can't stop me, Sadie. He's my son."

"That's right!" Sadie cried. "He's your *son*. Be a mother to him! I'm asking you to put his welfare first. It's not good for him to move in with Marlene and her boyfriend-of-the-week and her drugs, and you know it. If you cared about him, you wouldn't even *think* of it."

Sheila felt as she had in jail when someone had waltzed into her cell and stolen her hard-earned commissary items. "You have no right to talk to me that way. After all I've been through, the sacrifices I've made."

"The only sacrifices you've made have been forced on you," Sadie cried. "They've been because you were backed into a corner and you had no choices. You *have* choices now, Mom. You can do the right thing for Caleb. I'm old enough to make my own decisions, and I don't have to go with you. But so help me, if you take Caleb out of here and disrupt his life, you'll never see me again."

Sheila gaped at her. "You would turn your back on your mother and your little brother?"

"I wouldn't want to, Mom, but you've got to think about what you're doing. He's just a baby. He's seen some hard times, but he doesn't even remember them because the last few months have been so good. He doesn't need to go to some place where the people can't be trusted and he can't have any peace. He loves Morgan and Jonathan, and he loves me, and he doesn't even *know* you anymore!"

The words stung like the bite of a viper. "Sadie . . ."

Her daughter could hardly speak through her sobs. "I know it hurts to hear that, Mom, but it's true. You can't say you love him if you're going to take him out of this home. It would be a lie. I'm asking you to do the right thing. The hard thing. I want you to stay, but if you can't do that, leave him here. If you don't, you can quit calling me your daughter, because I don't want to have anything to do with you!"

The words slammed hard into Sheila's heart, almost knocking her back. She watched her daughter turn and run back down the stairs. The front door slammed. She looked out her window and saw Sadie running across the street to the beach, sobbing her heart out.

It only made her angry.

"You really gonna leave?"

She swung around and saw Karen standing in her doorway, her arms crossed.

Sheila wiped her face. "What's it to you?"

Karen came in, looked at the bag she'd been packing. "I'll tell you what it is to me. When I got out of jail I wanted to do the same thing. I had the choice of coming here or going back to the old neighborhood. I decided to go back. Wound up moving back in with my boyfriend, and every night he got high and slapped me around."

Sheila had been there. She hadn't forgotten what that was like.

"And then I went and got pregnant." Karen sat down on her bed. "And I kept telling myself that he was gonna change, because I was having his baby and he was gonna care. Only he had a few other women, and some of them had babies, too. One of them had her baby before me. She had to go back to work two weeks after the baby was born because he wasn't about to support her."

"Why are you telling me this? I didn't ask you to come in here."

"She left her baby with him while she went to work, Sheila. The baby was two weeks old when he took him on a drug deal with him, and somebody hurt him. That night he had a seizure, and his mama took him to the hospital. He had a cracked skull."

Sheila didn't want to hear this. It sounded too familiar. She thought of Sadie's broken ribs, her broken arm, the bruises on her face.

"That's when I knew my baby wasn't gonna make it if I stayed there. I had to make a choice, just like you have to make now. I decided to do what was best for my baby and get him out of that environment before he was even born. I showed up here nine months pregnant, begging them to take me in, and they did. The minute I gave my life back to God and started letting him call the shots, things turned around for me."

Sheila didn't want to keep crying in front of this woman she hardly knew. She turned back to the window and peered out. Sadie was long out of sight.

"It could happen to you, too. But if you choose to be stupid like I was stupid and go back to the place you came from—the same place that got your family torn apart and you thrown in jail—then you deserve to lose your daughter and your baby."

"How *dare* you?" Sheila bit out the words. "You don't know me."

"Oh, I know you. I know you because you're just like me. You could take Caleb out of here and back to that neighborhood. But you better know he's gonna grow up just like you—shooting up, snorting, beating women . . . in and out of jail. You need to decide if it's worth it."

Sheila jerked up the bag and shoved the rest of her things into it.

Karen got up, touched her shoulder, and made Sheila look at her. "Sheila, you do the right thing for your kids, and you'll be doing the right thing for you, too. You need to look at your sins, girl. You need to repent and thank God that he's stepped in as much as he has to break that cycle for your babies."

Sheila just gritted her teeth. "Get out of my way." She threw the bag aside and bolted out of the room. Morgan stood at the top of the stairs, and Sheila knew she'd heard everything. Sheila pushed past her and went down the stairs and out the front door.

CHAPTER

66

*F*ury propelled Sheila across the street and down the beach. Sadie was nowhere in sight, so she strode as fast as she could on the sand, cursing under her breath and replaying those conversations in her mind. Who did these people think they were? How did they know she couldn't do the right thing? How in the world could they anticipate the way she would bring up her child? They barely knew her.

The sun bore down on her, making her sweat. Summer was closing in. She wished she could move up north, where the summers were dry and cool. She could get a little house in the mountains and start over. All she had to do was work a while in Atlanta and she could make it happen.

She lifted her hair from her neck and slogged through the sand. The beach was four miles long, and she walked all the way down it, then up along the river. She was soaked and breathing hard as she went past the Bull Bridge.

She wasn't going to find her daughter.

But maybe that was best.

After all, she was letting her down again. She knew it from the depths of her heart, but she felt powerless to change it. She couldn't stay here. It was out of the question.

She walked and walked, hating herself more with each step. It would have been better for everyone if she'd stayed in jail. Her daughter had been settled, well adjusted, until she'd come back. Caleb couldn't have been healthier or happier.

If she went back to Atlanta, would she do what Karen predicted? Would she fall back into the habit of using again, bringing men home, letting them ruin her life again? Was that her nature? She didn't want to believe it, yet she knew it was true.

Sadie was right. How had her daughter gotten her head screwed on so straight? She thought about that day that Sadie came to see her in jail, with her arm broken and her eye swollen shut. Jack had beaten her, and she'd barely escaped.

Sheila felt so helpless and so frightened for her baby, still in Jack's care. She'd told Sadie to run, to get as far from him as she could.

That's how Sadie wound up in Cape Refuge.

Sheila had moments of repentance in jail. She went to religious counseling and talked the talk. She had even meant it at times. From inside her cell, she'd had clarity of mind and had seen the provisions that had been made for her children. She'd even been thankful.

Why now did she feel so angry, so out of control, so oppressed? After all this time, why couldn't she get Atlanta out of her mind? Why couldn't she let herself start over?

It would be so simple just to follow the rules and be there for her children, but she didn't know if she had the character to be what they expected her to be.

She followed the river through the trees, hoping Sadie had not come back here. It was near the place where that Jackson woman had been found. Sadie had shown it to her yesterday. She came to the flowers placed at the sight where the woman's car had gone in.

She paused for a moment, noting the tire tracks in the grass and trying to picture where the car had plunged into the water. It didn't look like a place of death. She'd seen places that did—crack houses and dirty hotel rooms and the alleys behind the strip clubs.

She'd kicked her crack habit once, when Sadie was a little girl, but when she'd started to gain weight, she'd changed her drug of choice to methamphetamine. That led her to Jack, a dealer with a lab, and she allowed him to come into her home and set up shop there.

What had she been thinking?

She stood at the edge of the water, staring down into it, and suddenly the reality of that horrible decision washed over her again—the shame that she felt when she was arrested in front of her daughter and taken off in handcuffs, the screams of her baby as she was driven away.

Her mother was an alcoholic, so Sheila always consoled herself with the idea that addiction was a family disease and she had no control over it. But the truth was that selfishness had more to do with her addiction than genes. She cared more about her drugs than she cared about her children.

That wasn't who she wanted to be.

She stared down the bank into the water. If she were to jump in right now, plummet straight to the bottom, Sadie would be the only one to mourn her passing.

She wanted to be a person people would miss when she was gone, someone for whom they would bring flowers, someone who left a legacy of good things and not bad.

But that was never going to be who she was. Maybe throwing herself in the river would be the noblest act she'd ever done. Though they'd probably never say it out loud, they'd probably secretly thank God that she wasn't causing problems anymore.

She stared at the water as it rushed by to join the sea. She wondered what it felt like to jump in. It was probably warm enough, and the river rushed fast and hard enough to keep her from changing her mind and struggling back to the bank. No, if she did it, she needed to make sure it worked. Her cowardice could be no excuse for living.

She thought of the water closing over her head, fighting to catch her breath as the current swept her down river and then out to sea. Would a shark come along and end things quickly? Would they think she'd run away, until her body washed up several days later?

No, that was no better for Sadie than going to Atlanta.

She stepped back from the river's edge and wiped the tears from her face. What had Karen said, about her having a choice? She'd said there was nothing noble about snatching Caleb and going back to Atlanta. She'd probably say there was nothing noble about making your daughter suffer through a suicide, especially after they'd exchanged harsh words, either. Sadie would blame herself. It would change the rest of her life. Nothing good could come of it.

What Karen was doing was noble—coming here and committing herself to starting a new life for the sake of her little baby. And now she was planning her wedding. Maybe the prison chaplain had been right. Maybe there were blessings in living right.

Breaking her daughter's heart for the hundredth time in her life was not noble. Staying here and submitting to Jonathan and Morgan's authority would be. The sacrifice would be theirs, not hers.

They'd offered her a life, a second chance, a new beginning. She'd thrown it back in their faces.

Her mind sorted through the possibilities. If she went back, begged their forgiveness, promised Sadie she would do better . . . would they let her stay? Or were they already making plans to throw her out?

She heard a screen door slam and looked up to the pier just around the bend of the river. There must be a house hidden in the trees there.

Then she saw him, coming through the trees, walking the path straight toward her.

Carson Graham.

He looked startled when he saw her standing there. She started to speak, but then she heard a woman's voice. "Carson! You forgot your wallet!"

He turned back, and Sheila saw a pretty blonde woman hurrying out to meet him. She handed him his wallet, then reached up to kiss him. Carson pulled back and nodded toward Sheila. The woman jumped away, then hurried back into the house. Carson followed her.

Was he fooling around? He'd told her that he lived in that Palm Reading house, and at the beach she could have sworn that his wife was a brunette.

It wasn't surprising that he'd have an affair. He'd certainly put out the signals with her, and she hadn't dissuaded him. In fact, she had told him to call her, even though she knew he wasn't single.

It didn't matter. Carson Graham's fidelity wasn't her concern. She had enough problems of her own.

She left the river to keep from walking through that yard, and followed the road back to Hanover House. Her feet hurt and she needed water. She hadn't meant to walk so far.

She'd been gone for over two hours by the time she made it back to Hanover House. She walked into the house and found everyone seated around the kitchen table. Sadie was home, but her eyes were swollen, and disappointment seemed etched into her young face.

It was an awful sight, that disappointment. That acceptance that her mother was a loser. Sheila wanted to erase that from her face.

They all looked up at her. They were angry, and she couldn't blame them for it anymore.

Caleb sat in his highchair between Morgan and Jonathan, feeding himself with a spoon. He was the only one who didn't look at her as if bracing himself. Instead, he ignored her, as if she had nothing to do with him.

Sheila drew a deep breath. "I used to think that all the bad things in my life were other people's fault, and I guess I blamed everybody but myself. But it's no one else's fault. It's just mine. I'm the one who's failed myself. I'm the one who's failed my children."

It clearly wasn't what they'd expected her to say. She went around the table to Sadie. Her daughter looked up at her, tears streaming from her red eyes. Sheila's mouth trembled. "Honey, I'm so sorry that I've broken your heart so many times. You don't deserve it. If you'll give me another chance, I'll do better. I promise."

Sadie just looked at her as if she'd heard this before, and Sheila knew she would have to prove it. She turned to Morgan and Jonathan.

"Morgan and Jonathan . . ." She looked away, ashamed to meet their eyes. "I made up my mind in jail that when I got out I was gonna be somebody. I was gonna turn my life around and start taking care of my children. But the fact is, Morgan, you take a lot better care of my children than I do, and I've been having a hard time with that."

Morgan sighed and looked at Jonathan. "Sheila, I appreciate your saying that. I know it's not easy."

"No, it's not easy, but it should be. I mean, why is it so hard for me to admit things? I ought to be down on my knees, thanking you."

Jonathan got up and stepped toward her. "Sheila, why don't we start over? If you'll commit to our program and stop seeing us as the enemy, then we'd love for you to stay."

A sob caught in her throat, and she covered her mouth. "I promise. Thank you."

"All right then. Welcome back."

Morgan got up and hugged her, and she wept against her shoulder. How could Morgan stand to hold her after the way she'd spoken to her, the things she'd said?

But Morgan wasn't like anyone else she'd ever known.

Sheila went to Sadie, touched her shoulder. "Will you forgive me, honey?"

Sadie was crying so hard she could hardly speak. She got up too, and came to put her arms around her mother. Sheila clung longer than she needed to. She almost didn't dare let her go. Sadie felt so small in her arms, so vulnerable, so broken. She swore to herself—and to God—that she would never hurt her again.

CHAPTER

67

"Curiouser and curiouser." McCormick came into Cade's office and sat down. "Another twist in this continuing saga."

Cade didn't need another twist. He'd been too busy trying to untwist the things they already knew. "All right. Let's hear it."

"We've got a match on the handwriting. Sam Sullivan wrote the letters to Lisa Jackson, all right, and his prints were all over them. He tried to disguise his handwriting, but the analyst says that it's definitely his."

Cade laced his fingers in front of his face. He couldn't say he was surprised. After all, he'd had enough suspicion to give Sam's sample to the analyst. Sam had been bonded for his work, so his prints had already been in the system.

"Okay, so we have Sam Sullivan, Jackson's opponent in the race, stirring up trouble for the front-runner. I guess the question is, how far was he willing to go? There are miles between mail fraud and murder."

"You want to come with me to question him?"

Cade thought that over for a moment. "No, I'd rather you picked him up and brought him in for questioning. That'll be better than getting his whole office involved. Meanwhile, I'll get on the phone with the DA and see about getting an arrest warrant for mail fraud. Anything to hold him."

Half an hour later, they brought Sam in, still wearing the Hawaiian shirt he'd had on during the debate that morning. His neck and face were sunburned after a full day of campaigning door-to-door. He announced that he didn't know what this was about, but he wasn't saying a word until his lawyer joined him. Sam clearly knew that he'd been found out—but just how deep did his guilt run?

His lawyer, Richard Mason from Savannah, got there an hour later, and they all assembled in the interview room, as if they were sitting down to negotiate a deal.

"What's this all about, Cade?" Sullivan demanded.

Cade pulled out the letters that had been sent to Lisa Jackson. "Sam, have you ever seen these?"

Sam glanced at his lawyer. A thin sheen of perspiration glistened on his lip. "No, I haven't. What are they?"

"They're letters that were sent to Lisa from someone who claimed to be Ben's lover."

Sam wiped his mouth. "So the rumors were true?"

Cade didn't answer. "Sam, your fingerprints are on these letters, and we have it on good authority that they're in your handwriting."

"No way!" Sam got to his feet and looked at his lawyer. "Why would I do a thing like that?"

Cade didn't move. "Sit down, Sam. Tell us where you were on the morning of May 16."

"Oh, you've got to be kidding me!"

His attorney touched his arm to silence him. "Chief, I'd rather my client didn't answer that until I've had the chance to confer with him."

Sam slapped his hand on the table. "No, I'll answer it. I have nothing to hide, Cade. I was in my office on the morning of May 16, and my secretary and a dozen others can vouch for it. In fact, that was the morning I had the cell phone people in." A sweat drop ran from his hairline to his jaw. "You gotta believe me, Cade."

"We'll talk to them, and if it's true, we'll find out. But for now, I'd like to know how you explain those letters."

His lawyer tried to silence him again, but Sam shook him off. "If I don't talk, they're going to think I'm guilty of murder!" He rubbed the sweat off of his mouth and took a deep breath. "Okay, Cade. I'm gonna lay all my cards on the table, because I don't need a murder rap. I did something stupid, but not *murder*. I sent the letters, okay? I admit it."

Cade met McCormick's eyes. Now they were getting somewhere.

"It was a lousy thing to do, I admit. I was trying to get a leg up in the race. I thought if I stirred up a little trouble in paradise, that might knock Ben's legs out from under him. If I'd known that Lisa was gonna wind up dead, I never would have done it. It was unethical, but it wasn't criminal."

"Ever heard of mail fraud?" Cade asked. "How about harassment?"

McCormick agreed. "How about murder one? Lining up things to make it look like Ben had a motive for killing his wife."

"I wouldn't be that stupid!" Sam sat back down and made an effort to calm himself. "I just wanted to start a rumor to sway opinion. I approached Vince Barr and tried to get him to write about it, but he wouldn't. Said he wasn't interested in local politics—and the *Savannah Morning News* wouldn't print it because they couldn't confirm it. I knew better than to approach Blair Owens with it. I never expected police involvement. If there hadn't been a murder, this would have been a harmless prank."

"A prank that might have broken up a marriage and ruined a man's life," Cade said.

McCormick chuckled. "And you didn't have much faith in the police department, did you, Sam? This Podunk outfit couldn't figure out anything that complicated."

"Oh, boy." Sam sat back hard in his chair. Despite his tanning-bed tan, he was beginning to pale. "Cade, I know you don't have good feelings toward me, after all I've said about you during the race, but so help me, if you try to pin this murder on me, I'll scream harassment so loud that they'll hear it all the way in Atlanta."

Cade leaned his elbows on the table and leveled his eyes on him. "That sounds like a threat, Sam."

Sam backed off. "That's not how I meant it, Cade. I'm just saying that people might *perceive* it wrong."

"They might perceive it right," McCormick said, "and then where would you be?"

When they'd finished questioning Sam, Cade realized holding him would invite accusations that Cade had worked things so Jonathan would win the election. If he let him go, they could keep an eye on him until they could corroborate his alibi. Cade watched Sam drive off with his attorney.

McCormick shook his head. "What a guy."

Cade looked around at the other cops in the squad room. They all watched him for a rundown of what they'd found out. "McCormick, I want you to check out Sullivan's alibi with every person he claims he saw that morning. Check his phone records, see who called him. Johnson, Caldwell, you interview everybody who talked to him, see if they spoke to him personally. I want this done before you go home tonight."

"So he did send the letters?" Caldwell asked him.

"Yeah, he sent them. He confessed to that much."

"You think he's the killer, Chief?" Johnson asked.

"He's got an alibi. We just have to see if it's real. At best, he's a scumbag who would lie and cheat to win an election. At worst, he's a murderer."

McCormick rubbed his hand over his bald head. "I say we leak it to the press. Let the voters know who they're dealing with before the election Tuesday."

"He's got a point, Chief," Johnson said.

Cade stared out the window. It was a temptation. A sure win for Jonathan. A way to ensure he kept his job. Didn't the voters have the right to know? Wasn't it critical information?

The room seemed to go quiet. The printers stopped printing, the radio ceased to crackle, the air-conditioner cycled off. Everyone waited for an answer.

"Hear me and hear me good, every one of you," Cade said. "Every bit of evidence we've uncovered is part of a criminal investigation. We don't do leaks, not in my department. If I hear of any, trust me, I'll find out who did it, and your career in law enforcement will be a thing of the past. Any questions?"

There weren't any.

"Good. Now get on it."

CHAPTER

68

The Sunday morning crowd for the Church on the Dock had already assembled as Cade pulled into the small parking lot. He'd thought of missing church again today, since there was still so much pressing business in the investigation, but it was the Lord's Day and he needed to worship.

He got out of his truck and heard the sound of believers' voices lifting in song. His spirit quickened, and he felt instant relief and power . . . a filling up . . . a drawing in.

He went in and saw that the pews were full. Dock workers and transient sailors sat among the longtime members, offering their sacrifices of praise.

And Vince Barr, the illustrious tabloid reporter and recent television star, was there among them. Cade knew he wasn't there to worship or seek the Lord. He was, no doubt, looking for more trouble to stir up, more rumors, more yarns to spin on his next television appearance, things that would keep the national media focused on him and his investigation.

Cade thought of leaving, but he wouldn't let that guy hinder his worship.

There was an empty seat beside Blair. Her eyes were closed as she sang to the Lord. He didn't want to disrupt her focus or distract her, so he waited at the back of the room until the song was finished. Then he slipped in beside her.

She smiled up at him, and his heart warmed.

Jonathan led them from the praise chorus into a hymn that filled Cade with comfort and reminded him of the joy of his salvation.

He was glad he had taken the time to come.

He'd half expected Jonathan to mention Tuesday's election, contend for the vote of the people in that room. But he never brought it up. He had to hand it to him. His friend would campaign outside of these walls, but this hour was only for the Lord.

When the service was over, Cade felt equipped to go back to the investigation.

Blair smiled. "Did you see our *Observer* friend?"

Cade shot him a look. He was already talking to some of the members in the corner. "Yeah, I saw him."

"At least he came to church."

"You think he learned anything?" Cade asked without hope.

"Nothing he could use to get on CNN." She looked back at Cade. "Want to get a bite to eat?"

He shook his head. "Better not. There's too much going on."

"Anything you want to share?" She grinned.

He matched it. "Can't think of anything."

"How about why Sam Sullivan was taken into the police station last night?"

His smile faded. "Blair, you know we've been interviewing everybody."

"Everybody didn't feel the need to get a lawyer."

Cade breathed a laugh. "This town. Nothing is sacred. Give it up, Blair. You know you're barking up the wrong tree."

"Just tell me if the handwriting matched his."

He leaned down, putting his face close to hers. "If I have something to say about this investigation, I'll call a press conference—and you'll get the first question."

Her grin crept back across her face. "All right, Cade. You win. Guess I'll go eat at Hanover House and figure it out for myself."

He watched her leave, then looked back toward the front of the chapel. Jonathan looked tired. Cade waited until Vince had followed some chatty resident out, and most of the congregation had left, then he approached his best friend. "How you doing, man?"

Jonathan sighed. "Okay. How about you?"

"Been kind of busy."

"Glad you were able to make it today."

"Me too. Your sermon was inspired, Jonathan. I don't know how you do it. So how's the campaigning going?"

Jonathan looked around. A few members still stood across the room, and Morgan was apparently introducing Sheila. "Let's talk outside."

"Sure." Cade followed him out to the boardwalk behind the warehouse, and Jonathan sat down on the bench that looked out over the river. He leaned his elbows on his knees, and his shoulders slumped, like they carried too much weight.

"What's up, buddy?"

"It's the election," Jonathan said. "Cade, I owe you an apology."

"For what?"

"For losing."

Cade grunted. "Jonathan, it's not Tuesday yet."

"No, but I can see the writing on the wall." Jonathan leaned down and picked up a stick from the planks and threw it into the water. "Sam Sullivan's the favorite. Mr. Cell Phone hero himself. I let you down, man. I'm really sorry."

"What do you mean, you let me down? Why would you say that?"

"Because if Sullivan wins the election, you're probably going to lose your job. I hate that for you, Cade. It's flat-out wrong."

Cade sat down beside him and looked out over the water. "I haven't sent out resumés yet, Jonathan. Don't give up. Things could turn around."

"That's easy to say now, but what are you going to do if he wins?"

"Deal with it, I guess." Cade squinted in the sunlight. "He's not going to fire me until I solve this crime, but I guess in a way a vote for him is a vote against me. Maybe it is time I moved on, if that's what the people want."

"You've got it all wrong, Cade. A vote for Sam is a vote for cell phones. It's as simple as that, I think."

"Hey, it's not like he's going to kill the deal for the phones if he loses the election. It's not one or the other."

"Yeah, well. I have two more days to get that word out."

Cade wished he could resolve this case in time for election day. It could only help. He thought about Sam's duplicity, his deceit, his cruel scheme to hijack the election. All he had to do was drop the secret to one person . . .

But that wasn't how he did business.

"I'll pray for you, buddy," he said, "if you keep praying for me. It's all in God's hands."

Jonathan couldn't argue with that.

CHAPTER

69

*E*lection day was grueling. Morgan and Jonathan had campaigned all day, standing in the hot sun with signs that made one last plea as voters drove down the road to the polling booths at the church gyms. Blair and Sadie had been manning both voting centers for the newspaper, polling people as they came out.

Blair conveyed to Morgan around midafternoon that the news might not be good. It was way too close and could go either way.

Still, Morgan had a party to throw that night. They'd invited dozens of people who had helped with the campaign to come and wait for the results. Melba Jefferson had done all the cooking, and hors d'oeuvres were passed around the house with abundance. Madelyn Short played piano in the corner, singing patriotic tunes, as if this were a national election. Several children raced through the house, balloons flying behind them. Everyone was in a festive mood.

Everyone except Jonathan.

The polls closed at seven, but the counting wouldn't be finished for several hours yet. The town's voting equipment was antiquated, so they had to be hand counted, hanging chads and all. Morgan hoped Jonathan had the chance to replace the equipment before they had to vote again.

She went into the kitchen to check on the food, and saw that Melba and several of the ladies from the church had things under control. She wondered where Sheila had gone with Caleb, so she started up the stairs to look for them.

She saw that the door to Caleb's room was closed. She leaned against it, listening, but heard nothing. Finally, she turned the knob and pushed it open.

Sheila sat in the rocker, singing softly as she held her sleeping son in her arms.

"Hey," Sheila whispered. "He was getting sleepy so I brought him up where it's quiet."

Morgan gave her a weak smile. "That's good. He's had a long day."

She watched as Sheila got up, laid him carefully in his bed without waking him, and then gently stroked his hair. "He's so beautiful, isn't he?"

Morgan got tears in her eyes and nodded. "Yes, he is." She swallowed hard. "He looks just like you."

Sheila's glistening eyes showed her gratitude.

"Well, I'll go back down."

Sheila smiled. "I'll be down in a minute."

Morgan stepped out into the hall, closing the door behind her, and leaned back against the wall, the reality of the moment washing over her. This was as it should be—Sheila mothering her child.

It was the best thing for Caleb.

She breathed a silent prayer that God would give her the strength to accept that, and a strange peace fell over her.

In that moment, she vowed to stop thinking of herself. She would decrease so that Sheila could increase.

Wiping the tear that rolled down her face, she forced herself to rejoin the party.

She found Jonathan sitting on the back porch with Cade and Blair.

She tried to look upbeat. "What are you guys doing?"

"Commiserating," Jonathan said. "Wondering what we'll do if they fire Cade."

"They're not going to fire him, Jonathan," Morgan said. "Because you're going to win."

Jonathan clearly wasn't holding his breath.

Blair groaned. "It's insane. It would be absolutely ludicrous if they fired you, Cade. We can't let this happen."

"I don't see what we can do about it," Cade said. "I'm going to be at the mercy of the mayor, whoever it is."

They heard the phone ringing inside, and Jonathan started to get up.

Melba burst through the screen door. "It's the early part of the returns, Jonathan!" She handed the cordless phone to him. The piano stopped playing, the children stopped laughing, and all of the soft conversations ceased.

"Jonathan Cleary." His voice was tight, nervous.

Morgan said a silent prayer as she waited for the verdict. Suddenly a smile broke across Jonathan's face. "You're kidding me! Thanks, man. I appreciate it. Keep us updated."

He clicked off the phone and looked at the crowd who had suddenly come to bottleneck in the doorway to the porch.

"The votes at the high school have been counted, and I'm a few dozen votes ahead."

Everybody sent up a cheer, and Morgan threw her arms around Jonathan's neck. He laughed and swung her around.

"Can you believe it? I thought it was impossible."

"Nothing is impossible with God," she said.

He let her go, then looked around at the others. "There's still several voting centers that haven't reported yet, so we need to be cautiously optimistic."

For the first time in over two weeks, a bubble of joy fluttered up inside Morgan, but it was a fragile joy. She prayed it would last.

The party atmosphere grew more tense as the night progressed. Each time Lance from the circuit clerk's office called with an update, that tension was turned up a notch. Sam Sullivan and Jonathan had been running neck and neck for the whole night. Sometimes Jonathan was a few votes ahead, causing a celebration at Hanover House. Then things would turn and Sam would be in the lead. No one could guess who might be the victor.

When Vince Barr showed up at nine-thirty, Morgan graciously let him in. Blair cut across the room and took her aside. "What is wrong with you? Why would you let *him* in here?"

"I can't tell him to go away. Besides, when you're in politics, you have to be willing to talk to the media."

"But he's here to dig up dirt about the murder. He doesn't care about our mayoral election!"

Morgan's gaze drifted across the room to the man who was already engaged in conversation with some of her guests. "Then watch him for me. I'm really busy, Blair. We're going to hear the returns soon. Maybe he'll be able to write about a victory celebration."

Blair said a few words to Vince, then excused herself and went back to Cade, who stood talking to Sheila.

"Did you see who's here?" she whispered harshly.

Cade glanced across the room at the reporter who seemed to be making his way toward them. "Maybe it's time for me to leave."

"You can't leave before we know the results," Sheila said. "Maybe somebody needs to get in touch with that fortune-teller. Maybe he could tell us who the winner's going to be."

Blair shot the woman a look. All night, she had flicked her hair as she'd followed Cade around like a groupie. Ever since Blair caught her sitting in Carson's van, she hadn't trusted her.

"Fortune-teller or not, that Vince guy's waiting for the returns just like we are," Blair bit out.

"But didn't Graham give you the information that helped you find that woman's body, Cade?"

The familiar way Sheila used Cade's name made Blair angry. She was being territorial, she knew, but Sheila was a flirt, and she was good at it. Sheila locked her blue eyes into Cade's with that sultry teasing look that sent Blair over the edge.

Cade was noncommittal. "I can't really comment on his involvement."

"Oh, of course you can't." Sheila touched his arm and leaned in. "Frankly, that guy's involvements seem to be all over the place. Some of them even extramarital, if you know what I mean."

Blair bristled. Was Sheila hinting she'd been involved with him? Would she admit that right here in front of Blair, knowing she would tell Jonathan and Morgan? "No. Why don't you tell us what you mean?"

Sheila crossed her arms and, with a coy grin, offered a shrug. "I'm just saying . . . I saw him with a cute little thing who was not his wife. Not unless she'd bleached her hair blonde since the debate that morning."

Blair looked at Cade. He was interested now, squinting as he stared at Sheila. "Where did you see him, Sheila?"

"I was walking around the island Saturday, trying to vent a little steam, and I was over there by the river. You know, where that woman's car was found? Sadie had shown it to me, and there were flowers marking the place. Just past that, there he came. The palm reader himself, bopping along the path, coming right toward me."

Blair felt Cade stiffening. "Where was he coming from?"

"From that house around the bend of the river."

Melanie Adams' house? Blair shot an alarmed look at Cade, then turned back to Sheila. "You say there was a blonde there?"

"Yes. He was walking toward me, and all of a sudden this Miss America type calls to him and she comes running and says, 'You forgot your wallet.' She kisses him right on the mouth, and then he sees me and disappears back into her house."

"Melanie Adams." Cade looked at Blair, a million thoughts running through his eyes.

"You don't think . . ."

Sadie called Sheila from across the room, and Sheila hurried away.

Blair watched the dots connecting in Cade's mind.

"If Carson's having an affair with Melanie Adams, then we may have an answer about how he got his vision."

Blair lowered her voice to a whisper. "Do you think he just witnessed the murder, or was he actually the one who committed it?"

"I don't know, but I'm sure going to find out." He pulled his keys out of his pocket. "I've got to go, Blair."

She started walking him to the door, when the telephone rang again.

A hush fell over the room again, and Cade froze, waiting to see what the news was.

Jonathan picked it up. "Jonathan Cleary. Yeah, Lance?"

There was a long pause.

Jonathan swallowed. "So that's it? The final result?"

Blair's heart plunged. She knew he'd lost.

He hung up the phone and looked around at the crowd. She felt sorry for him. These things should be handled in private, not with fifty people staring you down.

He set his hands on his hips and drew in a deep breath. "It's over. Sam won by fifty-two votes."

Reactions flared up from everyone in the room. Morgan started to cry.

Jonathan put his arm around her. "It's okay, everybody. Really, I appreciate all the work that you all did and all the confidence you put in me. I especially appreciate those of you who convinced me to run. Maybe God just knew that I'd bitten off more than I could chew, what with running Hanover House, running a tour business, and trying to be the pastor of a growing church. I'm fine, really."

Cade crossed the room and pulled Jonathan into a hug. "I'm sorry, man."

"Me too. I tried."

Cade stepped back as others descended on Jonathan with soft words of encouragement and loving hugs. When he looked back at Blair, he saw that her scars had gone crimson.

"I can't believe it," she said under her breath. "I can't believe that jerk won. What is wrong with the people of this town?"

Cade just shook his head. "The town needs a lot of prayer. And he'll take office within the week."

She threw her chin up in defiance. "It's not over, Cade. I'm going to fight Sam Sullivan tooth and nail. If he thinks he's going to replace you—"

Cade took her hand. "Leave it alone, Blair. I can fight my own battles."

"But he's going to fire you!"

"Until he does, I have a job to do, and I'm going to do it." He got his cane and headed for the door. "I'll call you later."

The rumor about Carson Graham's affair brought things into focus. Cade still couldn't see a motive, but Graham may well have lied about his whereabouts on the morning of May 16. They had never been able to confirm it. Either he witnessed the murder and saw Lisa's car going into the river from the vantage point of Melanie's property, or he'd been in place when Lisa came along, and had murdered her himself. And what was Melanie's part in the crime?

Carson Graham wasn't answering the door, even though his Palm Reading van was parked in his parking lot. Cade banged on the door. "Open up, Carson! We know you're there. We want to talk to you."

There was still no answer. He thought of having Caldwell kick the door in, but it was too visible from the busy street, and he didn't want to call attention to what they were doing. Besides, he didn't have an arrest warrant. Theoretically, Graham could evade them all he wanted until he got one.

But Cade wasn't going to let him off that easily. "Let's try the side door."

He led McCormick and Caldwell around to the side of the house, where a warped door sat above concrete steps. The window was broken out, and the glass had fallen into the house. Someone from outside had smashed it in.

McCormick frowned at him. "What do you think?"

"I don't know. Maybe a burglary. Question is, is he in there?" Cade drew his weapon and radioed for backup. Then, pulling a handkerchief out of his pocket, he tested the knob. The door came open easily.

He led with his gun, checking all around him. Stepping over the glass, he moved into the kitchen. McCormick and Caldwell spread out, checking the laundry room, the pantry. Cade moved into the living room . . .

Carson Graham lay in the middle of the floor, a pool of blood under his head.

"In here!" He went to Carson's side and felt for a pulse.

But it was too late.

The palm reader was dead.

CHAPTER

71

*T*he phone rang just as Blair was getting ready for bed. Hoping it was Cade, she grabbed it up.

"Hello?"

"Blair, this is Clara Montgomery." The woman sounded excited. "I'm so sorry to bother you so late, honey, but I thought I'd give you a heads-up. There's something going on across the street at Carson Graham's. Police cars everywhere. Even an ambulance, but no one's been brought out."

Blair caught her breath. She couldn't imagine what could have happened. Had Cade's men gone to arrest him? Had he resisted arrest?

She thanked Clara, then grabbed her camera and rushed out to her car. She turned on her police scanner and listened to the chatter.

". . . homicide . . . gunshot wound to the head . . . notify his wife . . ."

Was Carson Graham dead?

She made it to his house on Ocean Boulevard in just a few minutes and saw the glut of squad cars, a fire truck, and a rescue unit blocking the road. She pulled her car over and saw that Vince Barr had already beaten her there. He stood talking to a neighbor who stood in the street.

Blair bolted up to the first cop she saw, standing at the edge of the crime scene tape. "Ed, what happened?"

He hesitated. "Blair, I can't talk to you. You'll have to wait until Cade makes a statement."

"I know it was a gunshot wound to the head. What caliber weapon was used? Have they got a suspect in custody?"

Ed looked agitated. "No comment, Blair."

"Were they making an arrest, Ed? Was there gunplay between Graham and the police?"

"No. Absolutely not. They found him dead." Ed turned away, ending her interview, so Blair started snapping pictures.

She heard the screeching of tires, a door slamming, feet running. Carson's wife had come home from working at the hospital. Amber tore aside the crime scene tape and cut across the grass. One of the officers tried to stop her, but she wrestled away from him. "Carson!"

Blair just stood there, camera in hand, unable to photograph the woman in her terror. She watched as they escorted her into the house. Blair heard a loud, anguished scream and knew that Amber had seen her husband's body.

Suddenly, the spectacle turned from drama to reality. She knew how it felt to be notified by the police, led to the scene of the crime, and shocked by the sight of a loved one's lifeless body. She knew the grief that would follow.

She didn't know Amber very well, but she wished she could cross that tape and comfort her somehow.

"Where's Chief Cade?" a voice bellowed from behind her. She turned and saw Sam Sullivan stalking toward her. "I want to talk to him."

"He's kind of busy," Ed said.

"Go get him!"

"I'm sorry, but you'll have to wait until he comes out."

"Young fella, you must not know who I am," Sam bit out. "I am this town's newly elected mayor. You're my employee, and I told you to go in there and get Chief Cade, or I'll do it myself."

The young cop finally capitulated and went toward the house.

Blair stepped toward him. "Nice going, Sam. Way to flex those newly acquired muscles. You really know how to win friends and influence people."

"Hey, I influenced enough to win the election, Blair—and I do appreciate all the paper's support."

Blair bit her lip and walked away. She gave Sam ad space because he'd paid for it fair and square, but now she wondered at the merits of unbiased reporting. Maybe she should have given more of her opinion.

She knew better than that. She'd vowed when she bought the paper that she would be an old-fashioned reporter, the kind who was objective and factual. But sometimes it just didn't seem to pay.

She saw Ed coming back with Cade on his heels, so she slipped into the shadows behind some trees so her snooping around wouldn't set him off. Her heart surged with compassion for Cade. He looked as if he'd had about all he could take.

"What can I do for you, Sam?"

"I want to know what happened here."

"I'll be making a statement when I have something to say. You're welcome to wait here until I do."

"Do you know who did this?"

"Not yet, Sam."

"Does this have anything to do with the Lisa Jackson case?"

"We haven't ruled anything out. Everyone related to this case will be questioned—and since you're here, we can start with you."

She would have expected a calm response, an easy flowing of information that might help. Instead, Sam looked as if he'd been slapped. "I know you've checked out my alibi, Cade. You know by now that I was telling the truth about where I was May 16.

I've had a hundred people around me all night tonight. I didn't leave my victory party once until now, and I got to tell you, if you keep harassing me, you're going to be in the unemployment lines even faster than you thought."

She could see Cade's jaw popping. "Wait here," he said. "I'm sending McCormick out to question you."

"Cade, I'm warning you!"

Shaking his head, Cade just turned and went back into the house.

Sam kicked the sawhorse holding up the yellow crime scene tape and knocked it over. Then he thought better of it and quickly picked it back up.

McCormick came out a moment later, and Blair stayed in her hiding place behind the tree. "Cade said you were here," he said. "Why don't you come sit in my car with me and answer a few questions?"

She saw Sam looking around to make sure no one heard. Blair stayed hidden, but strained to hear. "McCormick, Cade isn't trying to connect me with this, is he?"

McCormick just looked at him. "Why do you ask that, Sam?"

"Because he knew that if I got elected I was going to fire him. Tell me that he's not misinterpreting my little letter-writing hoax. I never would have written them if I'd known it was going to make me a murder suspect."

"Of course you wouldn't. You only did it because you thought you wouldn't get caught."

"Hey, I was forthright with you people. I admitted everything. That's got to count for something."

Blair let the words sink in. So Sam *had* written the letters. He'd hung a motive on Ben. He'd made him look guilty—and he'd confessed to the police.

Could the mayor-elect be the killer?

She didn't know, but her readers were about to find out what kind of man they'd elected. It would be worth staying up all night to get out a special edition. Sam's first act as mayor would be picking up the pieces of his own character.

She looked around to make sure Vince hadn't heard the same thing. He stood in the next-door neighbor's yard, trying to take pictures of the palm reader's side door. He hadn't heard a word of the exchange.

She hurried back to her newspaper office. Normally, she would have confirmed this with at least two other sources, but she'd heard it from the horse's mouth. What could be greater confirmation than the man's own confession? As fast as she could type, she wrote the headline article about Carson's murder. She wrote furiously, trying to get everything down. At the bottom of the front page, she wrote about how Sam Sullivan had confessed to sending the letters to Lisa Jackson claiming her husband was having an affair. By morning, the residents of Cape Refuge would know what kind of man their new mayor was.

Half watching FOX News as she worked, she set about to paste in the articles that hadn't fit in yesterday's regular issue, including local club news and items about high school athletes and academic awards—anything to fill up this issue so it wouldn't look so sparse.

Then she heard the News Alert.

"We have breaking news in the Lisa Jackson case. FOX News has just learned that Carson Graham, the psychic who led police to Lisa's body, was found dead tonight in his home. Joining us now from our FOX affiliate in Savannah is Vince Barr of the *Observer*. Welcome back, Vince."

She turned from her computer and gaped at the screen. How had he gotten to them so quickly? She turned up the set, and held her breath, praying that Vince wouldn't report what she'd just spent the last hours writing.

"Good to be here, John. First, let me backtrack a little to explain that the police force of Cape Refuge had gone to question Carson Graham. It's not clear what information led them to that. When Graham didn't answer the door, they looked around and found that the glass on one of his doors had been shattered from the outside. When they went in, they found the psychic dead on the floor."

"How was he killed?"

"A gunshot wound to the head."

"Do they have any leads on who may have killed him?"

"If they do, they're not saying, John. My question, as I'm sure yours is, is why no one heard the sound of the gunshot. But his house is in a business district, if you will, and his next-door neighbors include an exterminator's office and an insurance office. Both of these offices were closed, so no one would have heard. There's also a lot of traffic on that street, so anyone across the street may not have heard, either."

"Any theories on who might have killed him and why? And do we know for sure it has anything to do with the Lisa Jackson murder?"

"If it doesn't, it's quite a coincidence," Vince said on a chuckle.

Blair leaned back hard in her chair, relieved that he didn't seem to know about Sam's writing the letters to Lisa. He would surely have told it if he'd known.

She had scooped him, she thought with a smile. And maybe now she had a chance to save Cade's job.

CHAPTER

72

*D*awn had just broken when Cade reported to the police station. He'd been at Carson Graham's all night, working with the detectives to gather enough evidence to determine his killer, but they made little progress.

Billy Caldwell met him at the door with a newspaper in his hand. "Chief, you need to see something."

Cade glanced at the paper. It was the *Cape Refuge Journal*, hot off the press. The headline read, "Psychic Found Murdered."

"Where did you get this?"

"Paper guy just delivered it. Special edition."

Cade scanned the article, saw that it had no surprises. "She's good. She had the scoop before the *Savannah Morning News*, or even the *Observer*. Guess she couldn't wait to get it out."

Caldwell pointed at the article at the bottom of the page. "Check *this* out."

Cade glanced at the secondary headline. "'Mayor-Elect Confesses to Fraud.' Aw, no!" He grabbed a chair and sank into it as his eyes ran over the article. "Tell me she didn't write that." Anger shot through him, stamping out his fatigue. "I want to know who leaked this."

"It wasn't me, Chief. I swear it."

Cade bolted into his office and grabbed the telephone. He dialed Blair's number, but she wasn't home, so he tried her at the office.

"*Cape Refuge Journal*," she said in a tired voice. "Blair speaking."

"I want to know where you got this information," Cade bit out. "Give me a name, Blair."

She hesitated. "What are you talking about?"

"Who leaked the Sam Sullivan story to you?"

"Nobody, Cade. I heard it for myself. Sam was spouting off to Joe, saying that he hoped you didn't think his letter-writing scheme connected him to the murder."

"Blair, you should not have reported this. It was police business."

"I found it out fair and square, Cade, and the voters need to know what kind of man they just elected. It's important news to this community."

"Blair, nothing good can come of this. He's going to think I leaked it in some feeble attempt to save my job. That's not how I operate."

"Cade, the article clearly says that I heard it myself. I'm sorry that you're not comfortable with it, but it's the truth—and it probably *will* save your job!"

"I told you to let me fight my own battles. Between you and Vince Barr, it's a wonder I still *have* a job."

That set her off. "Come on, Cade. This has all been a reporter's dream, but I'm not the one who's exploited it. I've been responsible with my reporting. You haven't seen me milking this into a national story, parading myself on the major news shows like that Vince jerk has done. I'm tired of taking the heat from you for the stuff he's doing. It's not fair, and you know it."

Maybe it *wasn't* fair . . . Maybe Vince *had* gotten famous over this, and maybe it was all making him look bad. Maybe he *was* taking it out on her.

But he was tired, and he didn't want to deal with these distractions anymore. He just wanted the case to be resolved.

"So where are we on Carson's murder?" she asked. "I've been listening to the scanner all night, but nothing seems to be happening."

"You're not getting a thing out of me, Blair. I don't want you reporting an arrest before it's even made."

With that, he hung up the phone and tried to swallow his anger so he could do his job.

CHAPTER

The facts about Carson Graham had filed in after his murder. His bank and phone records showed that he'd made a $30,000 deposit into his account on May 16—the day of Lisa's murder.

"So either somebody paid him for killing Lisa," Cade told McCormick, "or he witnessed the murder and was blackmailing the killer."

Cade looked at the phone records scrolling across his computer screen. From May 16 on, there were several calls to newspapers across Georgia, placed after the body was found. It was his attempt to make himself a hero, and it had pretty much worked. Had he exploited something he'd only witnessed? If so, had Lisa's killer murdered him?

Cade had plenty of questions by the time he went with McCormick to visit Melanie Adams. When she answered the door, it was clear they had woken her up. She clutched her robe shut and squinted out at them. "What's going on?"

"Melanie, we need to talk to you. Police business."

She opened the door further. "I'm not even dressed . . ." She stepped back to let them in.

Cade could see that the woman had been crying.

She turned on the light in her front room. Still clutching her robe, she sat down.

"Melanie, Carson Graham was murdered last night."

She swallowed hard and nodded. "I know. I saw it on the news." Her face twisted. "We were . . . friends. I couldn't believe it."

"Melanie, we know about your affair."

She just stared at them for a long moment, dread pulling at her expression. "My husband . . . he doesn't know. Is there any way to keep this quiet? He's out of town for a few more days. I really can't let him find out." Her lower lip began to quiver, and she started to cry. She covered her mouth, and her brow pleated as she stared at them.

"Do you think he knows already?"

She looked at them then, her eyes rounding. "You think . . . No, it wasn't my husband! He's not a killer. He's been in Canada on business for the last three weeks. He has no idea. It's not him, Cade."

"Do you have any idea who might have wanted Carson dead?"

She got up, grabbed a tissue. "I told him. I told him to be careful, that he was playing with fire."

Cade glanced up at McCormick. His muscles were rigid with attention. He looked back at the woman. "Melanie, what did he tell you about Lisa Jackson's murder?"

She was sobbing now, clearly losing control. "He was a witness. He spent the night with me that night. My husband wasn't home, and Carson's wife was working a double shift at the hospital. He walked over so no one would see his van here. He was leaving my house around ten that morning, walking home, when he saw someone pushing Lisa's car into the river." She looked at Cade through her tears. "That person has to be the one who killed Carson!"

Cade wanted to be careful now. He didn't want to frighten her away from giving him a name. "I think he could have been, Melanie. That's why your account is so important."

"I knew it." She got up again and walked across the room. "I told him! When Carson tried to get money out of him, I told him he was dealing with a killer. That he was putting his life in danger! He thought he had it all under control."

Cade's heart stopped. "So he was blackmailing the killer?"

"Yes! Only he wouldn't tell me who it was. I really don't know, Cade. You've got to believe me." She went to the front window as she spoke and peered out, as if she feared someone was watching her.

Cade shot McCormick a look. She knew who it was. She knew and wasn't telling, but her own fear spoke volumes.

"Melanie, I'm afraid we need to take you in to the station and take a statement from you."

She swung around. "You're arresting me?"

"Not yet. Not unless we think you're lying ... or withholding important information about a homicide case."

She grunted and looked at him as if she couldn't believe he distrusted her. "I'm telling you, Cade, I don't know a thing."

"Then why are you looking out that window like you know someone's going to come for you?"

"Because he might know about me. He might *think* Carson told me."

"Then you'll be safer at the police station anyway," McCormick said.

Her face changed as she saw the wisdom in his words. "All right. Let me get dressed, and I'll come with you."

CHAPTER

74

By the time they got Melanie back to the police station, there was a message waiting for Cade. "Chief, this woman named Kylie Hyatt said she needs to talk to you," Alex Johnson said. "She says she knows who killed Lisa Jackson."

Cade grabbed the message and stared down at it. "Who is she?"

"I don't know. She wouldn't say."

Cade called the number, and a man answered in a gruff, phlegmy voice. "Yeah?"

"This is Chief Cade of the Cape Refuge Police Department. I'm calling for Kylie Hyatt."

"She wants to talk to you in person," the man said. He gave him an address in Savannah.

Cade frowned. "All right, but first tell me who she is and what she has to do with this case."

There was a long pause, then, "She's Dr. Alan Sims' maid—and that's all I'm going to say until you get here."

The phone went dead in his hand, and he stared down at it. Sims' maid?

He rolled the tapes back through his mind, of his visit to Sims' house right after the murder. *"Excuse the mess. My maid is AWOL, and my wife has been in Europe for the past week. It doesn't usually look like this."* On his last visit, Sims had mentioned that his maid "up and quit."

Maybe there was a reason she was AWOL.

Maybe she'd witnessed a murder.

Cade hurried out of his office to the interview room where McCormick sat with Melanie. He motioned him out and closed the door.

"I just got a call from Sims' maid. She wants to talk to me. I think this might be our smoking gun. Let's leave Melanie here to stew in her juices while we go interview this woman."

CHAPTER

75

Kylie Hyatt lived in a neighborhood of HUD houses and low-income rental units in Savannah. It was early in the evening, but even now, several men loitered out on the street, and women who looked as if they had long ago traded in their dignity for a drug fix stood on the corners. They all scattered at the sight of Cade's police vehicle, as if he'd come to make a sweep.

Cade had notified Savannah police that they'd be questioning Hyatt, and invited them to escort him and McCormick since it was their turf. They opted out, since it was Cade's case. McCormick followed him to the ramshackle door, and he knocked. Heavy footsteps shook the house, and then the door came open.

An obese man with a dingy white tank top and a cigarette in his mouth looked out at them. "You're here."

Cade showed him his badge. "I'm Chief Cade, and this is Detective McCormick."

"Come in." The door opened, and a small, plump woman peered past the man. "I'm Kylie," she said as they came into the dimly lit house.

The place reeked of tobacco and mold, and had decades of dirt ground into the vinyl tiles. The paint on the walls was peeling. But there was no clutter. Everything seemed in its place.

The woman had a nervous tick that kept twitching in her cheek. "I should have called you sooner, but I was scared. After I heard about that woman's murder, I didn't know what to do. Now that there's a second murder . . . well, I just couldn't stay quiet any longer."

She sat down, and Cade sat next to her on the dirty couch.

"Excuse the way the place looks. This is my brother's house." She looked up at the obese man. "Roy isn't as neat as I'd like for him to be. I've been trying to clean up since I've been here."

"Don't go apologizing for my place, Sis. It ain't none of their business how I keep house."

Cade didn't want to get sidetracked. "Miss Hyatt, you said you had something to tell us."

Kylie went to the window and peered out as if she expected the killer to come walking up her porch steps. The nervous gesture was so similar to what Melanie had done this morning. "I was supposed to be off that day—"

"What day?" Cade asked.

"The day that lady was murdered."

"May 16," Cade said, and Kylie nodded.

"I hadn't left yet, though. Mrs. Sims went to Europe a couple of days before, and they'd given me a long weekend. Dr. Sims thought I was already gone, but Roy hadn't come to get me yet, and when that woman came banging on the door, I listened."

"What woman? Lisa Jackson?"

"Yes. He let her in, and she was hysterical. She called him a fraud and accused him of tricking her and deceiving her for money. Said he had robbed her of her childbearing years, that she was going to expose him. I felt like I was eavesdropping—and I didn't want Dr. Sims to get mad and fire me—so I went on out-side and waited for Roy on the street."

"Did you see anything else?"

"No, that's all. Just an argument. She was very angry."

"Was she still there when Roy came?"

"Yes. I was so glad to get out of there." Kylie burst into tears and covered her mouth with a trembling hand. "And then when I heard about her disappearance, and when she was found . . . I knew he killed her."

Cade's heart fell. "But you didn't see him do it."

She shook her head. "No, but she was so angry, and the things she was accusing him of were terrible. He must have snapped . . ."

He looked at McCormick. This was not the smoking gun they'd hoped for. Too bad she hadn't stuck around to see what else had happened, but the fact that Sims had lied about Lisa com-ing to see him didn't look good. If only they'd known all this ear-lier. "Miss Hyatt, why didn't you call the police before now?"

"I was scared. I didn't know what to do. I couldn't go back there, but I was afraid to come forward." She started to fall apart then, and her brother came over and put his arms around her.

"It's okay, Sis. You've done the right thing now." He looked up at them over her head. "You get him, officers. You lock him up so he can't hurt my sister."

Cade intended to do just that.

CHAPTER

76

*T*he waiting room in the fertility clinic was full of patients, both men and women, waiting for Sims to play God with their reproductive systems and give them hope—or take it away. They all looked up as Cade came in with two uniformed officers.

Armed with an arrest warrant, which the DA had finally granted him, he bypassed the receptionist's desk and pushed through the door into the back. A nurse was coming toward them, and she stepped back, startled.

"I need to see Dr. Sims," Cade said in a low voice. "Where is he?"

"He's with a patient right now."

"Which room?"

She pointed to the room, but stepped in front of him. "You can't go in there!"

"Knock on the door. Tell him to step out here."

She did as she was told, and after a moment, Sims stepped through the door. His face drained of color as he saw his visitors. "Chief Cade, what are you doing—?"

"Alan Sims, you are under arrest for the murder of Lisa Jackson. You have the right to remain silent . . ."

"You're out of your mind!"

One of the officers snapped a cuff over one of Sims' wrists, but he twisted away before he could click the other one into place. Cade's men descended on him, wrestling him to the ground.

"I didn't do it, you idiots! I didn't kill anybody!"

He fought to get away, but within seconds the other cuff snapped around his wrist, and Sims was jerked to his feet. His face was red and he breathed hard. "Elaine, call my lawyer! Tell him they're trying to frame me for Lisa Jackson's murder!" He swung back to Cade. "You're going to regret this, Cade! We're going to sue the socks off of you for this."

Cade grabbed his arm and led him back through the nurses. The doorway to Sims' waiting room came open, and the patients who'd put their faith in him watched, stunned, as their doctor was dragged away.

CHAPTER

O kay, she came to see me, but I didn't kill her."

Sims sat in the interview room at the police station, rubbing his sweating face with both hands. He'd finally confessed that he saw Lisa the morning of her death, but in the last hour of grilling, he hadn't confessed to anything else.

"Why did you lie to us when we asked you when you'd last seen her?" Cade demanded.

"Because I was scared. If you knew she came to see me that morning, you would have thought I did it. I'm not stupid. When I first heard she'd disappeared, I thought she'd gone off somewhere and killed herself."

"Why would she kill herself when Dr. Anderson had finally given her hope?"

"I didn't know. She was crazed with anger and rage, not thinking rationally. Then when she was found murdered . . ." He rubbed his face again. "I was shocked.

It was too much of a coincidence that it would happen on the same day."

"Coincidence, all right," McCormick said. "But I don't really believe in coincidences. You, Cade?"

"No, I don't. Not in murder cases."

"Come on," Sims said. "I know it looks terrible. It couldn't look worse, but I did not kill her."

"So she confronted you about lying to her."

"I made a mistake with her diagnosis."

Cade thought of the tape he'd heard of him trying to convince Morgan to mortgage her life to pay for IVF, the lies he'd probably told her about her fertility, and that same rage boiled up inside him. Slowly, he stood up and leaned over the table. "You didn't make a mistake with Lisa, Sims. You lied flat out. Falsified her test results. Exploited her fears to get money out of her. And you kept her from getting the help she needed so she could have a family."

Sims looked at the ceiling, shaking his head. "I'll fight this. I'll get the best lawyers money can buy."

"They won't help you, Sims. We have too much on you."

He considered that a moment, then his hand closed into a fist, and he gritted his teeth. "Even if everything you said was true, I did not kill her. She came to me rabidly angry, shouting threats and accusing me of . . . all those things. I never touched her. Then she left my house. I followed her out, trying to convince her it was a mistake, begging her not to go public with her accusations, but she got into her car and sped off. I never saw her again."

"Pretty convenient that she died before she could have you arrested."

"I didn't do it! But Ben probably did. She probably went home and had it out with him. I'm telling you, she was in a rage. Maybe he was defending himself, then didn't know what to do."

Cade believed she might have been killed in self-defense, but he was certain that Sims had been the one to do it. Nothing else made any sense.

A knock sounded on the door, and Cade looked up.
"Chief, can I see you for a minute?"

Cade got up and went out into the squad room. Caldwell nodded toward the television on in the corner. "Vince Barr is on again."

Cade moaned and limped over to the set. "Man, he doesn't waste any time."

"The drama continues to unfold," Vince said to Shepherd Smith. "But if Dr. Sims is the man, then he very well could have killed both Lisa and Carson Graham. Kylie Hyatt, the woman who worked as Alan Sims' maid, told me just a few minutes ago that she reported to police that Lisa Jackson paid Sims a visit the morning of her disappearance. She had just gotten the results of a second opinion she'd obtained from another doctor, and learned that Sims had been lying to her about her fertility problem for the last thirteen years ..."

Cade almost turned the set off. He turned back to the others in the squad room and saw that they all anticipated an explosion. "If one of you has been talking to this man, so help me ..."

"Though Miss Hyatt left before it came to blows, she feels certain that her employer is the one who strangled Lisa Jackson with a telephone cord, and then disposed of her body, in order to keep her from exposing him as a fraud."

Cade swung back around and stared at the set. How had Barr known about the telephone cord? They found it on the floor of the car, bagged it as evidence, and kept it quiet. Only McCormick and two of the detectives from the State Police knew about it. Cade hadn't even told his men.

It was something only the killer could know.

His heart started to pound, and sweat broke out on his
He turned back to the interview room and looked at that
possible ... could Sims and Jackson and Melanie
truth? Could the killer be someone else

the screen. Could it be someone who'd
story, who'd carefully orchestrated events
national attention? Could it be the man

who was reporting the story almost as fast as Cade was uncovering the facts?

"McCormick!" He limped to his office.

McCormick came out of the interview room. "What is it, Cade?"

"We've got more work to do. There's been a new development."

CHAPTER

78

*V*ince Barr's background only added to Cade's suspicion. The man had a history of blowing mediocre stories into spectacular headlines, but he'd failed at getting much attention out of any of them. Cade did a search for Barr's name on the Internet, and amid the hundreds of articles Barr had written, Cade found a few about the writer, himself.

"Take a look at this." Cade turned his monitor so McCormick could see it. "Here's an AP report that came out an hour or so ago about the Lisa Jackson case and the media coverage of it. They're talking about how a local case turned into a national drama, and they quote Barr. He says, 'The timing was perfect for this case to break. No war news, no terrorist attacks, no hurricanes, no interesting politics filling the news. So when this attractive woman is killed and her husband is the immediate suspect, it can't help pique national interest. And as awful as this sounds, even the murder of Carson Graham couldn't have come at a more perfect time. For those of us writing about it, it's like a dream come true.'"

McCormick rubbed his hand over his shaven head. "Okay, so let me get this straight. Didn't Sam Sullivan tell us that he went to Vince Barr with the rumor of Ben's affair?"

"Yes he did. Said Vince wasn't interested in local politics."

"But maybe that was the springboard Vince needed to set up the perfect story. One that he could help unfold, so he could give the national news shows a play-by-play."

Cade couldn't believe they'd been chasing down the wrong trails. "So you think he mulled this alleged affair over in his mind, then decided that it really would be a story if the candidate's wife turned up dead?"

"So he makes it happen—and he's on top of the story from Day One."

"What about Carson Graham?"

"I think he witnessed it, just like Melanie told us he did, and he seized the opportunity to blackmail the guy. Hence, the thirty thousand dollars that showed up in his account."

"Question is, did thirty thousand dollars leave Barr's account?"

"We'll soon see." He pulled up the man's bank records and studied them until he came to May 16. "Interesting. Looks like he had several accounts. A 401(k), a savings account, a couple of CDs. Pulled a little from each of them that day. And you'll never guess what it totals."

"Thirty K?"

"You got it."

McCormick drew in a deep, ragged breath. "Unbelievable."

Cade nodded. "So Graham agrees to keep quiet, and Barr agrees to use his own immediate fame to boost the reputation and notoriety of the psychic. They scratch each other's backs."

"Until we were about to bring Graham in for the murder. Then he was afraid Graham would cave. But how did he know we were going to do that? The timing was perfect. He got him before he could spill his guts to us."

Cade thought back over the night at Hanover House, the moment he'd realized that Carson Graham was having an affair with Melanie Adams. Sheila had been talking more loudly than she needed to . . .

"Vince Barr heard Sheila telling me about Graham's affair. He was at Jonathan's party. He knew that information raised a red flag in my mind, and he probably saw the writing on the wall."

"So he beat us to Carson Graham's house."

"Looks like it."

McCormick handed Cade his cane. "I think we have one more arrest to make."

79

*T*hrough Vince Barr's office at the *Observer*, they were able to locate him at the local NBC affiliate. He was gearing up to do a satellite-linked segment on MSNBC.

Cade and McCormick hoped to take him peacefully, without making a huge media circus out of it.

But Vince *was* the circus, and he wasn't ready to give up the center ring. The moment he saw Cade and McCormick coming in, he headed toward them. "Chief Cade, I'd love to interview you during my segment. How about coming on with me?"

Cade thought of acquiescing, getting on national television, and asking the man where he was on the morning of Lisa's death and how he knew about the telephone cord. He imagined reading him his rights and cuffing him as the cameras rolled. Vince Barr wanted to be famous—well, this would be news for days.

"Vince, this isn't a social visit. We're here to question you about where you were on the morning of May 16."

The smug look on Barr's face faded, and he frowned. "What do you mean where I was? The morning of . . . Lisa Jackson's murder?" Fear flashed across his face. "Oh, you've got to be kidding. No, you can't be serious."

"Where were you, Vince?"

Vince took another two steps back and almost tripped over a cord. "I was out doing a story. I don't remember which one."

Cade had expected as much. "Are you sure you weren't out *creating* a story?"

He laughed nervously. "I don't know what you're talking about. This is ludicrous."

"Vince, how did you know that Lisa was strangled with a telephone cord?"

His face turned white. The young blonde standing on the set looked fascinated, and one of the cameramen got interested, too.

"It was at the scene of the crime. In the car. I took pictures— didn't you see them?"

"There was no telephone cord in those pictures. No one had any way of knowing about that cord, except for the killer."

Cade wasn't sure, but he thought the cameraman had turned on his camera and was rolling now as Vince began to back further away.

"It was leaked to me. One of your own men told me about it."

"No one leaked it," Cade said. "You had inside information. Carson Graham knew, and that's why he's dead now. Where did you get the thirty thousand dollars to keep him quiet, Vince?"

He'd almost expected the man to break and run for it, but instead, he froze, staring at Cade, a stricken look on his face. A calm seemed to settle over him as he glanced back toward the set and realized the camera was rolling.

Vince was already miked up, so he turned to the camera. "As you can see, ladies and gentlemen, I'm here with Cape Refuge's finest, who've found a creative way of shutting up the press."

Cade glanced at the monitors on the wall, and realized that MSNBC had halted their normal reporting and was playing the unfolding scene. If Cade arrested Vince now, he would do it on national television.

Vince backed away and stepped onto the set and into the bright lights. "Well, you guys love drama. Here it is." He was starting to sweat. "As you've probably already seen, they're accusing me of creating a story by murdering Lisa Jackson myself. As ludicrous as that sounds, I find I have to defend myself." He turned back to Cade. "Chief Cade, why don't we hash this out right now, on national television? Step up here with me and interrogate me publicly."

Another camera came on and swung around to Cade.

"I'm not here to interrogate you, Barr. I'm here to arrest you—and grandstanding on television isn't going to save you."

"Okay, look—" Vince chuckled—"I don't mind explaining myself right here and now. This is all because of the information I had about the telephone cord. As I told you, one of your own men leaked that to me, but I cannot reveal my sources. So arrest me if you must, but the viewers know you're coming after me because you can kill two birds with one stone. You need a scapegoat, and you can shut up the reporter."

Cade stood there, knowing the cameras were on him. He figured by now all of the news stations had live coverage of the scene. Vince was trying to make him look stupid, figuring Cade would back off, not make the arrest.

But Vince had him all wrong.

Cade stepped up to the stage, into the lights, and went straight to the first camera. He pulled the plug that gave it power, and the red light died.

"Hey, you can't do that!"

"Watch." He walked to the other one and yanked it, too. The monitors went black, and then he saw the national anchors coming back on, commenting on what they'd just seen.

They were off the air.

"Arrest him," Cade said.

His men stepped onto the stage, fully armed, and surrounded the tabloid star. But Vince had no intention of going quietly. He bolted forward and knocked over the camera, leaped over it, and took off toward an exit door.

Cade had brought plenty of backup. "Freeze!" McCormick shouted, his gun aimed dead center.

Vince hesitated, then groped at the waistband of his pants just under his blazer.

"He's got a gun!" Cade yelled. "Drop it now, Barr!"

A camerawoman rushed in with a camera on her shoulder, recording Vince's panic as he backed up with that gun. "You're making it worse," Cade shouted. "You're resisting arrest on live television."

The word *live* startled Vince, and he lowered his gun long enough to look back at the monitors. His own panicked, sweaty face stared back at him. The camerawoman moved closer . . . showing the world Vince Barr's pathetic attempt to save himself.

Suddenly he sprang forward, knocking the camera out of her hands and shoving the gun to her head.

"Get your men out of my way, or I'll blow her head off!"

The young woman Vince had taken hostage screamed out her horror as he dragged her across the floor. "Get back, all of you." He backed up with her, toward a door behind the lighted set. "I don't want to kill her."

"Vince, please," the woman cried. "Please, let me go."

"No! I'm taking you with me. If they make one wrong move, your blood will be on their hands."

"What do you think you're going to do?" Cade inched toward him. "You'll never get out of this building."

"Watch me."

Vince opened the door behind him and backed into the hallway. Cade followed him, his gun trained dead center. But the woman was in the way.

Barr kept backing up the hall, heading toward the exit door.

"Let me go, Vince!" the woman screamed. "I'm not your enemy!"

Cade came toward him. "Don't make it worse for yourself, Barr."

But the reporter had a look of crazed panic in his eyes. He wasn't going to surrender easily. "You're not going to make me tomorrow's headline!"

"You've already made yourself a part of this story," Cade said, "but if you let her go, if you cooperate with us . . ."

Barr got to the exit door and tried to open the door, but it was jammed. He looked around, his arm clamped across the woman's neck as he kept the gun on Cade.

Cade lowered his gun. "All right, let's slow down and take a deep breath," he said in a calming voice. "You don't have to do this, Barr. Maybe a judge will show you mercy if you stop resisting. Just let her go."

Vince tried shoving the exit door again. This time it fell open. He pulled the woman out into the daylight—and found himself staring at dozens of guns, pointed straight at him. Savannah police had arrived on the scene and had cordoned off the area.

"Hold your fire!" Cade shouted. "He's got a hostage."

Barr thought better of his decision to leave the building, and pulled the woman back inside. He looked around and saw a staircase. Walking backward, he dragged the woman up the stairs, then backed into the stairwell, intent on escape.

Cade spoke softly into his radio. "Go up the other fire escape and cover every floor of the building."

He'd have no place to go except the roof. Where did he think he would go once he got there?

The woman screamed as her captor went further up, and McCormick and his men followed him, guns still drawn. Cade followed a few paces behind, his leg killing him as he made his way up four flights of stairs.

Barr got into daylight and dragged the fighting woman to the edge of the roof. McCormick stopped at the door, afraid to go further. "He's going to kill himself and take her with him."

"Oh, no, he's not." Cade pushed past him and went out on the roof. The woman's screams vibrated through his body.

"Let her go, Vince! Come on, let her go. We don't need a third murder."

But Vince wasn't listening. He was teetering on the edge of the roof, looking down at what lay below him. Finally, he pulled his cell phone off of his belt and made a call.

"Send me the helicopter, now. I'm on the roof of Channel 3—and hurry!"

Cade knew Barr had access to the *Observer*'s helicopter. But would they listen to him? Wouldn't they be keenly aware of what was going on?

Cade heard McCormick, still in the stairwell, making the radio call. "Get word to the *Observer* that any helicopter that touches down on this building will be fired upon."

"Vince, please let me go," the woman cried. "They'll come for you, and you'll be home free. Just let me go now."

"Shut up!"

He still stood dangerously close to the edge. Was he keeping open his option of jumping if the helicopter let him down?

Cade heard the sound of rudders overhead and saw the aircraft approaching. It had probably been en route even before Vince called, anxious to get the story as it moved outside the building.

Cade's hair blew wildly as the copter hovered overhead. McCormick and the others came out of the stairwell, some of their guns aimed high, and the others still trained on Barr.

"They're coming, Vince," the woman screamed. "Please, let me go now!"

Vince looked hopeful as the copter came closer, but it never got within gunshot range. Cade watched Vince's face as the man realized the *Observer* had not come to his rescue. Instead, they were filming his demise.

"No, you morons!" He raised his gun to fire on the helicopter.

Cade dove toward him, knocking the gun and the woman out of his hands and flinging him to the concrete. He screamed and struggled, but the other officers descended on him, fighting his arms behind him and grinding his chin into the roof.

Finally, Cade got off him and got up, jerking the man to his feet. Pulling his head back so that the helicopter's camera could get a good view, he said through his teeth, "Smile, Vince. Now you're really a star."

CHAPTER

*T*he calm after the storm left Cade feeling strangely empty and melancholy. If he'd thought the media circus was bad before Barr's arrest, it had been ridiculous since. They got footage of Cade's confrontation with Barr, then security tape that showed him dragging the woman through the building. Then from the helicopter they caught the drama on the roof. Every news station played the footage over and over, several times a day.

The story Vince Barr created had, indeed, made him famous.

Alan Sims was charged with medical fraud, then released on bond pending his trial. Meanwhile, the DA subpoenaed records from his office, and was building a rock-solid case that was sure to put Sims out of business and behind bars. Cade was finally able to let Ben go to finish grieving his wife's death.

And then there was Sam Sullivan.

Cade hadn't spoken to Blair since she'd written the piece about Sullivan in the paper, but the firestorm from that continued. The phone had rung off the hook since, mostly from local reporters who wanted Cade to confirm that Sullivan had confessed to fraud. He'd heard that Ben Jackson had filed a lawsuit against the mayor-elect. He hoped Sam got what he deserved.

He knew that the solving of the murder probably meant the end of his job. Any day now Sam would ask for Cade's resignation and put some yes-man in to replace him. He supposed it was inevitable. Though public opinion had shifted against the mayor-elect, he supposed he still had the power to take away Cade's position.

McCormick sat in his office now, helping him sort through all the papers on his desk. "Best I can figure, Chief, Barr killed Lisa in her own home. Must have been waiting for her there after she confronted Sims. Killed her right there with her own telephone cord. Piled her body into the car, grabbed a pair of Ben's shoes and his baseball cap, drove her to the river, not drawing anybody's attention, and pushed her car into the river. Must have put the shoes back in the house after the crime."

"We need to run the cap that was in the car through forensics. Maybe there's a hair or something—"

"Doubtful, Cade. It was underwater, remember."

"You never know. Doesn't matter, though. We've got enough to nail him. The DA says it's cut and dried. I guess the rumor Sam Sullivan started was what gave Barr the idea. The mayoral candidate who murders his wife for his mistress. Made a great story."

McCormick grinned. "We did it again, man. We're good."

Cade laughed for the first time in days.

"Hey, Chief, Art Russell from the City Council is on the phone." Cade looked up at Alex Johnson, leaning in his doorway. "Wants to talk to you."

"Well, here it comes." Cade grabbed a bottle of Tylenol out of his desk drawer. Pouring two pills into his hand, he shot McCormick a look.

"He said it was urgent."

"Yeah, I'll bet." Cade swallowed the pills and bottomed the glass of water on his desk. Finally, he picked up the phone. "Yeah, Art. What is it?"

"Cade, there's been a new development at City Hall, and I wanted you to be the first to know."

Cade closed his eyes. "All right."

"Sam Sullivan resigned this morning."

"He *what*?"

"Came in and resigned. He really had no choice. The phone has been ringing off the hook ever since Blair's article came out about him. Everywhere he went, he faced attacks about what he'd done. There was no way he could be effective as mayor under the circumstances."

Cade put his hand over the phone and told McCormick. McCormick started to laugh. Cade held up a hand to quiet him, so McCormick rushed out to tell the others. "So what happens now?"

"We may have to call another election, but we've got Judge Evers looking at things, trying to decide what the proper course of action will be. We hope he'll rule sometime today."

Cade thanked him for the information, then hung up and stared at the phone. Maybe his job was going to be saved, after all.

The phone rang again, and McCormick stuck his head back in. "Chief, I know you don't want to be bothered again, but it's FOX News."

Cade groaned. He wasn't in the mood to make a statement, but he supposed they needed information about the murderer-reporter they had helped make a hero. He picked up the phone. "Chief Cade."

"Chief, this is Mike Lassiter from FOX News. We wondered if we could get you to come on this afternoon and talk about Vince Barr."

"I don't think so. I'll give you a statement on the phone, but that's it."

The reporter grunted. "What is it with you people? We tried to get Blair Owens earlier, but she refused, too. You know, it served Chief Moose of Virginia well to come on our network when he solved the sniper case. Now he has a huge book deal, and there are rumors of a movie."

Blair had turned them down? When she'd had the chance to go on FOX News and comment on the story, she'd declined?

He leaned forward, setting his elbows on his desk. Why hadn't she seized that opportunity to build up her subscriber base?

"Chief? Did you hear me?"

"Yeah, I heard you. I'm not looking for a book or movie deal, Lassiter. I just did my job."

"All right, then we'll have to make do with the phone interview. Chief Cade, tell us how you learned that Vince Barr was the actual murderer in the Jackson case."

Cade told him about the interview their network had done with Vince, in which he'd mentioned the telephone cord. He explained how the media had played into the man's hands, aiding and abetting as he'd built himself into a media star, using the simple avenue of murder.

When he'd said all he was going to say and the man had stopped recording, he leaned back wearily in his chair. "So you say Blair refused to talk to you? Did she say why?"

Lassiter sounded amused. "She said she was too busy, but I'm guessing it was because of her scars. Who could blame her, really? She doesn't exactly have a face for television."

White-hot anger whipped through him at the remark, and he ground his teeth and thought of telling the man that he wouldn't know beauty if it bit his nose off, because if he had the slightest taste he'd realize that Blair Owens was the most beautiful woman in the entire state, and she didn't need some screaming news show to elevate her self-esteem.

Instead, he slammed down the phone. How dare he say that about her? Cade hoped Lassiter hadn't said those things to her face. She didn't deserve that.

He thought of all the things he'd said to her himself, when he'd chewed her out about her special edition that had wound up saving the day.

And he realized that solving the murders and closing the case meant little to him, after all, if he didn't have Blair to share it with.

CHAPTER

82

Morgan felt a little shaky when she came back to herself after the laparoscopy. She had been awake through the whole procedure, but couldn't remember a moment of it. The hypnotic drug they gave her in the place of anesthesia had an amnesiac effect.

Jonathan helped her get dressed, and they waited for the results.

Dr. Anderson looked sober as he came into the room. "How you feeling?"

"Fine." She clutched Jonathan's hand. "Did you find anything, Doctor?"

His smile was tentative. "As a matter of fact, I did. Morgan, the results of all of your tests—including your FSH—were normal. I'm afraid it was as we thought. Dr. Sims falsified the results he gave you."

Morgan caught her breath. "But if that's true, what caused my miscarriage? My infertility?"

Dr. Anderson's eyes had a pleasant twinkle as he regarded her. "It may be due to the small fibroids I found in your uterus."

"Fibroids?" Jonathan asked. "Tumors, you mean?"

"Benign tumors."

Morgan got tears in her eyes. It was structural, then. Physical.

"I'd like to schedule you for a procedure called a hysteroscopy. We can do it next week, if you'd like. We'll go in and remove the fibroids with lasers. I can't promise that this will solve your fertility problem, but the chances are very good that it will. It's worked for quite a few of my patients."

Morgan stared at him for a moment, letting the hope sink in. "Really, Doctor?"

Jonathan wanted to make sure he understood. "Are you telling us that this could be resolved in one minor surgical procedure? That after that, we might be able to have a family without problems?"

"Again, I can't guarantee anything, but that's my hope."

Morgan started to laugh and threw her arms around Jonathan. And the bright light of joy began to shine on their lives again.

That afternoon, Morgan came home to an early dinner cooked by the residents of Hanover House. Even Sheila had helped.

Sheila attended to Caleb over dinner. He had warmed up to her now, and sent her frequent smiles and giggles. The mother-son bond was renewing itself. It was a miracle of grace to Sheila, and as difficult as it was for Morgan, she found herself happy for Caleb.

When Blair burst in, everyone stopped what they were doing.

"I was just at the courthouse! The judge made his decision about the mayoral race!"

Jonathan groaned. "Don't tell me, let me guess. He's going to put us through another election."

"Wrong!" Blair crossed the room, took hold of his shoulders, and looked him squarely in the face. "Congratulations, Jonathan. You're the new mayor."

Morgan's mouth fell open, and she gaped at Jonathan. He stared at Blair as if he didn't believe. "But ... how can that be? Sam was elected. I wasn't."

"The judge cited the city's bylaws, which say that if something happens to a candidate-elect to keep him from serving, a new election would be held, *unless* another candidate had gotten at least forty-five percent of the votes. In that case, that candidate would win the race. Jonathan, you got forty-six percent!"

The residents sent up a loud cheer, whooping and hollering and congratulating the new mayor. Even Caleb joined in the celebration.

CHAPTER

83

*T*here was so much to celebrate, yet Blair found herself wanting to be alone later that evening. She left Hanover House as everyone fluttered into action preparing for Karen and Gus's wedding on Saturday. Church members filled the house to help decorate, insisting that Morgan not lift a finger after her procedure that morning. Karen seemed to walk on a cloud.

Blair wondered if that day would ever come for her.

The sun was dropping over the horizon, but it would still be light for a couple more hours. What was Cade doing? Was he floating in the aftermath of solving the murder? Had he heard that Jonathan was going to be his new boss?

Was he still nursing his anger toward her?

She went to the boathouse and fired up the boat. She hadn't used it in quite a while. They'd used it as a ski boat during her teenage years, but mostly her father used it for fishing. Jonathan kept the motor well maintained, so it started right up. She guided it down river, out toward the sea, and headed through the waves to Breaker's Reef. It was one of her favorite places on earth—a cavern you had to dive under water to get into. The payoff was inside, glorious in its beauty. Her father used to love anchoring his boat there and enjoying the quiet—and the occasional glimpse of a sea turtle—when he needed to think or pray. He used to bring her here sometimes to fish, and they would sit for hours in perfect stillness, listening to the whisper of the breeze stirring up frothy waves that hit the rocks of the cave. Sometimes he would forget she was there—or maybe he hadn't forgotten at all—and would talk aloud to Jesus, as if he sat in the boat with them. She hadn't recognized the value of that then, but now, as she looked out over the brilliant horizon, she knew it was true. Jesus had a thing for boats, after all.

Her boat rocked in the water as she looked up at the setting sun, its red-gold hues bursting across the water. It was glorious, like the grace God had bestowed on her ever since she had given her heart to Christ. She had no right to ask for anything else.

Still, she did.

"I never expected to have somebody fall in love with me," she whispered. "A girl like me with her face all disfigured, is happy just to live a normal life without people gawking and staring wherever she goes. But then Cade came along . . . and I guess I got my hopes up."

Tears came to her eyes and she blinked them back.

It wasn't just Carson Graham who had buoyed her hopes. She had hoped it before Graham uttered his predictions. That's why she wanted to believe him.

"I thought maybe you were behind this. After all, it was a miracle that Cade would even look twice at me. An act of God. But maybe I jumped the gun just a little."

She drew in a deep breath and closed her eyes. The breeze blew her tears dry. "I'll try to be okay with him not being my long-lost love, the future father of my children, the one I grow old with, if you'll just let him be my friend. Everyone who knows Cade is blessed to be his friend."

The tears came harder then, and she realized that friendship wasn't going to be enough. Not for her. The pain that would cause would be so deep that she didn't know if she could stay in town to endure it. Maybe she would have to leave, after all. Maybe she could sell the paper, start over somewhere else . . .

Then she heard a motor on the wind.

She turned, shaded her eyes, and saw another boat in the distance, coming toward her. As it moved closer, she realized it was Cade in the department's speedboat. Her heart burst.

He slowed and came to her boat, stopping beside her. "I figured you'd be here."

She hadn't seen him out of uniform since the night they'd gone to Carson's show. Now he wore a yellow tank top and a pair of navy shorts. He looked younger in the waning sunlight, more relaxed and at ease. But his face held a trace of tension.

"Jonathan said you were taking the boat out," he said. "Can I come on board?"

"Of course."

She watched him tie their boats together, and then he climbed over, careful not to bump his leg. The scar down his flesh was healing, but it would forever remind her of how close he'd come to death, not so long ago.

As he stepped into her boat, hope fired in her heart like a fourth of July display. He stood there looking at her, the boat rocking beneath his feet. Her heart constricted her throat as she waited for him to speak. Instead, he reached out, slid his fingers through the roots of her hair and pulled her into a kiss.

She melted into it, realizing that God had answered a prayer she wasn't even confident enough to pray. The kiss said things they'd never uttered, made promises they'd never made. Could it be that it wasn't over?

He pulled back, breathless, and touched those flaming scars as if he didn't even see them. His eyes were misty as he gazed down at her. "I'm sorry I yelled at you," he whispered. "Can you forgive me?"

She tried to blink back the tears in her eyes. It was stupid to cry right here in front of him like this. He would think she was some sappy heartsick teenager. But the mist in his own eyes was glistening. Did he feel the same way?

"Of course I forgive you."

"I had no right to jump on you like that. You saved the day. Instead of fighting with you, I should have trusted you. We've always made a great team before."

"We have, haven't we?"

His eyes were soft as he gazed into hers. "I'm tired of this surface dating game, Blair. I'm ready to put my cards on the table. The truth is, I think of you constantly. I want to be with you all the time, even when I'm mad at you. I want to assume that you're my girl, and that this is going somewhere."

She swallowed and breathed in a sob. "I want that, too."

"And the town, they'll know we're an item. They'll rib us, tease us, even try to marry us off before we're ready."

She grinned as a tear rolled down her cheek. "I'm tough, remember? I can take it."

He kissed her again, and she melted in his arms, thinking that if she fell over into the ocean and died right then, she would have had almost everything she'd ever wanted.

He broke the kiss and held her against his chest, his breath gentle against her ear. "I'm taking you to dinner tonight, and I'm going to hold your hand in public and let everyone know that I'm in love."

Her heart burst with the sheer grace of it. She started to cry so hard that she could hardly get the words out. "I love you, too."

She kept her head against his chest and watched as the sun melted into the water, sending a twilight of gold that beckoned the night.

It was like a smile from God.

AFTERWORD

*A*t this writing I've been crafting novels for over twenty years. People often ask me where I get my ideas, and I always tell them that my gift consists of a fertile imagination and an ability to see and hear things around me that others may miss. Like most other writers, I get ideas when I least expect them, then I "what-if" my way to a complete plot.

But it doesn't stop with those ideas. Writing a novel is a lengthy, meticulous process that might never end if it weren't for deadlines that force me to turn the book in. Though I've written a number of books over my career, I can tell you that each one is harder than the one before. And the work never gets easier.

I write each book several times over, printing out copies and writing all over it like a bitter teacher who finds fault with every essay her student turns in. I'm brutal with my own work, and never satisfied, and I spend sleepless nights worrying over plot twists and wondering if the story is too predictable or too boring. My mind wanders when I'm in places where it shouldn't as I work through problems and conversations and character interactions.

When I finally turn it in, I practically throw it into the mailbox and run away before I can change my mind. Once it's gone, I sweat until I hear from my publishers that they like it. But their praise is always tempered with criticism, and so—armed with their feedback—I tear into the book again, striving to take it to another level, to polish yet again, examining every plot device to see if it truly is the best I can do.

By the time it reaches publication, I practically have the work memorized. I know if one word has been changed in editorial, if one comma has been moved, if one apostrophe has been edited. And for all of my jealous protection of my work and my pursuit of excellence in my writing, I sometimes wind up with mistakes. I'm not the best writer around, nor am I the cleverest. I do the best I can, within the bounds of my own skill.

So why am I telling you this?

Because God is an author, too. He is the author of the most important, bestselling book of all time. And I believe that he is even more careful with his work than I am with mine.

With the advent of cable television, the world is bombarded with documentaries regarding the authenticity of the Bible, whether it's fiction or fact, whether all of it is true or just some of it. People make a smorgasbord out of God's Word and choose which things to believe—a little here, a little there. They decide that some of it—the parts they like—are inspired by God, and that the rest is written by flawed men and compiled by corrupt committees with their own selfish agendas.

In making those claims, they are saying that God is not powerful, that he doesn't care enough about us to watch over his Word, that he doesn't care if we're confused or lied to or misled. That he didn't even strive for as much excellence as I strive for in my work. That it's okay with him if it isn't quite right, because the basic gist of what he was trying to say lies within those pages. That the musings of David and the instructions of Paul and the history of Moses are all just myth and entertainment.

Proverbs 14:12 says, "There is a way that seems right to man, that in the end leads to destruction."

I believe the Bible is true, every word of it—so far as it's translated accurately. I believe our Lord chose every word with great care and precision, and that each verse holds layer upon layer of meaning, truths so deep it would take us a lifetime to mine them—and still we wouldn't have seen it all.

I believe God gave us his Word because of his great love for us and his desire to help us know him better. And I think he also cares about our entertainment. He gave us minds that like to puzzle, uncover, discover things we haven't seen before. The Bible is available to every level of intellect—it can be as meaningful to the mathematical genius as it is to the little child. It is full of connections, threads that tie one thing to another, prophecies made and revisited (many, many of which have already come true), and signs all along the way that point to Jesus. From Creation itself, to the sacrificial system, to the Law and the covenants, the Cross, and the description of the final days of earth and our entrance into heaven, the Bible has a running theme of God's sovereignty, his love for those who break his heart, and his plan for our redemption even though we don't deserve it.

"All Scripture is God-breathed and is useful for teaching, rebuking, correcting and training in righteousness, so that the man of God may be thoroughly equipped for every good work" (2 Timothy 3:16–17).

We can choose to discount it if we want, pick and choose the parts we'll believe, or even ignore it entirely so that it doesn't interfere with our lives, but our denial doesn't make it less true. The consequence of being wrong is destruction.

My prayer for my books is that God will use them to whisper truth into your ear, and stir your soul to a longing for him and his Word. I pray that the next book you open will be the one he wrote for you.

Then you will be richly blessed, and I will have succeeded.

May the God of peace, who through the blood of the eternal covenant brought back from the dead our Lord Jesus, that great Shepherd of the sheep, equip you with every good thing for doing his will, and may he work in us what is pleasing to him, through Jesus Christ, to whom be glory for ever and ever. Amen.

Hebrews 13:20–21

About the Author

*T*erri Blackstock is an award-winning novelist who has written for several major publishers including Harper-Collins, Dell, Harlequin, and Silhouette. Published under two pseudonyms, her books have sold over 3.5 million copies worldwide.

With her success in secular publishing at its peak, Blackstock had what she calls "a spiritual awakening." A Christian since the age of fourteen, she realized she had not been using her gift as God intended. It was at that point that she recommitted her life to Christ, gave up her secular career, and made the decision to write only books that would point her readers to him.

"I wanted to be able to tell the truth in my stories," she said, "and not just be politically correct. It doesn't matter how many readers I have if I can't tell them what I know about the roots of their problems and the solutions that have literally saved my own life."

Her books are about flawed Christians in crisis and God's provisions for their mistakes and wrong choices. She claims to be extremely qualified to write such books, since she's had years of personal experience.

A native of nowhere, since she was raised in the Air Force, Blackstock makes Mississippi her home. She and her husband are the parents of three children—a blended family which she considers one more of God's provisions.

#1 Bestseller!

Cape Refuge

Terri Blackstock

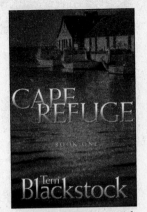

Mystery and suspense combine in this first book of an exciting new 4-book series by best-selling author Terri Blackstock.

Thelma and Wayne Owens run a bed and breakfast in Cape Refuge, Georgia. After a heated, public argument with his in-laws, Jonathan discovers Thelma and Wayne murdered in the warehouse where they held their church services. Considered the prime suspect, Jonathan is arrested. Grief-stricken, Morgan and Blair launch their own investigation to help Matthew Cade, the town's young police chief, find the real killer. Shady characters and a raft of suspects keep the plot twisting and the suspense building as we learn not only who murdered Thelma and Wayne, but also the secrets about their family's past and the true reason for Blair's disfigurement.

Softcover: 0-310-23592-8

Southern Storm

Terri Blackstock

The second book in the best-selling Cape Refuge suspense series.

Police Chief Cade disappears without a trace after accidentally hitting a man with his patrol car and killing him. While the rest of the police force looks for him and chases a series of clues that condemn Cade as a murderer, Blair Owens can't believe he is guilty of such a crime. Instead, she conducts her own search for the truth.

Softcover: 0-310-23593-6